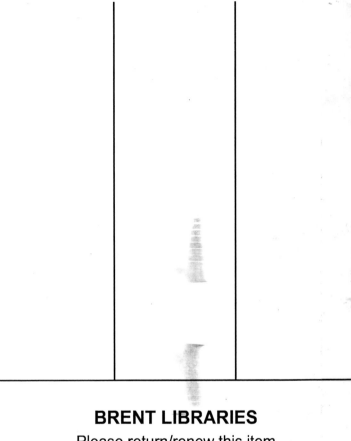

BRENT LIBRARIES

Please return/renew this item
by the last date shown.
Books may also be renewed by
phone or online.
Tel: 0333 370 4700

On-line w www.brent.gov.uk/libraryservice

Also by Jennie Lucas

Chosen as the Sheikh's Royal Bride
Christmas Baby for the Greek
Her Boss's One-Night Baby

Secret Heirs and Scandalous Brides miniseries

The Secret the Italian Claims
The Heir the Prince Secures
The Baby the Billionaire Demands

Also by Jackie Ashenden

Crowned at the Desert King's Command

Shocking Italian Heirs miniseries

Demanding His Hidden Heir
Claiming His One-Night Child

Discover more at millsandboon.co.uk.

CLAIMING THE VIRGIN'S BABY

JENNIE LUCAS

THE SPANIARD'S WEDDING REVENGE

JACKIE ASHENDEN

MILLS & BOON

First Published in Great Britain 2020
by Mills & Boon, an imprint of HarperCollins*Publishers*
1 London Bridge Street, London, SE1 9GF

Claiming the Virgin's Baby © 2020 by Jennie Lucas

The Spaniard's Wedding Revenge © 2020 by Jackie Ashenden

ISBN: 978-0-263-27814-9

MIX
Paper from
responsible sources
FSC® C007454

This book is produced from independently certified FSC™ paper
to ensure responsible forest management.
For more information visit www.harpercollins.co.uk/green.

Printed and bound in Spain
by CPI, Barcelona

CLAIMING THE VIRGIN'S BABY

JENNIE LUCAS

To Julie Sonveau and all my fellow travelers
to Mont St. Michel.
You know who you are. ;)

CHAPTER ONE

PANIC. FEAR. BITTER REGRET.

Those were the things that Rosalie Brown felt as she looked down at her seven-months'-pregnant belly.

She took a deep breath. She'd thought she could do this—be a surrogate mother for a childless married couple. She'd convinced herself that at the end of her pregnancy she'd be able to joyfully give the baby into the arms of his true, loving family.

She'd been a fool.

Burning tears lifted to Rosalie's eyes. Wrapping her hands over the wrinkled cotton of her sundress, she cradled her baby bump, her heart in her throat.

For the last seven months, as this baby had grown inside her, she'd felt him kick and move. She'd gone to ultrasounds and gotten in the habit of talking to him out loud as she took long walks along the edge of San Francisco Bay, morning and evening, rain and shine. As the winter fog rolled in, as the spring sunshine sparkled on the water, she'd come to love this baby.

Secretly.

Stupidly.

Rosalie blinked fast. When she'd seen the fertility clinic's ad looking for surrogates, she'd been in a bad place, grief stricken, newly unemployed and unable to ever go home again. When she'd seen the ad, she'd thought it was a miracle: a way not just to help pay her rent for a few months, but to truly do something good in the world. The best way—the only way—to get past her own blinding guilt and pain.

So she'd met the prospective mother, a beautiful, chic Italian woman who'd had tears in her eyes as she spoke of her husband's desire for a child. "Please," the woman had whispered in huskily accented English, "you're the only one who can help us." For the first time in months, Rosalie had felt something other than despair. She'd signed the surrogacy contract that very day.

It was only a few weeks later, when she'd first started to surface from the fog of grief, that she'd had second thoughts. She'd realized she'd be giving up her own baby, not just carried by her body, but even related to her biologically. Yes, she would conceive the baby in a medical clinic, and she'd yet to meet the biological father, but would that make the child any less hers?

After just one artificial insemination attempt, Rosalie had realized it was a horrible mistake. She'd known she couldn't be a surrogate after all. She'd decided to tell them to forget it.

But it was already too late.

She was pregnant. Pregnant on the first try. With a child that, by her own signed contract, she'd be forced to give away at birth.

For the last seven months, Rosalie had tried to convince herself the baby wasn't really hers. She'd told herself the baby belonged to Chiara Falconeri and her husband, Alex. This was *their* baby. Not hers.

But every part of Rosalie—heart and body and soul—violently disagreed. Until finally, she could bear it no longer. Last week, she'd gotten a passport for the first time in her life. She'd booked an international flight.

And she'd flown here today, to Venice, in an act that could only be described as pure lunacy. For how would

Rosalie ever convince the Italian couple to tear up the contract and let her keep her baby?

"Signora?"

She looked up at the smiling young Italian man in the striped shirt, holding his hand to help her out of the vaporetto, which had shuttled them across the lagoon from the Marco Polo airport. A hot gust of wind hit her yellow sundress, already wrinkled from being crammed into a middle seat in the airplane's back row for a fourteen-hour flight. The small ferry rocked beneath her, or maybe she was just dizzy from stress and lack of sleep.

"Help with bag?" the young man asked politely.

"No," she said, clinging to her small overnight bag on her shoulder. *"Grazie."* It was the only word in Italian she knew, other than food words like spaghetti or gelato.

"Ciao, bella." She felt the young man's eyes follow her as she went up the gangplank, and she felt self-conscious of her hugely pregnant shape. She obviously wasn't actually beautiful. Italian men must call every woman *bella*, she decided, as a mark of warmth and respect. She liked the country already.

At least she *would*, if she could just convince the Italian couple to let her keep her baby. How hard could that be?

Yeah, right. Rosalie had a hollow feeling in her chest as she followed the crowd of tourists off the vaporetto and into the city, past charming outdoor cafés and shops selling brightly colored glass and Venetian masks. For a moment, she looked up at the city—Venice, city of dreams, La Serenissima.

She'd grown up on a small Northern California farm, until she'd moved to nearby San Francisco for a job. She'd never imagined she might someday travel to the other side of the world. She was dazzled by the fairy-tale Renaissance buildings, the romantic Juliet balconies, the canals sparkling like diamonds beneath the hot Italian sun.

Narrowing her eyes, she shook her head with a sigh. Who cared about exotic locales or fairy-tale dreams? She was here for one reason: to try to keep her baby.

She had to convince them. She *had* to. Fiercely, Rosalie focused on the map on her phone. She left the crowds pushing south to Saint Mark's Square, turning instead onto a quiet narrow street, then another. She followed the directions to the address from the contract, crossing a narrow bridge, far beyond the tourist hordes to the quiet Piazza di Falconeri.

With every step, she felt sweatier and more wrinkled. She'd only met Chiara Falconeri once at the clinic in California, and she'd never met the husband at all. But she knew there was no way that Alex Falconeri would call her *bella* as the other Italian man had. Not after Rosalie asked to take his son.

She stopped in front of a wrought-iron gate within a tall stone wall. Behind it, she could see a leafy green courtyard filled with plants and trees, and behind that, a discreet palazzo. This was it. For a second, her knees went weak beneath her. Then she thought of her desperation. Tugging her bag more firmly on her shoulder, she pressed the bell.

A cold voice came over the intercom. *"Si?"*

Feeling awkward speaking to a stone wall, she said, "Um… I'd like to see—to speak to Mr. and Mrs. Falconeri, please."

"Mr. Falconeri?" The man's voice sounded scandalized, with an accent that reminded her of the English butler in *Downton Abbey.* "Do you have an appointment?"

"No, but they'll wish to see me." She hoped.

A sniff. "And who are you?"

"I'm—I'm Rosalie Brown. I'm their surrogate. I'm having their baby."

Dead silence on the other end of the intercom.

"Hello?" she ventured finally. "Is anyone there?" Still

no answer. "Please, I've come all the way from California. If you could just ask Mrs. Falconeri, she can explain—"

There was a buzzing sound, and the gate suddenly snapped open. With a gulp, she pushed inside.

The courtyard was shadowy, quiet and green, and seemed a world away from the rest of crowded, treeless Venice. She heard birdsong as she went through the small garden to an elaborate door. But even as she reached up to knock, the door opened in front of her hand. A supercilious white-haired man, who was bent over and looked as if he had to be at least a hundred and fifty years old, looked up at her.

"You may come in." She recognized the quivery British voice. Beneath bushy white eyebrows, his gaze fell to her pregnant belly with a frown.

"Um… Thanks." Nervously, Rosalie entered the foyer and felt the welcome relief of air-conditioning cooling her overheated skin. She bit her lip, then said hesitantly, "Are you Mr. Falconeri?"

"I?" The elderly man coughed. "I am Collins, the butler. The *conte* is my employer."

"Conte?" she repeated, confused.

"Alexander Falconeri is the Conte di Rialto," he replied pointedly. "Strange you do not know who he is, if you are having his baby." His voice indicated how doubtful he was of that claim.

"Oh." Great. So her baby's father was apparently royalty of some kind. Like she needed to feel more insecure than she already did. Tilting back her head, Rosalie looked up at painted frescos of angels above the antique crystal chandelier soaring high overhead.

"This way, Miss Brown." The butler led her past a sweeping staircase and down a wide hallway, then through double doors, ten feet high, into a gilded salon. She gaped, looking around her at the Louis XIV furniture, an oil portrait over the marble fireplace and large windows overlooking a canal. "Wait here, if you please."

After he left, Rosalie paced nervously in the salon, uncertain where to stand or sit or look. A palace like this was totally foreign to her experience, nothing like the tiny apartment in San Francisco she'd shared with three other girls, or before that, her family's farm in Northern California, with its hundred-year-old farmhouse, crammed to the gills with mismatched furniture.

All very flammable, as it turned out…

She felt queasiness rise inside her and pushed the thought away. She forced herself to focus only on the room around her. This furniture, too, looked as if it had been handed down through generations, but very differently than how her loving, lived-in family home had been. Every chair in here, every table, looked priceless, almost untouchable—she eyeballed a gilded antique settee—and very uncomfortable.

With a sigh, she looked up at the portrait above the marble fireplace. The man in the painting, no doubt some long-ago Falconeri ancestor, looked down at her even more scornfully than the butler had. *You don't belong here*, the bewigged man's sneer seemed to say to her. And shivering, she agreed with him. No. She didn't. And neither did her baby.

There was no way she could allow her child to be raised in a museum like this. Rosalie gripped the leather strap of her bag. She'd recently discovered that surrogacy was illegal in Italy. A fact which Chiara and Alex Falconeri had obviously known when they'd decided to hire a surrogacy clinic in more lenient California.

But the thought of trying to use that to her advantage made her knees shake. No. She couldn't. Could she? Absolutely not. She'd never threatened anyone in her life.

But to keep her baby—?

"Who are you and what do you want?"

Hearing the low growl behind her, Rosalie whirled to face the man who'd just entered the salon door.

He was tall, powerfully built, with broad shoulders and a muscular shape. His hair was dark and mussed. His eyes were black and they burned right through her. Rosalie gripped the edge of the marble fireplace mantel for support as her knees trembled beneath her.

"You are—Alex Falconeri?" she croaked.

His dark eyes narrowed as he stalked into the room, then stopped directly in front of her. He was dressed all in black, a button-down shirt, perfectly tailored trousers, and leather shoes with a dull shine. His stark clothing seemed perfect for a palace like this—and totally wrong for real life, for the hot, sunny Italian weather outside, on the last day in May.

"You didn't answer my question." The man's gaze was a weapon, freezing her in place as he slowly looked her over. "Who are you? What is this ridiculous story you told my butler?"

How many different surrogates did they have that he didn't immediately know who she was? Frowning, she blinked in bewilderment. "I'm Rosalie. Rosalie B-Brown."

"Well. Rosalie, Rosalie Brown," he mocked, "Is this some kind of joke? Are you truly claiming to be pregnant with my baby?"

Claiming? She frowned, bewildered. "You know I am."

"And how could that be?" he said scornfully, folding his powerful arms. "I never cheated on my wife, not in three years of marriage, not once, not even when she—"

He cut himself off, his jaw clenching.

Rosalie gaped at him. "I saw your signature on the surrogacy contract!"

"Contract?" he growled. "What are you talking about?"

Was it possible—he didn't know?

"Your wife—Mrs. Falconeri—I mean, the countess or

whatever she's called, hired me through the surrogacy clinic in San Francisco last November. She told me you were—" she hesitated "—um, too busy to leave Italy. But she said you were happily married, and all you needed was a child to make your happiness complete."

"Happy?" He looked at her incredulously. "You cannot have actually met my wife. She would never have said that."

"Well—she said that once I had the baby, you'd be happy, because a baby was all you wanted. And she said once I gave birth, she could finally be happy too."

Alex Falconeri stared at her coldly.

She licked her lips. "Just ask her," she said weakly. "She's the one who arranged everything. She—"

"I can't ask her anything," he bit out. His black eyes narrowed, hard as stone. "My wife is dead. In a car accident four weeks ago—"

"I'm so sorry—" Rosalie gasped.

"With her lover," he finished. "So I know everything you're saying is a lie."

Alexander Falconeri, the Conte di Rialto, stared at the beautiful young pregnant woman in the salon of his palazzo.

She was obviously lying. Her ridiculous story couldn't be true. Even Chiara wouldn't, couldn't, have done what this girl claimed. Create a child through a surrogate, without Alex's knowledge? No. Impossible.

Was it?

Impossible, he repeated to himself harshly. The girl claimed to have been impregnated in some fertility clinic in San Francisco. How could an American clinic even have gotten hold of Alex's DNA?

It had to be a trick.

Now *that*, he could believe. Chiara was—had been—clever and ruthless. For two years, she'd desperately wanted a divorce. Not just that, she'd wanted to take his fortune with her.

Alex had refused. He saw no reason to accept a divorce, much less tear up the prenup and meekly give her his inheritance. She'd done nothing to deserve it, and besides, he'd spoken vows. A man without honor was no man at all. For him, marriage, happy or unhappy, was forever.

Chiara had felt differently. After her wealthy father had died, a year into their marriage, she'd received her eagerly awaited inheritance and saw no reason to remain married to Alex. She'd been desperate to be free, so she could marry the penniless, drug-addicted musician she'd loved for years.

But she'd soon realized that even her large inheritance wouldn't last long, not the way she and Carraro bled money on their jet-set lifestyle. Her married lover had hinted that only a truly spectacular fortune could tempt him to leave his wife, and suddenly, a mere divorce wasn't enough for Chiara. She'd demanded that Alex forget their prenuptial agreement, and instead give her half his family's fortune.

When Alex had refused, she'd vengefully flaunted her affair, rubbing his nose in it, drunkenly partying with her lover in all the hot spots of Venice and Rome. She'd done everything possible to force Alex's hand.

But he'd refused to give in. Why should he?

Finally, in furious desperation, she'd threatened blackmail. Alex was scornful. He knew she had nothing to blackmail him with—he'd never betrayed her, never broken any law.

But a child.

She knew he wanted children. He was the last of his direct line. His family, powerful for five hundred years, had dwindled to only Alex and a distant cousin, Cesare. If he had no children, the title of Conte di Rialto would die with him.

But having an heir had seemed more and more unlikely,

as he and Chiara had stopped sharing a bed long ago. For the last two years, he'd grimly waited for her to come to her senses and return to their marriage. He'd thought they could still have a partnership. He didn't need to love her. In fact, it was better if he did not.

But Chiara must have known that if she'd surprised him with a biological child, Alex would have been willing to surrender anything—his honor, his fortune—to protect his own flesh and blood.

Could she have actually done what this girl claimed?

"I'm so sorry about your wife," the American girl said now, interrupting his thoughts. Reaching out, she put her hand gently on his wrist. "Even if you had…problems in your marriage—" she stumbled over the words, then took a deep breath "—I'm sure you loved her very much."

She was sure of *what*? Shocked, Alex looked down at the small hand over his wrist.

It was a conventional gesture, meant to offer comfort. But comfort was the last thing he felt. The touch of her hand caused a sizzle to spread through his body, from his fingertips to his toes and everywhere in between.

Why would his body react that way to this girl—this stranger?

There was no special magic in it, Alex told himself harshly. It was an instinctive reaction, nothing more. It had been too long since he'd had sex. Years. His marriage had never been about passion, even from the beginning. Their union had been about merging old families, old vineyards. He'd barely known anything about Chiara, except that she was beautiful and from a distinguished family, and that she brought the nearby Vulpato Winery as a dowry. The few times they'd made love it had felt mechanical, perfunctory. And within months of their wedding day, even that had stopped entirely.

That was nearly three years ago.

Was there any wonder his body was reacting now to the slightest touch? The slightest care?

He yanked his hand away. She blushed in pretty confusion.

She was almost *too* pretty, with her expressive brown eyes and dark hair pulled up in a long ponytail. She wore a yellow sundress that hugged her lushly pregnant curves. Her legs were tanned and slender, all the way to her simple leather sandals. Her face was bare of makeup, and she wore no jewelry at all.

"But—I don't understand any of this." She looked at the large, worn-looking bag hanging on her shoulder. "The clinic wasn't notified of your wife's death, or at least I wasn't. And she said you were happy together—" The girl took an unsteady breath. "I'm sorry. You don't have to talk about it. I can only imagine your grief."

"No. You can't." She couldn't, because he wasn't feeling any. His whole body felt tight. "And I don't know anything about your clinic."

"You said she died in—in an accident?"

"Yes." *If you could call it accidental to get drunk and stoned with one's lover and drive on a curvy cliff road on a rainy night.* "Four weeks ago. You didn't hear? It was in the news."

He watched the girl as he spoke, waiting for some hint of recognition. For weeks, Chiara's death had been reported gleefully in the Italian and French media. It was the perfect bit of gossip for the start of summer, a juicy scandal to see the proud Conte di Rialto, the former playboy who before his marriage had been the despair of every actress and debutante in Europe, for the last two years brought low by his wife's endless public betrayals. Chiara's death had been the perfect end to the gossipy news story, dying with her lover in a spectacular fireball on the French Riviera.

But even before that, everyone on earth, it seemed—

friends, acquaintances, total strangers—had asked Alex point-blank why he didn't just divorce her. He'd tried once or twice to explain about honor and the seriousness of vows, but even his friends didn't understand. *Promises are all well and good, Alex,* they'd said, shaking their heads, *but your wife is making a fool of you. Honor doesn't demand that you keep your wedding vows. Honor demands you divorce the cheating harlot!*

But this young woman's luminous dark eyes were full of anguished sympathy.

He hated her kindness.

It was an act. It had to be. There was no way she could be telling the truth about her baby's parentage, because there was no way a California clinic could have gotten his DNA without his knowledge or consent. Perhaps Chiara had found some struggling actress in LA who was already pregnant, and convinced her to play the role of a lifetime.

"I hope she paid you in advance," Alex said through gritted teeth. The girl blinked, her expression bewildered.

"What?"

"For whatever deal you made with my dear departed wife." He bared his teeth in a smile. "She hired you, did she not? To come to Venice and pretend you were pregnant with my child?"

Gripping the strap of her bag, which was digging into her bare shoulder beside the thin strap of her sundress, she said in a wavering voice, "You don't believe me?"

The tremble of her voice, the unshed tears shining in her eyes. Oh, the girl was good. He'd give her that. Such an accomplished little actress, he expected he'd probably see her on television someday, accepting a gold statuette. "That you've conceived my baby in a test tube?"

"Artificial insemination," she mumbled, her cheeks turning pink.

"Miss—what was your name again?"

"Rosalie Brown."

"Miss Brown." Alex lifted an eyebrow. "I'll pay you double what Chiara did, if you'll admit you're lying."

"Lying?"

"Admit I'm not the father of your baby." He paused, tilting his head as he considered her. "That is, if you're even pregnant at all."

"Not pregnant?" Her voice was indignant. "Feel this!"

Grabbing his hand, she placed it on the swell of her belly. He half expected to discover soft padding, nothing more. Instead, he felt her belly's warmth and firmness. He pulled his hand back in surprise.

She glared at him. "Of course I'm pregnant. Why would I lie?"

"Girl or boy?" he challenged, a little shaken.

"What difference does it make? A boy. He'll be born in two months. You're the father."

"And you've come for a payout," he guessed grimly. His mind was whirling. "You were already pregnant when Chiara found you. But she promised you a good deal of money if you could come to Venice and make me believe I was the father, so she'd get her divorce."

"She wanted a divorce?"

"But when you heard she was dead, you were afraid you wouldn't get paid," he continued relentlessly. "So now you're hoping I'll pay you to go away."

"What? No! You've got it all wrong!"

Alex turned toward the grand piano, topped by dozens of framed pictures his parents had taken with celebrities and politicians long ago. It was strange to see his mother and father smiling together in pictures, when he had no memory of them doing that when they were alive. "Then what do you want, Miss Brown?"

Rosalie stared at him, her lovely face pale. He was tantalized once more by his attraction for her, the shape of her,

her expressive eyes, deep pools of midnight scattered with faraway stars. She took a deep breath.

"I want *you* to go away," she whispered. "That's why I came. That's why I just got a passport and traveled across the ocean for the first time in my life. I want this baby to be mine. Because he *is* mine. He's my son."

Alex's jaw fell. He recovered quickly. "You mean, you want my money—"

"No. All I want is my baby." Reaching into her worn leather bag, she pulled out a small roll of dollar bills wrapped by a rubber band. She held it out to him. "Here's what your wife gave me for pregnancy expenses. You can have it back. All of it."

Bewildered, he took the wad of bills. He looked down at the money. It seemed a very small amount. He lifted his head.

"You don't want anything from me?" he said slowly.

Rosalie Brown shook her head. A beam of sunlight burst through the salon's large window, glazing all the old furniture with gold, making the room briefly seem warm and alive.

"Go, then," Alex said hoarsely. "I don't know anything about your baby. There's no way I can be the father. So just get the hell out."

He expected her to respond with angry words.

Instead, Rosalie suddenly flung her arms around him in a tearfully grateful embrace. With a sob, she kissed him fiercely and lingeringly on the cheek.

"Thank you," she whispered, her lips brushing his ear. "Oh, thank you."

Alex felt the softness of her full breasts against his ribs, the push of her belly against his groin. He breathed in the scent of her dark hair, like vanilla and orange blossoms.

Electricity sizzled through his body, like a burst of heat and sunlight of summer after a long, cold, dead winter.

Rosalie drew back, looking up at him, and he felt the rush of cold air against his body where her warmth had just been. Tears streaked down her cheeks as she choked out, "You don't know what this means to me. I was afraid to even hope." Reaching into her bag, she pushed a document into his hands. "Please sign that and send it to the medical clinic in San Francisco. Just so they don't give me any trouble." Wiping her tears, she tried to smile. "Thank you. You're a good man," she whispered, and turning, she left.

Alex stared after her in shock. Then he looked down at the paper in his hands. It was a legal document that would sever all his parental rights, according to California law.

Why would Rosalie Brown come all the way to Venice, claim to be the mother of his child, but not ask him for any money?

He looked at the small roll of American dollars in his hand. In fact, she'd given money to *him*. None of this made sense.

Unless her story was true.

But it couldn't be. Because however much Chiara might have wished to put a diabolical plan like this in motion, how could she? There was no way he could be the father. The San Francisco clinic couldn't have had access to his DNA. He hadn't been to California in years.

Unless—

With an intake of breath, Alex remembered his visit to a Swiss medical clinic, early in his marriage, when he'd still hoped for a child and had wondered why they hadn't conceived. He'd gone to get tested for problems, and agreed to let them keep the samples for the future, just in case. Could it possibly be—

His lips parted.

Yes, he realized. It could. His dead wife, so clever and ruthless, must have known he'd demand a paternity test. The baby would have to be provably his; blackmail would never work otherwise. She could have bribed her way to getting his sample from the Swiss clinic, and had it sent to San Francisco.

The thought was chilling. Had Chiara found a way to take her revenge, even from beyond the grave?

Could it really be possible that Rosalie Brown, a woman he'd never met before today, was pregnant with his baby?

CHAPTER TWO

"ARE THEY STILL HERE? Why won't they leave?" Rosalie's wizened great-aunt whispered in French as she stood in the kitchen doorway, staring at the tourists singing on the other side of her restaurant. Looking at Rosalie, she scowled, putting her hand on her hip beneath her frilly apron. "And for the last time, stop smiling! It's enough to curdle the eggs!"

"I'm sorry—I can't help it." But it wasn't just the singing tourists who were making Rosalie smile. The truth was, since she'd arrived at Mont-Saint-Michel two days ago, she'd barely stopped grinning.

Her baby was hers.

Well and truly hers. When she'd left San Francisco for Venice, she'd thought it an impossible dream.

But that dream had actually come true. Rosalie could keep her baby. Her child was hers alone. Now and forever.

Joy lit up her heart. Standing by an empty table, she did an impromptu little dance, hugging her huge belly.

We're a family, baby. You and me.

And she felt her unborn baby dance with her, turning over, kicking his joy.

"Do not dance in the middle of my restaurant!" Great-aunt Odette looked scandalized. "You are acting as drunk as the tourists!"

"Drunk on happiness, *Tatie*," Rosalie replied fondly, giving her a big kiss on the cheek. Her white-haired great-aunt pulled away, wiping her cheek.

"My sister never should have moved to America. You do not know how to behave! You are embarrassing yourself!"

But her words had no sting. In spite of her bluster, her aunt was hiding a smile. For about the hundredth time, Rosalie was glad she'd had a few extra days before her scheduled return flight to California. Since getting custody of her baby had been so unexpectedly fast and easy, she'd taken the train from Venice to see her great-aunt in France. Odette Lancel owned the most popular omelet restaurant on the tiny island of Mont-Saint-Michel, in the village beneath the medieval abbey, clinging to the rock jutting from the sea.

Not that Grande-tante Odette had been happy at first to see her only relative show up on her doorstep, unmarried and heavily pregnant. That first day had been filled with many French scoldings which, fortunately, Rosalie had been too happy to take to heart. But Odette Lancel had made it clear she thought her young great-niece exceedingly silly to have gotten pregnant via surrogacy, and even more naive to now plan to raise the baby alone.

"A baby needs two parents, ma petite," Odette had told her firmly. "And as foolish a child as you obviously are, I know you had a happy childhood. Your mother was a dear creature, and I know you loved your father. And they loved you..."

At the mention of her parents, Rosalie's joy had briefly dimmed. She couldn't bear to remember her wonderful parents who had died, and the happiness of her childhood home, all lost forever. Because of her.

And Chiara Falconeri, too, had died. Rosalie had met the beautiful, chic Italian woman only briefly in San Francisco. Such a tragedy, dying so suddenly. And apparently her marriage, far from being happy, had in truth been a misery. She'd died with her lover, cheating on her husband.

After she'd created the child without Alex Falconeri's consent—trying to force him into a divorce?

It was all so messed up. Rosalie was grateful and relieved she'd raise her baby away from all that, in a home that would be filled with love, not drama.

"A boy needs a father," her great-aunt had insisted.

"It's impossible," Rosalie replied with equal firmness. "The father of my baby is..."

Handsome. Darkly sexy. Powerful.

Images of Alex Falconeri flooded through her.

Resolutely, she pushed away the memory, finishing, "He's newly bereaved and not interested in raising a child."

"Still, he has responsibilities."

"I don't want his money," Rosalie replied, annoyed.

"Why?" Her great-aunt's dark eyes narrowed. "As a receptionist, do you make such a fortune?"

"No," Rosalie had admitted, then added reluctantly, "I have my parents' life insurance. And if I sell my family's land..."

"Sell your land?" Odette had been scandalized. "I never approved of my niece marrying an American farmer, but she spoke of the land with pride. Your father's family farmed it for generations. Just as this restaurant was started by my grandpère." She'd looked around the bustling tables of L'Omeletterie. "One should not cast aside a family legacy lightly."

"Of course I wouldn't. I'm not." A lump lifted in Rosalie's throat. "But—the farm's gone, Tatie. My parents are dead. I can never go back. I must accept that."

Her great-aunt's voice had trembled. "Rosalie—"

"I only have a few days before I go back to California. Why don't I help you in the restaurant?"

Rosalie couldn't have chosen a better way to distract Odette. Her great-aunt's face had lit up, for the busy tourist season was in full swing. And so Rosalie had spent the last two days clearing up dishes and chatting with customers in English and French.

She was almost regretful that today would be her last day, since tomorrow she must return to Venice, and take her ticketed flight back to San Francisco.

Then decisions would need to be made. Because she obviously could not raise a crying baby in a tiny two-bedroom apartment with three roommates. And could Rosalie really keep working as a receptionist after her baby was born, when the cost of childcare would be more than her actual salary?

Her parents' life insurance was not much, and would not last, even if she felt comfortable about spending it, which she didn't. But could she really sell her family's acres to the highest bidder?

As the tourists joyfully screeched their song about baseball across the restaurant, Rosalie blinked, relieved to be pulled from her thoughts. It was late, and all the tables had become empty but one. A group of rowdy American tourists was cheering and drunkenly singing, their arms looped around each other's shoulders. Their beloved team had soundly beaten some bitter rival. They were all gray haired and well past middle age, but their joie de vivre and energy was greater than most college students had. Watching them from across the restaurant, Rosalie couldn't stop smiling, no matter what her aunt said.

"Make them stop, *ma petite*," Odette whispered to her in French, her wrinkled face irritated.

"Why?" Rosalie gave a low laugh, looking around the darkened restaurant. The day-trippers from Paris had already departed on the last shuttle, leaving the island quiet, with only a few tourists remaining. The hotels on Mont-Saint-Michel were tiny, with just a few hotel rooms scattered across the steep island. "There's no one left here to bother."

"They're bothering *me*." Her great-aunt gave an expressive sniff. "It's past ten. The good heaven knows they should be headed to their beds. Do they expect me to cart them up the hill in a wheelbarrow?"

"I'll tell them to leave."

"Good."

But going over to the rowdy table, Rosalie impulsively joined them in the chorus, causing the tourists to shout their appreciation.

"Congratulations on your game, guys," she said in English.

"You're American," one of the women exclaimed. "What are you doing in Mont-Saint-Michel?"

"My great-aunt owns this restaurant." Taking the empty glasses of kir Normands and putting them on her tray, Rosalie gently set down the bill.

"I've never had such a good omelet!" a man said, patting his belly.

"I can see why they're so famous," another chimed in. "Thirty euros, but worth it!"

"How do you make them so fluffy?" a woman begged.

Rosalie leaned forward confidentially. "I'm not supposed to share this." Her great-aunt, watching from the doorway, rolled her eyes. She'd seen this before. Rosalie continued, "It's a family secret, but maybe I'll share it. Just this once." The entire table waited, rapt and breathless. She whispered, "It's love."

The tourists sat back in their chairs, groaning.

Rosalie grinned. In answer to their good-natured complaining, she replied firmly, "I'm serious. That's how everything truly special is created in this world. Love."

And she had to believe that. Sometimes life seemed like one heartbreak after another—but love existed. It was love that gave meaning and magic to everything.

And it worked in mysterious ways. How else to explain

that, in her darkest hour, filled with grief and despair, she'd become pregnant—she, who'd never even slept with a man before? How else to explain the miracle that she could keep her baby?

Rosalie knew how lucky she was. She had to fiercely cherish every drop of joy. She wrapped one hand around her baby bump. This was more than a drop. This was an ocean.

She didn't understand why Alex Falconeri had been willing to abandon his own child, but whatever the reason, she would be grateful to him for the rest of her life.

But even as she had the thought, she heard a husky voice.

"Miss Brown."

Frowning, she straightened, glancing behind her. Then her lips parted in a silent gasp.

Alex Falconeri stood in the restaurant's doorway, his broad shoulders blocking the light from the hallway entrance. His handsome face, half-shadowed in silhouette, was wreathed in a scowl.

Her body went weak. Trembling, she set down her tray.

"Thank you again. We'll tell all our friends about this place," the Americans said, and tossing money down on the table for the bill, they wobbled to their feet and wavered happily and drunkenly out of the restaurant.

But Rosalie barely heard them. She stared at the darkly charismatic man that she thought she'd left behind forever.

"Miss Brown," he said again, his voice low and husky. The vibrations curled around her like mist, and she swallowed, her teeth suddenly chattering.

"H-how did you f-find me here? What do you want?"

He blended with the shadows in his dark gray shirt and black trousers and long dark coat. "It was not difficult to find you. I called a few hours ago and spoke with your aunt."

"My—" She whirled around accusingly at Odette, who was scooping all the piles of euros from the table into her apron.

The elderly lady drew herself up haughtily to her full five feet. "He is the father. As I told you, he has a responsibility, *non*?"

"No," Rosalie informed her, then turned and glared at him. "You verbally terminated your parental rights in Venice."

Alex's eyebrows rose. "Is that what you think?" he said incredulously. "You just show up out of the blue and tell me some ridiculous story, and when I don't immediately believe it, you think I terminated all my rights to my child?"

Yes. That was exactly what Rosalie had thought. Her heart fell to the floor, and her knees trembled. She leaned against the table.

There was only one reason he could be here: he wanted to take her baby from her after all. And he could. With all his money and power, who could stop him?

"Please," she whispered. "Just leave me alone."

Alex Falconeri started to speak, then hesitated, glancing at her great-aunt. Narrowing his eyes, he turned back to Rosalie.

"Come with me."

Mont-Saint-Michel's tiny cobblestoned street, dark beneath the moonlight, was empty except for the departing group of American tourists.

Alex looked at Rosalie Brown, who was dressed as a waitress in a simple black shift dress and white apron. She looked angry—and terrified.

"Goodbye!" one of the tourists called back to her, waving. Rosalie didn't respond.

Alex set his jaw. He hardly wanted a bunch of strangers to hear what he had to say to her. Just as he hadn't rel-

ished having her great-aunt listening in, looking as if she
was memorizing every word to repeat to a lawyer later.

"This way," he told Rosalie grimly, leading her up the
nearest flight of steps. It led to the high stone rampart that
surrounded the steeply vertical island. Up on the ramparts,
all was quiet, except the wind and seagulls. Mont-Saint-
Michel, which had once been a fortress, a monastery and a
prison, seemed haunted beneath the moonlight, as it overlooked the shadowed beauty of the bay.

But it was when Alex turned back to look at Rosalie that
he truly caught his breath.

Standing next to him, she looked up at him with big
dark eyes that seemed to echo with ripples of moonlight,
like the tide. A cool wind blew her hair, and she was biting her deliciously full lower lip. Beneath her white apron,
her simple black dress showed off her full breasts and belly
swelling with his child.

His child.

Alex still couldn't believe it.

After she'd left his palazzo in Venice two days ago, he'd
called a private investigator, the best and most expensive.
Yesterday, Alex had called the fertility clinic in San Francisco and interviewed them at length. Now he knew everything.

But he hadn't just confirmed her story. He'd learned everything about Rosalie Brown—oh, yes—from the grades
she'd gotten in her rural school to the recent tragic deaths
of her parents in a wildfire.

Odette Lancel was her only remaining family. It hadn't
taken a genius to track Rosalie to Mont-Saint-Michel.

Which was good, because the last thing Alex felt like at
the moment was a genius.

He could hardly believe the depths of his dead wife's
betrayal. Or her determination to gain the upper hand. And
she would have. If not for her sudden, shocking death, she

would have gotten what she wanted. Because she'd found the one thing more important to him than his honor. More important than his fortune.

"Why did you come here?" Rosalie's voice was low. "In Venice you called me a liar and said I couldn't possibly be pregnant with your child."

"I was wrong."

She gave a bitter laugh. "Thank you." She looked away. "What did you tell my aunt? That you wanted to share custody?"

"Not exactly." As he looked at the beautiful girl standing on the haunted stone parapet, he thought she looked like a lost princess in a medieval fairy tale.

Obviously the shocking events of the last month were starting to take a toll on Alex. Because there was no such thing as magic. Fairy tales weren't real, and this girl, however beautiful she might be, didn't need a knight to save her. She was a young woman who'd agreed to bear a child for money.

But why? Knowing what he knew about her, money was the last thing Rosalie Brown needed. She had received multiple offers on valuable farmland in Sonoma County, famous for its vineyards. She could have sold it. Failing that, she could have asked him for a small fortune in Venice two days before. But she hadn't.

He knew everything, but he understood nothing.

"What do you want, then?" Rosalie demanded.

"I've had you investigated," he said slowly. "I've learned everything about you. But there are things I don't understand."

"Investigated?" She turned pale. "You had no right to invade my privacy—"

"Why did you agree to get pregnant by a stranger and give away the baby at birth? Was it really for the money?"

Her eyes flashed. "It was a mistake. I never should have agreed to be a surrogate."

"Why did you?"

"I thought," her voice faltered, "I could do something good in the world, something that would make up for... Well." Her jaw set. "I made a mistake when I signed the surrogacy contract. I changed my mind almost at once, but...by then it was too late."

"You were already pregnant."

She gave a single nod.

"How could you believe Chiara with her ridiculous story? Did you really believe that any man would be *too busy* to meet the future mother of his child?"

She suddenly couldn't meet his gaze. "That isn't actually what she said."

"What did she say?"

"She said...um..."

"What?"

Rosalie lifted her chin. "That you were impotent."

Alex stared at her, his mouth open.

Then he burst into a laugh. He laughed until the girl's defiant glare changed to bewilderment, then concern. As if she thought he'd suddenly gone mad.

And maybe he had. He thought of the years he'd put up with his wife's affair. The years he'd told himself she would eventually come to her senses and return to their marriage. How he'd convinced himself he could forgive her and take her back, when she would be chastened by experience, wiser, ready to finally become a decent partner and eventually, a good mother to their children.

Impotent.

It was almost amusing, how childish and vengeful she'd been, in her frustration at not getting her way. His lips quirked as he shook his head.

"I didn't particularly enjoy having sex with her, but I wasn't impotent."

Her cheeks turned red. "No?"

"We weren't close, and yes, she seemed cold, but I thought that meant she'd be a steady, practical partner for building a business and a family. When she didn't get pregnant after a few months, I went to a clinic in Switzerland to get tested. The doctors saw no problem." He paused. "Later I discovered she'd been on the Pill the whole time."

Rosalie's eyes widened. "She lied to you?"

"She'd only married me to please her father. As soon as he was dead and she safely had her inheritance, she was desperate to be free." He paused. "Chiara bribed a technician in California to forge documents and get my sample from the Swiss clinic."

"Just to get a divorce?"

"To hold me hostage," he said softly. "She meant to tell me I had a child, then hide him away from me, until I gave her what she wanted. Not just a divorce. She also wanted me to tear up our prenuptial agreement. She wanted to keep all her own money, but also take half of mine. It was the only way her lover said he'd marry her. If she could keep him in Ferraris and cocaine for the rest of his life."

Rosalie's eyes went big. "What kind of people marry for reasons like that?"

"Why else would anyone marry, except for financial reasons, or to create a home for children?"

"For—for love," she stammered. "That's the only reason. Isn't it? True love that lasts forever?"

He stared at her. "Do you feel that way about sex?"

Her blush deepened, and she suddenly couldn't meet his eyes. "Or course," she mumbled. "Love is the basis of everything. Or it should be."

"You're quite a romantic," he said finally.

"You say that like it's a bad thing."

Because it was. Alex drew closer to her in the moonlight. Standing by the rough-hewn parapets overlooking the sea, he heard the rush of the tide, the roar of the wind and the cries of seagulls overhead. He had that strange feeling again, like they were alone together in some strange fantasy world. "I don't understand. If love is so important to you, why would you agree to have a child for money?"

"Not for money. For love." Her voice caught. "I thought I could bring another family together, to try to make up for what happened to—" She suddenly shook her head, her eyes shimmering with tears. "Why didn't your wife just get pregnant herself?" she choked out. "Why drag me into your fight?"

"Chiara didn't want to be biologically related to the child. Apparently, not even she—" he looked at Rosalie "—could imagine abandoning her own baby."

She stared at him for a moment, and then he saw the moment his barb hit. Her nostrils flared.

"Well, I'm not abandoning this baby now. Not to you. Not to anyone." Rosalie hugged her belly over the black shift dress and white apron. "He's mine."

Alex decided to test her one last time. "Is there any amount of money I could pay you to give up the child? What is your price, Miss Brown? How much would it take for you to give me my son and disappear from our lives?"

"There is no amount!"

"A million euros? Ten?"

"No! Leave us alone!" she cried and whirled away. He grabbed her wrist.

"I can't let you go."

"You can't force me to stay." She wrenched her wrist from his grasp. "Surrogacy is illegal in Italy."

His eyes tightened. "You're right. Surrogacy with no biological connection is illegal in my home country." As he saw her exhale, he continued smoothly, "But that's not relevant in this case. You are the mother, Miss Brown, and I am the father—it's as simple as that. I have rights. I will not let you go."

"I will die before I leave my baby to be raised in that *museum*, with a father who has ice for a heart!"

Alex let her insult of his family home pass without comment, but— "Ice?"

She glared at him. "Your wife was desperate to be free of you. Desperate! Why couldn't you face reality? Why couldn't you just let her go?" Her eyes glittered. "If you'd just given her what she wanted, I wouldn't have been dragged into it. I thought I was doing something good in the world—something that would make another family happy, and that I'd feel…something…other than—"

Her voice choked off as she looked away.

Alex remembered what the investigator had told him about her parents' deaths. They'd died last autumn, just weeks before the girl had contacted the fertility clinic. There had been horrifying pictures of burned fields, her childhood home razed to the foundations. An entire farm village in Northern California had been lost by the raging fire. Sixty people had died, including Ernst and Mireille Brown.

Could that be why the girl had agreed to the surrogacy? Could she really be such an idealist—believing in *true love*, trying to save others to heal her own pain?

"You lost your parents," he said slowly. Her shoulders snapped back.

"I don't want to talk about it."

He came closer. "Your parents had just died in a fire. You felt sad and alone. So you decided to help strangers have a baby."

He saw her swallow, furiously blinking back tears. She looked away. "My mother used to say that if I was feeling sad, I should try to make someone else's life better, and maybe it would make my life a little better too." She looked up at him, and he saw the heartbreak in her beautiful face. "Then I realized what a mistake I'd made, thinking I could ever give up my baby. So I went to Venice. That's when the miracle happened."

"You discovered Chiara was dead."

She looked at him, her expression horrified. "No! Whatever she might have done, her death was a tragedy." She took a deep breath. "The miracle was when you said you didn't want my baby. When you accused me of lying and told me to get the hell out. Those were the sweetest words I'd ever heard in my life. Like angels singing."

Her words were so ludicrous they almost made him smile. His cursing had sounded like a choir of angels?

"But there are no miracles." Her voice cracked as she looked up at the highest spire of the thousand-year-old abbey crowning the island. "Just tragedy."

Alex stared at her. Up here on the ramparts with the wind blowing, he could taste the salt of the sea like tears.

When he'd first met Rosalie Brown, he'd imagined her to be like Chiara. She wasn't. He saw that now. She was a do-gooder, romantic and naive. She'd tried to channel her grief into making the world a better place.

It had been a long time since he'd met anyone so unselfish. Certainly not since his sister, Margaret, had died. No wonder he hadn't recognized it at first.

"Perhaps," he said slowly, "we can raise the baby together."

"Together?" He saw the flash of longing in her eyes, then dismay. She clearly wanted to be with her baby, but however much his opinion of her had improved, her opinion of *him* was obviously more dismal than ever.

Usually, he didn't care what people thought. But for some reason, in this case he did. "Why not?"

"How? I live in California."

"Not anymore. You will live with me in Italy until the baby is born. And after I get a DNA test, you will remain. Forever."

"What are you saying?" she whispered. She wiped a trembling hand over her eyes. "You—you want to marry me?"

He barked a laugh, which echoed across the ramparts. It was only when he saw her flinch that he bit it back. "Forgive me. But marry? No." He snorted. "I was married once. Never again."

"Then—" Rosalie blinked, confused. "I don't understand. What exactly are you suggesting?"

Alex lifted a dark eyebrow. "You will live with me. I will provide for you. I'll give you an allowance, more than you can possibly spend—"

"I'm not a gold digger! I'm not interested in your money!"

"Fine," he said, annoyed. Then he had a sudden idea. He gave her a grin. "As you wish. You can get a job and pay your own way, every step. You'll come to Venice and live with us." He tilted his head. "As the nanny."

CHAPTER THREE

Rosalie stared at him in shock. Then she lost it.

"The *nanny*?" she screeched.

"Is that a problem?" Alex replied.

She put her hands protectively over her belly. "I'm his *mother*. Not some employee!"

"A few days ago, you were just a hired womb. I'd think becoming the baby's nanny would feel like a promotion."

"Are you drunk?" she demanded. "You must be, if you think I'd ever agree to be my own child's nanny!"

Alex looked her over slowly, at her black shift dress and waitress's white apron. "Am I correct in believing you are not in possession of a trust fund? That you have no..." he paused "...*private estate*?"

Rosalie thought of her family's thousand-acre farm as it had been, and the warm golden patina on the hundred-year-old Victorian house she'd grown up in. Then she blinked, remembering it as it was now, nothing but a thousand acres of charred ash. She'd only looked at it for a millisecond, on the way to the funeral, but it would forever be burned into her mind.

Swallowing hard, she focused on Alex. He was looking at her strangely.

"No trust fund," she said shortly. She didn't mention her parents' life insurance, because it made her feel sick to think of it, and anyway it wasn't very much. "Just a job in San Francisco. Where I'm expected on Monday."

"I see." His sensual lips curved. "But since you've made

it clear you won't accept any handouts from me, you will need to earn money somehow while you're living in Italy, will you not?"

"I haven't said I'm moving to Italy, but if I did, I'd get an actual job—"

"It can be difficult for an American to get a job in the European Union without a work permit. Unless, perhaps, you are highly skilled in some technical field?"

She thought of her job answering phones for a seafood wholesaler on the Embarcadero. "No," she said tightly.

"You perhaps have the capital to start a business that will create jobs for Italian workers?"

Not without selling her land. Which she couldn't. Not yet. Maybe not ever. "No."

"Do you speak Italian?"

"No," she whispered.

He changed tactics. "Well, let's say, for the sake of argument, you still found a full-time job. Then you'd spend all your daytime hours away from our newborn son, and that would defeat the whole reason for you moving to Italy, would it not?"

Rosalie stared at him, feeling dizzy. His words were spinning her in circles, making her doubt herself, making her actually wonder if his argument was reasonable. "I haven't said I will live with you."

"Or here's another idea." He looked at her sideways. "You could simply allow me to support you."

"No," she cried. "I don't want your money!"

He shrugged. "Then—nanny it is," he said lightly. "It is a compromise. A way for us to raise our son in Italy together."

"Funny compromise. It seems I'm the only one making any sacrifices here, quitting my job and moving around the world."

Alex looked at her. "Would you really be giving up so much by leaving San Francisco?"

Rosalie thought of what waited for her there. A job where she felt anonymous to her bosses and was screamed at by customers. A tattered two-bedroom apartment with a re-volving door of roommates who worked long hours to pay the rent, and went out clubbing and brought home men whenever they weren't. She'd even found herself locked out of her own bedroom and forced to sleep on the lumpy sofa, whenever her roommate brought home one-night stands.

But even *that* was preferable to going home to Emmets-ville.

So sell, a voice whispered inside her. *Just sell the farm and you'll never have to see it again.*

The land was in wine country between Sonoma and Pet-aluma. She'd already received multiple offers, each more shockingly high than the last. With that much in her bank account, she could wipe that smug look off Alex's face in an instant. The nanny, indeed.

"The truth is," Alex said quietly, "You don't have any desire to return to San Francisco."

It was as if he was reading her mind. "Why do you say that?"

"Because if you enjoyed living in San Francisco, you'd have already sold the land you inherited from your parents in Sonoma County."

She stared at him in shock.

"I told you—I know everything," he said. "You could have sold the land to one of the big wineries and changed your life. Plenty of money to buy a fancy condo or get a college degree or take a luxury cruise around the world. But you haven't done any of those things."

She looked away. "No."

He shook his head. "You can't bring yourself to sell the land. But you can't bring yourself to go back to it, either. You're stuck. A detail that was made obvious to me when you didn't bring up the fact that you are, in fact, in possession of a large fortune. Just one you do not wish to spend." He looked at her. "Well?"

Rosalie's heart was pounding wildly. She looked longingly at the steps that led down to the cobblestoned lane, and the safety of her great-aunt's restaurant.

"I want you to come and live with me, Rosalie. You are the mother of my child. Let me support you." He gave a small smile. "As your aunt pointed out, it is my responsibility."

"No one gives something for nothing," she whispered. She didn't want to owe him anything. She took a deep breath. "Maybe I could be a nanny."

Alex blinked, looking surprised. "As you wish," he said softly. "You'll spend your days caring for our baby, exactly as you wish, without having to worry about your financial security, and knowing you have a safety net if I ever fire you…"

"*Fire* me?"

"Yes. We'll draw up a contract. You'll have severance, so there would be nothing to worry about. Or if you grow tired of motherhood, and leave us—"

"Are you crazy?"

"You'll still have all the benefits of an employment contract. And be protected."

Rosalie's only experience with a contract had been the disastrous one with the fertility clinic. That hadn't made her eager to sign another one. "Protected? From what?"

Pressing his lips together tightly, he didn't answer.

Rosalie repeated in a hard voice, "Protected from what, Alex?"

He said abruptly, "From me."

Her mouth went dry. "Why—why would I need protecting from you?"

Alex came closer to her and her heart quickened as his

powerful body stopped just inches from hers, his hard, handsome face half hidden in shadow.

"Because I might be tempted to seduce you," he said softly.

Her lips parted as a shiver went over her body. "What?"

"Having you living in my house, when you're not just so beautiful, but also the mother of my child…"

"You think I'm beautiful?" Rosalie felt dizzy.

His eyes fell briefly to her mouth, then lifted back up. "It would perhaps help us to draw clear boundaries. So there's no danger."

"Danger," she echoed. She felt it. Something about being close to him did strange things to her, body and soul.

Why? Because he was so darkly handsome? So rich and powerful? So sensual and wicked, with his cruel lips and husky voice, with its barest hint of Italian accent?

All that, and she was pregnant with his baby. It would be astonishing if she *didn't* feel shivery every time he was near.

But she couldn't believe he would call her beautiful. Even if she weren't heavily pregnant, she wouldn't be remotely in his league. His type of woman would be obviously more like Chiara—chic, pin thin, wickedly gorgeous, devastatingly clever.

While Rosalie was just an ordinary girl in a shapeless dress and waitress apron, who wore her heart on her sleeve. Of petite height and tending toward plumpness, she'd never cared much about fashion, either. She bought her clothes at the discount superstore and used coupons whenever she could.

She looked at Alex Falconeri. Whatever he might say about being tempted, there was no way *he* could be worried about losing control and seducing her.

There was only one explanation.

He'd seen how attracted Rosalie was to him, and was trying to let her down easy. How could he not see the impact he had on her, when her cheeks went red and her body trembled whenever he got close, whenever he even *looked* at her?

Gorgeous as he was, and a wealthy Italian count too, this type of thing probably happened to him all the time. Obviously, he was politely trying to warn her off.

Who could blame him when she'd just practically blurted out a marriage proposal? Her cheeks burned.

"So." He looked down at her. "You wish to be the nanny?"

She stared at him, then stubbornly shook her head. "I don't want to be your employee."

"You won't let me support you, you won't let me hire you—" Muttering in Italian, Alex rubbed the back of his head, looking as irritated as a man that handsome and suave *could* look, when he had the face of a dark angel. He bit out, "So what is the solution?"

Taking a deep breath, Rosalie said, "How about I keep my job in San Francisco, take two months' maternity leave, and we both chip in together and get a studio apartment there? Or if you prefer, you could get your own place, and I'll let you visit the baby. Whenever you want," she added generously.

Alex stared at her for a moment, then he snorted. "You've got guts. I'll give you that."

"I was just thinking the same about you." She paused. "*Guts* is such an American word. And you barely have an accent."

"My mother was American," he said coldly. "Like you."

"Oh, was she?" Rosalie opened her eyes wide in mock surprise. "*Your* mom was a farm girl who once took second place at the county fair for her pie crust? Or maybe you mean—" she tilted her head "—she, too, worked as a receptionist for minimum wage, and volunteered for Meals on Wheels in high school?"

His lips curved slightly as he considered her. "My mother was a debutante. A Cabot from Boston who attended Wellesley."

"Of course," Rosalie said, barely resisting the urge to roll her eyes. "*Exactly* like me."

She'd had enough. Turning on her heel, she started down the steep stone steps from the rampart, back into the little village behind the walls.

"Where are you going?" he demanded. "Nothing is decided—"

"Wrong." She looked back at him. "I've decided I'm going to bed. And don't worry, that wasn't an invitation."

"Rosalie—"

"Good night," she said firmly.

She went carefully down the steps back into the village, then went more quickly up the lane toward her great-aunt's door. Away from his presence, she felt like she could breathe again.

But as she reached the restaurant, Alex was suddenly beside her. He'd easily caught up to her with his long strides.

"I told you, you're not invited," she said uneasily. His sensual lips curved.

"I'm coming to help you pack."

"I'm not going to Venice with you."

"Oh, yes, you are," Odette said in French behind her. Turning, Rosalie saw her tiny, hunched great-aunt glaring from the doorway.

"Excuse me," she bit out to Alex, then stomped inside the restaurant, closing the door firmly behind her.

"You don't understand," she argued.

"I understand perfectly," Odette countered. "The father of your baby would like you to live with him, to get to know you, and help raise the child he never knew about. Alex Falconeri is handling this like a gentleman."

"A gentleman—are you crazy? He's bullying me into

living with him in Venice! In his palace!" Even Rosalie was aware of how ridiculous a complaint this must sound. Scowling, she felt herself on firmer ground as she argued, "He wanted to hire me as my own baby's *nanny*!"

"You refused, of course."

"Of course I did. I'm his son's mother, not his employee."

The elderly lady snorted. "As far as men are concerned, they don't often see any difference," she said tartly, then added, "You must get to know each other. Then, perhaps, for the child's sake, you will decide to marry."

Rosalie's cheeks burned. "I already suggested that."

"*Mon Dieu*, you are a fast worker."

"It was a misunderstanding, that's all. But he shot down the idea. He was married once already, and he takes his vows seriously. Perhaps a little too seriously," she added, thinking about all the problems this had caused.

Odette regarded her with bright eyes. "A man who takes his vows too seriously? There is no such thing."

"But *Tatie*—"

"You will give him a chance. The baby is his as much as it is yours. Does the child not deserve to have more family?"

"The baby has me. And you," Rosalie said desperately. Her great-aunt smiled.

"*Ma petite*, I will not live forever. And a boy needs a father."

"But it's not right—why should I go live with him in Italy? I don't know anyone there."

"Is there so much for you back in California?"

Rosalie thought of her childhood home, burned to ash. And her parents, who'd died in the fire, and it was her fault, all her fault. If she'd married the boy next door like they'd wanted, she would have been there to save them. She would have known to get them out before it was too late.

All that she had waiting for her in California was ash and regret.

So what if she went to Italy with her baby's father? What if, at least for a while, she agreed to live in his palazzo?

"But I don't want to be the nanny," she said in a small voice.

"Of course you do not," her great-aunt sniffed. "You are pregnant with a rich man's child. You will allow him to pay for everything."

Rosalie stared at her. "I couldn't!"

"Why?"

"It would be…charity! And my father always said, *No one gets something for nothing.*"

"Something for nothing indeed." Odette snorted. "You are pregnant with his baby, Rosalie, creating the child in your body. You will go through hard, painful labor to give birth. Then you will be up night and day, nursing the baby, rocking him to sleep, boiling bottles and so forth." Odette, who was childless, waved her hand vaguely. "If that is not work, what is? If anything, *he* is the one accepting charity from you. After all, what is he doing to help with all these tasks? Nothing! But nothing!"

Rosalie stared at her great-aunt. "You are crazy." But she suddenly leaned over and gave the wrinkled cheek a fierce kiss.

"You are welcome." Odette gave a satisfied nod. "That is why young people need the older ones. To tell you about life."

Taking off her apron, Rosalie hung it up on a hook and went back outside to where Alex waited, a hulking shadowy figure in the moonlight.

"I've decided I'll come with you."

His expression didn't change, but his shoulders relaxed. *"Va bene."*

"Just for a little while. Just so we can get to know each other."

"I will convince you to stay."

"Not as your nanny," she countered. "Since I'm agreeing to move to your city, you will pay for everything, food, housing, medical care. Even a stipend for extra expenses while I'm living in Venice."

"Yes," he said instantly.

She was astonished at how quickly he agreed. "And once the baby is born and you have your paternity test, you will always pay child support. Whether we live in the same house or not."

"Of course." Alex tilted his head. "Anything else?"

Rosalie thought fast. "And you must promise, if us living together doesn't work out for whatever reason, you will not try to bully me into giving you full custody."

"As long as you agree to the same."

She nearly choked a laugh, that Alex Falconeri, the wealthy, powerful Conte di Rialto, would think *she* could bully *him* into anything. But her smile faded as she looked at his face. She stuck out her hand. "Agreed."

"Agreed." He took her hand in his.

As his larger hand enfolded hers, she felt the warmth and roughness of his palm. His fingers pressed between hers, pushing down against her own. Electricity coursed through her body, making her breasts heavy and nipples taut.

Alex abruptly pulled his hand away.

She exhaled. Had she done it again? Revealed her pathetic desire, embarrassing herself and making him uncomfortable?

His handsome face was inscrutable.

Cheeks hot, she turned, muttering, "I'll go pack."

He was suddenly there beside her. "I'm coming too."

"Why?" She could barely bring herself to look at him. She tried to joke, "Are you afraid I might try to climb out the window?"

"The thought had crossed my mind."

"You obviously haven't seen the window. But fine, do what you want."

Inside the empty restaurant, Rosalie led him up the stairs in the back, then up another flight, and another flight still, each set of stairs more slender and vertical than the last. At the last flight, he frowned. "Are you sure this is safe for you? I can go get your things, if you tell me where they are."

Alex was being protective of her? For a moment she was touched and surprised. Then she realized it was his baby he was worried about, not her. Falling down a flight of stairs two months before her due date might lead to an onset of early labor. "I'm fine," she said stubbornly. "I've done this tons of times over the last two days. Come on."

At the very top was the tiny garret of her aunt's small hotel, an attic room far too undesirable for any paying guest.

Rosalie switched on a small lamp, which cast a soft glow on the slanted walls, barely reaching into the shadows. A single lonely bed was stuffed against the slanted wall next to a bare clothing rack. Leaning awkwardly, she pulled her overnight bag from beneath the bed, then swiftly packed it with her few items of clothes, blushing when she packed her extra bra and underwear over her rumpled paperback copy of *Murder on the Orient Express*.

Coming into the room behind her, he made no comment. Because of the slanted roof, he could only stand up straight in the middle of the room. Just having him so close to her made her feel a flash of heat across her skin.

Taking a deep breath, she glanced out the window, which she'd pushed open earlier for fresh air in the stuffy room. Trying to calm her heart, she looked at the tiny village clinging to the rock beneath her, and beyond the ramparts, the moonlit sea. In the distance, she heard a seagull's plaintive cry, like a lost soul searching, searching, searching and never finding.

"Alex—" Turning abruptly in the tight space of the room, she was suddenly pushed up against him.

"Yes?" He looked down at her. It was just the two of them alone beside a single bed.

Her whole body flushed hot beneath her black shift dress. Awkwardly, she turned away, yanking the sheets off the tiny bed. "I just need to drop these in the laundry room."

"Allow me." As he took her bag, then the sheets and blankets, his fingertips brushed hers. She swallowed.

What was wrong with her? Why was he having this effect on her? She'd never felt this way before about anyone. Certainly not Cody, the one time he'd tried to kiss her on that disastrous date, or any of the men she'd met in San Francisco, or the boys from high school. Was it pregnancy hormones?

Or was it just the fact that Alex Falconeri was the most obscenely sexy man she'd ever met?

Pushing past him, she fled the tiny garret. After going back down the stairs, she led him to the laundry room, then to the bathroom she'd shared with her aunt. Gathering up a small toiletry bag, she tucked it into the overnight bag still on his shoulder, then paused, knowing she should take the bag and carry it herself. She carried her own burdens, always.

But as she started to reach for the straps, she remembered her aunt's stern admonition. Okay. She was seven months' pregnant. Maybe she could accept help. But it wasn't easy.

Clenching her hands at her sides so she wouldn't be tempted to take the bag, she faced him with all the dignity she could muster. "I'm ready."

Rosalie just prayed he couldn't see the impact he was having on her. If he did…it would be even more embarrassing than when she'd blurted out the question asking if he was proposing to her. She could only imagine how humiliated she'd feel if he felt he had to explicitly tell her he wasn't interested in her physically. Again.

From now on, she told herself firmly as they headed downstairs, she would focus on one job. And it might be the most difficult job she'd ever had.

She would stop wanting Alex Falconeri.

CHAPTER FOUR

ALEX'S BLOOD WAS PUMPING as he watched Rosalie hug her great-aunt farewell. He'd gotten what he wanted. She was returning to live with him in Venice.

He didn't begrudge the deal they'd made. A stipend? Negligible. Child support? Obviously. Custody? He was relieved they'd promised not to battle each other with underhanded tricks. Yes, he had far more money for a protracted custody fight, but courts tended to be swayed with sympathy for a loving mother. And Rosalie's love for her unborn child was clear.

As was her incredible charisma. Her petite, curvy frame, her luminous brown eyes, so soulful and alive, her plump lips, her dark hair with streaks of sunlight around her heart-shaped face—

No judge alive could resist a plea from a woman like this, and a jury even less so. Any case Alex took to court against her, he would lose.

He would have paid any price to get her to willingly move to his palazzo in Venice. He could not easily have moved to California for a multitude of reasons. His vineyard was one. His inability to get on a plane was another. He was relieved she'd given in, and was going to let him support her. He'd only suggested Rosalie become a nanny because she'd been so strangely reluctant to let him pay her way. What did he care about money? He was glad to support both her and the child. *Of course* he should support them.

But he hadn't lied about wanting to create firm boundaries. Making her his employee would have helped with that. But now, there was nothing to prevent him from acting on his desire and making her his mistress. He'd be living in the same house with her. Wanting her with this ravenous hunger.

But he could never allow himself to have her.

Because a woman like Rosalie Brown only wanted true love. She'd said so. For her, it was the only reason for marriage, the only reason for sex.

Love is the basis of everything. Or it should be.

She'd been raised in a loving home. She actually believed that was *normal*. It was why she'd become a surrogate. To bring another family together, to try to heal her own grief over the parents she'd lost. For love, all for love.

While Alex had no love to give.

Just learning to be a father would be hard enough. He sucked in his breath.

All this time, he'd wanted a child, but that had been theoretical. He'd wanted to continue the family name.

But in two months, he was going to be responsible for a real flesh-and-blood little boy. How would he know what to do? He'd assumed he'd love his child, but what if he didn't? After the way he'd been raised, how would Alex possibly know how to be a good father?

"It's nearly midnight," the elderly French lady said as she pulled away from her great-niece's embrace in the restaurant. "Are you sure you don't want to wait to leave until morning?"

Rosalie glanced back at him questioningly. Alex thought of her tiny bed in the garret, of the way it had felt with the two of them pushed together in such a tight space. He wouldn't last two minutes without trying to kiss her.

"We should leave," he replied. "We will sleep in Paris.

Goodbye, *madame*." He gave Odette Lancel a small bow. "Thank you again for your assistance."

The white-haired Frenchwoman's eyes narrowed as she looked up at him. "Take good care of her, young man. Or you'll have me to deal with."

"I would not wish to tangle with you, *madame*." It was not a jest. She reminded him of his Italian grandmother, who'd been fierce and almost diabolically clever. A woman not to be crossed.

"I have your word?"

He paused. He was careful with his word. It was no longer in his soul to give flimsy promises. "Yes."

The older woman nodded, satisfied, then gave her grand-niece one last admonition. "Remember. Let him pay for everything."

"Tatie!" Rosalie seemed scandalized and her cheeks blushed deeper than ever as she threw him a nervous glance.

Ah. So that was why she'd had a change of heart about letting him pay. Her aunt had convinced her.

Alex was glad. He wanted to pay. It made things easier. And money meant little to him. Just piles of gold in the bank reminding him of things of which he did not want to be reminded. He hefted Rosalie's bag higher on his shoulder. "We should go."

She nodded. Giving her great-aunt's wrinkled cheek one last kiss, she followed him out of the restaurant. Holding her hand so she wouldn't fall, he led her down the steep hill and through the dark, deserted village.

They exited the town gate. Rosalie stopped abruptly on the flat sandy beach between the ramparts and the cause-way.

"What," she breathed, "is that?"

"This?" He casually continued walking toward the red Lamborghini. He glanced back at her. "It's our ride."

"How did you get permission to park it here?" She looked at him accusingly. "There are rules."

He shrugged. "I have friends."

"I bet," she muttered as he opened the passenger door. He supported her arm as she lowered herself heavily into the black leather seat. She glared up at him. "Does everyone do what you say, wherever you go?"

"Usually," Alex said. He thought the lie sounded more modest than the actual truth, which was *Yes*.

Tucking her bag into the tiny trunk, Alex got into the driver's seat and started the engine. The low purr built to a roar as he whirled the sleek red sports car back down the empty causeway. Silence fell as he drove onto the mainland, then away across the fields of Normandy.

"Why are we driving to Venice?" she asked finally, looking uncomfortable in the supple leather seat, as if she was afraid to touch anything in the expensive car. "It would be much faster to fly."

"I don't care for planes," he said shortly, looking ahead at the empty road.

"I'm surprised you don't have a private jet."

He didn't answer. He felt her gaze on him.

"You do, don't you?" she said slowly. "You have a private jet."

"I inherited it. I allow my employees to use it. Or to bring people to me in Venice."

"Why don't you like to fly?"

Focusing fiercely on the road, he said, "My father loved it. He thought himself quite a pilot, until he crashed his Cessna into the Alps, with my mother and brother aboard."

She sucked in her breath. "Oh, no! Were they—all right?"

"No," he said flatly.

"They died?" Rosalie choked out, "I'm so sorry."

So much sympathy she had for people who hadn't been good or kind. "We were never particularly close."

"No wonder you're nervous about flying."

"I'm not nervous. I just don't do it."

She hesitated. "There are courses, classes you can take to help—"

"Yes," he cut in. "I took them. I was in the middle of one when my sister died three years ago. In a plane crash in South America." He glanced at her coldly. "I lost my entire family to plane crashes, Miss Brown. Perhaps you won't harass me if I prefer to remain on the ground."

She took a deep breath.

"I'm sorry," she said quietly. "It's awful. I know."

You don't know, he wanted to snap at her. How could she?

But her parents had died too. Maybe she did know.

Rosalie looked out the window, but before she turned her head he saw a tear streaking down her cheek.

She pitied him.

Alex wondered what Rosalie would think if she knew the whole truth. How he'd indirectly caused his family to die.

His sister, Margaret, the middle child and only daughter, had been Alex's ally growing up. She'd been the peacemaker in an angry family. Thomas, the eldest brother and heir, had all the worst qualities of their parents—a hair-trigger temper, a chip on his shoulder and a habit of screaming at the slightest insult. Alex, the youngest, had learned to keep his own resentments bottled up beneath silence and sarcasm.

As Thomas would inherit the title and the responsibility for running their family's company, Margaret had buried her head in books and research. Alex similarly had fled, to study viticulture at Cornell, and he'd dreamed of starting his own wine label in America. After graduation, he'd promised his mother he'd go home for Christmas, especially since Margaret had just started her new job as a research scientist in Antarctica. But, unwilling to face the family drama, Alex had broken his promise and stayed in New York.

And so his parents and older brother, finding the holidays unmanageable without the emotional buffer of Margaret or Alex, had decided at the last moment to go skiing in the Alps.

After their deaths, Alex had found himself unable to get on a plane, even a big commercial jet. Margaret had been sympathetic at first, but as years passed, she'd finally demanded that he get his problem *sorted out* because, as she'd said during a satellite phone call from Antarctica, "I can't help you. You can only help yourself."

"I will. I promise," he'd told her.

He'd returned to Italy, where he'd focused on the old vineyard owned by the Falconeris for generations. He knew he should take an interest in the financial institution his mother had inherited in Boston, which provided the bulk of their family's fortune. But when it was threatened with a hostile takeover, he'd wanted to sell their shares, and let it go.

"You can't," Margaret had begged him from Antarctica. "It's mother's only legacy. Promise you'll go to the shareholders' meeting in two weeks and fight it. You have to convince them not to sell!"

"I promise," Alex had told her reluctantly.

But the day before the meeting, when she'd called to make sure he'd made it to Boston, he'd been forced to admit that he was, in fact, still in Italy with no intention of getting on a plane.

Margaret had been upset. "Fine, I'll go. Even though this is a really bad time to try to leave. You should have told me from the beginning that you had no intention of going."

"I'm sorry," he tried, "I never meant to—"

"Whether you meant it or not, you lied to me. I'm disappointed in you, Alex. I'll call you when I reach Boston."

It was the last time he'd ever spoken to his sister.

Everyone said the two crashes were totally unrelated. His father had been piloting a private jet, and drinking, and likely arguing both with his wife and with his eldest son, screaming as he always did, causing them to scream back. While Margaret had been traveling to Chile on a chartered jet when a bird strike blew through the engine. There was no obvious connection between the two incidents.

Only Alex knew that there was.

Him.

If he had been honest with himself about his fear of flying, he could have booked passage on a ship to Boston in plenty of time for the shareholders' meeting. If he'd been honest with his sister, he could have told her frankly that he'd never intended to help run the investment firm. Either way, he'd broken promises, forcing his sister to leave her research station in Antarctica. Just as he'd broken that promise to his mother to come home for Christmas.

At Margaret's funeral in Venice, dry-eyed, numb, Alex came to a decision. He obviously had no idea how to love anyone. But he would never break a promise again. For any reason.

His family's investment firm had been lost in the hostile takeover, and Alex had let it go. He'd quietly accepted a fortune in cash for his family's shares. He'd tucked away the money and buried himself at the vineyard, blocking everything from his mind except the need to produce a truly stellar wine—as if that could save him.

A month later, he'd married Chiara Vulpato.

Now, as Alex drove his red Lamborghini through desolate French valleys, he looked at the beautiful woman beside him. She'd fallen asleep beneath the quietly vibrating hum of the engine. Even as she slept, her arms were cradled tenderly around her belly.

Rosalie thought she shared the same grief, because she, too, was an orphan. But her heart was full of love, and she had the naive belief that she could make the world a better place. Her parents had died in a wildfire. It hadn't been Rosalie's fault.

So she had no idea how Alex felt. At all.

And he intended to keep it that way.

Hours later, as he pulled the sports car into the grand entrance of his favorite Parisian luxury hotel, he looked at her. She'd slept fitfully for hours as they'd traveled across the north of France. She was so beautiful, so unconsciously sensual. He wanted her.

But he could not have her.

Of all women on earth, Rosalie was the most forbidden. The stakes were too high, with a child that would bind them for the rest of their lives. She was a romantic with a loving heart. If Alex seduced her, all he would do was break that heart and wreck her life. Just as he'd wrecked so many others.

Turning off the car engine, he looked at her again, seeing the tired circles beneath her eyes as she slept. He thought of how much she had gone through over the past year. No wonder she'd been so deliriously happy when, in Venice, he'd told her she could keep her baby. No wonder she'd pulled him fiercely into her arms. He could still feel the electricity of her lips brushing against his earlobe as she'd whispered, *Thank you. You're a good man.*

But her horrified, traumatized expression when he'd shown up at her great-aunt's restaurant today told a different story. He'd made her dream of keeping her baby come true.

Then today, he'd taken it away.

He took a deep breath. He could not let her take his child

away. Nor could he be the man she needed. He'd never be a romantic partner or a husband.

But there were other things he could do for her. Other ways to comfort her after all her grief. She was pregnant with his baby. She deserved every ounce of his care.

And she would get it. He thought suddenly of her wistful words. *I just got a passport and traveled across the ocean for the first time in my life.* He remembered the Agatha Christie paperback he'd seen in her satchel.

Reaching out, Alex gently shook her awake in the stopped car beneath the illuminated porte cochere. "We're here."

"Here?"

"Paris. Our hotel."

Yawning, Rosalie blinked groggily. "What time is it?"

"Three in the morning." Looking at her sleepy expression, he smiled. "I can carry you inside, if you like."

That seemed to wake her up. She drew back, alarmed. "No. I'm awake."

As the hotel's valet rushed forward, Alex carried her bag, and his own, as he led Rosalie inside the luxurious hotel.

Even Paris was quiet at this time of night. They walked together through the elegant lobby.

He would take care of her, Alex reiterated to himself. He would give her the world.

And he would not seduce her. He could resist. Of course he could. He could resist anything.

But when they reached the registration desk, as the manager's face lit up and greeted him by name, asking if he'd like his usual room, Alex refused. He asked instead for a two-bedroom suite.

He thought of himself as tough. He'd even been accused of being heartless. But even he could feel his weakness where Rosalie Brown was concerned.

Against her sensual beauty, he was only a man.

* * *

Rosalie woke slowly. Her eyes fluttered, then opened.

She'd slept in late. She saw it by the slant of gray light in the magnificent Paris hotel suite, all pale pastel furniture and matching silk wallpapers. She looked at the elegant clock above the marble fireplace mantel and saw it was almost noon.

She'd slept better than she'd ever imagined. But then, Alex had insisted on giving her the only bed.

Sitting up, she looked across the open suite. But on the other side of the large, spacious room, the sofa was empty.

Last night, the manager had regretfully informed them that all the two-bedroom suites were occupied. "But," he'd added hopefully, "we do have your regular room available, *monsieur le comte*. Room 847."

With a sigh, Alex had agreed. Refusing the offer of assistance with the two small satchels, he'd signed the receipt then taken her up to the hotel room himself. She'd been dazzled by the vast, beautiful room, which seemed to her as elegant as Versailles, with its enormous bed and marble fireplace. Then she'd looked again at the bed. Just one bed.

"You will take it," Alex had told her. When Rosalie had tried to refuse, he'd asked her, with a gleam in his dark eyes, if he needed to physically lift her onto the bed himself.

The idea of having Alex hold her so closely against his body had made her afraid—afraid of herself, afraid of what she might do when faced with such temptation. So she'd agreed. Just the hours together in the tiny space of his sports car had been bad enough. She'd spent a long time pretending to be asleep, until she had actually fallen asleep.

But in the intimacy of the hotel room, after she'd already changed her clothes, brushed her teeth, climbed into the bed and pulled the blankets up to her neck, she'd heard him take off his clothes in the darkness. The slight gleam of light from the windows had caressed his naked chest as he walked to the sofa. Even though the lights were off, even though she was on the other side of the room, she still felt him. Every step. Every breath.

As she'd squeezed her eyes shut, she'd known she wouldn't sleep a wink. But she'd been more tired than she'd realized. Now, waking up so late, she felt guilty. He obviously hadn't slept nearly so well. "Alex?"

He came in from the sliding door that led to a wrought-iron balcony. "Good morning."

He looked handsome, freshly showered and shaved and wearing clean clothes, a charcoal tailored shirt and trousers. His hair was still a little wet. Unconsciously, she licked her lips. She could only imagine how she looked, with sleep-mussed hair, probably with a little drool left on her pillow. As if she didn't feel ungainly enough, at seven months' pregnant and wearing an old T-shirt that stretched over her belly like a beach balloon. "Why did you let me sleep so late?"

His dark eyes were warm as they trailed over her. "I thought you needed it."

Why? Did she look that bad? "I'm sorry."

"About what?"

"It's bad enough that I made you take the sofa—"

"You didn't make me—I insisted."

"But also, because of me, we'll get a late start on the road back to Venice. I'm sure you have more important things to do than wait for me."

"Yes," he said, "speaking of that…"

She sat up straight on the bed. "What?"

"I've decided I'm not in such a hurry." He smiled. "You said earlier that this is your first trip to Europe."

"Yes," she said, feeling suddenly guarded. "So?"

He came closer to the bed, looking down at her in a way that made her feel like the stretchy T-shirt and blanket covering her body weren't nearly enough, because she could feel him, even without him touching her.

"I've made plans."

"P-plans?" she stammered, her cheeks flooding with heat. Her gaze fell to his thighs so close to her mattress, his muscular, powerful body seeming barely tamed by his civilized clothing. "What plans?"

"Would you like to see Paris?"

Her lips parted as she looked at him. "Um?"

"I'm guessing you haven't seen much of the city."

"That's true." After she'd left him in Venice three days before, she'd gotten the cheapest flight she could to Paris. She'd stumbled out of Charles de Gaulle Airport, exhausted from jet lag, and caught the first train to Rennes, then taken the bus to arrive in a heap on her great-aunt's doorstep. She said honestly, "Last night was the most I've seen of Paris."

He snorted. "Since you were asleep, that isn't much." He paused, tilting his head as his black eyes glinted. "Get up."

Nervously, she pushed back the covers. She felt his eyes skim over her stretchy T-shirt and shorts, and her body reacted as if he'd caught her naked. She said defensively, "It's the only thing that still fits to sleep in."

"I will buy you new clothes."

She started to protest, then realized he was likely wanting to buy her new clothes just for self-preservation. For a man as sleekly sophisticated as Alex Falconeri, seeing her in an old, worn T-shirt and tiny shorts likely hurt his eyeballs. Remembering Great-aunt Odette's adjuration to *let him pay*, she sighed. "If you must."

Alex slowly looked her over again. "I must." He abruptly looked away. "But not today. Today we…"

"We what?"

"Today I'm going to show you Paris."

And Alex did. After they came out of the five-star hotel on the Champs-Élysées, with Rosalie wearing just a simple blouse and flowing skirt against the cool, drizzly gray day, she discovered a Rolls-Royce and French-speaking driver, who tipped his hat.

"Mademoiselle."

She looked at Alex in surprise. "What happened to your Lamborghini?"

"I had it sent on," he said.

"Sent on? All the way to Venice?"

He shrugged, then held out his hand. "We have other things to do."

For the rest of the day, they saw the most famous sights of Paris. Traveling in luxury and comfort, they bypassed lines. Doors fell open to them as if by magic. The Eiffel Tower was first, followed by lunch at the most difficult-to-book restaurant in the City of Light. Afterward, they enjoyed a speed tour of the Louvre, including the *Mona Lisa*. Then they visited the Arc de Triomphe, the bookstores of Saint-Germain-des-Prés and ate buttery fresh-baked croissants in the Marais.

Through it all, Alex was beside her, telling her stories about the history of the city, about this shocking general, or that scandalous queen.

"How did you learn all this?" Rosalie blurted out in the back of the Rolls-Royce as twilight finally fell across the city.

"I lived here long ago, studying wine." He shook his head. "But don't ask me about that, or I will bore you to tears with stories of vintners that are not quite so interesting, unless you're fascinated by the Great French Wine Blight of 1871."

"Fascinated," she repeated, staring at the curve of his sensual lips.

"In the mid-nineteenth century, the phylloxera aphid blight destroyed most vineyards in France, forcing wine-makers to try an American's crazy idea of grafting hardy

Texas rootstock onto their vines. It worked, the vineyards were saved, and a cowboy was awarded the Légion d'honneur by the French government…"

She watched his lips move as he spoke, wondering what it would feel like if he kissed her.

"Rosalie." His voice was suddenly low and hoarse. "Don't."

She looked up. "What?"

"Just don't. I want to take good care of you. But there are some things I cannot do." He looked abruptly out the window. "We're almost there."

Humiliation made her cheeks blaze. Why did she keep doing this, revealing her desire? They'd spent a lovely day together, he'd been gentlemanly and kind, and she'd wrecked it all by staring at his lips!

Why did she keep embarrassing herself, forcing Alex to remind her that she could never be more to him than the mother of his child, a partner, or maybe if she was very lucky, a friend?

"Thank you for showing me Paris." She looked out at the twinkling lights of the city beneath the rising purple night. Her stomach rumbled. "Are we going to dinner?"

"Yes. But you'll have to wait for it." The car stopped outside the Gare de l'Est. "Here."

As she got out of the Rolls-Royce, she tilted her head back to look at the nineteenth-century building. "We're eating at the train station?"

"We'll be eating on the train." He grinned. "Call it fast food." Looking at her expression, Alex gave a low laugh. Taking the two satchels from the driver, he said, "Follow me."

He led her into the train station. When she finally saw their train, her jaw dropped. It was a good thing she wasn't carrying a bag, because her knees went weak.

"Our train is…is…" She swallowed hard, then breathed, "The Orient Express?"

Alex smiled almost shyly. "I saw your book, and I thought…"

Putting her arms around him, Rosalie lifted up on her tiptoes and kissed him.

It was meant to be a quick kiss, just to express her over-whelming gratitude for what he'd done for her today. His actions had gone beyond kindness. That he had noticed her paperback, and on a whim, changed their plans for re-turning to Venice!

Her kiss was meant to simply thank him. Nothing more. Or so she told herself.

But when their lips brushed, she felt a sizzle of electric-ity that shook her deep inside. She quickly pulled away, and their eyes locked on the platform of the Gare de l'Est, where they stood next to the shining carriage of their lux-ury train.

The two satchels fell from Alex's shoulders. Looking at her intently, he cupped her face with both his large hands and lowered his head swiftly to hers.

His kiss was not gentle. It had nothing to do with grati-tude.

His lips seared hers, burning her. She gasped as her whole world swirled around her, around the train platform in Paris, as the most handsome, powerful man she'd ever met held her tightly to his muscular body and plundered her mouth in the most amazing kiss of her life.

When he finally pulled away, Rosalie was dazed, lost. Sprinkles of stars, a penumbra of rainbow-colored fairy dust, hovered on the edges of her vision.

"What—was that?" she breathed.

"Don't you know? Haven't you guessed?" Alex looked down at her. Running his fingertips along the edge of her cheek, he said huskily, "I want you, Rosalie."

For a moment, she was lost in the dark fire of his gaze. She heard a loud whistle, and a conductor calling out in French before he said in English, with good humor, "Young lovers, do you need help with your bags?"

Blushing, Rosalie turned back to Alex.

"We're supposed to board," she said, somewhat lamely.

"Yes. I heard him." A lazy smile lifted to Alex's lips. He picked up the two satchels from the platform. "Shall we?"

She followed him, feeling like she'd fallen into an alternate universe. Alex Falconeri, the Conte di Rialto, had kissed her. He'd said he wanted her.

No. It couldn't be true. She had to be dreaming!

But as he helped her up the train steps, Rosalie felt his hand against the curve of her lower back. And she shivered, caught between desire and fear, as they boarded the Orient Express bound for Venice.

CHAPTER FIVE

HE NEVER SHOULD have kissed her.

As the evening passed, and they'd boarded the train and found their separate compartments, Alex despised himself for his weakness. Even as he'd escorted Rosalie to their dining car and they sat across from each other for the elegant four-course meal, an underlying sexual tension had filled in all the spaces between their awkward dinner conversation, and he'd seen the unspoken question in her eyes.

What about his kiss? What did it mean? And above all: *Would it happen again?*

He would not let himself seduce her. He could not give her the love or the kind of marriage she clearly dreamed of. But he intended to make her happy. So he'd spent the whole day in Paris trying to charm her, to make her glad she'd agreed to move to Italy—while at the same time, keeping his emotional and physical distance.

Then he'd ruined it all by kissing her at the Gare de l'Est.

No matter how beautiful Rosalie had looked, no matter how wildly his body had reacted when she'd thrown her arms around him and pressed her soft lips to his, he should never have lost control and kissed her back.

After that kiss, he'd desperately needed a cold shower, and sadly his private compartment on the refurbished 1920s-era train did not have one. He deliberately hadn't booked the grand suite for two, with its anachronistic large bed and en suite shower. He was grimly determined to keep his distance.

Especially at night.

After sharing the hotel suite with Rosalie in Paris, Alex had known he could not endure another such night, tossing and turning on the sofa, aware that just a few steps away in the darkness, this beautiful, half-naked woman was wrapped around the pillows of a king-size bed. Just seeing her yesterday morning in a thin T-shirt which showed the detailed shape of her belly, her nipples and swollen breasts, and the little knit sleep shorts that rested below her pregnant tummy, clinging to the very edge of her hips as if they might fall off!

It was torture.

To be fair, in his overheated state, anything and everything felt like too much. Throughout their Paris tour yesterday, he'd been constantly aware of her, sitting beside him in the back seat of the Rolls. So he'd talked too much, tried to distract himself from his desire by telling one absurd tale after another. Even now, he could hardly believe he'd told Rosalie about the wine blight of 1871.

He'd never felt so out of control.

Alex could not seduce her. It would cause a world of hurt—not just for him, not even just for her, but for their child. Warm and sweet as she was, Rosalie would inevitably end up offering him her heart, and he would just as inevitably break it, because he had no heart of his own to offer in return. And their child would be the one to suffer most from his parents' unavoidable warring.

Alex's own parents had hated each other. For the entirety of their marriage, they'd screamed at each other, threatening divorce. His mother had cried, throwing dishes and jewels—whatever was close to hand—whenever she caught his father in another affair with a trashy stripper. His father, for his part, yelled that his affairs were her fault, because she was a drunkard, a cold harpy without a soul. They'd both started divorce proceedings multiple times, holding splashy, emotional press conferences accusing each other of cruelty and adultery, before ultimately deciding to remain together, *for the children*. The newspapers had loved the Conte and Contessa di Rialto. Already renowned for their wealth and beauty, they'd become the Italian Liz Taylor and Richard Burton, infamous for their marital battles.

But the experience had been not so enjoyable for their children.

All that drama. All that emotion. Alex had heard his parents had loved each other passionately when they wed, before all their love turned to hatred, and their vows to broken promises.

He wanted no part of that life. He'd vowed to be different. And he was. He had rules. He was honorable. For the last three years, he'd made absolutely sure to keep every single promise he made. At any cost. It was better to have no emotion at all, than risk that kind of destructive chaos.

He never should have kissed her.

And now he was paying the price. As much as he'd wanted Rosalie before, after last night's kiss on the railway platform, he could now think of nothing else but the sweet, hot fire of her lips. The desperate ache set his entire body aflame. He hungered for her like a starving man.

It had taken all Alex's strength to leave Rosalie after their dinner last evening, bidding her good-night at the door of her compartment, with its large window and folded-down twin bed. She'd seemed shocked, even hurt, as he'd simply left her with nothing more than a courteous bow.

His sleep last night, in his lonely berth beneath the steady hum and shake of the train, had been troubled with sensual dreams. The next day, after brooding over a continental breakfast of hot coffee and orange juice and freshly baked croissants served in his compartment, Alex went to the restaurant car to meet Rosalie for lunch at noon, as they'd previously agreed.

Arriving first at the small table, Alex looked out at the magnificent view flying past the train windows as he waited for Rosalie. They'd left all the gray drizzle of Paris behind, and now he could see the green Alps and sparkling mountain lakes beneath a blue sky.

He could hear the excited, happy chatter of other Orient Express passengers, many of whom had booked this expensive trip to mark an important occasion. Half the couples around him seemed to be celebrating their wedding anniversary.

Feeling suddenly surly, Alex drank black coffee, bitter as the brew.

Looking up, he saw Rosalie in the doorway. She looked fresh and pretty, wearing a yellow sundress. Her dark hair flowed over her shoulders, and her long, tanned legs ended in open-toed sandals. People's eyes turned to her, and he rose to his feet.

Smiling shyly, she came forward and let Alex help her into her chair. The waiter came to take her drink order. *"Madame?"*

"Orange juice," she responded with a warm smile. "With ice, please."

Not just the restaurant car, but the whole world seemed suddenly brighter to Alex as he looked at Rosalie's beautiful face, listening as she exclaimed how much she loved the train, how well she'd slept last night, how breathtaking the view was outside.

Alex's coffee no longer tasted bitter as he drank in his own view of her. His gaze traced down the curve of her cheek, to the edge of her chin, to her long, graceful neck.

"It's a good thing I packed sundresses and not jeans." Rosalie turned to him with smiling eyes. "Everyone is so dressed up—"

"You could wear anything or nothing," he murmured, "and you'd still be the most beautiful woman here."

Her smile faltered as electricity crackled between them. Their table for two was an island of sparks and fire, surrounded by the happy conversations, and beneath it all, the steady hum of the train.

"I'm glad you slept well." Against his will, Alex leaned forward. "Did you dream?"

Rosalie's cheeks turned pink, and she looked up with visible relief as the waiter appeared with her glass of orange juice. She seemed afraid to meet Alex's eyes. Sipping her drink, she looked out at the sharp green mountains and vivid blue sky. Her hand seemed to tremble.

He was torturing her, Alex realized. Torturing them both. It was unfair, even cruel of him to ask about her dreams. Why had he told her she was beautiful? In this one case, honesty did not seem like the best policy. Especially since she seemed so innocent. He knew from her dossier that she was twenty-five. He wondered how many lovers she'd had. Perhaps only three? Four?

"Where are we now?" she asked him, lifting her glass to her lips. For a moment, he was distracted. Then he realized she was asking a literal question, not a metaphorical one.

"Austria, almost to the Italian border." He tried to change the subject. "I have a second cousin who lives not too far from here, in the Italian Lake District."

"A cousin!" Looking astonished, she set down her glass as the waiter served the first course of their lunch, braised artichokes *à la barigoule* served with hot, flaky rolls. "I didn't know you had any family."

"Family is relative," he said grimly. He looked at her in surprise when he heard her snort.

"You made a joke," she pointed out.

He rolled his eyes. "Hardly much of a joke."

"True, but who am I to judge?" Taking a bite, she sighed in pleasure, then tilted her head. "What's your cousin like?"

"*Second* cousin. I barely know him." That wasn't entirely

true. Alex and Cesare had been friends as boys, when their parents had summered together in the Alps. But Cesare's parents being what they were, and Alex's parents being what they were, it didn't last long before the summer dissolved into bickering, shouting and drunken accusations of adultery.

But before that, for a few weeks, Cesare had been the older brother Alex had always wanted. While his real brother Thomas ignored or bullied him, his much older cousin had been gruffly kind, taking Alex fishing, skipping rocks across the lake, biking. Looking back, it had been the best summer of his life.

After that, he didn't see Cesare for years. The man had been busy building his hotel empire, and later, Alex had heard he'd gotten scandalously married to some American maid or housekeeper or something like that.

But by then, Alex's parents and older brother had died, and his sister was living in Antarctica. Alex had retreated into his own pursuit of winemaking. It was easier to think of himself as having no family than remember the one summer when he had.

Cesare had come to his family's funerals, but the two men hadn't spoken much. And Alex had invited him to his wedding, of course. The man was powerful, not to mention a prince, so Chiara had begged to include him. Why not?

At first, when he'd seen Cesare across the grand ballroom during the wedding reception, Alex had been honestly glad to see him again.

Then he'd met Cesare's wife, Emma, the lovely darkhaired woman looking up at her husband with eyes glowing with love. He'd seen Cesare's two children, a toddler and a fat, chortling baby, both of whom clung to their father. He'd seen the way Cesare circled his family with his powerful arms, loving them back with all his heart, strength and devotion.

Then Alex had looked at his own new bride. Chiara had been drunk before she'd even spoken her vows, and avoided being near him as much as possible, including at their reception. And something had cracked inside him.

He'd spoken to Cesare and his family politely at the reception that day—but only just. And ever since, he'd avoided them. He'd evaded Cesare's attempts at organizing get-togethers, ignored Princess Emma Falconeri's chirpy Christmas cards, full of happy pictures of their growing family, and handwritten notes: "Alex, we'd love to see you!"

As if he'd ever want to visit their home at Lake Como, to see what Cesare had become. All that sloppy, ridiculous happiness. It was obscene. It wouldn't last. Any moment now, the man's marriage, his family, would all fall apart, devolving into screams and accusations and plates exploding against walls. It would. Because it always did.

Brooding, Alex stared out at the last of the Alps flying past them.

"You're not close to your cousin?" Rosalie sounded disappointed.

"Second cousin," he repeated stiffly, "and no. Not since we were boys. He's busy. He runs a large company. He has a wife. Children."

"I'd think that would make you want to see him more, not less."

"It doesn't," Alex said shortly.

She waited patiently for him to explain. He didn't.

Narrowing her eyes, Rosalie looked at him, almost as if she could see into his soul. He shifted uncomfortably in his cushioned chair. Luckily, they were interrupted by the second course.

She took a bite of lobster in butter and gasped, closing her eyes at the taste. She licked her plate before the waiter took it. Which almost made *him* gasp.

Next, the main course was served, beef in truffle sauce

and fingerling potatoes. Alex noted the delicious flavor indifferently. The tantalizing pleasure he truly wanted was the woman sitting across from him at the table. The woman now moaning softly in pleasure as she ate.

A silent curse went through him. To distract her, he reintroduced the conversation. "Cesare and I have hardly seen each other since my childhood."

Rosalie blinked, slowly pulling the fork from her mouth. It nearly made him groan aloud. "But he lives so close to Venice."

"They are often in London and Rome. He came to my sister's funeral three years ago. And my wedding a month later."

"I'm so sorry about your sister." She paused. "You were married just a month after her funeral?"

Again she waited; again, he didn't explain. He said only, "My second cousin and I lead very different lives."

She looked at him narrowly as the train hummed around them, and the dappled sunlight shone briefly on his face.

"But still," she said finally, "you're family."

"That doesn't mean anything."

"Of course it does."

Alex shrugged. "Just because someone is family doesn't mean they can't also be strangers."

Rosalie's forehead creased. "You can't be serious."

"Why?"

"Because it's messed up!" Good mood evaporated, she dropped her fork with a clatter against her empty plate. "Your cousin lives within driving distance of Venice, but you can't be bothered with him. While my great-aunt lives in France, on the other side of the world from California, but I still make an effort, phone calls, even letters! I would do anything to stay close to her. Anything!" She shook her head at the waiter, refusing the cheese plate. "She's all I have!"

She looked near tears. Reaching out, Alex gently put his hand over hers.

"That's not true. Not anymore," he said in a low voice. He looked at her belly. "We have our son."

He felt her hand tremble as she looked up at him.

"And you?" Rosalie whispered. "Will I have you?"

A shiver went through him. He pulled his hand away.

"I never should have kissed you, Rosalie," he said quietly. "It was a mistake."

"*Madame? Monsieur?* Dessert? Coffee?"

She shook her head at the waiter, as did Alex. The waiter, looking disappointed, swiftly departed.

Looking down, Rosalie twisted the linen napkin in her hands. "I wondered why you did that. Because you can't possibly—" her voice dropped so low, it was almost inaudible "—want me."

"You're wrong," he said huskily. "I want you. As I've never wanted anyone."

For a moment, their eyes locked.

Then he shook his head. "But I can never give in to it. For your sake."

She stiffened. "For—my sake?"

"Forgive me," he said softly. "But I do not think you could give me your body without also giving me your heart. You would want a commitment. You would want a lifetime of love."

Alex realized he was holding his breath, waiting for her answer. Why? Because he hoped she would deny it? Because he hoped she would immediately inform him that he was being insufferably arrogant and she could easily, *easily*, enjoy time with him in bed with no repercussions to the future? How wonderful it would be if—

"You're right," Rosalie said. She blinked fast, trying to smile. "I think I do want forever."

It was exactly what he'd known she would say. But still, he felt unaccountably disappointed.

"I have no desire for a one-night stand," she continued. "It would feel empty. I want…more."

"You want love," he agreed.

She looked up. "I want a marriage like my parents had. I know that probably sounds silly. But that's why I've waited."

"What do you mean—waited?" He rolled his eyes, shaking his head. "It's not like you're some untouched virgin…"

She looked studiously at the white linen tablecloth. "Yes."

He frowned, confused. "Yes what?"

"I'm—" Blushing, she ducked her head as she whispered, "What you said. I've never…" She looked away, her eyes affixed on a random chalet on the other side of the mountain valley.

The world dropped from under his feet.

"You cannot mean," he croaked, "you've never had sex?"

Glancing sharply to the right and left, as if she feared one of the long-married couples nearby might have heard his words, she shook her head.

"But you can't be a virgin," he stammered, still unable to comprehend it. "You're *pregnant*."

"Yes." He must have looked comical, because looking at him, she gave a rueful laugh. "I wondered a little, that no one at the fertility clinic stopped me from being a surrogate. I gather it's usually a problem. But your—Chiara must have paid them to look the other way." She said wistfully, "I wanted to wait for true love. To be intimate with only one person. For a lifetime." She looked up at him with a crooked smile. "Silly, huh?"

Alex's heart was pounding, his body burning. Rosalie was pregnant with his child. And yet no man had ever touched her. Not even him. She was a virgin.

He looked at her downcast eyes. She was afraid he would laugh at her. Scorn her. "Rosalie. Look at me."

Nervously, she lifted her gaze. He saw her self-consciousness. She thought he would insult her as—what? As a freak? A throwback to the Victorian age? Her eyes gleamed with fear of being hurt.

"You're right," she said suddenly. "It's stupid." She started to turn away, to rise from the table—

He grabbed her arm, knowing he couldn't let her go like this. "I honor your choice," he said quietly. "I respect it."

Her shoulders relaxed a little as she stayed in her chair. She looked at him over the table. "You do?"

Alex gave a nod. "You think of sex as part of marriage. As something to be shared with only one person."

"Yes."

"I honor sex in marriage, as well. It's part of the vows. 'To keep only unto her as long as you both shall live.' It's why I wouldn't divorce Chiara. It's why—" he lifted his eyes to hers "—even though she cheated on me for years, and we quit sharing a bed shortly after we were wed, I never betrayed those vows."

Her lips parted. "But—that would mean you've been celibate for…"

"Almost three years." Alex held his breath. Knowing well how his friends would react, he'd never shared that fact with anyone.

Rosalie stared at him with something like horror. For a moment, she closed her eyes, as if she'd just received some heavy blow. Then she slowly opened them.

"Finally," she whispered. "I understand."

And Rosalie did understand.

Ever since they'd left Mont-Saint-Michel, she'd fought

her desire for him as a matter of course. Any woman would want a powerful, gorgeous, ridiculously sexy man like Alex Falconeri. But it wouldn't make any sense for *him* to want her.

And yet, innocent as she was, she'd noticed the way his gaze had lingered on her. And then, on the platform at the train station in Paris, the way he'd kissed her!

His embrace had been a wonder, magical. As he'd kissed her, all the world had whirled around them like a storm, lightning crackling through her veins. When he'd finally pulled away, she'd been lost, knowing that if they shared a compartment on the train, she could no longer resist his seduction any more than she could resist breathing.

But Alex hadn't tried to seduce her. He'd kept his distance, leaving her to read her book and sleep alone, nervously looking out at the gorgeous Alpine scenery, wondering when he'd appear, when he'd explain. After an early breakfast, she'd walked the length of the train and said hello to other smiling passengers, all of whom seemed happy to be here, as if this trip was the fulfillment of a lifelong dream. And no wonder. She could only imagine how much it cost.

But Alex had arranged it on a whim. Because he'd noticed the old Agatha Christie paperback in her satchel.

He pretended to be cold and ruthless, but on the inside, she saw the streak of kindness that he tried to hide. He wanted to take care of her, because she was carrying his baby.

But he didn't actually desire her, Rosalie Brown of Brown Farm in Emmetsville, California. Now she finally understood.

He'd kissed her because he was *starving*.

A man like Alex Falconeri, with that level of sensual appeal, should have been well-fed sexually. But he hadn't had sex in years. No wonder he was looking at her like a starving man might look at a buffet table.

"What do you mean, *you understand*?" Alex demanded now.

"It's not me you want," she whispered, glancing around the restaurant car of the train, which luckily had started to thin out from the lunchtime crowds. "You're just starved for sex. That's the only reason you kissed me. *Any* woman would be desirable to you right now. I was just handy."

He pulled away, his dark eyes serious. "Do you truly believe that?"

Rosalie thought again of the way he'd dropped the bags on the platform and taken her in his arms with such passion when he'd kissed her, such yearning and need.

But which made more sense—that Alex, a gorgeous, aristocratic Italian billionaire, would actually desire an ordinary girl like Rosalie? Or that she was simply nearby, and he was taking what was easily available, like a starving man would grab a handy bag of chips?

She looked away. "I'm not your type."

"What's my type?"

"Blonde," she said. "Thin and beautiful and regal."

"You just described Chiara," Alex said flatly. "And I never wanted her. Not even on our wedding day. Kissing her was like kissing a flagpole in winter."

Rosalie caught her breath. He really felt that way about someone so stylish, so effortlessly beautiful? "Then why did you marry her?"

"We both came from a similar background. I thought a marriage would work." He paused. "And her family's winery was next to mine."

"You make it sound so cold-blooded. Like a business merger."

"That's what it was. There was very little desire in it, for either of us. She was in love with another man."

"Why did she marry you, then?"

"Because her father had threatened to disinherit her if she threw her life away on some penniless musician. And if there was one thing that Chiara valued even more than her lover, it was having money."

"And that's what you think marriage is?" Rosalie recoiled. "You all sound so awful."

"Yes," he said.

She suddenly hated that her unborn baby had anything to do with any of them. "If I'd known—"

"If you'd known," Alex agreed.

For a moment, Rosalie felt a bittersweet lump in her throat. "I wish I'd conceived this baby the old-fashioned way," she said wistfully, looking at her belly. "I wish I'd waited for a husband I could trust and believe in."

"You can believe in me," Alex said. She looked up. "I promise you, Rosalie. I will always be there for our son. I will be the best father I can."

She exhaled. She knew what such a promise meant to him.

"Thank you for that, at least." She hesitated. "And if I someday find a man I want to marry?"

His dark eyes widened, then he gave a small smile. "All I ask is that he is worthy of my son. And of you."

Rosalie was still thinking of those words much later that afternoon, when the Orient Express finally crossed the causeway into Venice.

The sun was setting, leaving the sky aflame with red and orange that reflected back from the lagoon, and the Grand Canal outside Santa Lucia station as they arrived.

Alex helped her down the steps from the train, lifting their satchels against his powerful shoulder. "My driver is waiting outside."

Rosalie looked at his powerful frame in the expensively cut shirt and trousers. The hard lines of his jaw, dark with five o'clock shadow, his sculpted cheekbones, his black eyes that seemed at times as fathomless as night, containing all the mysteries of the universe. They all made up Alex. The greatest mystery of all.

He hadn't wanted Chiara, as beautiful as she'd been. Was it actually possible...somehow...that he wanted Rosalie? Not just because she was handy, but because...

Because why? Why on earth would he want her?

She pondered the question silently as his driver, at the helm of a luxurious speedboat rather than a car, drove them through the canals back to Alex's palazzo.

Why would a sexy billionaire like the Conte di Rialto want her, when no ordinary man ever had?

Although that wasn't entirely true, she realized. A few boys in her rural high school had competed for her attention. Then there was Cody from the farm next door, whose awkwardly sweet proposal had set her parents' hearts racing—and Rosalie fleeing to San Francisco. During her time in the big city, she'd been far too busy and too overwhelmed to be thinking of dating anyone, especially as she'd watched her roommates engage in one empty hookup after another. But Rosalie had to admit she *had* been asked out by customers and coworkers. Only she'd thought of those attempts as something to be evaded. The last thing she'd wanted to do was hurt anyone's feelings. So she'd kept her head down, avoiding any man's attention.

As the speedboat pulled up to the private dock behind the palazzo, Rosalie glanced at Alex from beneath her dark lashes. Could he actually want her? Was it possible?

Then as he helped her out, and they walked through the private gate into the luxurious, formal rooms of the palazzo, she abruptly decided it didn't matter.

Because as he'd said, their kiss had been a mistake. He didn't intend to marry again, and *she* wasn't interested in a one-night stand. Their baby deserved a stable home, a stable family.

Even if Rosalie did not. Not really. Not after the way she'd abandoned her parents to their fate. A lump rose to her throat.

Alex turned to her at the bottom of the sweeping staircase, beneath the chandelier and painted frescoes. "I'll show you to your room."

He led her upstairs to a long hallway, and then pushed open one of the doors. Inside, she saw an enormous four-poster bed, and a flower-strewn balcony that overlooked the canal.

"Will this do?" he asked quietly.

She looked from the antique writing desk, to the elegant chair beside it, to the shelves filled with leather-bound books. A portrait of some supercilious Circe in seventeenth-century clothes stared down from the marble fireplace. "Who is that?"

He shrugged. "Some ancestor. Or perhaps a painting bought by one for its intrinsic value. I can't keep track of them all." He opened the enormous, empty closet. "For your clothes."

As he set down her small satchel, she stared at him incredulously. "I don't need all this."

Alex smiled. "You will. I'm taking you shopping tomorrow. Right after you get a checkup with the doctor." He held up his hand to stop her protests. "I'm sorry, Rosalie, you cannot survive in Venice with just a few sundresses and a single pair of sandals. Dinner will be in one hour in the dining room. I'll leave you to freshen up. My room is next door if you need me." He paused at the door. "Thank you for coming here."

His intense gaze made her heart race faster. "You didn't leave me much choice," she said, and despised the tremble in her voice. He shook his head.

"There is always a choice." And he closed the door behind him.

Always a choice.

As Rosalie went into her en suite bathroom and took a long, hot shower, she thought about his words. Brushing out her wet hair, she took her last sundress out of the satchel, grateful it had been washed and pressed by the hotel staff in Paris. She would wear it for dinner tonight, then perhaps tomorrow, as well.

Perhaps Alex was right. At least for the foreseeable future, her life had changed. It was time to accept that. She didn't just need new clothes. She needed to call her boss and roommates in San Francisco and let them know she wouldn't be coming back.

But how long would this last? Once her stay here was finished, where would she go to start over, yet again? How would it even work for her and Alex to share custody after the baby was born?

So many questions, so few answers. With a sigh, Rosalie glanced at herself in the mirror then went downstairs to find the dining room. She stopped on the staircase when she heard voices from the foyer below.

She saw Alex speaking to a beautiful blonde woman in a tight, sexy dress. The woman was moving toward Alex with a low, intimate laugh, pressing her hand against his chest, as she said something in Italian.

Rosalie must have made a noise, for they both turned to her.

She blushed. A moment before, she'd been feeling almost pretty in the white cotton sundress, but now, compared to the other woman, she felt hugely pregnant and ungainly as a whale.

Stop it, she told herself angrily. She wasn't Alex's wife or girlfriend. Who cared if the blonde was looking at Alex like a Persian cat looked at a bowl of fresh cream? It didn't matter to Rosalie. She had no claim on his romantic life.

Forcing her lips into a warm smile, she came forward.

"Hello." She held out her hand. "I'm Rosalie."

The blonde just stared at her as if she had two heads. Her eyes dropped to Rosalie's pregnant belly, then she turned to ask Alex a sharp question in Italian.

He responded coolly in the same language.

"Fine," the woman snapped in English. "Who is this?"

"I'm Rosalie," she repeated, dropping her hand. "Rosalie Brown. Are you one of Alex's friends?"

"One of Chiara's friends," the woman said, looking at her as if she were some dog poo she'd just discovered beneath her sleek designer high heel.

"Rosalie and I just arrived home," Alex said smoothly. "So as you can see, we're busy now, Giulia. Perhaps you can visit some other time—"

"Yes, I can see how busy you've been." The blonde's heavily made-up eyes focused with laser-like focus on Rosalie's baby bump. With a sweet smile, she asked him, "The baby is yours?"

"Of course he is," Rosalie said indignantly.

Giulia gave Alex a pointed smile. "Ah, you're a sly one. All this time, everyone criticized Chiara, and thought you were so noble and long-suffering, but you didn't mind her affair at all, did you?" She looked at Rosalie's belly. "All that time you were buried in the country, you weren't just squeezing grapes."

Rosalie's jaw dropped. She'd never once imagined that anyone could think that she and Alex had conceived the baby the old-fashioned way—that they'd had some kind of adulterous affair while he was still married!

"You've got it wrong," she said indignantly. "Alex and I only met last week. I'm a surrogate. This baby was conceived in a fertility clinic in California. Chiara hired me."

"She hired you?" The other woman was incredulous. "Are you telling me that Chiara is the actual mother of your baby? That you're only the oven, as it were?"

"No," Rosalie was forced to admit. "The bun—I mean the baby—is mine, but it was Chiara's idea—"

The woman gave a low laugh. "It's the most ridiculous story I've ever heard. How delicious." Looking up at Alex, she purred, "You will still come tomorrow, won't you? You won't be too *busy* to attend an event in honor of your dead wife?" She glanced at Rosalie's belly, then gave a wicked smile. "If you don't show up, people will think you're hiding something."

"I have nothing to be ashamed of," he said coldly.

"Good. Oh, and bring her, won't you?" Giulia waved her red-tipped hand toward Rosalie. "Everyone will be dying to meet her."

Going to the door, he opened it. "Ciao, Giulia."

"Ciao."

After he closed the door, Rosalie ventured, "What was that?"

Alex gave a grim smile. "*That* was Giulia Zanella. Chiara's best friend." He rolled his eyes. "Though that didn't stop her from throwing herself at me multiple times throughout my marriage. Even on the night of Chiara's funeral."

"*What?* What kind of horrible friend—?"

"She is holding a charity ball tomorrow night in honor of her *dear dead friend*, to raise money for a local musicians' fund. Really just in honor of herself, if you ask me…"

"So why would you go?" she cried.

"If I don't, they'll say I was afraid. That I was ashamed." He glanced at Rosalie's belly ruefully. "Especially now."

"Why wouldn't she believe me about the surrogacy?" she said, frustrated.

He shrugged. "Because it's more amusing for her not to

believe it." He gave her an unwilling smile. "Besides. Even you have to admit the truth is hard to believe. It seems far more likely that I seduced you, than that Chiara created a baby I didn't know about on the other side of the world."

"Seriously? There's no way it's more likely you'd seduce me."

"What do you mean?"

"Well, look at you." Rosalie motioned vaguely toward his Greek-godlike beauty and sleek suit. Then she looked down at herself, with her still-wet hair leaving damp marks on the cotton bodice of her white sundress. She mumbled, "And look at me."

For a moment, silence fell in the foyer.

"I am looking at you, Rosalie," he said softly.

Electricity filled the air as she glanced up. Their eyes met. He came closer.

Suddenly, her mouth went dry. She licked her lips. Saw his gaze fall to the motion of her tongue.

"Why won't you believe you're beautiful?" He brushed back some tendrils of hair from her face. "All the more beautiful because you're not even trying to be. You just are."

Her lips parted and her heart was pounding as she looked at his sensual mouth. He was going to kiss her again. She knew it...

His hands tightened on her upper arms, then he dropped back. "I'm sorry Giulia was rude. I will not, of course, bring you with me to her charity ball to be gawked at and gossiped about." His black gaze was ferocious. "I would never wish you to endure such a thing. Come. Dinner is waiting."

But as Alex led her into the dining room, Rosalie was forced to admit what her senses had been screaming at her for days. She didn't know why, or how. But for whatever reason, it was true.

Alex wanted her.

In the elegant, oversize dining room with its chandeliers over its table for twelve, Alex pulled out a chair for her, his eyes hungry. As she came forward, no matter how she tried to tell herself that their desire didn't matter, that it was forbidden, all she could hear was the husky echo of his words.

There is always a choice.

CHAPTER SIX

First thing the next morning, as threatened, Alex took Rosalie to the best obstetrician in Venice, who'd opened up her private clinic two hours early for them.

When he first heard his baby's heartbeat and saw the sonogram, he was overcome in a way he'd never expected. He actually felt tears in his eyes. He blinked them away before either Rosalie or the doctor could notice. But as she was stretched out on the examination table, looking at the ultrasound pictures of their son, Alex reached for Rosalie's hand and held it very tight.

But other than that, he was careful not to touch her. It was too dangerous, tempting him to do more. Instead, after she'd gotten a clean bill of health from the obstetrician, who'd told them the baby would arrive in early August, Alex introduced her to her new city. They explored Saint Mark's Square early in the morning, before the cruise ships arrived. He watched her laugh as she saw the pigeons flying up against the sky.

After breakfast, they went to luxury clothing boutiques, at his insistence, and he bought her and the baby anything he wanted, anything Rosalie's gaze lingered on, even for a moment. When she protested, Alex reminded her of his promise to her great-aunt that he'd take care of them. "I do not intend to cross her."

"Probably wise," Rosalie sighed, but she seemed to find shopping uninspiring, even when he insisted on buying her a formal ball gown "just in case."

"I just don't see the point," she argued. "I don't know how long I'll be staying in Venice. It's not like I'll need any ball gowns after I leave. I doubt I'll even need one here."

Alex didn't like to think of her leaving. "I'm buying it."

"It's not necessary—"

"Pick out some dresses. Or I'll pick them for you. Then I'll drag you to the jewelry boutique and force you to pick out diamonds to match."

Faced with such an awful threat, Rosalie dutifully picked out a fancy ball gown, as well as a cocktail dress, both of which were bagged up by the delighted shopgirls. "I chose the most expensive dresses in the store," she grumbled. "I hope you're happy."

"Very," he said, but as they passed a lingerie shop, he thought he would have been even happier to buy her everything in that particular store. He resisted. After a few more shops, as his bodyguard discreetly arranged for all the packages to be sent home, Alex turned to her with a smile. "All right. I suppose you've suffered enough. Shall we explore?"

As they explored the tiny alleys and winding byways, he entertained her with the history of the city, which had been a republic for a thousand years—even in the Middle Ages, when all the countries around them had been feudal kingdoms.

She asked him questions about what a doge was—apparently the elected leader of the council. She wanted to know when Venice had become a republic—697—and how it had ended—Napoleon.

"This city has always been fought over, by men who lusted after it to the death. It's ironic that Venice is called La Serenissima when men have gone mad trying to take it. Men have gone mad," he said in a low voice, looking at Rosalie, "trying to possess what they cannot have."

Her eyes became dreamy. "I think it's beautiful."

"Yes." The city *was* beautiful, Alex thought. But growing up here, it had always felt cold. Beautiful and cold. Like his family's palazzo. Like Chiara.

Rosalie was not cold. She was warm, like the earth. Being around her made him feel like himself, the man he really was beneath the title and vast fortune and expensive designer suits. Just as he felt most himself while overseeing the vineyards of his country estate, ninety minutes outside the city.

Venice, as beautiful as it was, had never truly felt like his home. For many reasons.

It was when they stopped for a late lunch at the most exclusive restaurant in the city that Rosalie first noticed they were being followed. As they went inside, she glanced nervously behind them at the people who were stopped by the man at the door.

"Are they following us?" she whispered.

"Yes," Alex answered grimly, as they were led to his preferred table, private in the back.

But even here, inside this elegant *ristorante*, some of their fellow diners were surreptitiously watching them. One young woman at a nearby table lifted up her phone to take a photo.

"Why are they looking at us?" Rosalie asked uncomfortably.

Alex shrugged. "People have been following us ever since we left the doctor's office. It is normal."

"Normal?" Her lovely face was shocked.

But as he enjoyed the house specialty, *spaghetti alla carbonara*, Alex looked again at the crowd outside the window, on the edge of the square. The number of people had grown exponentially since they'd arrived. *This* size of crowd was not so normal.

Suddenly, his bodyguard crossed the restaurant, whispering urgently in his ear. Tossing money on the table, Alex rose to his feet.

"I'm not done yet," Rosalie protested, holding up a fork thick with *linguine alle vongole*.

"We must go."

"Why? What's wrong?" she asked, bewildered as the bodyguard led them out the back exit.

"Someone posted a photo of us on social media," he said grimly. "And it's already gotten picked up on television and online. There's interest."

"In what?"

"In you. In us. In our apparent juicy affair during my marriage that led to your pregnancy."

She looked back at their half-eaten lunch. "But—it's not fair!"

Alex snorted incredulously. "Fair?"

He spoke the word mockingly, as if expecting fairness in the world was a fantasy believed only by children and fools. Her cheeks went red.

In the alley behind the restaurant, another waiting bodyguard whisked them into the docked speedboat. His driver Lorenzo sped them away down the canals, turning quickly from one to another. Once they were out of the sun, away from prying eyes in the cool shadows of the deep, they reached the palazzo's private gate. Behind them, in the distance, boats were desperately trying to catch up with them, but they would be too late. Alex helped her climb out of the speedboat, where Collins was waiting inside the open gateway. He locked it behind them.

Once they were in the quiet privacy of the courtyard, Rosalie exhaled with relief. "I can't believe you deal with that all the time."

He glanced back at her as they entered the grand hallway of the palazzo. "I don't. It's why I spend most of my time in the countryside."

"You? In the country?" Her expression was doubtful. He smiled.

"I'm a farmer. I grow grapes. I make wine."

"But—aren't you this billionaire aristocrat?"

He snorted. "Have you ever heard the joke about the best way to make a small fortune in winemaking? You start with a large fortune." Tilting his head, he sighed. "Luckily I don't need to make a living." He didn't like to remember how he'd gotten the huge fortune now sitting in worldwide investments—by losing control of his mother's company. And losing his sister. His throat grew tight. "I don't chase money. That's what I like about farming. The sun and rain and earth don't give a damn about my title. They're *real*."

She looked up at the frescoes, at the grand chandelier. "But—you live in this palazzo…"

Alex motioned toward the gilded salon. "Chiara lived here. She liked the grandeur, and being close to her boy-friend and the Venice music scene. But I haven't really lived here since I was a boy. The only reason I'm here now is to tie things up."

"What things? You mean me?" Rosalie's voice quiv-ered a little.

"I mean all the things that need to be done after some-one is dead," he said flatly. "Chiara didn't leave a will. All her remaining fortune was left to me as her husband. She must be turning in her grave. And there were other legal complications to be dealt with." He paused. "Her lover left behind a wife and children."

"Wait—the man was *married*?"

He shrugged. "That's why Chiara didn't just want a di-vorce—she wanted my fortune to go with it. Carraro hinted that nothing less could induce him to leave his wife. My guess is he enjoyed having them both. He seemed to have no morals, but then—" he gave a grim smile "—I think that's what Chiara liked about him."

Rosalie's eyes were huge with shock. Her mouth was open, as if she could not find any words.

"I have a few things to finish sorting out with the lawyer over the next few weeks. I'll attend Giulia's charity ball, so no one can say I did not pay my respects to Chiara's memory. But after that, I'm going home." He looked at her, then added gently, "But if the city feels like home to you, we can stay."

"Home." Rosalie's voice was unexpectedly bitter. "Venice is beautiful, but it's not my home." She looked away. "I called my boss in San Francisco from the train. Told him he'll need to find a new receptionist. I left a message for my roommates too. My rent is paid till the end of the month, but I'll need to go get my stuff."

"My people can arrange it. Just give me the address."

"Thank you." She sighed. "I just wish I knew where I'll be living in the future."

"Here with me," he said, thinking it should be obvious.

Rosalie gave a rueful laugh. "Yes, but after the baby is born..."

"Here with me," he repeated firmly.

"For a while, yes," she agreed, then said in a small voice, "Then I want to find my place in the world. My permanent home."

Permanent home.

Alex wanted to tell her that her permanent home should be with him. Then he'd never need to grudgingly allow some other man into his child's life. Into Rosalie's bed.

But how could he even consider saying that, when he knew she wanted more than he could give?

How could he say it, with the memory of three miserable years of marriage still ringing in his brain?

"Was it hard to quit your job and tell your roommates goodbye?" he asked.

"No. I never felt really at home in San Francisco, either."

"Where is your home, then?"

She gave a low laugh. "Emmetsville, I guess." Her expression grew sad. "But our farm is gone. Burned. I saw it, when I went to my parents' funeral…" She shuddered. "I can never go back."

"Why not?"

She turned away, her face half-hidden by shadow. For a moment he thought she wouldn't answer. Then she said, in a voice almost too quiet to hear, "Because it's my fault. My fault my parents died."

"How can that be true? It was a wildfire, caused by lightning. Do you control the skies?"

Turning away, she started up the stairs. "I'm tired. I'm going to rest. I'll see you for dinner later."

Alex thought of pressing her, of persuading her to see that her parents' deaths obviously weren't her fault. But how could he? He himself had many things he never, ever wanted to discuss with anyone. And unlike Rosalie, the things he felt guilty about were actually his fault, and if he let himself remember, anguish would snap its bloodthirsty jaws right through his heart—

"I will be gone tonight," he said.

She stopped on the stair. "The charity ball."

He gave a single nod. "You'll be on your own. Maria can prepare any dish you like. She is a very good cook. Collins will serve it wherever you prefer, in the dining room or more casually in the breakfast room."

She shuddered a little. "And you'll have to face that awful woman, and her friends…" Biting her lip, she looked at him. "Are you sure you don't want me to come with you?"

Alex gave a rueful laugh. "*Cara*, the night is unlikely to be an enjoyable one. The last thing I'd wish to do is inflict it on you. No. Stay here, and have a peaceful evening. That will give me some solace, at least. I will see you in the morning."

"All right." She looked uncertain. "Will you come to my room to say goodbye before you leave?"

"Of course."

"Are you worried?"

He gave a small smile. "Not at all."

The truth was that Alex thought of the upcoming event with utter dread. There was sure to be a scene. But he'd be damned if he'd stay home, and let them have the satisfaction of thinking he was afraid.

After an afternoon spent on the phone with lawyers, then the manager of his vineyard, Alex reluctantly went upstairs to get ready for the ball. He paused at Rosalie's closed bedroom door, but hearing nothing, he went into his own room and took a shower.

Once dressed in his tuxedo, he again paused at her door, and this time thought he heard some movement. He lifted his hand to knock, then lowered it again. He paced back and forth in the hallway, then finally, hands clenched at his sides, he went downstairs.

In his study, he poured himself a drink, gulped it down and paced some more.

His desire for her was almost unbearable. The last thing he wanted to do was enter her bedroom.

How would he manage to live in the same house as her; how could he see her every day? How would he raise his child with her, knowing he could never touch her, knowing she could never be his?

Because Rosalie Brown wanted love, which he could never give her. He had no heart to share. If he had the capacity, wouldn't it have revealed itself by now?

He paced another three steps, his whole body tense. But how could he endure his desire for her without satiating it? How?

His friends would tell him to take a lover, he thought suddenly. Yes. A lover. A very good idea. That would be the obvious medicine for this disease. He knew dozens of women he could easily invite to his bed, if he wished. Women he could seduce with little effort.

Unfortunately, he didn't want any of them.

Exhaling, Alex stopped, clawing back his hair.

He only wanted Rosalie. But he couldn't have her. Not without destroying what chance they might have at a peaceful partnership, raising their child together.

I want to find my place in the world. My permanent home.

He had to put it from his mind. He would take care of her for the next two months until the baby was born. And then he'd take care of both her and his newborn son.

But sometime after that, he would have to let Rosalie go.

He'd always be their baby's father. But he could never be Rosalie's man. He'd have no choice but to allow her to find a husband who could love her, and love their child.

Alex's hand tightened on the glass.

He wished love had never been invented. He desired Rosalie, but more than that—he liked her. They were having a child together. They could have gotten on well together as partners. As lovers. Perhaps even as spouses.

How much better would it be for their child to be raised in a secure home, with married parents who were stable, reasonable friends, who'd never been in love so could never be in hate? Who would never scream or threaten divorce?

If Rosalie weren't so fixated on love—

The grandfather clock in his study gave a ponderous chime. It was time to leave. He set down his empty glass.

"Alex."

Hearing Rosalie's voice, he went out to the foyer.

She stood on the sweeping staircase, illuminated by the twilight, warm rose and gold, from the large window behind her. Her long dark hair tumbled down her bare shoulders. The pink satin cocktail dress showed off the curves of her pregnant body, showcasing her overflowing breasts. Her tanned legs led down to high-heeled sandals.

He was transfixed by her beauty. To his hungry gaze, she looked like a pregnant goddess, symbolizing everything sexual and feminine.

Men have gone mad trying to possess what they cannot have.

As she came down the stairs, he couldn't take his eyes off her. All he wanted to do was take her in his arms. To lift her up against his chest and carry her straight back up the stairs.

"Why are you dressed like this?" he said.

Rosalie smiled, her brown eyes glowing beneath her dramatic sweep of dark lashes.

"I couldn't let you face them alone," she said simply.

He stared at her, overwhelmed. She felt protective—of him?

The noble thing would be to refuse, to tell her to stay here. But that seemed a churlish response to such a gesture.

Besides, Alex was forced to admit, he wanted her near him. Even though her sensual beauty tortured him, just seeing her, having her next to him, somehow made his world a better place. Selfish or not—he could not refuse her.

With a deep breath, Alex held out his arm. "So," he said with forced cheerfulness, "into the fiery pit?"

Rosalie took his arm, putting her hand lightly over the sleeve of his tuxedo jacket. She gave an awkward laugh. "There will be dessert, right? And music?"

"Yes," he said a little grimly. "There will be music."

He looked down at her fingers resting on his arm. Even that slight touch made him tremble. Three years, he thought. Nearly three years without a woman. And he wanted *this* woman more than he'd wanted any other.

Rosalie wanted him too. He could see that by the way she looked at him, the smile sliding from her face as her fingers tightened around his arm. It would be so easy to seduce her. He could take her right back upstairs and—

No. No, damn it. He could not. Would not. She wanted love. She wanted marriage. It would be dishonorable of Alex to lure her into accepting less.

He could not do love, he thought suddenly. But marriage?

Marriage…

Outside in the palazzo's courtyard, the warm twilight enfolded them. They went through the back gate, where Lorenzo waited with the speedboat. Alex gently helped her into the vehicle. As his driver accelerated the engine, the gleaming boat moved forward, slicing through pink-and-violet waves. The wind blew against Rosalie, whipping her dark hair against Alex's cheek.

This was unwise, he thought. He expected Chiara's friends to be brutal, even cruel. He never should have let Rosalie come with him tonight. He should tell Lorenzo to turn around and take her back to the palazzo, where it was safe.

But in the Venice sunset, as Rosalie turned to face him with eyes like stars, something cracked in his soul. And he could not let her go.

Alex wanted her to be his. Tonight and forever. He didn't just want her in his bed. He wanted to live with her. As his partner. As his friend. He wanted to raise their child together, in a stable, permanent home. She'd had loving parents. She could show him how to give their son a happy childhood.

He wanted Rosalie to be his wife, he realized. And to hell with the consequences.

As Rosalie stepped onto the dock near the grand palazzo where the charity ball would be held, she had a hard time taking a full breath. It had to be due to her formfitting pink cocktail dress, she told herself. She wasn't nervous. She wasn't. Her high-heeled shoes tottered as Alex led her toward the red carpet and paparazzi waiting in front of the palace's grand entrance.

But Rosalie knew she was lying to herself. She was afraid.

Because Giulia Zanella had seemed so spiteful and mean when they'd met yesterday. The woman had already spread gossip far and wide. Rosalie had heard Alex's bodyguard telling him it had been Giulia's posts on social media that had snowballed, brought crowds outside their restaurant and forced them to flee out the back door. Rosalie could only imagine how bad tonight would be, being surrounded by people who'd loved Alex's dead wife, and come together to honor her. Would all of them believe Alex had been unfaithful, and Rosalie was some kind of trashy mistress-slash-home wrecker?

And her a virgin!

It was so unfair. But remembering how Alex had mocked her for that admittedly childish complaint earlier, she didn't say that aloud.

"Are you ready for this?" Alex asked quietly, tucking her hand around his arm as they faced the crowds outside the door. With a deep breath, she nodded. Because as nervous as she was, she was totally sure about one thing: she couldn't let him face this alone.

As they walked by the paparazzi, she ignored the shouted questions and Italian words that sounded vaguely like insults, and kept her head held high. She exhaled with relief as they entered the building. But she relaxed too soon. As he led her into the grand ballroom, she quickly discovered it was a case of out of the frying pan, into the fire.

Crowds of party guests, mostly young and dressed creatively, in wild, bright colors, or else scantily, barely covering themselves, all turned to stare, some with hostility, others merely curious. A few men in tuxedoes, clearly Alex's friends, came and spoke with him quietly. They spoke in Italian, obviously astonished he'd come to enemy territory. They looked at Rosalie with something like pity.

"You made it!" Giulia was suddenly in front of them with a sharp, gleeful smile. With her extremely thin frame and tiny tight black-and-white dress, she made Rosalie think of Cruella de Vil.

"Hello," she replied politely. "Thank you for inviting me."

"Darling, you're the star attraction. Come." The blonde took Alex's other arm. "Let me show you to your table."

As they passed through the crowds, Rosalie watched as people came forward, speaking tauntingly to him in Italian. They didn't even look at Rosalie's face, only her belly. Her hands clenched. It was all she could do not to yell or run away.

A red flush crept up Alex's neck. But he did not rise to the bait. He responded to each person coolly, even coldly.

Giulia gave each interlocutor plenty of time to corner them before she moved on through the ballroom at a glacial pace.

"And here is your table," the blonde chirped finally. "Just for you lovebirds, to have some private time!"

It was a table for two, set directly beneath the podium on the stage. They were surrounded by ten-person tables.

Without comment, Alex pulled out a chair at the tiny table. As Rosalie sat in it, Giulia added with a vengeful smile, "After dinner, Alex, you'll come up on stage and say a few words about Chiara—won't you?"

If she thought she could rattle him, she was disappointed. "Of course," he replied calmly. "Whatever is needed for—what is your organization again?"

"The Venice Association for the Promotion of the Musical Arts," she said sweetly. "Chiara was a beloved bene-factress."

His handsome face held no expression. "Right."

Alex sat down with Rosalie. Feeling the eyes of the other guests in the ballroom from all the larger surrounding tables, she whispered indignantly, "I'm just surprised they haven't put a spotlight on our table, to help people know where to throw their tomatoes!"

He gave a low snort, then put his hand gently over hers. "Are you all right?"

"Yes," she sighed. "And in a way, I'm glad we have our own table. But it's just so unfair! They're acting like you did something wrong when you didn't!"

"There's no point in fighting. We could show them a report from the fertility clinic and it wouldn't change their minds. People will believe what they want to believe. And besides—" he looked at her quietly "—who told you life was fair, Rosalie?"

She looked away, suddenly in tears. "My parents," she said. "They told me if you always do the right thing, try to help and be kind, that people would be kind in return."

Alex gave a low laugh. "I had a very different education in my childhood."

"What was it?"

"Kill or be killed."

She gaped at him. "You don't mean that."

As dinner was served by a bored-looking waiter, Alex looked at her with a brief smile that didn't meet his eyes. "No. Of course I don't." He looked down at the plate of food, which seemed like a very weak, pasty meal of over-boiled green beans and bland chicken. "And after this, I will make a speech extolling Chiara's virtues."

"Was she really such a benefactress to music?" she asked, looking at the bohemian crowd around them.

"She was to one musician," he said wryly, before taking a sip of red wine.

With a gulp, Rosalie looked up at the podium. "Are you going to say that?"

He shook his head. "What would be the point of insulting her to her friends, especially now she's dead?" He looked away. "There are better ways to honor her."

"Honor? But you hated her."

"She hated me. I felt nothing for her." With a humorless smile, he murmured, "I think that's what I liked most about her."

That didn't even make sense to Rosalie. But for the rest of the evening, as she watched him endure rudeness so calmly and politely, she marveled at his self-control. After the dinner dishes were finally cleared away, and the coffee poured, Giulia made a speech in Italian from the stage. Rosalie's eyes kept creeping toward Alex, as he watched with a faint smile on his lips, looking so handsome and powerful in his tuxedo.

He could have tossed this table, screamed, vowed to destroy everyone who insulted him. But he didn't. He showed restraint. He was a good man, she thought. And against her will, a tiny, stubborn thought crept through her brain, twisting and turning like a serpent until it was like a thick, unbreakable knot inside her soul.

She wished Alex was hers.

That she could have a husband that steady. That loyal. That honorable and kind.

Rosalie jolted out of her reverie when Giulia switched to English in her speech on the stage.

"And now, to accept the prize, is Chiara's husband—the Conte di Rialto! Who's even come here with his pregnant *friend*," she added spitefully.

Rosalie sucked in her breath, her cheeks burning red as

her worst fear came true and a spotlight, indeed, did fall on their small table.

"Don't be shy," Giulia called. "Come up on stage, Alex, to accept Chiara's award!"

The ballroom fell silent as Alex stood up from the table and walked up the steps to the stage. Going to the podium, he put his large hands against it and spoke in English, looking out at the crowds.

"Thanks," he said with a casual smile. "I know Chiara valued the musical community in Venice. It's why she chose to live here. She valued Riccardo Carraro's genius above all." His voice was mild. Looking out at the crowd, he raised his voice. "And so, I have decided that my late wife's estate should go to support the musicians of Venice, with a million euros of it going directly to Carraro's wife—"

Total uproar took over the ballroom. Giulia, standing behind him, had a shocked, slack-jawed expression as Alex turned and took the small crystal "award" from her limp hands. Smiling, he kissed her on the cheek, as if to say *Checkmate*.

Coming down from the stage, it was a very different affair. People who'd glared and hissed earlier now stampeded over themselves to shake Alex's hand vigorously, thanking him for his generosity and telling him what a fine fellow he was, leaving Rosalie to wonder if it all, really, was only about money. It took some time for Alex to reach their tiny table. His dark eyes glinted as he held out his hand.

"Let's go."

Rising from her seat, Rosalie took his hand gratefully and let him lead her through the crowded ballroom. He didn't stop to speak to anyone, until a plump, dark-haired woman threw herself desperately into his path, pleading in Italian.

"Yes," Alex replied in English. "I meant it."

Looking at Rosalie, the woman switched to English.

"Thank you. Thank you so much." She seemed near tears. "You don't know what this will do for us. My husband, he left no money, you see, and we have two young daughters—"

"Signora." His voice was gentle as he took the woman's hand. "I am glad to help you. My lawyer will contact you tomorrow. I wish you and your children well."

Then he pulled away, leaving her in grateful tears. Crowds of well-wishers started to gather around her as they left through the door.

Rosalie looked at him. "That was Carraro's widow?"

He shrugged. "She was innocent in all of this."

They left the building through a quiet side entrance, into the deepening night. She felt the welcome blast of cool air against her overheated skin. Above them, stars twinkled.

Alex didn't let go of her hand. They walked in silence down the slender sliver of Venetian alley. When they reached a deserted bridge crossing a dark canal, she stopped and looked at him.

"So you're just giving away Chiara's money."

"Yes."

"What about her land, where you've already invested so much time in the vineyard?"

"Ah. That's different." He gave a smile. "But even that, I will buy from her estate at a fair market price. And it will go to the musicians."

"Buy back something you already own…" she breathed. She shook her head, bewildered. "Why?"

Alex looked down at her. "Because I want to be free of her. Truly free. And it's the right thing to do."

Rosalie felt tears rising in her own eyes. "You're driving me crazy, do you know that?" she choked out. "Why are you so amazing? Why are you everything I've ever wanted, everything I know I'll never have? It's not—"

But she cut off the last word, because Alex was right. Life wasn't fair. She should have learned that long ago.

She turned away, trying not to let him see her tears. Alex stopped her, roughly pulling her into his arms.

"But you do have me, Rosalie," he said huskily. "If you want me, I'm yours…"

And he lowered his head hungrily to hers.

His kiss was passionate, hard, full of desperate yearning that matched her own, as she clung to him on the moonlit Venice bridge.

When he finally pulled away, he said words she never imagined she'd hear from him in a million years.

"Marry me, Rosalie," he whispered.

Her lips parted in a gasp. "You said you'd never marry again…"

"I never intended to." Alex cupped her cheek. "But I want you in my life. Not just for a one-night stand. You are the mother of my child. I don't want you to find some other man. I want you to be mine. My wife. Now and forever."

Forever. Her heart turned in her chest. "But you don't… love me."

"Not like you've been dreaming of," he said softly. "Our marriage won't be a fairy tale. Not like the poets say. But I want you, Rosalie. And I know you want me." He drew closer to her in the moonlight, pressing her hands against the white shirt of his tuxedo. "We can be good together. Raise our son together. We can be happy. Friends. Parents." He kissed one cheek, then the other. "Partners. In life." He ran his thumb slowly across her lower lip. "In bed."

Her body trembled at that touch. Her gaze fell unwillingly to his beautiful mouth as she heard herself whisper, "All right."

Alex blinked and pulled away. He looked down at her. "Think about what you're saying, Rosalie. Can you really be happy without a grand, romantic love? Because I take promises seriously. Happy or unhappy, marriage is forever. I'll never divorce you. Once we speak our vows, we're wed for life."

She swallowed. Her heart was pounding.

Was she making a terrible mistake? A corner of her soul was terrified and shrieking for her to slow down, to back away, to stop, to consider. But the rest of her just wanted Alex, at any cost. And that part was arguing even louder.

Rosalie wanted a real home, and knew she could never return to Emmetsville. She was tired of feeling sad and unsure about her future. *Put other people first if you want to be happy*, her mother had always said. How better to start than by putting their son first? And how better to do that than by marrying her baby's father?

For her whole life, she'd dreamed of having a loving marriage like her parents had. Wasn't that why she'd fled to San Francisco—because she hadn't been willing to settle for less?

But after her parents had died, everything changed. The light inside Rosalie had died. She was no longer sure she'd find that kind of love. No longer sure she even deserved it.

And so she'd agreed to be a surrogate. To help someone else. Because, in her soul, she'd given up hope.

How many times over the last year had she wished she'd married Cody Kowalski? Wishing she hadn't refused him because she'd wanted to wait for true love?

Her parents had paid the price for her selfishness. And if she refused Alex's proposal now, wouldn't she be doing the same to her baby? Holding out for some impossible dream of romantic love, that deep at her core, she no longer believed in?

We can be good together. Raise our son together. We can be happy. Friends. Parents. Partners.

Yes. Wasn't that what her baby deserved—a stable home and two parents living together not just for a few months but for always?

Partners. In life, he'd said huskily. *In bed.*

Rosalie shivered. It was the best offer she'd ever had in her whole life. She wanted it more than anything. So why was she hesitating?

"I'm not a man who is comfortable sharing feelings," Alex said slowly. "I will never sing you love songs. If that is what you need—"

"It isn't." She didn't need love songs, Rosalie told herself desperately. She needed a home. She needed a partner. She needed a lover and friend. It would be enough—more than she deserved. She had to stop dreaming of some unreachable star. Alex wanted to marry her—wasn't that enough of a miracle? How could she possibly be greedy enough to cry out for more?

She was no longer a child, to believe in fairy tales, or expect life to be *fair*. She didn't need love. She didn't think she'd find it, anyway.

Reaching up her hand, Rosalie cupped his rough jawline. "I'll marry you, Alex."

With a rush of breath, he turned her palm to his lips and kissed it, causing electricity to sizzle up and down her body beneath the pink satin dress.

And as Alex pulled her into his arms, as he kissed her on the bridge, all her last doubts, all her soul's fearful cries, melted away like mist beneath the power and force of his hot, brilliant sun.

CHAPTER SEVEN

THREE WEEKS LATER, Rosalie held her breath as she looked at herself in the full-length mirror.

Her bridal gown was simple, a long white slip dress with a bias cut. The low-cut bodice, held up with spaghetti straps, caressed her full breasts and pregnant belly. Her long hair tumbled down her bare shoulders, crowned by a long translucent veil that stretched all the way to the floor, edged with lace. She looked like the perfect pregnant bride.

Except the face in the mirror looked scared.

The sweep of eyeliner accentuated her dark lashes above worried brown eyes. She'd already had to retouch her scarlet lipstick three times, because she kept biting her lips and smearing it.

How Rosalie wished she had someone here with her, to tell her she was doing the right thing in marrying Alex. If only her parents could be here, or childhood friends from back home. But the only person who might have come was Odette, and when she'd phoned her great-aunt to invite her to today's wedding, she hadn't exactly been reassuring.

"A wedding? So fast? What's the hurry?" her great-aunt had demanded.

Rosalie could hardly explain that her fiancé had refused to make love to her until their wedding night.

I cannot give you everything, but I can at least give you that dream, Alex had said, before kissing her until she was dizzy.

She could absolutely, positively never discuss *that* with

her great-aunt. So she'd stammered, "We want to be married before our baby is born."

"That is when I will come visit," Odette had replied grandly. "In the autumn, when I can meet my great-great-nephew. *Zut*, that is a lot of *greats*," she muttered under her breath.

"But why wait? Why not come now? Alex can send his jet…"

"Oh, can he?" Odette had replied with asperity. "But he cannot cook my omelets or run my restaurant. I cannot leave Mont-Saint-Michel at the height of tourist season. We have yet to get a single bad review and I intend to keep it that way. Euros and good reviews, do you think they grow on trees?"

"Please, *Tatie*," Rosalie had whispered. "I need you."

Her great-aunt had paused. She said in a different voice, "You are sure about this marriage?"

"Of course," Rosalie said, putting every bit of certainty she could into her voice.

"Then *bon courage, ma petite*. And I will see you in September."

Courage and luck. Rosalie would need both today.

For the last three weeks, she and Alex had done everything legally required to wed. They'd procured documents, going to the American Consulate and the lower court, and waited for the banns. They'd signed a prenuptial agreement. At any moment, Rosalie had half expected that something would happen to stop the wedding, or that Alex might change his mind. But nothing had happened, and he hadn't.

Whenever she was with Alex, she was happy, her brain and body and heart all drugged with desire. Like last week, when he'd taken her to watch a glassblower on Murano. She'd watched the artist roll his fingers over the pole that he placed into the fire, twisting the glass into shapes at the end. She should have been paying attention to the creativity, to the artistry. Instead, she'd been distracted by Alex's powerful body sitting close to her own, and the glassblower's sensual dance of molten glass made her imagine what it would be like to have Alex's hands moving similarly over her body—over her breasts, her hips, her thighs…

She shivered, remembering.

It was only when she was alone, and it was quiet, like now, that she felt the uncertainty in her heart whenever she remembered Alex's stark words.

Our marriage won't be a fairy tale. Not like the poets say.

And no matter how many times Rosalie repeated to herself that she wasn't a child and didn't believe in fairy tales anymore, she would remember her parents. They'd had such a loving marriage. Her father, early in the morning before he left on his tractor, had always started a pot of coffee for her mother, so it would be waiting when she woke. Her mother had responded by making his favorite dessert. And every evening, after dinner, her parents had danced to the old record player as they washed dishes together. Her dad would twirl Maman around the small kitchen, crooning old love songs by Bing Crosby and Nat "King" Cole. "La Vie en Rose" had been their particular favorite. Her father would sing it in English. Her mother would sing it in French. They would dance across the worn linoleum, with her mother's head pressed tenderly against his chest. Sometimes, they would see Rosalie watching, and they'd hold out their arms, pulling her into their tight circle of love.

Her heart hurt to remember.

I will never sing you love songs, Alex had told her. Looking at herself in the mirror, Rosalie suddenly couldn't breathe.

Was she making the worst mistake of her life?

There was a soft knock at the bedroom door.

"Cara?" She heard Alex's low voice as the door cracked open. "Are you ready?"

Was she?

Her heart was pounding.

She was doing the right thing, she told herself. She and Alex would be good partners and provide a loving home for their baby. She couldn't be selfish enough to hold out for romantic love, putting their baby's future at risk, especially when she no longer believed it would even happen. She took a deep breath.

"Yes. Come in." Leaving the mirror, she turned to face him. Pools of morning light from the high windows of the bedroom frosted her long bridal veil with gold.

Alex pushed open the door, then gasped when he saw her in the wedding dress. *"Rosalie."*

She looked at her future husband in the doorway. He was devastatingly handsome, his muscular body sheathed in a civilized tuxedo that masked the savagery of his powerful physique. But his face was awed as he slowly looked over her wedding dress, his gaze for once utterly devoid of mockery or cynicism.

Clearing his throat, Alex came forward, holding out a flat black velvet box. He opened it. "For you."

Rosalie's lips parted as he held up a beautiful diamond tiara that sparkled and shimmered in the morning light.

"This has been in my family for generations." Setting down the black velvet box, he placed the tiara lightly on her head, crowning her tumbling dark hair and translucent white veil. Stepping back, he looked at her, his dark eyes warm. "Now it is yours."

Shocked, Rosalie looked back at the mirror. She hardly recognized herself, with her bold red lips and hair that looked almost black against the white gown. She looked like a princess. Reaching up, she touched the tiara with a trembling hand. The stones twinkled in the mirror, but felt hard and cold to the touch. "But—but what if I lose it?"

"The tiara is yours to keep or lose." Tilting his head, he said huskily, "I cannot wait to marry you."

Holding the tiara to her head, she ran to the bathroom and stuck in a bunch of bobby pins to hold it tight. With all the pins, and beneath the weight of the tiara, her scalp hurt, and her temples ached. Her heart was still pounding with fear for the commitment she was about to make.

A life with diamonds. But without love.

She would die without ever hearing a man tell her he loved her.

But how could it be a mistake, when it would allow their son to have two parents in a secure home…forever? How could it be a mistake, when it meant that tonight and for always, Rosalie would sleep in Alex's bed?

"Cara?" he said quietly. He held out his arm.

Her gaze fell on his antique cuff links, solid gold engraved with the Falconeri family crest. He had large, sensual hands, which she yearned to have on her body. His every teasing kiss, every passionate caress, made her burn until she thought she'd die. She had to marry him. *Had* to.

Picking up her bouquet of red roses, Rosalie placed her hand around his arm. He kissed her gently on the temple and led her downstairs.

They left his palazzo at the back, going to the private gate at the canal. She'd expected to see the speedboat. But instead…

"A *gondola*?" she gasped. He gave a sheepish grin.

"The speedboat left twenty minutes ago with decoys to draw away the paparazzi. Gondolas are only used by tourists. With luck, no one will even look at us."

As his burly-looking bodyguard, dressed as a gondolier, steered the picturesque boat down the canal, Rosalie looked out at Venice in the bright early morning. The golden rays of the sun burst over the water, gilding the edges of the streets, the alleyways peeking out from between the orange-and-red-stucco buildings. The Venice of dreams.

It was almost as good as a love song, Rosalie thought. A lump rose in her throat.

A light breeze blew against her bare shoulders, against her hot skin, causing her hair and translucent white veil to flutter behind her in the gondola. She gripped her small bouquet of blood-red roses.

"*Cara?*" Alex said incredulously. "Are you crying?"

She looked at him, blinking fast. She couldn't wipe her tears without wrecking her mascara. She tried to smile. "Of course I'm crying. It's our wedding day."

It was the most romantic moment of her life. The streets were still quiet, as it was early. To an observer, Rosalie probably looked like Cinderella getting whisked to a palace with a handsome prince.

But amidst all the beauty, all the glamour and romance, she knew what she was losing today, losing forever.

I have no choice, she told herself desperately.

Then she was tortured by the memory of Alex's earlier words.

There is always a choice.

She'd made hers, and she would have to forget about what she was losing today—the last hope of being truly loved. She didn't care. It wouldn't have happened anyway. She would wrap up her yearning in an iron box and dump it into the lagoon, never to be found again.

When they arrived at the palazzo where Venice's civil weddings were held, she kept her face frozen in a smile as Alex helped her out of the gondola and onto the dock.

His eyes were dark, his words simple.

"Are you sure?"

"I'm sure," she told him.

But was she?

Taking a deep breath, she went forward.

Inside the palace, Collins and Maria were waiting to be witnesses. Rosalie turned to Alex in surprise.

"You didn't invite your cousin, Cesare?"

"I changed my mind." Alex's expression became hard. "I barely know the man."

"But he's family!"

He shrugged. "He attended my last wedding, and it didn't help anything. Besides—" his hand tightened over hers "—you're my family now."

So their butler and cook would be their only witnesses. Rosalie wished her great-aunt could have been there. Or anyone from her hometown. Or most of all, her parents—

But thinking of her past only reminded her of everything she didn't want to remember. She lifted her chin.

"Maybe you're right," she said. "Let's keep the ceremony simple."

She turned to Collins and Maria, praying they wouldn't see her heart was crumpling inside her.

For my baby, she told herself, clutching the bouquet of red roses tightly. *For my baby*.

She flinched. Pulling back a hand from her bouquet, she saw a drop of blood on her finger. A single thorn, missed by the florist, had pricked through her skin.

"What is it?" Alex reached for her hand. Pulling a handkerchief out of his pocket, he wiped the blood from her finger. She looked at him in amazement as he tucked the handkerchief back into the pocket of his tuxedo jacket. A handkerchief? Was he from the nineteen hundreds?

Still holding her hand, he brought it to his lips. She felt the heat of his breath, the caress of his sensual lips as he kissed the back of her hand.

She shivered.

Desire. That was what they would have, instead of love. Longing and lust. As their eyes met, her fear was silenced beneath the pounding heartbeat of desire, like a drumbeat that drowned out everything else.

Desire. His hand tightened on hers, and he led her up the stairs of the grand palazzo. He didn't let go of her hand as they went into the small room where the official waited to marry them.

Rosalie barely listened to the Italian ceremony or the English translation. She didn't want to hear, didn't want to understand. All she had to do was make it to tonight. Then she'd let forever take care of itself.

Afterward, they signed the papers. An enormous diamond ring was added to Rosalie's left hand. They kissed. They stood. And suddenly, Maria and Collins were congratulating them.

Just like that, they were wed. All her worries no longer mattered. She was his wife. Now and forever.

As they left the building and went out into the sunlight, Alex took her left hand with its heavy new diamond. He cradled it against his powerful chest, and she held her breath as her bridegroom looked down at her.

"Well, wife," he said softly, "shall we go home?"

Before Rosalie could embarrass herself with a reply like *Yes, yes, yes,* or *Oh, please, yes,* Collins cleared his throat behind them. Alex looked back at the elderly butler. "Yes?"

"Your staff from the winery has a surprise for you, sir. They've rented out a nearby restaurant to celebrate your nuptials."

A flash of annoyance crossed Alex's face. "Tell them no."

"Of course." The butler bowed his head. "Though they've spent some time on it, sir."

Maria, the cook, added something in rapid Italian.

"Alex," Rosalie said. Putting off consummating their marriage was the last thing she wanted, but she could not imagine snubbing his employees after they'd made such an effort. "We can't be rude on our wedding day."

With a sigh, he said through gritted teeth, "It was very kind of them." He looked down the street. Crowds had started to form, holding up cameras, straining to see them. "It seems the world has already found us." He turned to Collins. "The reception is nearby?"

He pointed. "Across the bridge, signore."

"Make sure the bodyguards are close when we want to leave."

They walked the short way across the slender bridge to the party eagerly awaiting them in a local trattoria. Rosalie found herself engulfed by hugs and greetings as she met the employees and farmworkers from his vineyard.

"Welcome, *contessa*."

"So happy to meet you, *contessa*!"

Rosalie looked up at Alex in astonishment. "I'm—a countess?"

He encircled her with his arms. "That's how it works."

"Me!" An incredulous laugh bubbled up as she looked back at him. "A farm girl from Emmetsville—an Italian countess! How did I get so lucky?"

Alex kissed her.

"I'm the lucky one," he said huskily.

For lunch, they were served traditional Venetian dishes such as *caparossoi a scota deo*—clams in lemon pepper—and *risi e bisi*—risotto with peas—at the long, rough wooden tables. Alex toasted his bride with champagne, holding out his flute and speaking in rapid Italian, translating his words into English for her benefit.

But Rosalie needed no translation. Sitting at the table of the trattoria, surrounded by new friends, she felt happy, from her fingertips to her toes, to be Alex's wife. She listened to the timbre of his voice, watched the movement of his body. Her gaze lingered on his large, capable hand holding the stem of the crystal flute. She watched his lips move as he spoke, noted the mesmerizing way they pressed together, lifted, laughed. Though it was only early afternoon, she noticed the five-o'clock shadow along his jawline, the thickness of his neck. As he took off his tuxedo jacket and rolled up the sleeves of his white shirt, her gaze lingered on his powerful forearms, laced with dark hair.

With his broad shoulders and muscular body, he seemed like a man who could lift a horse on his shoulders, or perhaps a car, or perhaps the whole world.

His low-slung trousers were trim against his slim waist. And as he turned to speak to someone who had come up to congratulate him, Rosalie's gaze fell to his backside, so taut and shapely beneath the fabric that her mouth went dry. As lovely as this reception was, she could hardly wait for it to be over. Because once they were alone, she would be able to see him. She would be able to *touch* him. She would be able to—

"Don't you think, *cara*?" Alex said, turning to face her, to include her in the conversation with his estate manager. Her cheeks went red as they waited for her reply.

"Um…yes—yes, of course," she stammered. Then, "Er… what?"

"I was saying we do not wish to post a wedding photo online, not even on the winery's social media accounts. Our celebration is private." He frowned at her, and she knew her behavior must seem strange; she must look like a fool. Then, looking at her more closely, Alex suddenly grinned, as if he knew exactly what she'd been thinking about—and liked it.

Her cheeks felt radioactive with heat. What was wrong with her? She was a virgin, but felt totally wanton, utterly in her husband's sexual thrall.

Her husband. Alex was her husband.

"Are you ready, *cara*?" he murmured hours later, holding out his hand as they finally left the trattoria.

This time, there was no hesitation in her answer, no doubt, no question. Looking up at him, she was vibrating with need.

"Yes," she said.

They took the speedboat back to the palazzo, going very fast to evade paparazzi hovering in their wake, and taking five wrong turns to throw them off the scent. Instead of going to the back gate on the canal as expected, Lorenzo dropped them at a dock a little way from the front of the palazzo. Taking Rosalie's hand, Alex led her down a tiny, winding alley, as they both laughed with joy at their escape.

Rosalie's heart pounded as she looked at her darkly handsome husband. When they reached the rarely used kitchen door of the palazzo, she was still laughing as she started to go through it. Alex stopped her.

"Wait," he said huskily.

Lifting her in his arms, he carried her over the threshold. She expected him to immediately put her down in the kitchen, because after all, at nearly eight months' pregnant, she wasn't exactly a waif. Instead, he carried her all the way through the kitchen, down the hall, into the grand foyer and up the stairs.

His footsteps never faltered. He carried her as if she were a feather.

Only when they were in his master bedroom, the room she'd never even been inside before, he slowly lowered her to her feet.

No. His bedroom no longer. *Theirs.*

Her eyes fell on the enormous four-poster bed, and she bit her lip nervously. She was about to experience what all the fuss was about. She would make love to the man whose child she already carried…

They'd done everything backward, she thought suddenly. Getting pregnant. *Then* marrying. *Then* making love. The last thing should have been falling in love—because really, that should have come first, before anything else. But now it would come never.

This was close enough to love, Rosalie thought as he looked down at her, burning her with his hot gaze. It *was*.

Outside the windows, past the balcony, the sun was beginning to set, leaving a soft rose hue over the lush, warm Venetian buildings.

Reaching out, Alex pulled the diamond tiara slowly from her dark hair. As the pins disappeared, the long, translucent white veil, too, dropped to the floor. She shivered.

Cupping her face with his hands, Alex lowered his head and kissed her.

His lips burned hers, moving languorously, as if he had all the time in the world. His hands moved in her hair, stroking down her back. Her lips parted as he deepened the kiss, taking command, luring her tongue with his own.

Slowly, he unzipped the back of her wedding dress. It fell in a crumple of silk, gleaming on the marble floor with a pearlescent sheen. Pulling back, he looked down at her with wide eyes, his lips slightly parted.

The girl at the lingerie shop had practically forced her to buy this. "Perfect for a wedding night, *signorina*! It will make your *sposo* mad with desire!" That had sounded good to Rosalie, so she'd taken it, in spite of her blushes: a strapless white silk demi bra, which she saw now barely contained her overflowing, pregnancy-swollen breasts. Beneath her prominent belly, matching white silk panties clung to her hips. A white lace garter belt held up thigh-high sheer white stockings, which had seemed unnecessary in the warm Italian summer, but the salesgirl had insisted were absolutely necessary.

And now, looking at her bridegroom, Rosalie agreed.

Because the expression on Alex's face was one so over-whelmed with shock and desire, it was almost comical.

"What," he breathed, "is that?"

"Lingerie," she said shyly, peeking at him. "Do you like it?"

With a low growl, he gripped her shoulders, pulling her into his arms, plundering her mouth with his own. A soft sigh came from the back of her throat as she wrapped her arms around him tightly, pulling him down against her.

He yanked off his tuxedo jacket, then dropped it to the floor. His antique cuff links came next. As he unbuttoned his shirt, she placed her hands against his bare chest, feeling the warmth of his skin over his powerful muscles, his flat belly, laced with dark hair. The shirt fell to the floor.

Gently, almost reverently, Alex lowered her to the bed.

Climbing beside her, where she reclined against the pillows, he kissed her. Slowly, softly, his hands caressed her, working his way down her body with the lingering stroke of his touch.

"My wife at last," he whispered huskily against her skin, and the words burned through her, nearly as much as his touch.

She wrapped her hands around him, exploring the muscles of his back, feeling the strength of his biceps as he cupped her full breasts over the tactile silk bra, running his thumbs over her taut, aching nipples. Moving the fabric aside, he stroked the sensitive reddish-pink tips with his fingertips. Her lips parted in a silent gasp as he touched where no man ever had before.

Reaching beneath her, he easily unhooked the clasp of her bra, and the white silk fell to the bed, fluttering like a flag of surrender. He bent his head, and she felt the heat of his breath, then the electricity of his lips on her nipple as he suckled her, drawing her deeply into his warm, wet mouth. She moaned aloud as pleasure crackled down the length of her body. Tension coiled low and deep in her belly.

He moved to her other breast, cupping the weight with his large hand, squeezing it softly as he drew the large, aching nipple deeply into his mouth. She moaned again as he stroked her body. Lifting his head to plunder her lips, he ran his hands down her bare shoulders, through her hair tumbling over the pillow, then very gently over the swell of her pregnant belly.

Her hands traced the contours of his powerful chest, down his flat belly to the waistband of his tuxedo trousers. She felt the hardness of him beneath, pressing against her. He froze.

With an intake of breath, she looked up, her cheeks burning. "I… I don't know what I'm doing."

He cupped her cheek, his dark eyes burning through her. "You are wrong, *cara*," he said huskily. "You're driving me mad." Lowering his head, he kissed her naked shoulder, whispering against her skin, "Your every touch intoxicates me…"

Moving down her body, his fingertips lightly caressed her arms, her belly, to the edge of her white silk panties. They paused, then continued moving downward, to her hips, and her thighs beneath the white silk stockings. He unhooked the white lace garters, one by one, then slowly peeled the stockings like a whisper down her legs, first one, then the other. After he dropped them to the floor, he kissed the hollow of one foot, then the other. She shivered at the feel of his lips in that sensitive spot.

He moved slowly back up her legs, kissing as he traveled, and she felt the caress of his lips, of his hot breath, at the hollows of her knees, then her tender thighs, then higher still…

He unhooked her white bridal garter belt from around her waist. His hands moved over her silk panties, stroking over the fabric. Then he pulled those, too, slowly down her legs, tossing them aside.

She was finally naked on the bed. Her eyes squeezed tightly shut. Her breath came in sharp little gasps as he moved away from her. For the briefest moment, she felt nothing but cool air where the heat of his powerful body had been.

Then he lowered himself back against her. She felt his muscular legs, rough with dark hair, moving against her smooth ones, and she realized that he, too, was now naked.

"Rosalie."

She opened her eyes. His hard, handsome face looked down at her in the shadowy bedroom. His dark gaze burned her like fire. Stroking back her hair from her forehead, he gave her a wicked smile.

"You're mine," he whispered. He stroked down her full breasts, tweaking one of her taut, sensitive nipples, gently caressing her enormous belly. He kissed her forehead, her eyelids. He whispered against her trembling lips, "Every part of you belongs to me…"

Wonderingly, she stroked his bare chest. She marveled at the feel of him beneath her palm, his flat nipples, the tight muscles, like steel beneath satin. Her hand moved slowly downward, echoing his earlier exploration of her body. She traced the line of dark hair that arrowed down his flat belly, and down further still. She paused, then with a deep breath, she explored there, as well.

His shaft was rock hard, jutting from his body, enormous in length and width. She heard his quiet groan and hesitated. Then, with determination, she allowed her fingertips to caress the entire length, from the root to the bulbous tip, glistening with a single pearlescent drop. Curious, she wrapped her small hand around him, then stroked up, then down.

With a choked exclamation, he stopped her.

"What is it?" she said, pulling back her hand, looking up at him. "Do I not please you?"

"You please me too much." His deep voice was hoarse. "My bride. I want to make this last. I want to make your first time amazing. I want this to be…" He ran his hand through her dark hair. "The night we remember, as if it were the night we conceived our son…"

Lowering his body next to hers on the mattress, he kissed her slowly. His lips were hot velvet, as his tongue entwined with hers. She sighed as her lips parted in surrender.

His hand trailed lightly down her body as he brushed her shoulder, then cupped her breast. His hand stroked across her belly, then her hips. Pushing her thighs apart, he deliberately reached between her legs. She gasped as he stroked her wet satin core with a fingertip, sliding against her, swirling.

Breaking their kiss, he moved abruptly downward. Kneeling between her legs on the bed, he lowered his head to where she could not see, beyond her pregnant belly. She felt his warm breath against her tender inner thighs.

Pushing her legs apart, he lowered his head. And he tasted her.

Pleasure exploded inside her. It was so intense, it made her hips shudder beneath him. He held her, swirling her with his tongue. Tremors exploded up and down her body. Her back curved off the bed as she held her breath, her eyes closed, her lips parted in a silent gasp.

His tongue was rough, lapping her with its full width, then softly, twirling her, feather soft with only the tip. Her whole body felt tight, arching off the bed once more as she exploded with a scream of ecstasy.

That cry was still ringing in her ears as he moved. Positioning his hips between her thighs, he pushed himself inside her in a single thrust. She gasped, feeling him suddenly so deep inside her. Shockingly, new pleasure built, twisting around her, soaring her even higher, swirling around until she felt dizzy, whirled by a storm of intense pleasure. The hurricane buffeted her up, down, spinning her in circles, leaving her light-headed. He pushed inside her again, his whole hard length, moving slowly, so she felt every inch of him. As he filled her completely, she flew higher, and higher as he rode her, until her breaths came in soft desperate pants. She lost all awareness of identity, of time.

There was only pleasure. There was only *this*.

There was only him.

CHAPTER EIGHT

ALEX HAD NEVER felt like this before. He'd never known pleasure like this even existed.

He'd nearly exploded three times already. When he first took off her wedding dress. When he first touched her naked body. When he'd first felt her touch him, wrapping her hand around the length of his shaft.

But none of that had prepared him for this.

Pushing so deep inside her, he felt an intensity he'd never imagined. Though she was a virgin, there were no physical barriers, just the waves of pleasure he felt as he thrust deep into her tight, wet sheath.

He felt as if he, too, were a virgin.

But this was caused by more than just his long period of celibacy. Far more. It was as if he'd never even experienced sex before. Why? Was it because she was pregnant with his baby? Just seeing her swollen breasts and belly, and knowing she was ripening with his child? Was that what was causing such an overwhelming reaction inside him, body and soul?

No. It was more than even that.

It was *her*.

From the moment he'd first seen her, standing uncertainly in the salon of his palazzo last month, he'd hungered for Rosalie. For her beauty, her warmth, her light.

And now she was his. Truly and forever. She would be his until the end of time.

Just that thought caused a rush through his body. Holding himself up from her belly, with his hands pushed against the bed, he thrust inside her a second time, even deeper, and groaned. Pleasure swirled around him in crashing waves, making him struggle for breath. He pushed inside her again, and again, knowing he was on the razor-thin margin of control, barely keeping himself from exploding.

Then he heard his wife cry out with new ecstasy, felt her tighten around him as her fingernails pressed into his skin. He held himself still, his eyes squeezed shut, battling to hold himself back. He wanted to last, damn it. He wanted to bring her to fulfillment not just twice, but an infinite number of times. He wanted their wedding night to last in this moment of pure joy…

But even as he had the thought, he knew he could not endure for much longer. Her hips undulated beneath him. He was so close—

Abruptly, he rolled off her, onto the bed. Her eyes opened, but before she could ask the question he saw forming in her mind, he lifted her, carefully placing her on top of him.

For a moment, she hesitated, and he thought she might refuse to take the lead, that she might be too shy in her inexperience. Then she took a breath, and, watching his face, she lowered herself deliberately, drawing him deeply inside her.

But that was when it really fell apart.

He'd thought being in this position might make it easier, might help him hold on to his shreds of self-control. But as he looked up at his bride leaning over him on the bed, as her breasts swayed over her pregnant belly, he gave a choked gasp. She rode him, slowly at first, then quickly building up speed. Her lips parted, her expression fervent, almost glowing, illuminated by the soft light of the Venice night.

Looking up at her beautiful face, he saw her eyes had closed with a new intensity as she rode him harder and faster, gripping his shoulders tight, pushing herself against him, harder, deeper—

She screamed, even louder than the two times before. An answering growl rose from deep in his throat. Feeling dizzy, he gripped the bed beneath him with white-knuckled hands to keep himself from flying up into the sky. She pushed down harder, pulling him more deeply inside her as his growl built into a hoarse scream echoing and crashing against the walls of the bedroom—

He exploded, as his soul shattered and broke into a thousand chiming shards.

Alex was only dimly aware of her falling beside him on the bed, exhausted. Only dimly aware of cuddling her beautiful, sweaty body, pulling her back against his chest in a tangle of limbs, hardly knowing where she ended and he began.

Afterward, he only gradually came back to awareness. He remembered where he was. In the palazzo. Who he was. Alex. When he was. His wedding night.

He tenderly kissed his wife's temple. Her eyes were closed, her breathing even. She was asleep, he thought. As well she should be. He'd never felt so spent—as if every drop of him had been wrung dry. He had nothing left.

Or so he thought. Until about ten minutes later, when, feeling her delectably round backside nestled naked against his groin, to his shock he started to stir again. Even as a teenager he'd never felt like this, so full of endless hunger and need. For Rosalie. His wife. *Forever*.

Brushing back her dark hair, Alex kissed her cheek, then nuzzled her ear. He nibbled the tender corner between her neck and shoulder. With a delicious sigh, she turned to him, wrapping her arms around his neck as her eyes fluttered open. He felt her glorious naked breasts pressing against his chest, thrusting upward toward his chin. In devoted obedience to their demand, he lowered his head in worship, cupping their magnificent weight in his hands, lifting a full, red nipple to his lips. Tugging it into his mouth, he felt the soft, sensual tip pebble against his tongue, as he suckled her, until he felt her body rise with sweet new desire.

Then he lifted her leg up over his hip, and he took her right there, pushing himself deeply inside her, filling her every inch. Fulfilling her every need. He heard her gasp as she gripped his shoulders, straining against him, pressing harder, deeper. He squeezed his eyes shut as she filled his senses, his soul, his every dream. She was his.

And he was hers.

The next morning, when Alex woke in the magnificent bedroom of his Venice palazzo, he looked down at Rosalie, curled up in his arms beneath the soft rose-gold light.

How was it possible that she'd come a virgin to his bed? He still didn't understand such a miracle.

She'd saved herself for love.

The treasonous whisper went through him with a stab of guilt.

No, Alex told himself firmly. She'd saved herself for *marriage*. She'd given up the ideal of love, for the sake of a stable home for their baby, companionship and passion. And he would give all those things to her. She would never have cause to regret her choice.

And as he kissed her bare shoulder, incredibly he felt himself stir yet again, even after all their lovemaking the previous night. With a soft sigh, Rosalie woke, turning in his arms to say shyly, "Good morning."

"Good morning." Her smile was so beautiful that it made his throat ache. Leaning forward, he kissed her lips, her cheeks, her forehead as he murmured, "I can hardly believe you're mine, that some other man didn't marry you before now."

Her expression changed, and Alex wished he hadn't

brought it up. Both of them were still naked in bed, facing each other. And yet a wall suddenly separated them. She looked away.

"Someone proposed to me once. The boy who lived at the farm next door. My parents were thrilled." Her voice was quiet. "But I didn't love him, so I refused."

"I understand," he said, thinking of Chiara and how he'd married her for her acreage. He reached for her, intending to change the subject with a kiss.

She pressed her hand against his naked chest, stopping him. "No. You don't. It wasn't just my parents who thought Cody and I would marry. It was everyone in Emmetsville. We'd dated in high school. We were perfect for each other. He said he loved me. He proposed. But—"

"But?"

"I never felt like I thought I should feel." She looked away. "My parents were shocked. Everyone asked how I could refuse him, when he was so perfect for me, when he loved me so much. I couldn't take it. So I left. I moved to San Francisco, to be a receptionist, and live with strangers."

"You did what you had to do," he said gently. His hands tightened as he thought how grateful he was that she hadn't married some farmer in California. "It was fate—"

"No," she whispered. She suddenly wiped her eyes. "It was selfishness. I should have been there for them."

"Rosalie."

"No," she choked out. She sat up in bed. "My parents died because of me. If I'd done what everyone expected me to do, they would still be alive now—"

Her voice broke on a sob. Sitting up on the bed, Alex pulled her to his chest without a word. As she cried, he stroked her hair, her back, murmuring soft words in Italian. He stroked her until the sobs subsided, until there were no tears left, falling cold against his bare skin.

Outside the balcony window in the fresh air of morning, he could hear the distant cry of gulls, the sound of a speedboat on the canal and a low buzz of voices. Apparently the tourists were out early.

Rosalie felt good, too good, in Alex's arms.

"How can you say it was your fault, Rosalie?" he asked in a low voice. "How could it be?"

"If I'd been there, I would have insisted my parents leave town immediately, at first word of the wildfire. I would have forced them into the car and driven them out of the valley before the fire picked up speed and crushed both sides of the road." She wiped her eyes in a rough, jerky movement. "But I wasn't there. I abandoned them, just because I didn't love Cody and..." She turned away. "I was selfish. Evil."

Stroking her hair, Alex said in a gentle voice, "Seeking your own happiness doesn't make you evil."

She shook her head wildly, her eyes glistening in the morning light. "My parents made the wrong choices without me. They tried to pack their things, they waited too long, until there was no escape. *Cody* managed to get his parents out. *They* lived. My parents...they died."

Her voice choked off as she looked away.

Alex could hear the anguished love and loss in her voice. "It wasn't your fault."

"But—"

He kissed her cheeks, her forehead. "Your parents loved you, Rosalie," he whispered. "They never would have wanted you to suffer. You did nothing wrong. It wasn't your fault."

He held her, comforting her, until he finally felt her relax in his arms, pressing her cheek against his shoulder. Then Rosalie looked up, her stunning brown eyes swimming in tears. "You know how it feels."

He gave a single nod. "I lost my family too." Even to his own ears, his voice was cold. "My older brother and parents died at Christmas." Looking at the tears still glistening in her eyes, he forced himself to go on. "I'd promised to go home. But I couldn't face their yelling and screaming. So they decided to take a ski trip instead, and crashed into a mountain." He paused. "The jet I took to their funeral…it was my last one. After that, I suddenly couldn't stand the sight of a plane, any plane, big or small." He looked away. "And that was before birds flew into the engine of my sister's plane in Chile. A plane she wouldn't have been on if I'd gone to Boston in her place."

His throat was so tight he couldn't say more.

"No wonder you're afraid of flying," Rosalie murmured.

"Yes," he said quietly. "I'm afraid." He wondered if she had any idea how much that admission cost him. It was something he'd never said out loud before. "I lost them. All of them."

"But the crashes weren't your fault." She put her hand on his cheek. "They were accidents. Tragedies. Why can't you believe that?"

Looking at her, he said in a low voice, "Why can't you believe that about the wildfire?"

For a moment, they looked at each other, cuddled so close together on the bed.

Dropping her hand, Rosalie said, "But your cousin—"

"*Second* cousin," he corrected.

She scowled. "Why do you insist on doing that?"

"What?"

"Emphasizing that he's a distant cousin. Pushing him away." She shook her head, her beautiful face puzzled. "Is he such a horrible person?"

"No," he was forced to admit.

"A liar? A thief?"

"No."

"Then it's his family you don't like. His wife?"

Alex paused. He hadn't thought too hard about why he

avoided Cesare. He still didn't want to think about it. But with his wife looking at him, in the early-morning light, he wanted to please her. He wanted to distract her with anything that wasn't forcing him to explain how he'd destroyed his own family. He scrambled to think of a reason that might satisfy her about Cesare.

"It's complicated" was the best he could come up with.

She waited. Alex tried to think of something else, but his mind was unhelpfully blank.

"I already told you why I didn't invite him to our wedding," he said irritably. "He'd been to my first one. There was no point in inviting him to another."

Rosalie stared at him incredulously. "That doesn't make any sense."

No, it didn't, and he didn't want to explore it further. "Rosalie, *cara*, I don't want to fight." Pulling her into his arms, he nuzzled her close. "It's our honeymoon, and..."

"What's that noise?" she asked, turning away.

Alex realized the low buzz of noise he'd noticed earlier had built to a roar. It sounded like a vaporetto with a fully gunned motor. Rising from the bed, he looked out at the small canal, three stories below. He saw a few boats, hanging out conspicuously near his private gate.

"Paparazzi," he said grimly. "On boats."

"They're making all that noise?"

Still naked, he padded to the opposite window in the corner bedroom. Looking downward and to the right, he could just barely see into the square.

There, he saw people with cameras, reporters, all shoved into the tiny square, as if ten cruise ships had dumped all their passengers on the doorstep of his palazzo. As if his life were a mere entertainment for others.

"Oh, no." Rosalie stood beside him, her body wrapped in a sheet. Her face was almost that same color as she looked up at him. "What do they want from us?"

"A story," he replied, his jaw tight. He looked at her. "I'm sorry. Paparazzi have been following me for years, because my parents were well-known, but especially since Chiara's death. And now, with social media…and the new story about a mysterious pregnant woman, and now our wedding…they're more voracious than ever."

She looked panicked. "We're trapped. Prisoners."

Alex glanced out at the crowds. It was worse than ever. But the truth was, he'd put up with being a story for a long time. He'd thought he didn't have a choice. For years, Alex had told himself he didn't care. His strategy had been to hide out at his vineyard and ignore everyone and everything.

But Rosalie couldn't. She cared too much about other people to ignore them. She had no protection against this kind of onslaught. He hated the fear he saw on her face. It was even worse than tears.

"We're not trapped," he said grimly. "We're leaving. Now."

And so it was that, four hours later, they were driving toward his country villa outside the city in a vintage blue Fiat.

It hadn't been easy to escape from the palazzo unnoticed. They'd had to enlist not just Alex's two regular bodyguards, but the men's girlfriends as decoy versions of Rosalie, to lead the paparazzi away on two separate merry goose chases via speedboats on the canal. An hour later, their housekeeper and butler had staged themselves in the top bedroom window of the palazzo, moving like shadows to deceive the remaining crowds, while Alex and Rosalie crept out the side door, hunched beneath drab brown coats.

But now, they were finally free. Rosalie sighed happily as Alex stomped down on the gas of the tiny two-seater car, zipping through the Italian countryside.

"I can't believe you even own a car like this, that can actually blend in!" she said with a big smile.

"This is Maria's car." He grinned. "I asked for a loan, but she says it was a straight-up trade and she's permanently keeping my Lamborghini." He paused. "She probably deserves it, after all that time pretending to embrace Collins behind the window."

Rosalie gave a low laugh, running her hand along his shoulder. Her warm brown eyes danced as she looked at him. Her dark hair was tucked back behind a jaunty yellow scarf, and she wore a white cotton sundress in the heat of the Italian summer. He felt her happiness and an answering lift in his heart. Then her fingertips brushed his neck, the tender flesh of his earlobe, and he felt a different sort of lift slightly lower down.

"Don't do that," he said.

"Why? You're my husband. I own you."

He growled, "You'll make me pull over and take you right now."

"In this tiny car?" She gave a low laugh that sounded impossibly sensual. Her dark eyes challenged him. "I'd like to see you try it."

Put like that, Alex had no choice. He abruptly pulled over on the side of the road, where he kissed her until they steamed the insides of the windows. Then he discovered to his regret that his wife had been correct. There was no good way to make love in a two-seater car. Luckily Collins had packed a picnic lunch in the back before they made their escape from Venice.

Finding a quiet spot on a lonely lane, Alex parked the car behind a copse of trees. Lifting the picnic basket to his shoulder, he led her to a small clearing on the gentle incline of the hill. Spreading the blanket on the soft grass, he kissed her until she was trembling with need. He made love to her right there, pulling off her panties from beneath her dress, unzipping his trousers and lifting her on top of him on the blanket, until she gasped and screamed, and so did he, with only the birds to hear them.

Afterward, once they'd recovered, they had a delicious lunch of antipasto, sandwiches and sparkling water. Then, refreshed, they drove the rest of the way to his estate.

"That's it," Alex said finally, pointing.

"That?" she said in awe, looking at endless hills all covered with vines, beneath a wide blue sky with gray clouds in the far distance. As they drove past the vineyard's gate, where he nodded at the guard, Rosalie looked out at row after row of vines, stretching as far as the eye could see. "It's beautiful."

"I'm glad you like it." He smiled at her. "Chiara hated it here. She wanted to sell it from the beginning."

"Did you get her land sorted out?"

"I spent an exorbitant amount to purchase it, yes. The musicians of Venice will be dining on lobster and champagne for quite some time."

Rosalie looked forward, then saw the elaborate, gracious villa, surrounded at a distance by the outbuildings of the winery. Her eyes were huge in the dappled light as she turned back to him. "That's the house?"

"It is."

She bit her lip. "But it seems so…quiet. Where do you hold wine tastings? Where do the tour buses park, so people can visit your winery's fancy restaurants and art galleries and…?"

"I don't have any of those things." He remembered that she'd come from Sonoma, famous for its own wineries. So she knew how they worked. "You should see what some of the other wineries around here do. Offer tourists hot air balloon rides. Golf. Climbing walls and goat yoga. Trying to sell as many bottles as possible."

"What do you do?"

"Nothing."

"Nothing?"

Alex shrugged. "I'm not trying to build a fortune. I already have one. All I care about is making wine. I let it speak for itself, no gimmicks, and produce only a limited number of bottles. La Tesora is my private home. Tourists are not welcome here."

Rosalie gave a laugh. "I guess that explains the marketing strategy of the big no-trespassing sign at the gate."

"We don't even advertise."

"So where do people buy your wine?"

He gave a low laugh. "Anywhere but here."

When they finally pulled in front of the villa, he helped her out of the car as two smiling employees, whom she'd met at her reception the day before, whisked away their bags. Taking her hand, Alex led her toward the entrance of the sprawling, elegant villa. Her eyes were huge as she tilted back her head.

"It's so grand," she breathed.

"It looks old, doesn't it? But my great-great-grandfather built it for his wife in 1905. It was meant to evoke the romance and drama of the eighteenth century, only with the modern comforts of plumbing and hallways. I've added other things too. Technology. Solar paneling. There's a few people you haven't met yet. Gabriele," he called. "Come meet my wife."

Several older men with rumpled clothing and ready smiles came over and introduced themselves shyly, touching their caps as they spoke to her in Italian. She spoke to them in English, but somehow everyone got along just fine.

She glanced back at Alex, her eyes dancing. She was so beautiful in this moment, with her white sundress—a bit wrinkled by their interlude on the hillside—and bright yellow scarf in her hair, that he impulsively took her in his arms and kissed her.

When Alex finally drew back, he saw his employees glancing at each other with raised eyebrows. They clearly thought their boss had lost his mind. But he didn't care.

In the distance across the vineyard, the dark clouds in the far sky came closer as a summer thunderstorm approached.

Rosalie drew back from his embrace, looking up at him with flushed cheeks. The emotion in her deep brown eyes pierced his heart. He felt an answering flash sizzle through his soul like lightning, but he pushed it away. Desire, this was desire, nothing more. As he lowered his head back to hers, he buried all other emotions, walling off his heart. And he ignored the low roll of thunder trembling the earth beneath his feet.

CHAPTER NINE

SUMMER PASSED SWIFTLY in Veneto, one of the largest wine-growing areas in Italy, rivaling the more famous regions of Tuscany and Chianti. As June turned into July, then August, the weather was invariably sunny and hot; with the buzzing of bees in the golden light as in the vineyard, the grapes grew.

Rosalie, too, grew riper in the warm sun. Each day, she felt more relaxed, strolling lazily in the hot sun, as her belly expanded until she felt bigger, yet more contented, than she ever had before.

She'd never had such a wonderful summer. As Alex had promised, there was no one to bother them here. No paparazzi, no cruise ships, no tourists. Each day, Alex put on his work clothes—here, jeans and a T-shirt, not a bespoke suit—and got his hands dirty, toiling alongside his farm workers.

The very first day, when Rosalie had appeared at his side to walk his rounds, similarly dressed in pregnancy overalls and a white T-shirt, her hair bound up in a ponytail, ready to work, he'd been astonished.

"You forget—I'm a farm girl," she'd said with a smug grin, pleased to surprise *him* for a change.

Nine months before, when she'd conceived this baby via surrogacy in San Francisco, she could never, ever have imagined a life this wonderful was in her future. She'd thought then that she'd be lonely and grief stricken forever. She'd never dreamed she could be this happy.

Now as the three-wheeled Ape truck took them out to the edges of the estate, she put her hand over her forehead, blocking the sun from her eyes, and felt her whole body relax beneath the warm hazy light.

She'd forgotten how much she missed this, being out on the land. For two years, she'd been cooped up in an office in the big city. She was comfortable here as she hadn't been in San Francisco, or even in glamorous Venice. She *liked* wearing farm overalls. This was so much like her childhood. So much like home. So much like before—

Rosalie caught the thought in its tracks, shoving it away before it could clutch at her heart.

No. She wasn't going to think of the past anymore, only the future. She looked at her husband, driving the two-seater pickup truck beside her. Everything had changed. Their baby was due any day now.

In the last few weeks, she'd learned so much, living in a new country, meeting new friends. But farm life had felt somewhat familiar, at least, and she'd started to learn Italian, thanks to daily lessons arranged by the villa's housekeeper.

"You feel this land," Alex said, watching her as she walked through the even lines of growing vines. Stopping, she looked at him.

"I love this place," she said honestly. "It's almost like home."

Almost. Her family had raised crops like alfalfa and melons. She still didn't know much about viticulture or *vendemmia*, the autumn wine harvest. But she could only go forward, not back. She'd try to accept this new country as her own.

She'd never think of what she'd left behind. Never.

With a sudden frown, Alex tilted his head. "Should you be walking so much?"

"Waddling, more like," she sighed.

Coming closer, her husband pulled her into his arms. "You've never looked more beautiful."

Rosalie let him hold her, accepting his comfort and warmth. She was already three days past her due date. Her Venice doctor had been temporarily lured to a small private hospital nearby, at an exorbitant rate. The doctor was checking on her daily now. If Rosalie didn't go into labor soon, she'd been warned she might need to be induced, which sounded like no fun at all. To be honest, nothing about labor sounded terribly fun. Except the end, when she'd finally hold their baby in her arms.

Pulling away, she gave her husband a rueful grin. "Walking is good for me. Dr. Rossi said exercise might help me go into labor."

Lifting a dark eyebrow, Alex looked down at her wickedly. "She suggested other things that might help too."

She snorted a laugh. "You can't mean—"

Cupping her face with his hands, he lowered his lips passionately to hers. His embrace was fierce as his strong arms wrapped around her tenderly. When she finally pulled away, she looked up at his handsome face in wonder.

Warm golden sunlight was bathing the countryside, making it glow. And it gilded Alex most of all. He looked so handsome, gazing down at her, almost as if he—

As if he—

No. Rosalie couldn't let herself believe it. Just the thought caused a twinge deep inside her.

"Let's go back to the villa," he whispered, running his hand suggestively down her back.

"In the middle of the day?"

"Why not?"

"Gabriele and the rest would be shocked if—"

But as she turned to walk away through the vines, she felt the hard twinge again, and a moment later, she sensed it a third time. There was an ache in her lower back that she'd been ignoring all day. She suddenly realized what it was. She stopped in the middle of the row. She turned back to him with an intake of breath, her eyes wide, holding her belly.

Alex looked at her face. She didn't have to say a word. He rushed to her, scooping her up in his arms.

"I can walk," she tried to tell him, but he was implacable.

"No, *cara*," he said gently. "Let me help where I can."

Rosalie thought of the upcoming labor and was terrified of the unknown, the pain, everything she'd have to go through before she could hold her baby. "Promise you'll stay with me."

Alex's gaze went straight to her heart. "I promise."

Rosalie knew what a promise meant to him. Looking into her husband's face, held by his steady, powerful arms, she was suddenly no longer afraid.

Alex had just witnessed a miracle.

Sitting in a private suite of the small, modern hospital, he looked down at his newborn baby son in awe.

Tiny. So tiny. He looked at the minute fingers. He'd arranged for the DNA test, as a matter of form. He trusted Rosalie completely, but he'd wanted to make sure the California clinic hadn't made some mistake. But now, even with the baby's scrunched-up face, he saw the exact resemblance to his own baby pictures.

For so long, Alex had dreamed of having a child to carry on the family name. And now it had happened at last. He had an heir.

But it wasn't just an heir. This was a living, breathing child. His heart pounded as he looked down at his son.

Sitting in a soft chair by the window overlooking the lush Italian countryside, Alex had been shirtless for the last twenty minutes. When the baby had started whimpering and crying, the nurse had recommended that Alex comfort him with skin-to-skin contact. Pressed against his father's warm chest, cuddled beneath a blanket, the baby had swiftly quieted, then fallen asleep.

Alex looked at his wife, who was sleeping in the bed. He thought of everything she'd gone through to give birth. The pain, the fear. It had been a long night. He'd been at her side the whole time, ordering ice chips, raging at her doctor to do something, anything to ease her agony.

"It is too late," the doctor had replied crisply. "The baby is coming too quickly."

"I can deal with the pain," Rosalie had panted, her forehead sweaty, her eyes glazed. "Please, Alex. Just stay with me."

She'd reached out her hand. He'd taken it. He'd held it for two hours.

Now, he stretched out his hand ruefully. His bones seemed to creak. He could still feel the bruises.

But how proud he was of her. He was in awe of her courage and strength. He didn't know if he could ever endure what she just had.

And now, the room was quiet. Both his wife and son slept. Their breathing was even and soft, the sweetest music he'd ever heard.

Alex looked around the private hospital suite. The light from the window was golden, just as it had been yesterday, when he'd kissed her in the vineyard. The room was filled with bouquets of flowers, sent by his acquaintances from around the world, and by the estate staff, who already loved her.

Somehow, this summer had been the best time of his life. He'd never imagined any marriage could be so…happy. Not something to be endured, but actually enjoyed. And not just at night, when they set the world on fire, but during the day too. Rosalie had become not just his companion, but his friend. His true partner.

As he held his newborn, whom they'd named Oliver Ernst Falconeri after Rosalie's father, Alex looked across the room at his sleeping wife. And the emotion in his heart was so strong he almost couldn't bear it.

It was too much. He couldn't care this much. His heart started to race, going faster and faster. He couldn't have this much to lose. If he failed them—

So much could happen. To this tiny, fragile baby. To his tender, openhearted wife. How could he prevent any possible disaster? How could he keep them safe? His hands tightened around the sleeping bundle in his arms.

Alex had never felt like this before. Certainly not with Chiara. Marrying his first wife had been easy. Without passion, without love, there'd been no fear, no jealousy, no heartbreak, just coldness—his own personal Antarctica, right here in Italy.

His own childhood had been full of drama as his father argued hatefully, always going for the jugular, and his mother gave them all the silent treatment for days, both of them forcing their children to endure the endless cycle of misery. His older brother, Thomas, had soaked up their malice like a sponge, and learned to fight with the same weapons. They'd still died, and so had his sister, though she'd tried to flee and start a new life. And look at Rosalie's parents—they'd died in a fire.

Anything could happen, at any age, even to people who were rich. Even to people who were loved. Even to people who were good. There was no safety net. He could lose Rosalie. They could lose their child.

Alex suddenly felt dizzy. He took a deep breath, trying to control the frantic pounding of his heart.

He couldn't let anything happen to either of them. He had to hold it all together. To be tough. To be strong. To be steel.

He couldn't let his emotions take over, leaving him afraid

and weak, with his heart pounding like this, his breath a shallow gasp, and all from fear. Knowing his wife and child could be taken from him at any point. Knowing they could die.

Knowing they could leave.

A man was only as good as his strength. As good as his promises. Alex had to protect his family. And himself.

The only way to keep them all safe was to stay vigilant. To stay strong. To imprison his feelings, chaining them beneath walls of iron, chiseling them beneath stone.

He took a deep breath, forcing his heart to ice.

The only way to love his family…was to not let himself feel anything for them at all.

For the first few weeks after Oliver was born, Rosalie's days and nights blended into a haze of waking and sleeping.

She was tired, so tired. Her nipples were sore from nursing. Her shoulders ached from holding her newborn baby in the same position for hours as he slept, afraid of waking him, as she herself dozed upright in the rocking chair.

"We should get a nanny," her husband had told her multiple times, every time he saw her drugged-looking expression and the dark circles beneath her eyes. "A night nurse, at the very least."

But Rosalie had refused. This was her precious baby, and he deserved all her attention and love. She held him for hours, both because he cried when she set him down and also because she wanted to. She cradled his warm, tiny body close to her chest, and breathed in the scent of him, baby powder and sweet skin. Her baby needed her more than anyone ever had.

Oliver's birth utterly and completely changed her life. In more ways than one.

Labor had been difficult, especially since she'd been forced to do it without an epidural. For hours, she'd endured the worst physical pain of her life. She didn't know how she would have gotten through it if she hadn't been able to grip Alex's hand. "I'm here, *cara*," he'd murmured softly, his dark eyes glowing. "I'm here."

Afterward, exhausted, she'd cuddled her sweet newborn, and then slept. But when she'd woken, she had opened her eyes and had seen everything she'd ever dreamed of.

There, on the cushioned chair beside the window of the private suite, Alex sat cuddling their tiny baby.

He was shirtless, holding their son against his powerful, tanned chest, rippled with muscle and laced with dark hair. Both of them were half-covered by a knitted baby blanket sent overnight by her great-aunt from France.

And it was in that moment, buried beneath an avalanche of emotions, that Rosalie suddenly realized what she really felt.

She was in love with her husband.

All summer, she'd denied her growing feelings. They were merely partners, both in the vineyard, and as parents-to-be. Yes, they were lovers, and every night he brought her to shuddering, gasping fulfillment.

But that didn't mean they were *in love*. Even though he'd become her best friend, the person she kissed before she fell asleep at night, the one who made her smile when she opened her eyes each morning. The man she wanted to spend time with; the one she wanted to talk to. But that didn't mean she loved him. Of course it didn't.

But when she saw him holding their baby son, her heart had simply exploded. And she could no longer deny the feeling or pretend it was anything else.

She was in love with Alex.

Totally, recklessly and utterly in love.

It terrified her. She tried not to think what it could mean for their future. Love had never been part of the deal. In fact, when she'd married him, he'd warned her: there would be no love. And there would be no divorce.

After they'd left the hospital and returned to the villa, she'd been almost relieved that, in those very early days of motherhood, she'd had no time to think about it.

But now, with Oliver nearly two months old and sleeping in four-hour chunks at night, she'd slowly resurfaced from the haze. Coming up from the baby undertow, Rosalie's brain began to function again. And she was forced to face the cold, hard fact of her love.

And she was afraid.

Because now, for the first time, she also saw how her husband had grown increasingly distant since Oliver was born, spending very little time with them. Her husband never volunteered to care for their baby. In fact, after that miraculous afternoon in the hospital when he'd cradled him to his bare chest, he'd barely held his son at all.

It was almost, Rosalie thought with a shiver, as if he was purposefully trying to push her away. As if he *knew*.

But he couldn't know she'd fallen in love with him, she told herself desperately. His emotional distance had to be a coincidence. When she'd been busy, utterly focused on the baby, exhausted and barely surviving, she hadn't asked him for help. And in fairness, he'd been nearly as busy himself, with harvest. Harvesting grapes was labor-intensive, as Alex still insisted on the traditional method, harvesting by hand, with sharp shears and baskets. So it was all hands on deck. Alex always paid the top wages in the game, so he had no problem finding employees, and he himself worked hardest of all, from dawn till dusk, harvesting first the white grapes, mostly pinot grigio, and now the red, pinot nero and merlot.

An entire season of growing could be undone if the grapes were harvested too soon, or too late. So it was an intense, stressful season, until the grapes were all safely harvested and brought to the winery on the estate, where they'd be sorted, destemmed and crushed. Harvest was the most important time of a vintner's year.

That had to be the reason he seemed so distant now, so hostile almost, whenever Rosalie tried to speak to him. She hadn't even been able to tell him about the latest offer she'd received from a corporate American winery, asking to buy her family farm.

If she was truly never going back to California, she should sell, rather than continue to pay taxes on land that was going to seed, left a fallow ruin. The town deserved better. But every time she tried to force herself to accept the generous offer, she couldn't. She couldn't face it alone.

But Alex never talked to her. They hadn't shared a single meal together since the baby was born. She tried not to take it personally. But it was hard. Especially since they hadn't made love since the baby was born. They'd been separated not just by day, but by night too.

At first, after her difficult labor, and exhausted and zombielike from lack of sleep, sex had been the last thing on Rosalie's mind. She'd even moved out of their bedroom to sleep on a cot in the baby's nursery. She was waking up so continually with the baby; it seemed cruel to disturb Alex's sleep, as well. After all, *he* wasn't able to take catnaps with the baby throughout the day, but had to go out into the vineyard to put in fourteen-plus hours of hard physical labor.

But now Rosalie was getting more sleep, and she'd been given the all clear by her doctor two weeks ago, after her six-week checkup. But she was still sleeping alone in the nursery.

Her great-aunt Odette, who'd arrived three days earlier for her long-promised visit to see the baby, had looked at the lonely cot in the nursery and said, "Are you a single mother now, *ma petite*?"

"No, we're married, of course I'm not!"

"Then why are you sleeping alone?"

Rosalie had blushed. "I've been busy, and so has he…"

Odette had narrowed her eyes, looking intently up at her niece, then shaken her head with derision. "You must change this, Rosalie."

"I don't know how."

"You simply go back to his bed."

"I'm…" Swallowing hard, she'd admitted quietly, "I'm not sure if he wants me there."

Her great-aunt's dark eyes had glinted. "Then you should find out."

Find out. Right. It should have been the easiest thing in the world. All Rosalie had to do was ask her husband if he still wanted her.

Except she was afraid she already knew the answer. He hadn't so much as kissed her since their baby was born, beyond an occasional disinterested peck on the cheek.

"I can't," Rosalie had whispered. She half expected Odette to offer a scornful response. Instead, her great-aunt put a gentle hand on her arm.

"When you're stuck, Rosalie, the only way to move forward is to change. Take a risk. Be bold."

Thinking about it now, as she walked through the long downstairs hallway of the villa with her baby on her hip, Rosalie was wistful.

Take a risk. Be bold.

Easy for her Aunt Odette to say. She'd never been afraid of anything. But Rosalie—

How could she just climb back into her husband's bed, when for two months, he hadn't touched her? When they'd barely spoken? They'd become like two strangers, living in the same house. When she had news to share, she sent him a text.

Her aunt was right, she thought in horror. What had happened to their marriage?

But at least tonight, harvest would end. It was the final night of *vendemmia*, with the last grapes picked. At dusk, all the workers would celebrate by gathering around a bonfire, indulging in a feast, telling stories and polishing off last year's wine.

Take a risk. Be bold.

Maybe she could find a way to—

"Contessa, there is a phone call for your husband," called the housekeeper anxiously.

"He is out in the fields…"

"*Sì*, but the man says the *conte* does not return his calls, and it is urgent. Would you speak with him, *per favore*?" Rosalie hesitated until the housekeeper added, "He says he is his cousin."

"His cousin!" Rosalie brightened. "Of course I will speak with him!"

Propping Oliver against her hip, she reached for the house line in the kitchen. Cesare Falconeri did not seem surprised when Rosalie introduced herself as Alex's wife.

"Yes," the man replied. "My wife told me Alex was married. She read about you online. And I've heard you have a child?"

"Yes." She smiled down at her tiny baby, who was making *ba-ba-ba* sounds. "His name is Oliver."

"We are leaving for London next week and won't be back until spring. My wife has been dropping hints that we should visit you and drop off your wedding gift."

"You didn't need to get us a gift," she said, blushing. Cesare laughed.

"You don't know my wife, obviously, or you'd know that isn't true."

"I'm sorry we didn't invite you to the wedding…"

"You don't need to explain." And Rosalie got the feeling that she really didn't—that he understood. As she exhaled in relief, he continued, "But we'd love to see you now. I've been leaving my cousin messages for the last few days, but he hasn't responded."

"Alex has been busy with harvest," she said awkwardly, embarrassed.

"Oh, yes, of course—I should have remembered. Perhaps it's not a good time. You could come visit us in London this winter…" His voice sounded doubtful, as well it should. Rosalie couldn't imagine Alex traveling all the way to London when he couldn't be bothered to visit them here. "Or we could arrange for our families to meet in spring? By then, we'll have another one." Cesare's voice was fond. "Our fourth."

"Fourth!" she gasped, astonished.

"I'd like my other three to meet their new baby cousin. Not to mention you and Alex."

"Your kids have never met Alex? That's ridiculous!" She looked down at her own baby, who desperately needed cousins. Her child had so little family. So did she.

Take a risk. Be bold.

"I have an idea," Rosalie heard herself say. "Tonight is the last night of harvest, and we're having a bonfire with all his employees and staff to celebrate with dinner and wine. Why don't you join us?"

"Are you sure Alex would want us there?"

"Of course I'm sure," she lied stoutly. "After all, it's a party! Please come at eight, if that's not too late for your family."

"Wonderful. We'll make sure the children take a nap beforehand. We look forward to it. *Grazie mille*, Rosalie. And thank you." He paused, and added, "Oh, and my wife wants me to tell you her name is Emma, and she can't wait to meet you, because the wives of Falconeri men need to stick together. I can't believe you made me say that," she heard him grumble affectionately to his wife as he hung up.

Smiling, Rosalie put her baby down for a nap and took

a long, hot shower. Afterward, she looked at herself in the mirror. Her great-aunt was right. She was already feeling more hopeful. All she needed to do was be brave enough to make some changes. How hard could that be?

Instead of her usual jeans and T-shirt, she reached into her closet for a red dress she'd never worn before. It was a soft knit fabric, forgiving of the few pounds of baby weight she had yet to lose, while flattering her curves. The scarlet fabric looked striking against her dark hair, which tonight, instead of pulling into a ponytail, she let tumble over her shoulders, brushing it until it shone.

Tonight, things would change, she vowed. They'd come together as a family. She and Alex would finally reconnect. Now that he was done with harvest, he could wake up from his trance, as she had. He'd take her in his arms and kiss her, really kiss her. She'd be back in his bed tonight.

Maybe, if she was really brave, tonight at the bonfire she could even tell Alex she loved him. Rosalie looked at herself in the mirror.

Maybe not.

But everything was going to be fine. So she was in love with her husband. That wasn't such a disaster, surely? They had so much to be grateful for. A good harvest. A happy, healthy baby. Long-lost family coming to visit. What could possibly go wrong?

CHAPTER TEN

THE BONFIRE LIT UP the autumn night as wine flowed from oak casks and tables groaned beneath enormous bowls of pasta, antipasto and freshly baked bread, as well as luscious desserts. Laughter ran through the small crowds of farmworkers, winery staff and house staff, all of them gathered together in a raucous, joyful celebration of a bountiful grape harvest. *Vendemmia* had come early this year, at the very end of September, after the hot summer.

Rosalie had been nervous when Cesare, Emma and their three children had arrived at the villa earlier that evening. Alex was still out in the fields; he had no idea she'd invited his cousin's family to their home. But she'd discovered, talking to the villa's housekeeper, that Cesare wasn't just a billionaire hotel tycoon, but also a prince.

She'd been briefly nervous, wondering if the Falconeris would scorn her. But as soon as Rosalie welcomed them into the library, she'd swiftly realized she had no reason to be scared.

"Me, scorn you?" Emma said later, after Rosalie confessed her fear. "Why would I ever do that?" She gave a low laugh. "Don't you know I used to be a maid at Cesare's hotel?"

When Rosalie met them, she discovered Cesare was tall and dark, with the Falconeri good looks, in his midforties with streaks of gray at his temples. His American wife was lovely and kind, perhaps in her midthirties. She'd immediately given Rosalie a big hug and put her at ease with a warm smile. "So you're Rosalie! I'm so happy to meet you at last. And this is your baby?"

"Oliver," she'd replied, holding her yawning child close. "He's nearly two months old."

"Adorable," Emma sighed, stroking his dark tufts of hair. Then she'd looked back at her own brood with an impish grin. "And these are our little monsters. That's Sam—" she motioned toward a studious dark-haired eight-year-old poring through the leather-bound books on the library's shelves "—and Elena—" a pouting little girl who was vigorously thumping her older brother with her teddy bear "—and Hayes—" a toddler who was frantically pulling on the shirts of both his elder siblings. Emma put her hand on her belly, which only had the slightest curve. "And there's this angel, due next spring."

Rosalie looked at her in amazement. Emma Falconeri seemed so calm and put-together, so effortlessly chic and lovely, while for the last two months, contessa or not, Rosalie had felt like a zombie in yoga pants with baby spit-up on her shoulder. Today was the first day in ages that Rosalie had felt like herself, rather than just a baby accessory. In her flowy red dress and red lipstick, she almost felt pretty. But she had only one child, while Emma had nearly four. She blurted out, "How do you manage?"

Smiling at her children, Emma looked back at her handsome husband fondly. "With help."

Coming close to his wife, Cesare took her in his arms and kissed her tenderly. "Nothing makes me happier."

The way Cesare looked at his wife…

Rosalie's throat suddenly hurt.

"Well, come on," she told them finally. "Alex is outside. The party has just started. He will be surprised to see you!"

"Surprised?" Cesare's dark eyebrows lifted.

"Happy," Rosalie amended quickly.

Alex was surprised, all right. But he wasn't happy. After

a brief stop to introduce the Falconeris to her great-aunt Odette, who'd decided to skip the party in favor of a good book and glass of cognac by the fire in her room, Rosalie led the family outside. Still holding her yawning baby, she went out into the field between the villa and the winery, where the bonfire was being held, beside fairy lights and a few heaters in the rapidly cooling evening.

Her husband's dark eyes widened when he saw Rosalie in the red dress. His sensual lips curved and he started to come toward her.

Then he saw Cesare, Emma and their children behind her. And from his expression, Rosalie suddenly knew, with a chilling certainty, that she'd made a horrible mistake.

"Look who's come to visit," she said lamely.

"I see." Alex looked at her, then at his cousin. "How did it happen?"

She lifted her chin almost defiantly. "I invited them."

"Ah."

"It seemed past time for our children to meet."

"Of course." Reaching out, Alex shook his cousin's hand, asking Cesare how he was, as if it had been merely days since they'd met, rather than years. He then politely extended his hand to Emma, who pushed it aside to give him a warm hug.

"It's good to see you again. I'm sorry we missed—" Pulling back, Emma finished awkwardly "—so much."

So much, indeed, Rosalie thought. They'd missed their wedding, and for all these months, though living so close, they'd never even spoken.

The Falconeri children, after dutifully saying hello to their baby cousin Oliver, ran off to look more closely at the bonfire—and more important, the food table—as their father shouted a warning, "Don't break anything," and their mother called with a smile, "Be careful, cuties, stay close."

"So…how are you, Alex?" Cesare said.

"Fine," he snapped.

Three pairs of adult eyes turned on him in amazement.

Alex added politely, "The grape harvest was excellent. The hail did no damage."

"That's good." Cesare cleared his throat. "The hotel business has been solid. We now facilitate owner-operated homestays, for those who want a different kind of luxury experience."

Silence fell. Their two wives glanced at each other with chagrin.

"I need to feed Oliver and put him to bed," Rosalie said. "I'll be back in a bit…"

"I need to keep an eye on my children," Emma said. "With all the farm equipment around, you never know when Elena might try to convince one of her brothers to jump into a vat…"

The two women's eyes met, then they deliberately left the Falconeri men alone.

But forty minutes later, after Rosalie tucked her sleeping baby into his crib, leaving Odette to listen to the baby monitor, she went back outside, only to find the Falconeri men on opposite sides of the bonfire, still not talking.

"Did you and your cousin have a fight?" she asked Alex. He turned on her, the fire leaving a red flicker in his dark eyes.

"He's my *second* cousin."

"Why do you always insist on adding that? What difference does it make?"

"You shouldn't have invited them here, Rosalie."

"They're your family," she said stubbornly.

"Like I've told you before—just because they're family doesn't mean they're not strangers."

"That's ridiculous." When he didn't answer, she demanded, "Why are you being so rude?"

"If I'm rude, it's your fault," he replied coldly. "I never

invited them here. You did. So you can entertain them. Excuse me. I have work to do."

And Alex left her standing alone on the edge of the bonfire, as he stomped into the winery across the field.

So Rosalie spent the next hour talking to his employees, thanking them for all their hard work, and trying to entertain the Falconeris in such a way that they wouldn't notice Alex's incredible rudeness. The party started to wind down, as people wandered half-drunkenly back to the village or the staff quarters behind the villa. Finally, Cesare came to Rosalie by the dying bonfire.

"Thank you for inviting us," he said quietly. "We should go."

The Falconeri children were all yawning, and the toddler, Hayes, was actively crying, being comforted by his mother, who, being newly pregnant, looked rather tired herself.

Looking at them, Rosalie suddenly felt like crying too. This wasn't how she'd thought the evening would go.

Holding her two-year-old on her hip, Emma came to them. "Thank you, Rosalie. It was fun."

"No, it wasn't," Rosalie said, wiping her eyes. "I'm sorry. I don't know why Alex…"

"Don't worry about it," Cesare said. But it was obvious he was a little affronted by his cousin's coldness.

"Well, meeting you and the baby was fun, at least," Emma added cheerfully.

"And I got to spend the evening with you." Cesare looked at his dark-haired wife. "Every moment with you is pure pleasure."

"*Every* moment?" Emma said teasingly, glancing at her tired toddler and bickering children.

"Yes. Every one." Pulling her close, Cesare then kissed her softly on the lips. Rosalie saw the love in their eyes as they pulled apart, the two of them so obviously crazy about each other, even after three, almost four children and many years of marriage.

Looking at them made Rosalie's heart hurt. She would have given anything to have her own husband look at her with that kind of love in his eyes.

But he didn't. Instead, for the last two months, Alex had barely glanced at her at all.

Rosalie shivered in the deepening autumn night. She suddenly felt very cold.

"Here, I'll take him," Cesare said to Emma, lifting the toddler to his shoulder, where the boy laid his head to rest with a snuffle. "Good night, cousin," he told Rosalie, smiling, as his wife gave her one last hug.

"We'll see you again soon."

With many farewells and promises to meet in the future, the family left. For a long moment, Rosalie stared after them, her heart yearning. That was exactly what she wanted. A large, noisy family. A loving marriage. That was happiness.

Could she ever have that?

She didn't know if she deserved it, after the way she'd abandoned her parents. But whether deserved it or not, Rosalie wanted it. So badly it made her heart ache and swell until pain was all she felt and all she was.

And suddenly, she clearly saw the truth of her great-aunt's words.

The only way to change everything was to risk everything. To be brave enough to speak the truth from her heart.

As the bonfire died down to embers, after the employees had all left, Rosalie went to where her husband was putting out what remained of the flames. Reaching out her hand, she put it on his shoulder.

Alex looked at her coldly. His handsome face was half-hidden in the shadows of the fading firelight.

"What is really going on?" she asked quietly.

He looked down at the last embers and ash. His hands tightened. "Cesare and I have nothing in common. There's no reason for us to be friends."

"And us?" She lifted her gaze to his. "Is there any reason for us to be friends?"

Frowning, he straightened, still holding on tightly to the water hose. "We aren't friends. We're married."

"Yes. Married." With a deep breath, she forced herself to be brave. "I've missed you, Alex. Talking to you. Sleeping beside you—and all the rest of it. What's happened to us?"

For a moment, his dark eyes looked haunted. Then his jaw tightened, and he looked away. "Nothing."

Take a risk, her great-aunt had said. *Be bold.*

"Well, something's changed for me." Rosalie took a deep breath. "I'm in love with you, Alex."

Alex stared at her in shock.

A ripple went through his body, a seismic tremble, causing his heart to shake.

Rosalie loved him? How could she love him?

His knees felt weak. He staggered back a single step as he looked at her.

Her brown eyes were bright beneath the moonlight. A cool autumn wind mussed her long dark hair, blowing against her red dress, moving the knit fabric sensually against her small waist and legs. Her lips were parted. She seemed to be holding her breath.

She loved him.

Shock waves reverberated through him, sinew and bone. He wasn't worthy of her love. He didn't have the ability to love her back.

"Rosalie," he began hoarsely. Then he stopped.

"Yes?"

Seeing his wife's beautiful face turned up to his so hopefully, so bravely, he felt sick. The last thing he wanted to do was hurt her. It was one of the reasons he'd kept his distance. He had to protect her.

And he had to protect himself. He couldn't weaken. Not now. Not ever.

As he put out the final flames of the bonfire and watched the last embers die, Alex felt rising despair. He couldn't love her—couldn't she see that? He had to be tough and strong to be able to keep his promise to protect them.

But how could he say that without hurting her?

Rosalie waited silently with tortured hope. Then, slowly, her expression changed. He saw disappointment. Then pain.

Soon her love would turn to hate. Their marriage, their lives, would be destroyed. Along with their child's—

Fear pounded through him, surging like rain. He'd somehow known this would happen, from the first moment he'd seen Cesare's family tonight. His distant cousin was, to all appearances, utterly lost in playing his sickeningly sweet role of devoted family man, as his wife clung to him like he was Christmas and joy and heaven all wrapped into one.

But their dream world couldn't last. Soon—or perhaps even already, behind closed doors—his second cousin's marriage would dissolve into screams and accusations. And their three innocent children would be the ones to pay the price. They would suffer for their parents' love. As everyone suffered, if they believed romantic love could actually *endure*.

"I love you," Rosalie said again, helplessly.

Alex's shoulders sagged. He looked down at his hands. The last embers of the bonfire were gone. He pushed through the ashes with the tip of his boot to make doubly sure.

Turning away silently, he walked back to the barn with the hose and turned off the water. He took a deep breath. Gripping his hands at his sides, he walked back to her. He found her by the villa, beneath the windows. She turned, her body visibly shaking as he stopped her.

"I'm sorry, *cara*," he said in a low voice. He had to force himself to look at her. "I'm just not made that way."

Her face started to crumple. She took a deep breath, looking gorgeous in her red dress, her tumbling hair streaked with moonlight.

"I can be patient," she said. "I can give you time—"

"No," Alex said savagely. He had everything he'd ever wanted. A son to carry on his name. A beautiful wife who loved this land as much as he did. A partner. A friend. But it had come at a price. "It can't happen."

"I can wait." Coming forward, she put her arms around him. He stiffened, his heart pounding as he felt her soft body against his own. Standing on her tiptoes, she pressed her cheek to his, whispering once more against his skin, "I love you."

Every time she said those three little words, it felt like a gut punch.

He drew back from her almost angrily.

"Stop it, Rosalie. I told you from the beginning. I can't. And you agreed to marry me anyway. You agreed!"

"I know." She closed her eyes. He saw the single tear falling down her cheek, heard the tremble in her voice. He blocked a rush of emotion from his heart.

"You made your decision." His voice was hard. "You can't go back on it now, or ask for more than I can give. It's not fair."

Looking up at him, she tried to smile. "Weren't you the one who told me life isn't fair?"

She looked pitiful, in spite of her lush beauty. Begging for his love. He hated himself. The villa that had been their home looked dark behind her, dark and empty and cold.

"You made your bed," he told her coldly. "Now you must lie in it."

A light went out of her eyes. He couldn't bear it. Urgently, he yanked her into his arms, searching her gaze.

"I can give you anything else you desire, Rosalie. Diamonds. Yachts. Palaces. More children." Cupping her cheek, he looked down at her fiercely. "We can be happy enough. If you'll just let us…"

He lowered his lips to hers, trying desperately to burn through her love, to crush it to dust, to leave it in ashes like the bonfire. *Passion.* It was the one thing that had never failed them. For the last two months, he'd tried to keep himself distant, because he was afraid of his own feelings. But now, he feared something more—he feared hers.

He tried to deepen the kiss, pushing her lips apart, plundering her mouth with his tongue. He wanted to prove to her that a loveless marriage didn't mean a sexless one, and could be very pleasurable indeed. He tried to entice her, to punish her, to force her to match his fire. She always had.

But for the first time, her lips were strangely lifeless beneath his. Pain gutted him that he couldn't control. He ripped away from her.

"I can't love you or anyone." His voice was a frustrated shout in the darkness. "Why can't you accept it?"

"I have." Her voice was dead.

"Why can't you be happy, like you were?"

"Because—" She looked away. "I want more."

Alex stared at her. Taking a deep breath, he looked down, gripping his hands at his sides.

"I know you're scared," she whispered. "So am I."

"You don't know what you're asking."

"I know the risk." Rosalie met his gaze. "I know the cost."

Angry, defensive words rose to his lips, his usual defensive mechanism, to be sarcastic, to be cold, to create distance. Then he looked at her, remembering her pain over her parents' deaths.

He said in a low tone, "Love doesn't last. It only leads to anger, to yelling and coldness and hate."

"With Chiara?"

"I never loved her. She was safe. But my parents. They used to yell and scream and—I've seen it too many times, with everyone I know. However happy Cesare and his wife look now, it will end that way with them too. Love always ends. Either in hatred, or in death."

Reaching out, she grabbed his hand. "You're right. Life ends in death. Hatred is optional. So is love. But if we're afraid to feel either one, what are we left with except emptiness? What is that, but killing ourselves while we're still alive?"

For a moment, Alex felt the magnetic pull of her, of the emotional longing in her lovely brown eyes. All he had to do was surrender. All he had to do was give in—

But if he let himself feel, thirty-five years of repressed emotion might swallow him whole, drown him.

He looked away. "I can't be like you. Perhaps you can love like that. I cannot. I don't have the capacity. I never learned how."

"That's not true. If you'd only—"

"I can't," Alex cut her off. "I'm sorry." He exhaled, then looked down at her. He repeated in a low voice, "I'm sorry."

"All right." With an intake of breath, she tried to smile, even while her eyes were luminous with unshed tears. "I'll try to live without it."

Without love? Alex looked at her beautiful yet miserable face.

Could she? And could he let her do it?

CHAPTER ELEVEN

"YOU'VE BECOME A DOORMAT, *ma chérie*."

The next morning, after Rosalie had stumbled out of the small cot in the nursery, exhausted from a night tossing and turning and getting up twice to feed the baby, she came downstairs with Oliver to see if the housekeeper had made coffee. She looked out the windows and saw bright sunlight pouring over golden fields and clusters of trees in vivid autumn reds and oranges.

So beautiful it hurt.

She found Odette alone in the kitchen. The white-haired Frenchwoman handed Rosalie a steaming china cup of coffee laden with sugar and cream. But as she breathed her gratitude and took her first sip, her great-aunt had said those words that burned through her heart.

Swallowing hard, she looked down at her baby prattling happily against her hip.

"I'm not a doormat," Rosalie told them both.

Odette shook her head. "You look like you need something for strength. I'm making you an omelet." Pulling down a copper pan from a hook, before whisking eggs and then adding ingredients, her aunt said, "Last night, I had my window open. For fresh air."

Rosalie swallowed. "What did you hear?"

Her aunt met her gaze. "I heard my precious niece beg for the love of her husband, and accept it meekly when he refused her."

Rosalie blushed, horrified. Setting the china cup down

on the counter, she said in a low voice, "What else can I do? Alex is right. He told me from the beginning he could not love me."

"Why did you marry him, then?"

Rosalie gaped. "You were the one who said I should!"

"I said your baby needed a stable home and father," the older woman corrected. "I never said you had to marry him."

Hadn't she? Rosalie struggled to remember.

Odette looked at baby Oliver, with his chubby cheeks and good nature. "Do you want your son to grow up thinking this is normal in a marriage? That he should have no feelings and ignore his wife and child?"

Rosalie sucked in her breath. "I cannot force Alex to love me. So what choice do I have?"

"Plenty."

"I made my bed—I must lie in it," she said, echoing her husband's words.

Her great-aunt gave a low curse in French that made her blush.

"Tatie!" Rosalie said, scandalized.

"You made your bed, *oui*. But you can change the sheets. You can sleep on the sofa. You can decide not to sleep. You have many choices." Her dark eyes gleamed beneath the wrinkles as she placed the hot omelet on a china plate in front of her. "But what you must not do is sleep on a cot in your child's room, accepting a sexless marriage, or crawl back in surrender to your husband's bed, accepting a loveless one."

"He'll never divorce me."

"Who is speaking of divorce?" As Rosalie ate the omelet, her great-aunt tilted her head. "You told me you received another offer for your land in Sonoma. A very generous one."

"Yes," she muttered as she ate. She still hated the thought of selling her parents' land. But she couldn't just abandon it forever, lying fallow and forlorn. "They want an answer. I need to decide, one way or the other."

"Go home," Odette told her firmly.

Finishing the delicious omelet, Rosalie realized she'd been hungrier than she'd thought. "You want me to come back with you to Mont-Saint-Michel? I'm not sure if I could…"

"No. Home." Her great-aunt looked at her. "California."

Go home?

A whoosh of fear went through Rosalie, making her light-headed.

Odette put her wrinkled hand over hers and said very gently, "It's time.

It was an uncharacteristic display of sentimentality for her fierce great-aunt, and one that Rosalie was still thinking about two hours later, after Odette had departed in a chauffeured Rolls-Royce on her scheduled return to France.

Her aunt had only been at the villa for a few days, but immediately, Rosalie missed her. She felt more alone than she had since her parents had died.

Go home, her aunt had said.

Could she? Could she finally face it?

The last time she'd been to Emmetsville had been for her parents' funeral. She'd tried to erase that from her memory. The smell of ash in the air. The blurs of anguished faces. The sound of crying, including her own. And worst of all, the awful thump as dirt hit the coffin lids. Her parents had been buried together, for eternity, leaving Rosalie alone.

Cody Kowalski, the neighbor who'd once asked to marry her, had tried to approach her at the graveside service. He'd started to say something, then stopped, red faced. Stammering, *I'm so sorry*, he'd simply fled.

But Cody didn't need to say anything. Rosalie's guilt filled in the blanks. If she'd married him, if she'd stayed in town, she could have saved her parents, as he'd saved his.

Even after all this time, the thought was radioactive inside her.

While the baby took his early-afternoon nap, Rosalie went into the empty study inside the villa. It was a very masculine room, with wood and black leather. Sitting at the dark wood desk, she drew out her laptop computer from the bottom shelf. After opening it, she reread the email from the California corporation offering to buy her family's land. She should just accept it. They'd send a check to Italy, and she'd never have to go back. Never have to face her fear.

Her fingers hovered over the keyboard.

Alex came into the study. "Where have you been? I was…" Then he saw her stricken face. "What's wrong?"

Heart pounding, she looked up at him. "I need to go home."

His face shut down. "This is your home."

She shook her head. "I've had another offer for my parents' land."

"So?"

"I've been putting off the decision."

"You don't have to do anything."

"But I do," she whispered over the lump in her throat. She glanced out the window toward the lush Italian countryside. "Everything you feel about this vineyard—I feel the same about our farm. My family's lived there for a hundred years. And Wildemer just offered me a fortune for it."

"Wildemer!" He scowled at the name, one of the largest wineries in the world. "Don't sell to them. You don't need the money." He paused. "I would suggest we build a vineyard there ourselves, but this business is too personal to me." He gave a humorless laugh. "I could hardly oversee a vineyard in California, traveling by ship and train."

"Of course not." But suddenly, Rosalie wished they could. If Alex was with her, she thought she could face anything. Replant. Regrow. Rebuild.

She shook her head, shaking the foolish dream from her mind, along with her dream that her husband could ever love her. How many fantasies must she have, and all of them doomed to fail? She took a deep breath.

"If I never intend to go back, I must sell. I can't just leave it a ruin. It's not fair to the town, or to my parents' memory." She looked back at her computer, then squared her shoulders. "I must go."

"To California?"

"I have been hiding from this too long. I have to face it, for the baby's sake." She looked up from the desk. "If I can't be brave, how can I teach Oliver to be?"

Alex was looking at her strangely in the slanted light from the blinds.

Rosalie swallowed. "Will you…" She hesitated, then said in a rush, "Will you come with me?"

If he came with her, she wouldn't be so scared. She could hold his hand, until she got through it, like she had when she'd given birth to their son.

Glancing away, her husband said softly, "I can't."

"We could take a ship—"

His face was like stone. "*No*, Rosalie."

Her heart cracked as her last hope faded. "You really don't care at all, do you?" she said slowly.

He didn't meet her eyes. She thought of his earlier words: *Just because someone is family, doesn't mean they can't also be strangers.* He'd meant it, she realized. Every word. And it was killing her.

Rosalie was his family now. She was his wife. But to Alex, she'd always be a stranger.

She was utterly, completely alone.

Looking at her in the shadows of the villa's study, Alex couldn't bear the pain in his wife's eyes.

You really don't care at all, do you?

If only she knew!

Ever since his son had been born, he'd done everything he could to keep his distance from Rosalie, not just emotionally, but physically. Even after the doctor had given her the all clear, he'd stayed away. He'd feared, if he made love to her, he would surrender. Afraid he'd fall apart.

If he gave in to weakness, gave in to his feelings, then how would he defend against the decades of repressed pain he'd barely kept at bay? He'd end up sobbing in some corner, totally useless to anyone. Now more than ever, he needed to be strong for his wife and child.

So he'd tried to stay in control, cold as ice. He'd tried as hard as he could to keep his promise to take care of Rosalie and their son.

Alex had done everything he could to make her happy. But since last night, when she'd outright begged for his love, he'd realized how completely he'd failed.

She'd asked for his time and attention, and he'd refused. She'd asked for his love, and he'd refused. Finally, today, she'd asked for him to come to California with her. To be her comfort, her shield. It was a simple enough request. It should have been easy.

But even that, he could not do.

Rosalie was counting on him for strength and protection. How could he show her all the ways he was less brave, less strong than she?

His word was all he had. All of Alex's family had died—because of him. Because Alex had broken his word.

But now, he suddenly realized that Chiara had died because he'd *kept* it.

What did that mean? He put his hand against his forehead as his brain whirled. And then he suddenly knew.

There was no protection. There was no defense. No matter what Alex did, he destroyed anyone who got too close.

Rosalie and the baby would be better off without him.

It was a cold, ruthless thought. But though it filled him with despair, he could not argue with its truth.

All this time, he'd been so determined to keep his promises, as a means of saving his broken soul. But he'd been living in a dream.

He'd already broken his word to Rosalie. He'd promised to care for her. He'd promised she'd never regret marrying him. He hadn't. And she did. He looked at her.

"Go to California," he said hoarsely.

"All right," she said softly, not meeting his eyes.

All right, as if it meant nothing. Just as she'd said it last night, when he'd told her he'd never love her back. Simple as that. *All right*.

"And don't come back," he heard himself say.

She blinked, rising slowly from the desk. "What?"

Once, nothing had been more important to Alex than vows. Than honor.

But if he forced her to stay in this marriage, as he'd done with Chiara, then sooner or later, he'd ruin Rosalie's life—and their child's. Just like he'd ruined everyone else's.

He couldn't be that kind of monster.

"My jet will take you to California immediately," he said in a low voice. She couldn't know how much even that cost him. Allow her and the baby on a plane?

But then, Chiara had died in a car. It wasn't the means of transportation that ruined people's lives. It was being close to Alex.

Rosalie looked confused. "What do you mean, don't come back? It's only for a few days. Will you be joining us in California?"

"No." His throat hurt. He couldn't destroy her. He had to let her go.

"I don't understand."

"I don't want you here anymore. Neither you nor the

baby." Alex took a deep breath, clenching his hands at his sides. Looking straight into her beautiful, warm, loving eyes, he said in an expressionless voice, "I want a divorce."

Divorce?

Rosalie recoiled. It was the one thing she'd never, ever expected Alex to say. The man who'd absolutely refused to divorce his first wife, even when the woman had blatantly cheated on him in public, wanted to divorce Rosalie, who'd done nothing but support and love him?

She staggered back as the world collapsed beneath her feet. Their marriage was the one thing she'd assumed she could count on. No matter what.

"What about *happy or unhappy, marriage is forever*?" she choked out.

"I changed my mind," he said flatly.

"And our baby?"

For a moment, Alex didn't speak. Then he said in a low voice, "We'll come to some custody arrangement."

Rosalie could barely breathe. "I don't want that."

Alex stared at her coldly. His hard jaw was tight, and so was his posture. Every inch of his powerful body seemed about to snap. "Too bad. Because I do."

She wasn't going to beg. She *wasn't*. She'd done enough of that last night at the bonfire. She wasn't going to—

"Please, Alex," she heard herself say in a small voice. "Whatever the problem is, we can work through this. We have to stay together—"

His dark eyes looked through her as if she were a stranger. "I cannot be what you need me to be."

"Just try." Rosalie felt like the lights and shadows of the study were spinning around her in a whirl. She felt like she was drowning in tears. "We can go to counseling. We can—"

"No."

"People can change. Just look at what I'm doing now. The thing I'm scared of most. I'm going home."

"Yes. You are." His voice was hard, yielding nothing.

"Please don't make me do this alone," she said, and she didn't just mean her trip to California. "Come with us."

He drew back, clenching his hands. Then he shook his head. "You're better off without me."

Rosalie didn't want a divorce. As unhappy as she'd been lately, giving up on her marriage was the last thing she wanted to do.

But neither could she be the way Alex had been, when he'd coldly refused to set his first wife free. If Alex wanted this divorce—so much he was willing to sacrifice his honor and the sanctity of his promise—then Rosalie had no choice but to give him what he wanted.

But oh—she thought it would kill her.

Because she didn't want to face reality. She wanted to hope. She wanted to believe.

She wanted him to love her.

Standing in the shadows of the study, with her arms folded tight around her body as if she could somehow protect her heart, she gave a tearful laugh. *Love* her? Alex thought so little of her that he was willing to break his word for the first time in his adult life, just to get out of their marriage!

If even *he* couldn't keep his marriage vows, then there was nothing left for her to hope for. It was over.

"All right," Rosalie whispered.

At those two words, Alex looked away, his jaw tight.

Tears streamed down her face as she gazed at her husband for the last time. She said thickly, "I would have stayed married to you forever."

"I know," Alex whispered. Taking a deep breath, he cupped her cheek. "That's why I'm letting you go."

CHAPTER TWELVE

THE MOMENT THE DOOR closed behind Rosalie and his son, the villa went silent. More silent than any house had ever been.

Alex hadn't been able to watch her pack their suitcases. An hour later, his driver took her and the baby away, off to the airport near Venice where his private jet waited.

It was deadly quiet. To celebrate the end of harvest, he'd given his house staff the day off. He went to his study, the last place he'd spoken to Rosalie. He pretended to write emails and read business reports. But he understood nothing he read. His mind was with his wife, replaying the scene over and over, remembering her expression when he'd asked for a divorce.

Now she was gone. Both Rosalie, and his son.

Alex was alone.

He paced the hallways. The villa had never felt so empty before. This place had always been his home. But now, it felt more haunted and desolate than the palazzo in Venice.

Perhaps he should go there, he thought. At least in Venice, he wouldn't hear the echo of his wife's laughter, or his child's babbles. But as he started walking toward the door, he stopped.

No. He had memories of her at the palazzo, as well. It was where they'd first met. Where they'd gotten to know each other. Where he'd first made love to her on their wedding night. No. He couldn't possibly go there, either. His hands clenched at his sides.

Then where?

He should contact his lawyer. Order him to start divorce proceedings. Alex would make sure that Rosalie and his son never wanted for anything, ever. He would give her far more than the prenuptial agreement required. He'd give her half of everything he possessed.

But he knew that was never what she'd wanted from him.

I love you. I would have stayed married to you forever.

Stumbling past the library, he stopped when he saw a dark shadow on the hardwood floor. One of Oliver's toys? Frowning, he went into the room. It was indeed a child's toy, but not his son's. It was a well-loved teddy bear he'd never seen before. Whose could it be?

Then he knew.

"Your wife deserves better than how you're treating her, Alex," Cesare Falconeri had told him last night, when the two men were alone at the bonfire. "You can do better."

It was something that Alex had already known in his heart, something he was trying desperately not to know, so hearing the words spoken aloud had enraged him.

"Your marriage won't last," Alex had responded in a bitter counterattack. "Your children will see your family fall apart. See you break your vows."

"You're wrong." Cesare's eyes had calmly met Alex's. "I'd sooner cut out my own heart than betray those I love."

Now Alex looked at the stuffed teddy bear. He wondered which of Cesare's children it belonged to. Tomorrow, he would ask his assistant to send it on to Lake Como.

But as he was about to set it down, he stopped, looking at the teddy bear, so soft in his hand. For a moment, his heart pounded as he stood in the cool silence of the darkened villa.

His throat hurt.

He would take it himself. Why the hell not? Where else did he have to go?

Anything to get away from the memories of her—

Three hours later, after getting lost twice in the winding roads through the mountains, Alex arrived at the beautiful villa by the lake.

"Alex." Cesare's face was startled when the butler escorted him into the salon. "What are you doing here?"

Yes, what?

"This," Alex stammered, holding up the teddy bear awkwardly. Cesare took it with a rueful grin.

"You can't imagine how much trouble we had last night, convincing Elena to sleep without it. Thanks."

"Good. Great," Alex said awkwardly. "So. That's it. I'll go."

"Wait." His cousin smiled. "We're about to sit down for dinner. Join us. Come say hello."

And so it was that Alex greeted the Falconeri children, who seemed far more excited by the teddy bear's appearance than his. But Cesare's wife, Emma, hugged him close, before she glanced behind him.

"Where are Rosalie and Oliver?"

"Gone," he said. "Back to California."

His voice was strangled. He'd had to force the words from his throat.

"What? Why?" Emma cried.

Cesare, looking at Alex's face, intervened, "Emma, my dear, would you mind starting dinner without me?" Grabbing a bottle and two highball glasses, he looked back at Alex. "Let's go out on the terrace."

An hour later, deep into his second glass of forty-year-old Scotch, Alex found himself sitting on a terrace overlooking sparkling Lake Como, beneath the setting sun with a slight chill in the air, spilling his guts.

"Don't you see?" Alex finished. "They all died. No matter what I do. Whether I keep my promises or not, I destroy the life of anyone who gets close to me." He'd never thought he'd share the story with Cesare. "I tried to keep my promise to Rosalie," he said in a low voice. "I failed. I can't take care of her like she needs. I can't love her. I don't know how."

"I didn't know how, either," Cesare admitted, looking out at the water. Then, with a smile, he glanced behind him at the joyous villa, full of life. "But then I did."

Alex swallowed against the lump in his throat. "How did you get past it? Everything that happened? The way we were raised?"

Cesare poured his own second glass of Scotch. "You never really get past it." He looked at his cousin, then deliberately held up his glass. "Unless you want to."

"It can't be that simple."

"It isn't." He looked at his raised toast. "And it is."

Tilting back his head, Cesare drank deeply.

Alex looked at his cousin. He suddenly envied the man with all his heart. "It is easy for you to say," he growled. "I saw how you and Emma love each other, but I told myself it wouldn't last. I had to believe that. Because I don't know what love is or what it's supposed to feel like. That's why I couldn't stand to be around you, Cesare. Because it showed me—"

"What you thought you'd never have?" He leaned forward in his chair on the terrace. "I realized I loved Emma when I understood her happiness was more important to me than my pride. More important than anything."

"But I don't love Rosalie. That's the whole problem. I can't."

"You know you're in love not just by the way you feel, but by the way you act. For the first time in my life, I cared about someone else more than myself."

"Then I definitely don't love her," Alex said flatly. "Because all I've done is break her heart."

His cousin tilted his head. "So why did you let her go?"

"Because—because I couldn't stand to see her so unhappy. Because she deserves better than me. Because…"

"Because her happiness is more important to you than your own."

Alex stared at him.

Could it really be that simple?

He'd set her free because he couldn't bear for her to be unhappy. He'd sacrificed not just his honor, not just his comfort, but everything he'd ever wanted—a family, a home, a child, a wife.

He thought again of the loneliness of the villa after she'd left. His total misery. But he'd been willing to live like that.

For her.

Some people proved their love by proposing marriage, he realized. He'd proved his by asking Rosalie for a divorce.

"Do you see?" Cesare said, leaning forward intently. His eyes crinkled. "Do you finally understand?"

Alex sucked in his breath. "Yes," he whispered.

His actions proved his love.

All the emotion he'd been afraid of feeling, he suddenly felt all at once. It was as if his heart cracked open. He saw the beauty of the Italian lake beyond the villa's terrace, in a whirl of blue and gold and red and green. He saw his older cousin's concern, which Cesare had always had for him, ever since he was a child. Closing his eyes, he saw his own baby's sweet face.

And Rosalie's. Her beautiful eyes, her open heart, her joy in the world.

I love you. He heard the echo of her trembling voice.

She'd known great pain, but she'd still been brave enough to risk her heart, in spite of all Alex's demands to the contrary. In spite of the way he'd neglected and avoided her so he wouldn't have to face his own feelings. She'd loved him through it all.

And now she'd gone back to California alone, to face

her grief over her parents' deaths and the devastation of her childhood home. She was actually thinking of selling land that had been in her family for a hundred years. She'd asked him to go with her, to be her comfort and support. He'd refused like a coward.

So she'd had the courage to do it alone.

Part of Alex had always seen her strength. It was why he'd chased her to Mont-Saint-Michel. Why he'd brought her back to Venice. Why he'd married her, in spite of having believed he'd never marry again. Because some part of him had known, from the very beginning, that Rosalie was braver. That she was stronger and finer than he.

Some part of him had known, even then, that he needed her.

"I love her," Alex breathed, rising unsteadily from his chair.

His cousin, still seated with his hands folded, looked up at him quietly. "Of course you do."

"I have to see her now, today," Alex said. "I have to reach her before she makes a decision she'll regret—"

"Call her."

He shook his head, a lump in his throat. "If she hangs up, it's over. I have to see her in person. I can't let her face everything alone." He remembered how she'd insisted on accompanying him to the charity ball that he'd dreaded. How she'd endured labor, how she'd needed him there, how she'd squeezed his hand so hard. "But how can I show her? How can I prove—" His eyes went wide. "I'll take a plane."

The thought made his heart race, and not in a good way. But even as he started to turn, intending to run toward his Ferrari, he stopped. "It's too late."

"What?"

"My jet is gone. She's taking it back to California right now." Alex set his jaw. "I'll get a commercial flight." Even as he spoke the words, the horizon seemed to swim in front of his eyes. "But that will take too long, maybe even another whole day—"

"Need a plane?" Cesare asked with a lazy grin. "I might have one around."

Alex turned to him eagerly. "Yes. If you don't mind… I've had some…trouble." He licked his lips. "I know it's not rational. But for the last ten years, I haven't been able to get on a plane."

"No wonder, after what happened," his cousin said quietly. He brightened. "Perhaps I can help with that too."

"How?"

Cesare gave a low laugh. "I can punch you in the face till you pass out, then tie you up and toss you on my plane. If you want."

For a moment, Alex actually considered it. Then he shook his head.

"No?" Cesare pretended to sigh.

"I will do it sober," Alex said. "For her. Even if I'm scared out of my mind." He clenched his hands at his sides. "She's proven how brave she can be. So can I. For Rosalie. For our son."

And he thought of them, every moment, as he got on Cesare's plane thirty minutes later. As the jet took off, as he thought of his family members who'd died, his fingernails dug into the leather armrests of his seat.

Alex thought of Rosalie. He thought of how desperately she needed him to be strong. How they needed him to be *there*.

And he did it. Without alcohol, sleeping pills or being punched repeatedly in the face by his cousin. Sweating bullets, he arrived at the San Francisco airport fourteen hours later and stepped out into the California sunshine, knowing he'd just changed his world. He'd proved he could be brave too. He could do anything, if it meant he could win his wife back.

But what if Alex was too late?

Stepping out of the rental car in the midmorning light, Rosalie looked out at the ruins of her family farm in the California countryside.

She'd arrived at the San Francisco airport some hours earlier. Exhausted and filled with despair, she'd gotten a hotel room that overlooked the bay so she could try to rest for a while. From the window, she'd looked down at the path where she'd walked when she was pregnant, talking to her unborn child and wishing desperately that she could keep him.

Now she had everything she'd wanted.

What was wrong with her that it wasn't enough? That she still wanted more—that she so desperately wished her husband could have loved her?

I want a divorce.

Every time Rosalie thought back to that moment, she felt sick with grief. Part of her had hoped he would call her on the plane and tell her he'd made a mistake.

But he'd made his decision. He would not, could not love her.

Perhaps Alex had done the brave thing, letting her go, rather than letting their marriage die a slow, painful death. Because she never could have left him. Even if he didn't love her.

I know. That's why I'm letting you go.

Alex had done what she could not do. He'd been willing to face the truth and end the pain.

Now Rosalie prayed she could do the same.

She'd already stopped by the Wildemer Company's office in downtown Sonoma. The office was going to prepare a contract of sale immediately. But before she could force herself to sign it, she knew she had to be brave enough to go to the farm and say goodbye, one last time.

But as she'd come out of the Wildemer offices, pushing her baby in a stroller, she'd passed by a red-haired man coming toward the door.

"Hello, Rosalie."

Shocked, she gasped, "Cody?"

"I heard you were in town. Is this your baby?" Husky in a flannel shirt and jeans, with a wide, friendly face, Cody Kowalski knelt briefly by the stroller, smiling. "And I heard you were married…"

"What are you doing here?"

He straightened. "The same as you, I guess." He looked up at Wildemer's picturesque nineteenth-century office building. "I'm here to pick up the check." He tilted his head. "We're done. We sold."

"You sold your farm?" she cried. "But why?"

"My parents want to retire to Florida." Cody grinned. "And I hate farming. I always have."

"What?" she exclaimed.

He shook his head. "For my whole life, I tried to be brave enough to tell my parents I didn't want to do it." He looked at her. "All this time I've been wishing I could have been brave enough to do what you did, Rosalie."

"But I never should have left." She looked down at her baby in the stroller, feeling suddenly near tears. "At least you were here, to help your parents escape the fire…"

"No, Rosalie. It wasn't me." He came closer, his freckled face sad. "Your parents did that."

"My parents?"

"They helped us escape. I was in the basement, playing video games. My parents were in the kitchen, arguing. Your parents came and pounded on the door, and told us to leave. If not for them, we wouldn't have known. We wouldn't have made it. They said they were going back to try to save all their animals... They knew about the danger. But they didn't care."

"They knew?" Rosalie whispered.

Cody looked down. "I wanted to tell you at the funeral. But I was scared."

"Why?"

"Because it was my fault," he said in a low voice, wiping his eyes. "My fault your parents died. If I'd just been honest with my parents that I didn't want the farm, they would have sold up long before." He paused. "And your parents would still be alive, because they wouldn't have wasted time coming to warn us."

"It's not your fault."

"But—"

"It was never your fault, Cody. Never. Just be happy. It's what they would have wanted. It's what I want too." She hugged Cody hard as she whispered, "Thank you for telling me."

Now, remembering, Rosalie looked out at the land.

All this time, she'd thought of her parents' deaths with guilt and shame, blaming herself. Now she was able to see they'd died as they'd lived—on their own terms, making the world a better place.

Just as Rosalie could, if she tried. She took a deep breath.

Everything had burned. Nothing was left, except the house's foundation buried deep in the earth, and even that was covered with ash and scarred by smoke. Looking down at her baby, she said, "This is where I grew up, Oliver. Your grandparents and their grandparents too. I wanted you to see it. Even though it's gone."

Rosalie couldn't run the farm alone. She couldn't. It was the people she'd loved who'd made the land beautiful to her. Without them, there was nothing. She'd lost them forever. Her parents. Her dreams. And Alex—

Looking down, Rosalie saw tiny green shoots, pushing through the rubble and debris.

Or were they really gone?

She'd come to say goodbye.

But she couldn't.

Because she suddenly realized the people she loved were still here, in her heart. In her memory. She could feel her parents' love, all around her.

Love never died. Even her love for Alex, regardless of their divorce, would always be a part of her heart.

Rosalie looked up at the sky. "I will do everything I can," she whispered to her parents. "For you. And Oliver will know how much you would have loved him."

She couldn't sell. She had to stay. It was what her parents would have wanted.

No. It was what *she* wanted.

Turning as she wiped her tears, she saw Alex standing quietly behind her.

Was he a dream? He had to be. Because Alex Falconeri couldn't possibly have come across half the world on a ship in a single day…

"Rosalie," he said huskily, coming forward. He stopped when he was just two feet away from her.

"What? How?"

"I took a plane."

"A plane?" she gasped.

"I couldn't let you go." Taking her into his arms, he looked down at her, his dark eyes intent. "I've been waiting here for you. Because I knew you wouldn't sell. Not without coming to say goodbye."

"How did you know?"

"Because I know you." Alex gave a crooked smile. "I know your heart. And you would want Oliver to see your home. You'd want to know you'd faced it."

"You knew that?" Rosalie hadn't been sure herself that she'd be brave enough.

"You're the strongest person I know." He cradled her cheek. "When you left Italy yesterday, it nearly destroyed me. All I want is to be the man you deserve. The man you fell in love with. So I got on a plane to tell you." He paused, then said in a low voice, "Loving you gave me courage."

"What?" she said through numb lips. "What did you say?"

Alex smiled down at her. "I love you, Rosalie." He ran his hand through her dark hair. "It took losing you for me to realize how stupid I've been. And talking to my cousin…"

"You spoke with Cesare?" she said, astonished. At his nod, she added, "I thought he was your *second* cousin?"

"A cousin is a cousin." He grinned, then sobered as he took her hand in his own. "And family is family. I thought I didn't have the capacity to love because my parents hated each other. But the truth was, I was just afraid to care, after losing everyone I cared about. I was a coward."

"Coward?" She looked up at him in shock. "You got on a plane."

"I couldn't lose you. That's the only thing that made me brave enough. I'd face anything, do anything, to win you back. I want to be your family, Rosalie. Not a stranger." Looking at her, he whispered, "I want to give you everything."

Trembling, she looked up at him.

"But am I too late?" Alex's soul was vulnerable in his dark eyes. "Have I destroyed any chance to win you back, to love you forever? Can you ever forgive what I've done to us?"

With a choked sob, she lifted up on her toes, autumn

leaves crunching beneath her boots as she cupped his un-shaven cheek.

"There's nothing to forgive. You're mine, as I am yours. My friend. Lover. Partner. Husband." Glancing down at their baby in the stroller, she smiled through her tears. Looking up at Alex, she said, "I love you."

"I'm so in love with you, Rosalie—" With an intake of breath, Alex pulled her to him tightly. And as he lowered his lips to hers, to ravage her in a kiss, Rosalie heard the birdsong and soft sigh of the wind through distant trees, and she knew that, beneath the ash and ruin of her home, new life had just begun. It would grow back, even better and brighter than she'd ever dreamed.

The secret of life, as in making omelets, was love.

Spring had come to Venice at last.

Alex looked out the window of the palazzo. After a cold, dark, wet winter, the city had burst into the flowers of May. In the courtyard below, the leaves were green, and the canal sparkled blue against the sky.

His palazzo, too, had changed.

Looking around the salon where he'd first met Rosalie, when she'd been a panicked, pregnant stranger, Alex smiled. The floor was covered with his son's toys. Oliver was almost nine months old now, and a very fast crawler. He was already learning to walk.

Their family had only arrived a few weeks ago. They'd spent most of the winter planning their new vineyard in Sonoma, where they were rebuilding Rosalie's childhood home, and had passed the early spring at his vineyard in La Tesora. They looked forward to splitting their time between California and northern Italy, and had excellent employees to help manage both.

But Rosalie was his true partner. He'd never felt so alive as he did now. Their marriage had lots of laughter and joy by day—and by night, they set the world on fire. Alex shivered. Saying he loved his wife was insufficient. She was his life.

Everywhere he looked now, he could see her influence. She made everything joyful. The palazzo that had once been so empty and barren had become a comfortable, warm home.

Even Alex's work had changed. She'd convinced him to stop trying to be an anonymous wine genius, losing money every month, and start trying to market Falconeri wines, and turn it into a viable business.

"I know you're a billionaire and don't actually need the money," she'd said, rolling her eyes, "but if we're going to all the trouble of making it, why don't we also try to actually make people want to buy it? Just for fun?"

So they'd returned to Venice to open a tasting room for tourists. Just yesterday, they'd met with an architect to discuss plans for a tasting room and retail store at La Tesora. They might even sponsor next year's Venice Film Festival, to build the Falconeri brand. It made him nervous, but as his wife had said, the paparazzi were following them anyway—why not take that publicity and turn it into something positive? They were making wines. Instead of keeping it a closely held secret, why not go big, and see if the rest of the world liked their wines too?

It was risky. It involved putting his heart, and his wine, on the line. But in spite of that—or maybe because of it—Alex had never been happier.

In the palazzo's salon, above the marble fireplace, the painting of his haughty ancestor had been replaced by a beautiful new oil painting of his wife, holding their baby in her arms. After he'd begged, Rosalie had arranged it as a gift for his thirty-sixth birthday. Alex looked up at the painting, at her dark, spectacular beauty, at the glowing warmth of her deep brown eyes.

Then he heard her voice behind him. "There you are."

Turning, Alex saw his wife, even more beautiful in person. Coming forward, he kissed her. "Is everything ready?"

"Yes. Just in time too." She gave him a sideways glance. "Are you sure you're ready for this? There are four now, you know. *Four.*"

He paused. He'd invited Cesare and Emma and their children to stay not just for dinner, but for an entire weekend. If it went well, Alex and Rosalie and Oliver would go stay for a whole week with them in Lake Como later this summer. "If this works, our children will grow up as best friends."

"But there will be five children in our house at once," she pointed out. "All under the age of nine. Are you ready for that?"

"Absolutely," Alex said.

She hesitated, then watched his face. "And six?" she said slowly. "Could you handle six?"

Alex frowned. "What do you—" Then his expression changed. He breathed, "Are you saying…"

Rosalie nodded shyly. "Around Christmas."

"A baby!" With a shout, he pulled her into his arms, then kissed her cheeks and eyelids and forehead until she pulled away with a laugh.

"You're squashing me!" Her eyes grew wistful. "Are you truly happy, Alex?"

"So happy, *cara,*" he whispered, holding her tenderly. "So very, very happy." He gave a low laugh. "And I'm happy that this time, we did it the old-fashioned way."

"This time," she said huskily, her dark eyes warm. "And all the times to come."

And as Alex lowered his head to kiss her, he was thinking that six children wasn't such a bad idea. Because there was only one thing in the world more important than making wine, more important than promises, more important even than land that had been in the family for a hundred years. Only one thing would last forever, until all the stars went dim in the sky.

Love.

* * * * *

THE SPANIARD'S WEDDING REVENGE

JACKIE ASHENDEN

To Justin Alastair, Duke of Avon,
and Leonie de Saint-Vire.
Thanks for the inspiration!

CHAPTER ONE

THE LAST THING Cristiano Velazquez—current duke of an ancient and largely forgotten dukedom in Spain, not to mention playboy extraordinaire—wanted to see at two in the morning as he rolled out of his favourite Paris club was a gang of youths crouched in front of his limo as it waited by the kerb. He wanted to hear the distinctive rattle and then hiss of a spray can even less.

God only knew where his driver André was, the lazy *bastardo*, but he certainly wasn't here, guarding his limo like he should have been.

The two women on Cristiano's arm made fearful noises, murmuring fretfully about bodyguards, but Cristiano had never been bothered with protection and he couldn't be bothered now. Quite frankly, some nights he could use the excitement of a mugging, and at least the presence of a gang of Parisian street kids was something out of the ordinary.

Although it would have been better if they hadn't been spray-painting his limo, of course.

Still, the youths were clearly bothering his lady-friends, and if he wanted to spend the rest of the night with both of them in his bed—which he fully intended to do—then he was going to have to handle the situation.

'Allow me, ladies,' he murmured, and strolled unhurriedly towards the assembled youths.

One of them must have seen him, because the kid said something sharp to the rest of his friends and abruptly they all scattered like a pack of wild dogs.

Except for the boy with the spray can, currently graffitiing a rude phrase across the passenger door.

The kid was crouched down, his slight frame swamped by a pair of dirty black jeans and a huge black hoodie with the hood drawn up. He didn't seem to notice Cristiano's approach, absorbed as he was in adding a final flourish to his artwork.

Cristiano paused behind him, admiring said 'artwork'. 'Very good. But you missed an "e",' he pointed out helpfully.

Instantly the kid sprang up from his crouch, throwing the spray can to the right and darting to the left.

But Cristiano was ready for him. He grabbed the back of the boy's hoodie before the kid could escape and held on.

The boy was pulled up short, the hoodie slipping off his head. He made a grab for it, trying to pull it back up, but it was too late. A strand of bright hair escaped, the same pinky-red as apricots.

Cristiano froze. Unusual colour. Familiar in some way.

An old and forgotten memory stirred, and before he knew what he was doing he'd grabbed the boy's narrow shoulders and spun him around, jerking his hood down at the same time.

A wealth of apricot-coloured hair tumbled down the boy's back, framing a pale face with small, finely carved features and big eyes the deep violet-blue of cornflowers.

Not a boy. A girl.

No, a woman.

She said something foul in a voice completely at odds with the air of wide-eyed innocence she projected. A voice made for sex, husky and sweet, that went straight to his groin.

Not a problem. Everything went straight to his groin.

The grip he had on the back of her hoodie tightened.

She spat another curse at him and tried to wriggle out of his hold like a furious kitten.

Cristiano merely tightened his grip, studying her. She was quite strong for a little thing, not to mention feisty, and he really should let her go. Especially when he had other female company standing around behind him. Female company he actually wanted to spend time with tonight.

Then again, that familiarity was nagging at him, tugging at him as insistently as the girl was doing right now. That hair was familiar, and so were those eyes. And that lush little mouth…

Had he seen her before somewhere?

Had he slept with her, maybe?

But, no, surely not. She was dressed in dirty, baggy streetwear, and there was a feral, hungry look to her. He'd been in many dives around the world, and he recognised the look of a person who lived nowhere but the streets, and this young woman had that look.

She had the foul mouth that went along with it, too.

Not that he minded cursing. What he did mind was people spray-painting his limo and interrupting his evening.

'Be still, *gatita*,' he ordered. 'Or I'll call the police.'

At the mention of police she struggled harder, producing a knife from somewhere and waving it threateningly at him.

'Let me go!' she said, and added something rude to do with a very masculine part of his anatomy.

Definitely feisty, and probably more trouble than she was worth—especially with that knife waving around. She was pretty, but he wasn't into expending effort on a woman who was resistant when he had plenty of willing ones who weren't.

Then again, his tastes were…eclectic, and he liked difference. She was certainly that. A bit on the young side, though.

'No,' he said calmly. 'Your customisation of my car I could have ignored. But you have interrupted my evening and scared my friends, and that I simply won't stand for.'

She ignored him, spitting another curse and slashing at him with her knife.

'And now we're dealing with assault,' Cristiano pointed out, not at all bothered by the knife, since it managed to miss him by miles.

'Yes,' she snapped. 'You assaulting me!'

He sighed. He didn't have a lot of patience for this kind of nonsense and now, since it was late—or early, depending on your point of reference—he wanted to get to bed, and not alone. He really needed to handle this unfortunate situation.

So let her go.

Well, he should. After he'd figured out why she was so familiar, because it was really starting to annoy him now.

Though that was going to be difficult with her still swinging wildly at him with a knife.

Amongst the many skills he'd become proficient in on his quest to fill the gaping emptiness inside him was a certain expertise in a couple of martial arts, so it wasn't difficult for him to disarm her of her knife and then bundle her into his limo.

He got in after her and shut the door, locking it for good measure so that she was effectively confined.

Instantly she tried to get out, trying to get the doors to open. It wouldn't work. Only he could open the doors from the inside when they were locked.

He said nothing, watching her as she tried futilely to escape. When it became clear to her that she couldn't, she turned to him, a mix of fury and fear in her big cornflower-blue eyes.

'Let me out,' she demanded, breathless.

Cristiano leaned back in the seat opposite her and shoved his hands into the pockets of his expertly tailored black dress pants. It might have been a stupid move, since it wasn't clear whether she had another knife on her somewhere, but he was betting she didn't.

'No,' he said, studying her face.

Her jaw went rigid, her small figure stiff with tension. 'Are you going to rape me?'

He blinked at the stark question, then had a brief internal debate about whether he should be annoyed she'd even had to ask—especially since the latter part of his life had largely been spent in the pursuit of pleasure, both his own and that of any partners he came into contact with.

But in the end it wasn't worth getting uptight about. If she was indeed on the streets, then not being assaulted was likely to be one of her first concerns. Particularly when she'd been bundled into a car and locked in by a man much larger and stronger than she was.

'No,' he said flatly, so there could be no doubt. 'That

sounds like effort, and I try not to make any effort if I can possibly help it.'

She gazed at him suspiciously. 'Then why did you shut me in this car?'

'Because you tried to stab me with your knife.'

'You could have just let me go.'

'You were graffitiing my car. And it's an expensive car. It's going to cost me a lot of money to get it re-painted.'

She gave him a look that was at once disdainful and pitying. 'You can afford it, rich man.'

Unoffended, Cristiano tilted his head, studying her. 'It's true. I am rich. And, yes, I can afford to get it re-painted. But it's inconvenient to have to do so. You have inconvenienced me, *gatita*, and I do so hate to be incon-venienced. So, tell me, what are you going to do about it?'

'I'm not going to do anything about it.' She lifted her chin stubbornly. 'Let me out, *fils de pute*.'

'Such language,' Cristiano reproved, entertained de-spite himself. 'Where did you learn your manners?'

'I'll call the police myself. Tell them you're holding me against my will.'

She dug into the voluminous pockets of her hoodie, brought out a battered-looking cellphone and held it up triumphantly. 'Ten seconds to let me out and then I'm calling the emergency services.'

Cristiano was unmoved. 'Go ahead. I know the po-lice quite well. I'm sure you'll be able to explain why you were crouching in front of my car, spray-painting foul language all over it, and then pulling a knife on me when I tried to stop you.'

She opened her mouth. Closed it again.

'What's your name?' he went on. That nagging familiarity was still tugging at him. He'd seen her before—he was sure of it.

'None of your business.'

Clearly she'd thought better of calling the police, because she lowered her hand disappearing her phone back into her hoodie.

'Give me back my knife.'

Cristiano was amused. She was a brave little *gatita*, asking for the knife he'd only just disarmed her of after she'd tried to stab him with it. Brave to stand up to him, too—especially considering she was at a severe disadvantage. Not only physically but, given her dirty clothes and feral air, socially, too.

Then again, when you lived at the bottom of life's barrel you had nothing to left to lose. He knew. He'd been there himself—if not physically then certainly in spirit.

'Sadly, that's not going to happen.' He shifted, taking his hands out of his pockets and very slowly leaning forward, his elbows on his thighs, his fingers linked loosely between his knees.

A wary look crossed her face.

And that was good. She was right to be wary. Because he was losing his patience, and when he lost patience he was dangerous. Very dangerous indeed.

'I'll ask one more time,' he said, letting a warning edge his voice. 'What's your name, *gatita*?'

The man sitting opposite Leonie—the rich bastard who'd scooped her up and put her in his limo—was scaring the living daylights out of her, and she wasn't sure why.

He wasn't being threatening. He was simply sitting there with his hands between his knees, eyes the same kind of green as deep, dense jungles staring unblinkingly at her.

He was dressed all in black, and she didn't need to be rich to know that his clothes—black trousers and a plain black cotton shirt—had been made for him. Nothing else explained the way they fitted him so perfectly, framing wide shoulders and a broad chest, a lean waist and powerful thighs.

He reeked of money, this man. She could virtually smell it.

And not just money. He reeked of power, too. It was an almost physical force, pushing at her, crowding out all the air in the car and winding long fingers around her throat and squeezing.

There was another element to that power, though. An element she couldn't identify.

It had something to do with his face, which was as beautiful as some of the carved angels on the tombs in the Père Lachaise Cemetery. Yet that wasn't quite it. He seemed warmer than an angel, so maybe more like a fallen one. Maybe a beautiful devil instead.

Night-black hair, straight brows and those intense green eyes...

No, he wasn't an angel, and he wasn't a devil, either. He seemed more vital than a mythical being. More...elemental, somehow.

He was a black panther in the jungle, watching her from the branch of a tree. All sleepy and lazy... Until he was ready to pounce.

That frightened her—but it didn't feel like a threat she was familiar with. Sleeping on the streets of Paris had given her a very acute sense of threat, especially the threat of physical violence, and she wasn't getting that from him.

No, it was something else.

'Why do you want to know my name?'

She wasn't going to just give it to him. She never gave her name to anyone unless she knew them. Over the past few years she'd developed a hearty distrust of most people and it had saved her on more than one occasion.

'So you can call your friends in the police and get them to throw me in jail?'

She shouldn't have vandalised the car, since as a rule she liked to keep a low profile—less chance of coming to anyone's notice that way. But she'd been followed on her way to the little alley where she'd been hoping to bed down and, since being a woman on her own at night could be a problem, she'd attached herself to the crowd of homeless teenagers she'd been with earlier. They'd been out vandalising stuff and she'd had to prove herself willing to do the same in order to stay in their company. So she hadn't hesitated to pick up the spray can.

To be fair, she hadn't minded targeting this man's limo. The rich never saw the people on the streets, and she rather liked the idea of forcing her existence to at least be acknowledged in some way. Even if it did involve the police.

'No.'

His voice was very deep, with a warmth curling through it that made a part of her shiver right down low inside. There was a lilt to it, too…a faint, musical accent.

'But you were vandalising my car. Your name is the least you can give me in recompense.'

Leonie frowned. What had he done with her knife?

She wanted it back. She didn't feel safe without it. 'Why? Don't you want money?'

He raised one perfect black brow. 'Do you have any?'

'No.'

The man shrugged one powerful shoulder in an elegant motion and she found her gaze drawn by the movement. To the way his shirt pulled tight across that shoulder, displaying the power of the muscles underneath.

How odd. She'd never looked at a man that way before, so why was she doing so now? Men were awful—especially rich men like this one. She knew all about them; her father was one of them and he'd thrown her and her mother out on the streets. So no wonder she'd taken an instant dislike to this guy—though maybe it was more hate than dislike.

Hate was the only word strong enough to describe the disturbingly intense feeling gathering inside her now.

'Then, *gatita*,' he said, in his dark, deep voice, 'your name it will have to be.'

'But I don't want to give you that.'

Her jaw tightened. Resistance was the only thing she had on the streets and she clung to it stubbornly. Resistance to anything and everything that tried to push her down or squash her, grind her into the dirt of Paris's ancient cobbles. Because if she didn't resist then what else did she have? How would she even know she existed?

By spraying rude words on a limo?

Yes, if need be. It was all about the fight. That was all life was.

He gave another elegant shrug, as if it was all out of his hands. 'Then sadly I must be recompensed for my inconvenience in other ways.'

Ah, of course. She understood this, at least. 'I'm not paying you in sex. I'd rather die.'

His mouth twitched, which she found disconcerting. Normally men got angry when she refused them, but he didn't seem angry at all. Only...amused.

For some reason she didn't like it that he found her amusing.

'I'm sure you wouldn't,' he said lazily. 'I happen to be very good at it. No one has died having sex with me yet, for example.'

Leonie ignored the way her stomach fluttered. Perhaps that was hunger. She hadn't eaten today, and although a day without food was fairly normal for her, she didn't usually find herself chucked into a limo and kept prisoner by...whoever this man was.

'But,' he went on before she could argue, 'I know what you're talking about, and rest assured my recompense won't be in the form of sex. Though I'm sure you are, in fact, very desirable.'

She gave him a dark look. 'I am, actually. Why do you think I carry a knife?'

'Of course. What man wouldn't want a feral kitten?'

His mouth curved and she found herself staring at it. It had a nice shape, firm and beautifully carved.

She shook herself. Why was she staring at his mouth?

'You'd be surprised what men want,' she said, dragging her gaze to meet his, though quite frankly that wasn't any better.

His amusement abruptly drained away, the lines of his perfect face hardening. He shifted, sitting back against the seat. 'No. I would not.'

Leonie shivered, the interior of the car feeling suddenly cold. 'What do you want, then? I can't pay you, and

I'm not telling you my name, so all you can do is call the police and have me prosecuted. And if you're not going to do that, then isn't it easier to let me go?'

'But then how would I be recompensed for my inconvenience?' He shook his head slowly. 'No, I'm afraid, *gatita*, I can't let you go.' He paused, his green eyes considering. 'I think I'm going to have to put you to work instead.'

CHAPTER TWO

THE LITTLE REDHEAD treated this suggestion without obvious enthusiasm—which Cristiano had expected.

He still didn't know why exactly he'd said it. Because she was right. He could afford the paltry amount it would take to get his limo repainted. And as for his supposed inconvenience…

He glanced out through the window to the two lovely women he'd wanted to join him for the night. They were still out there, waiting for him to give them the word, though for once he felt a lessening of his own enthusiasm for their company.

It was a bit mystifying, since he never said no to anything or anyone—still less two beautiful women. Nevertheless, he found himself more interested in the little *gatita* sitting opposite him. She was a puzzle, and it had been too long since he'd had a puzzle.

He wanted her name. And the fact that she wouldn't just give it to him was irritating. Especially when that familiarity kept tugging on him, rubbing against his consciousness like a burr in a blanket.

Women never denied him, and the fact that she had was annoying.

And then she'd muttered that thing about men, and

he'd realised that letting her go meant letting her go back on the streets at two in the morning. Admittedly she'd been with a crowd earlier, but they'd all vanished, so she'd be on her own.

That she was used to looking after herself was obvious, but it didn't mean he was going to let her. He wasn't a gentleman, despite the fact that he came from an ancient line of Spanish nobility. Not in any way. But he was enough of a man that he couldn't leave this young woman alone in the middle of the night.

Because, no, he wouldn't be surprised at what men wanted from such a delectable little morsel such as herself. He was one of those men after all.

That left him with only one option: to keep hold of her in a way she'd accept.

He could, of course, simply ignore her protests and take her back to his Paris mansion and keep her there. But, again, dealing with the protests that would no doubt entail would be tiresome, and he preferred to avoid tiresome things. Things that left less time to do the things he liked doing. His own personal pleasure always took priority.

It would be easier all round if she agreed, therefore work it was.

If only he had something for her to do…

He had estates and a *castillo* back in Spain—which he avoided going to whenever possible—and numerous companies he'd invested his considerable fortune in. But he already had a number of staff managing all those things—and besides, they weren't the kinds of things a Parisian street urchin could manage, no matter how feisty she was.

No, the only work he could conceivably give her was

domestic, by adding her to his housekeeping staff. He already had a large contingent, but one more wouldn't hurt. House-cleaning, at least, required no extensive training, and it would keep her close until he'd uncovered her mysteries.

Which he was going to do, since he currently had a dearth of mysteries in his life.

'What kind of work?' she asked, still suspicious.

'I need someone to clean for me.' He tilted his head, studying her. 'I have a house in Paris that's very large and needs attention. You may work out what you owe me for the car and my personal inconvenience there.'

'But I—'

'Did I mention that I have rooms set aside for my staff? You will be required to live on-site for the duration.'

'Don't guys like you already have a lot people doing your dirty work for you?'

'Yes.' Her scorn didn't bother him. He tried not to let anything bother him, since it was very dangerous for all concerned when he was bothered. 'But I could always do with one more. Plus, I pay my staff very well for doing my "dirty work".'

At the mention of pay, something changed. Her eyes lost that wary look, and a calculating gleam sparked in their depths.

He knew that gleam and he knew it intimately. It was hunger. And not in the physical sense, of needing food, but in the sense of wanting something you could never have and wanting it desperately.

Money—she wanted money. And who could blame her when she didn't have any? Money was power, and she didn't have any of that, either, he'd bet.

Sure enough, she said, 'Pay? You pay them?'

'Of course. That's why they're my staff and not my slaves.'

She leaned forward all of a sudden, losing her wariness, all business now. Her violet eyes were focused very intently on him. 'Would you pay me? Once I earned back for the car? Could I have a proper job?'

Something shifted in Cristiano's gut. Something that, again, he was intimately familiar with.

She was lovely. And he could imagine her looking at him just like that, with a pretty flush to her pale cheeks and a flame in her eyes and all the beautiful hair spread over his pillow. Hungry for him as he buried himself inside her...

A nice thought, but a thought was what it would stay. She'd never be one of his partners. Apart from the fact that the distance between them in power, money and just about everything else could not have been more vast, she was also much younger than he was.

And he was betting she'd either had some bad experiences with men or she avoided men completely.

Again, dealing with all that sounded like work, and he tried to avoid work whenever he could. He didn't want anything hard, anything difficult, and he avoided complications like the plague.

This small *gatita* was certainly a complication, but he found he was willing to expend a bit of effort on figuring out why she was so familiar to him. After all, it had been a while since he'd let himself be interested in something other than physical pleasure. It certainly couldn't hurt.

'Do you want a job?' he asked, teasing her a little just because he could.

'Yes, of course I want a job.' Her gaze narrowed further. 'How much do you pay?'

A good question—though he was sure she couldn't afford to turn anything down.

'My staff are the best and I pay them accordingly,' he said, and named a sum that made her pretty eyes go round.

'That much?' All her earlier wariness and suspicion had dropped away. 'You really pay people that much just to clean your house?'

'It's a very big house.'

'And you'd pay me that?'

It wasn't a lot of money—at least it wasn't to him. But for her it was clearly a fortune. Then again, he suspected that a five-euro note left on the street would be a fortune for her.

'Yes, I'd pay you that.' He paused, studying her. 'Where do you live? And what are you doing on the streets at two in the morning?'

Instantly her expression closed up, the light disappearing from her face, the shutters coming down behind her eyes. She sat back on the seat, putting distance between them and glancing out of the window.

'I should go home. My...mother will be worried.'

Which didn't answer his direct question but answered the ones he hadn't voiced. Because she was lying. Her slight hesitation made him pretty certain she didn't have a mother and neither did she have a home.

'I think not,' he said, watching her. 'I think you should come directly back to my house and spend the night there. Then you can start work first thing tomorrow morning.'

'I don't want to come back to your house.'

'Like I said, I have quarters for my staff and there will be more than enough room.'

'But I—'

'There will be no argument.' Because he'd decided now, and once he made a decision he stuck to it. 'You have two choices. Either you come back to my house tonight or you spend the night in a police cell.'

'That's not much of a choice,' she said angrily.

'Too bad. You were the one who decided spray-painting my car was a good idea, so these are the consequences.' He liked her arguing with him, he realised. Probably too much—which was an issue. 'So what's it to be, *gatita*?'

She folded her arms. 'Why do you keep calling me that?'

'It means kitten in Spanish.'

'I'm not a kitten.'

'You're small and feral and you tried to scratch me—of course you're a kitten. And a wild one at that.'

She was silent a moment, not at all mollified. Then, 'Why Spanish?'

'Because I'm Spanish.'

'Oh. What are you doing in Paris?'

He stared at her, letting her see a little of his edge. 'That's a lot of questions for a woman who won't even give me her name.'

'Why should I? You haven't given me yours.'

That was true—he hadn't. And why not? His name was an ancient and illustrious one, but one that would soon come to an end. He was the sole heir and he had no plans to produce another. No, the Velazquez line, the dukedom of San Lorenzo, would die with him and then be forgotten. Which was probably for the best, considering his dissolute lifestyle.

Your parents would be appalled.

They certainly would have been had they still been alive, but they weren't. He had no one to impress, no one to live up to. There was only him and he didn't care.

'My name is Cristiano Velazquez, Fifteenth Duke of San Lorenzo,' he said, because he had no reason to hide it. 'And you may address me as Your Grace.'

A ripple of something crossed her face, though he couldn't tell what it was. Then she frowned. 'A duke? Cristiano Velazquez…?' She said his name very slowly, as if tasting it.

He knew she hadn't meant to do it in a seductive way, but he felt the seduction in it all the same. His name in her soft, sweet husky voice, said so carefully in French… As if that same sense of familiarity tugged at her the way it tugged at him.

But how would she know him? They'd never met—or at least not that he remembered. And he definitely hadn't slept with her—that he was sure of. He might have had too many women to count, but he'd remember if he'd had her.

'You've heard of me?' he asked carefully, watching her face.

'No… I don't think so.' She looked away. 'Where is your house, then?'

Was she telling the truth? Had she, in fact, heard of him? Briefly he debated whether or not to push her. But it was late, and there were dark circles under her eyes, and suddenly she looked very small and fragile sitting there.

He should get her back to his place and tuck her into bed.

'You'll see.' Moving over the seat towards the door, he opened it. 'Stay here.'

Not that he gave her much choice, because he got out and shut it behind him again, locking it just in case she decided to make a desperate bid for freedom.

He made excuses to the two patiently waiting women, ensured they were taken care of for the evening, then went to find his recalcitrant driver, whom he eventually found in a nearby alley, playing some kind of dice game with a couple of the kids who'd been standing around his car.

How fortunate.

Getting his wallet out of his pocket, Cristiano extracted a note and brandished it at one of the youths. 'You,' he said shortly. 'This is yours if you tell me the name of the woman with the pretty red hair who was spray-painting my car.'

The kid stared at the note, his mouth open. 'Uh... Leonie,' he muttered, and made a grab for the money.

So much for loyalty.

Cristiano jerked the note away before the boy could get it. 'You didn't give me a last name.'

The kid scowled. 'I don't know. No one knows anyone's last name around here.'

Which was probably true.

He allowed the boy to take the money and then, with a meaningful jerk of his head towards the car for his driver's benefit, he turned back to it himself.

Leonie. Leonie...

Somewhere in the dim recesses of his memory a bell rang.

Leonie blinked as a pair of big wrought-iron gates set into a tall stone wall opened and the car slid smoothly through them.

On the rare occasions when she'd ventured out of the

area she lived in she'd seen places like this. Old buildings surrounded by high walls. Houses where the rich lived.

She'd once lived in a house like this herself, but it had been a long time ago and elsewhere, when she'd been a little kid. Before her father had kicked her and her mother out of their palatial mansion and life had changed drastically.

She still remembered what it had been like to have money, to have a roof over her head and clean clothes and food. Nice memories, but they'd been a lie, so she tried not to think about them. It was better not to remember such things because they only made her want what she could never have—and wanting things was always a bad thing.

She stared distrustfully out into the darkness, where the silhouette of a massive old house reared against the sky.

The driver came around the side of the car and opened the door. The duke gestured at her to get out.

She turned her distrustful attention to him.

A duke. An honest-to-God duke. He didn't look like one—though she had no idea what dukes were supposed to look like. Maybe much older. Although, given the faint lines around his eyes and mouth, he was certainly a lot older than she was. Then again, his hair was still pitch-black so he couldn't be *that* old.

His name had sounded faintly familiar to her, though she couldn't think why. The fact that he was Spanish had given her a little kick, since she'd been born in Spain herself. In fact maybe she'd met him once before—back in Spain, before her father had got rid of her and her mother and her mother had dragged her to Paris.

Back when she'd been Leonie de Riero, the prized only

daughter of Victor de Riero, with the blood of ancient Spanish aristocracy running in her veins.

Perhaps she knew this duke from then? Or perhaps not. She'd been very young, after all, and her memories of that time were dim.

Whatever he was, or had been, she didn't want to remember those days. The present was the only thing she had, and she had to be on her guard at all times. Forgetting where she was and what was happening led to mistakes, and she'd already made enough of those since ending up on the streets.

If she hadn't been so absorbed in getting the lettering just so as she'd graffitied his car, she wouldn't be here after all.

You certainly wouldn't have had a bed for the night, so maybe it wasn't such a mistake?

That remained to be seen. Perhaps she should have fought harder to escape him. Then again, she hadn't been able to resist the lure of a job—if he actually meant what he'd said, that was.

The duke lifted that perfect brow of his. 'Are you going to get out? Or would you prefer to sit here all night? The car is quite comfortable, though I'm afraid the doors will have to stay locked.'

She gave him a ferocious glare. 'Give me back my knife first.' She liked to have some protection on her, just in case of treachery.

He remained impervious to her glare. 'I'm not going to hurt you, *gatita*.'

Kitten. He kept calling her kitten. It was annoying.

'I don't trust you. And I don't want to sleep in a strange place without some protection.'

His jungle-green gaze was very level and absolutely

expressionless. 'Fair enough.' Reaching into the pocket of his jacket, he extracted her knife and held it out, handle first.

She took it from him, the familiarity of the handle fitting into her palm making her feel slightly better. Briefly she debated whether or not to try and slash at him again, then bolt into the darkness. But she remembered the high walls surrounding the house. She wouldn't be able to get over those, alas. She could refuse to get out and sleep in the car, but she didn't like the idea of being locked in. No, it was the house or nothing.

With as much dignity as she could muster, Leonie pocketed her knife then slid out of the car. Behind her, the duke murmured something to his driver and then he was beside her, moving past her up the big stone steps to the front door of the mansion.

Some member of his staff was obviously still up, because the door opened, a pool of light shining out.

A minute later she found herself in a huge vaulted vestibule, with flights of stone steps curling up to the upper storeys and a massive, glittering chandelier lighting the echoing space. Thick silk rugs lay on the floor and there were pictures on the walls, and on the ceiling far above her head was a big painting of angels with white wings and golden haloes.

It was very warm inside.

She was used to being cold. She'd been cold ever since she was sixteen, coming home after school one day to the rundown apartment she'd shared with her mother only to find it empty, and a note from her mother on the rickety kitchen table informing Leonie that she'd gone and not to look for her.

Leonie hadn't believed it at first. But her mother hadn't

come home that night, or the next, or the one after that, and eventually Leonie had had to accept that her mother wasn't coming home at all. Leonie had been evicted from the apartment not long after that, and forced to live on the streets, where she'd felt like she'd become permanently cold.

But she hadn't realised just how cold until now. Until the warmth from this place seeped up through the cracked soles of her sneakers and into her body, into her heart.

Immediately she wanted to go outside again—to run and never stop running. She couldn't trust this warmth. She couldn't let her guard down. It wasn't safe.

Except the big front door had closed, and she knew it would be locked, and the duke was gesturing at her to follow the older woman who stood next to him, regarding her with some disgust, making her abruptly conscious of the holes in her jeans and the stains on the denim. Of the grimy hoodie that she'd stolen from a guy who'd taken it off to fight someone in the alleyway where she'd been sleeping one night. Of the paint stains on her hands.

She was dirty, and ragged, and she probably smelled since she hadn't found anywhere to clean herself for weeks. No wonder this woman looked disgusted.

Leonie's stomach clenched and she gripped the handle of her knife, scowling to cover the wave of vulnerability that had come over her. Never stop fighting. Never show weakness. That was the law of the streets.

'Go with Camille,' the duke said. 'She will show you—'

'No,' Leonie said. 'Just tell me where to go and I'll find my own way there.'

Camille made a disapproving sound, then said something in a lilting musical language to the duke. He replied in the same language, his deep, rich voice making it sound as if he was caressing each word.

Leonie felt every one of her muscles tense in resistance. She couldn't like the sound of his voice. She had to be on her guard at all times and not make any mistakes. And she didn't want to go with this Camille woman and her disapproving stare.

Much to her surprise, however, with one last dark look in Leonie's direction, the woman turned and vanished down one of the huge, echoing hallways that led off the entrance hall.

Without a word, the duke turned and headed towards the huge marble staircase. 'Follow me,' he said over his shoulder.

He didn't pause and he didn't wait, as if expecting her to follow him just as he'd said.

Leonie blinked. Why had he sent the other woman away? Was he just leaving her here? What if she somehow managed to get out through the door? What if she escaped down one of the corridors? What would he do? He wasn't looking at her. Would he even know until she was gone?

Her heartbeat thumped wildly, adrenaline surging through her—both preludes to a very good bolt. And yet she wasn't moving. She was standing there in this overwhelming, intimidating entrance hall, not running, watching a tall, powerful rich man go up the marble stairs.

He moved with economy and a lazy, athletic grace that reminded her even more strongly of a panther. It was mesmerising, for some reason. And when she found herself moving, it wasn't towards the doorway or the corridor, it was towards him, following him almost helplessly.

Was this what had happened in that fairy-tale? Those children following the Pied Piper, drawn beyond their control by the music he made. Disappearing. Never to be seen again.

You're an idiot. You have your knife. Pull yourself together.

This was true. And nothing had happened to her so far. Yes, he'd kept her locked in the car against her will, but he hadn't hurt her. And apart from the moment when he'd grabbed her, he hadn't touched her again.

She didn't trust him, or his offer of a job, but it was either follow him or stay down here in the entrance hall, and that seemed cowardly. She wasn't going to do that, either.

There was a slim possibility that he was telling the truth, and if so she needed to take advantage of it. If she was going to achieve her dream of having a little cottage of her own in the countryside, away from the city, away from danger, then he was her best chance of that happening.

Slowly Leonie moved after him, going up the winding marble staircase, trying to keep her attention on his strong back and not gawk at all the paintings on the walls, the carpets on the parquet floors, the vases of flowers on the small tables dotted here and there as they went down yet another wide and high-ceilinged corridor.

Windows let in the Parisian night and she caught glimpses of tall trees, hinting at a garden outside. She wanted to go and look through the glass, because it had been a long time since she'd seen a garden, but she didn't dare. She had to keep the duke's tall figure in sight.

Eventually, after leading her through a few more of

those high-ceilinged corridors, he stopped outside a door and opened it, inclining his head for her to go on through.

He was standing quite near the doorway, and she wasn't sure she wanted to get that close to him, but she didn't want him to know it bothered her, either, so she slipped past him as quickly as she could. But not quickly enough to avoid catching a hint of his aftershave and the warmth of his powerful body as she brushed past him.

It was only an instant, but in that instant she was acutely aware of his height looming over her. Of the width of his broad shoulders and the stretch of the cotton across his muscled chest. Of the way he smelled spicy and warm and quite delicious.

A strange ripple of sensation went through her like an electric shock.

Disturbed, Leonie ignored it, concentrating instead on the room she'd stepped into.

It was very large, with tall windows that looked out on to trees. A thick pale carpet covered the floor, and up against one wall, facing the windows, was a very large bed, made up with a thick, soft-looking white quilt.

The duke moved past her, going over to the windows and drawing heavy pale silk curtains over the black glass, shutting out the night. The room was very warm, the carpet very soft under her feet, and she was conscious once again of how dirty she was.

She was going to leave stains all over this pretty pale bedroom. Surely he couldn't mean for her to stay here? It didn't look like a cleaner's room. It was far too luxurious.

'This can't be where you put your staff,' she said, frowning. 'Why am I here?'

He adjusted the curtains with a small, precise move-ment, then turned around, putting his hands in his pockets. 'Not usually, no. But Camille didn't have a room ready for you, so I thought you could use one of my guest bedrooms.'

'Why? Why are you doing this?'

He tilted his head, gazing at her from underneath very long, thick black lashes. 'Which particular "this" are you talking about?'

'I mean this room. A job. A bed for the night. Why are you doing any of it? Why should you care?'

She hadn't meant it to come out so accusingly, but she couldn't help it. Men like him, with money and power, never did things without wanting something in return. Even charity usually came with strings. There were bound to be strings here, if only she could see them.

But the duke merely gave one of those elegant shrugs. 'What else does one do with a feral kitten but look after it?'

'I'm not a kitten,' she said, for the second time that night.

His mouth curved and once again she felt that electric ripple of sensation move through her. It came to her very suddenly that this man was dangerous. And dangerous in a way she couldn't name. He wasn't a physical threat— though those strange little ripples of sensation definitely were—but definitely a threat of some kind.

'No,' he murmured, his gaze moving over her in a way that made heat rise in her cheeks. 'You're not, are you?'

She lifted her chin, discomfited and not liking it one bit. 'And I didn't ask you to look after me, either.'

'Oh, if you think I'm doing it out of the goodness of my heart you are mistaken.' He strolled past her towards the door. 'It's entirely out of self-interest, believe me.'

'Why? Just because I vandalised your car?'

Pausing by the door, he gave her a sweeping, enigmatic glance. 'Among other things. The bathroom is through the door opposite. A shower or a bath wouldn't go amiss, *gatita*.'

'Don't call me that,' she snapped, annoyed that he'd obviously noticed how dirty she was and how she must smell, and then annoyed further by her own annoyance— since why should she care if he'd noticed?

'What else am I to call you?' His eyes gleamed. 'Especially since you won't give me your name.'

Leonie pressed her lips together. He might have strong-armed her into staying in his house, but her name was the one thing he wouldn't be able to force out of her. That was hers to give.

Again, he didn't seem offended. He only smiled. 'Then *gatita* it will have to be.'

And before she could say another word he walked out, closing the door carefully behind him.

CHAPTER THREE

THE LATE-MORNING SUN poured through the big windows of Cristiano's study, flooding the room with light and warmth, but he didn't notice. He wasn't interested in the weather.

He'd got up early that morning, despite not having slept much the previous night, and gone straight to his study to see if the memory that learning Leonie's name had generated was correct. After a couple of calls and a few strongly worded orders he'd had his confirmation.

She was exactly who he'd suspected she was.

Which should have been impossible, considering she was supposed to be dead.

He leaned back in his big black leather chair and stared at the computer screen on the desk in front of him. At the photo it displayed. An old one, from years and years ago, of a tall, dark-haired man, holding the hand of a little girl with hair the distinctive colour of apricots. At the side of the little girl stood a lovely slender woman with hair exactly the same colour.

It was a loving family portrait of the ancient and illustrious de Riero family—Spanish aristocrats who'd fallen on hard times and lost their title a century or so ago.

Leonie had turned out to be Leonie de Riero, Victor de Riero's prized only daughter, who'd disappeared along with her mother fifteen years earlier, rumoured to have died in an apartment fire in Barcelona not long after she'd disappeared.

It was a scandal that had rocked Spain for months and he remembered it acutely. Especially because Victor de Riero, whose family had been blood enemies of Cristiano's, had become his mentor.

Victor had been grief-stricken about the loss of his wife and child—at least until he'd found himself a new family.

Your family.

The deep, volcanic rage that Cristiano had thought he'd excised from his life shifted in his gut, hot enough to incinerate anything in its path, and he had to take a minute to wrestle it back into submission. Because he couldn't allow himself to feel that—not any more. He couldn't allow himself to feel anything any more.

It had taken him years to put that rage behind him, but he had. And he'd thought he'd found some measure of peace. Until Leonie had appeared.

Cristiano pushed his chair back and got to his feet, walking over to the bookshelves opposite his desk before turning and pacing back to the desk again, needing movement to settle himself.

His thoughts tumbled about in his head like dice.

Of course Leonie had been familiar to him. He *had* met her. But it had been years ago, and she'd been that little girl in the photo—a kid of around two or three, initially, when her father had first approached him.

He'd been seventeen at the time, and had just lost both his parents in a car accident. Victor de Riero had paid him a visit not long after the funeral, ostensibly to bury the hatchet on the ancient feud the Velazquez and de Riero families had been pursuing for centuries.

Cristiano had been only too happy to do so, having no interest in old feuds and still grappling with the deaths of his parents and the shock of suddenly having to take on the responsibility of a dukedom. He'd welcomed Victor's interest in him gratefully, listening to the older man's advice and accepting his help, thinking the other man was doing it out of the goodness of his heart.

But he hadn't known then that there was no goodness in Victor's heart, or that the flames of vengeance for the de Riero family still burned in him hot and strong.

In fact it hadn't been until Cristiano had married, three years later, that he'd discovered the truth about Victor de Riero's interest.

In that time, though, he'd met Victor's wife and his small, sparky daughter. Cristiano hadn't taken much notice of the daughter—kids hadn't been on his radar back then—but then Victor's wife had disappeared, taking the girl with her, only for both to be discovered dead in a fire a week or so later.

Cristiano had tried to be there for Victor the way Victor had been for him, after his parents had died, but he'd been in the throes of first love, and then early marriage, and hadn't paid as much attention as he should have.

He hadn't paid attention a year or so after that, either, when he'd gone to Victor for advice when his marriage to Anna had run into trouble. If he had, he might have noticed how much his wife had enjoyed Victor's company—how, at social occasions, she'd spent more time talking to him than she had to Cristiano.

He might have become aware that Victor had never

planned on burying the hatchet when it came to their family feud but had only been lying in wait, lulling Cristiano into a false sense of security, waiting for the right time to take advantage of a vulnerable young man.

And finally he had found that advantage in Cristiano's wife. Because it had been his lovely wife Anna that Victor had wanted, and in the end it had been his lovely wife that he'd taken—Cristiano's already pregnant wife.

Along with Cristiano's son.

Cristiano paced to the bookshelves again, memories he'd long since suppressed flooding like acid through him.

Victor turning up at Cristiano's Barcelona penthouse, flanked by bodyguards and cloaked in triumph, revealing the final piece of his plot like a pantomime villain. Rubbing salt into Cristiano's wound by telling him that his seduction of Anna had all been part of their blood feud, and then rubbing glass into that same wound by telling him that Anna was pregnant and the child was Cristiano's.

He would bring up Cristiano's child as his own, Victor had said. He would take something precious from a Velazquez after a Velazquez had ruined the de Riero family a century earlier, by stealing the dukedom from them.

Cristiano had barely heard the man's reasoning. He'd been incandescent with rage and betrayal. It had been wise of Victor to have brought bodyguards, because he hadn't been at all sure he wouldn't have launched himself at the other man and strangled him.

Your anger has always been a problem.

Yes, and he'd been on fire with it.

For two years he'd used almost the entirety of his

fortune trying to get his son back, but Victor had falsified the paternity tests Cristiano had demanded, paid any number of people off, and Cristiano hadn't had a leg to stand on.

Eventually he'd crashed a party of Victor's, intent on stealing back his son from the man who'd taken him— but when he'd approached the boy, the child had run from him in fear. Straight to Victor.

'This is the reason, Cristiano,' Anna had flung at him, as she'd tried to calm the hysterical child in Victor's arms. *'This is the reason I left you. You're dangerous and you only end up scaring people. Why can't you leave us alone?'*

Well, she'd got her wish in the end. After that—after seeing the fear in his son's green eyes—he'd left the party. Left Spain, vowing never to return.

For his own sanity he'd excised all knowledge of his son from his heart, scoured all thoughts of revenge from his soul. He had found other ways to kill the pain lodged inside him like a jagged shard of broken glass. Pleasure and lots of it had been the key, and soon enough the edges of that piece of glass had dulled, making him look back over the years and marvel at how it had ever been sharp enough to hurt.

But it was hurting now. Because of her.

He came to the bookshelves and turned around, pacing back to the desk once more.

If he'd had any sense he'd have got rid of her the moment that sense of nagging familiarity had hit him, but he hadn't, and now she was here. In his house. And he was certain it was her.

A member of his staff had managed to track down the man who'd told Victor that Leonie and Hélène de Riero had died in a fire, and the man—once some money had been waved in his face—had admitted he'd lied. That Hélène de Riero had paid him to report her and her daughter's death to her ex-husband for reasons unknown.

Of course Cristiano would need DNA confirmation, which he'd get easily enough, but he was sure already. No other woman he'd ever met had had hair that colour or those jewel-bright violet eyes.

He had Victor de Riero's daughter in his grasp.

Tension gathered inside him and a vicious anticipation twisted through it, the rage he'd never been able to conquer entirely burning in his heart. Whether it was fate that had brought her to his door, or merely simple chance, it didn't matter.

What mattered was that here was an opportunity. A very unexpected opportunity.

Isn't revenge a dish best served cold?

After his parents had been killed, the old family feud with the de Rieros had seemed like something out of the Middle Ages. A hold-over from a different time. But he'd been young back then, and naive. He hadn't yet learned that people lied and that they couldn't be trusted. He hadn't yet learned just how far the depths of grief and loss could go.

He'd learned eventually. Oh, yes, he'd learned that lesson well.

And now here was his chance to pay that lesson back in kind.

Tension crawled through him, making his jaw ache as he came to the desk and turned around to the bookshelf again.

He couldn't deny that he liked the thought. Relished it.

Victor de Riero had taken his son, so wouldn't it be

the sweetest revenge of all if Cristiano took his daughter? The daughter who'd been presumed dead for fifteen years?

An eye for an eye keeps the feud alive.

Perhaps he wouldn't have considered it if Leonie hadn't turned up. Perhaps he'd have gone through his life pretending he didn't have a son and that he'd never been married for the rest of his days. But she had, and now he could think of nothing else.

It seemed the old Spanish warlord in him wasn't as dead as he'd thought.

Maybe he'd make her his duchess. Invite de Riero to the wedding. He'd pull up her veil and then there she'd be—the daughter de Riero had thought was dead, marrying the man he'd once thought he could humiliate in front of the entire world.

And maybe to really pay him back Cristiano would have an heir with her after all. Pollute the pure de Riero bloodline with Velazquez blood.

After all, if de Riero could do it, why couldn't he?

He stopped mid-pace, his fingers curling inside his pockets, vicious pleasure pulling tight in his gut.

And then you can move on.

Not that he hadn't moved on already, but that jagged shard of glass was still embedded deep inside his heart, ensuring it could never heal. Perhaps if he took the revenge he was owed it finally would.

Certainty settled inside him like the earth settling after an earthquake, forming a new landscape.

First on the agenda would be Leonie—because she was vital to his plan and would have to agree to it. Which might be a problem when she was so stubborn, wary and distrustful. Not so surprising, given the circumstances under which he'd found her, but not exactly conducive to his plan. Then again, money seemed to motivate her. She could consider being his bride part of her job, for which she'd receive a very healthy bonus.

Revealing that he knew who she was could be a concern, however. She hadn't given him her name for a reason, and everything hinged on how she felt about her father. Had she ever wanted to return to him? Did she even know she was supposed to be dead?

He frowned at the wall opposite. Perhaps telling her about his discovery immediately would be a mistake. Now she was here, within his grasp, he couldn't afford for her to run, and he'd be at risk of scaring her away if he wasn't careful. No, maybe it would be better to gain her trust before he let her in on his secret—an easy enough task to accomplish with a beautiful woman. All it would require was a bit of careful handling.

Galvanised in a way he hadn't been for years, Cristiano turned towards the door, heading out of his study and going in search of the newest member of his staff.

He found her, as he'd expected, in the big library that faced onto the walled garden at the rear of the house. She was kneeling on the floor before one of the big bookshelves with her back to him. Her dirty clothes were gone—clearly Camille had found her something else to wear—and she now wore the staff uniform of plain black trousers and a fitted black T-shirt. Nondescript clothes that should have made her blend in, and yet the skein of silken hair that fell down her back in a sleek ponytail effectively prevented that. The colour glowed against her black T-shirt, a deep red-gold tinged with pink.

Beautiful.

His hands itched with the urge to run his fingers

through it, to see if it felt as soft as it looked. To touch that vibrant colour, wind it round his wrist, examine the contrast against his own skin…

Except that was not what he wanted from her. Her name, yes. Her body, no. He might find her more attractive than he'd expected, but he could get sex from any of the women in his extensive little black book. He didn't need to expend any effort on a skittish, homeless, much younger woman, no matter how pretty her hair was.

But what about your plans for an heir?

Ah, yes, but there would be time for that later.

He hitched one shoulder up against the doorframe and gazed at her.

It was clear she wasn't actually cleaning, since her cloth and polishing spray were sitting next to her. Her head was bent, as if she was looking at something, and it must be very absorbing since it was clear she hadn't heard him and he hadn't exactly been quiet.

That was what had got her into trouble the previous night, hadn't it? She'd been totally caught up in the 'art' she'd been creating on his limo door and hadn't run when she should have.

What would that attention be like it bed? Would she look at you that way? Would she touch you like—?

Cristiano jerked his offending thoughts out of the gutter, irritated with himself. Perhaps he needed to contact those two lovely women he'd been going to take home the previous night and finish what they'd started. Certainly he'd have to do something with his wayward groin—especially if he kept having thoughts like these about Leonie.

He shifted against the doorframe and said finally, 'Find some interesting reading material, *gatita*?'

* * *

The duke's deep, rich voice slid over Leonie's skin like an unexpected caress, making her jump in shock, then freeze in place, the book she'd been reading still clutched in her hands. She stared at the shelves in front of her, every sense she had focused on the voice that had come from behind her.

A small cold thread wound its way through her veins.

Her employer had caught her reading on the job on her very first day. Not a good look. Ugh—what had she been thinking?

Everything had been going extremely well since he'd left her the night before, too. She'd availed herself of the shower, even though everything in her had wanted to spend hours soaking in the vast white marble bath. But it had been very late and she'd needed some sleep. So she'd given her body and hair a decent scrub before falling into that outrageously comfortable bed naked, since she hadn't been able to bear putting on her filthy clothes again—not when she was so clean.

Her sleep had been fitful, due to the comfortableness of the bed—she was used to sleeping on hard surfaces covered with nothing but pieces of cardboard or, if she was lucky and had managed to get a night in a shelter, a hard mattress covered by a thin blanket—and she'd kept waking up. Her sleep was always light, in case of threats, but even so she'd felt okay when she'd woken this morning.

There had been a set of clothes left outside her door, which she'd snatched up and put on, glorying in the feel of soft, clean cotton against her skin. Coffee and a fresh warm croissant had been left along with the clothes, and she'd devoured both in seconds. She had still been hungry, but then Camille had come, a little less scornful than she'd been the night before, and given her an introduction to her duties.

There'd been no time for more food.

She was supposed to have spent no more than half an hour in the library—concentrating on dusting the shelves, since the duke was most particular about them—before moving on to the formal sitting room next door. But she had a horrible suspicion that she'd been in here longer than half an hour. And she hadn't even touched the shelves yet.

She'd just got very interested in some of the books, and hadn't been able to resist taking one off the shelf and opening it up.

Back when she'd been smaller, when her mother had still been around, she'd used to love going to the library and reading, and books were something she'd missed on the streets. And back further still, when she'd been very young, her father had read to her—

But, no, she wasn't going to think of her father.

She needed to be more alert to her surroundings, that was what she needed to be, because this wretched duke was always sneaking up on her.

Quickly, she closed the book and put it back. 'I wasn't reading,' she said, picking up her cloth and polish. 'I was just polishing the shelf.' She ran the cloth over the already gleaming wood a couple of times. 'It's very dirty.'

'Which book was it?'

Again that voice—a deep, dark purr that felt like soft velvet brushing against her skin. It made her shiver and she didn't like it…not one bit.

Clutching her cleaning equipment, Leonie got to her

feet and turned around, only to have the words she'd been going to say die in her throat.

The duke was leaning one powerful shoulder casually against the doorframe, his hands in his pockets. He was in perfectly tailored black suit trousers today, and a pristine white shirt with the sleeves rolled up to his elbows, revealing strong wrists and sleekly muscled forearms. It was plain, simple clothing that set off his sheer physical beauty to perfection, accentuating the aristocratic lines of his face, the straight black brows, the sharply carved mouth and the deep emerald glitter of his eyes.

He seemed different from the man he'd been the night before. There was an energy about him that hadn't been present the previous evening. It was oddly compelling and that made her wary.

Everything about this man made her wary.

He raised a brow in that imperious way he had. 'You were going to say something?'

Leonie was irritated to feel a blush rising in her cheeks, because she had a feeling he'd noticed her reaction to him and was amused by it.

'No,' she said, wishing she had her knife on her. Because although he hadn't made a move towards her, she felt the threat he presented all the same. 'Is there anything you need…uh…*monsieur*?' She couldn't quite bring herself to say *Your Grace*.

A smile curled his mouth, though it didn't look like an amused smile. More as if he was…satisfied.

'Not at all. Just coming to see how my newest staff member is settling in. Is everything to your liking?'

'Yes, thank you.' She kept a tight grip on her cloth and

polish. 'Camille said she would find me another room to sleep—'

'I think not,' he interrupted, with the casual arrogance of a man who was used to his word being law. 'You'll stay in the room you're in.'

Leonie wasn't unhappy with that—especially when she hadn't had a chance to use that amazing bath yet, and also didn't like being in close proximity to a lot of people—but she didn't like his automatic assumption that she could be told what to do.

And your need to fight is what gets you into trouble.

This was very true. And there was also another problem. A problem she'd foreseen the night before and yet had dismissed.

In accepting a bed for the night, and now a job, she'd had a tiny taste of what her life might be like off the streets.

Having a shower whenever she wanted it…having clean sheets and clean clothes. Having food brought to her and having something to do that wasn't figuring out how to shoplift her next meal or begging for coins. Being safe behind walls and locked doors.

Just a tiny taste. Enough to know she didn't want to give it up—not just yet.

This is how they suck you in. You should have run…

She swallowed, clutching her cleaning implements even tighter. It was too late to run now—too late to decide that life on the streets was better than being in this house and working for this duke. Like Persephone from the myth, she'd had a bite of the pomegranate and now she was trapped in the Underworld.

Which makes him Hades.

And a very fine Hades he made, too. No wonder she

found him dangerous. He was the snake in the garden, offering temptation…

'I don't need a special room,' she said, because her need to fight was so ingrained she couldn't stop herself. 'I'm happy to sleep wherever the other employees—'

'As I said, you will stay in the room you've been given.'

'Why?'

'Because I said so,' he replied easily. 'I'm the duke and what I say goes.' That smile was still playing around his fascinating mouth. 'Which reminds me—I usually have a formal job interview with my employees, and since you didn't have one, I suggest we schedule one for to-night. Over dinner.'

Instantly all her alarm bells went off at once. A job interview over dinner? That didn't sound right at all. Not that she had any experience with job interviews, but still…

She gave him a suspicious look. 'Job interviews are usually in offices during the day, not over dinner.'

'Astute, *gatita*. If being in an office would make you more comfortable, I can have dinner served to us there.'

Leonie scowled. 'I'm not sleeping with you.'

He raised both brows this time. 'Have I asked you to sleep with me?'

'No, but when a man asks a woman to dinner he expects certain things. Men always do.'

'You appear to have a very poor opinion of men—though I suppose that's understandable. We're not especially good examples of the human race.' His eyes glittered strangely. 'It's also true that I'm a particularly bad example. But I don't have any sexual designs on you, if that's what you're worried about.'

She *had* been worried about it. The threat of sexual violence was ever-present for a woman on her own on the streets. So why did him telling her that he had no sexual designs on her make her feel almost…disappointed?

'That's all very well,' she said, ignoring the feeling, 'but I don't trust you.'

He shifted, drawing her attention to his powerful body, making her aware of him in a disturbingly physical way.

'Fair enough. We've only just met after all. Bring your knife with you. And if I try anything romantic feel free to cut me with it.'

'Or you could just decide we don't need to have an interview,' she suggested. 'After all, you've already employed me.'

'It's true—I have. But the process is the process. I can't just let anyone into my house. Security checks need to be done…reference checks, et cetera. It's all very tiresome but absolutely necessary.' He paused, his gaze sharpening on her. 'Especially when said employee hasn't even given me her name.'

Leonie took a silent breath. She should have given it to him last night when he'd asked. What did it matter if he knew? She'd only wanted to retain a little bit of autonomy, but now she'd turned it into a big deal and maybe he thought she was trying to hide something, or that she was on the run from something.

Not the actual truth, which was that she was only a girl who'd been discarded by both parents. A girl nobody wanted.

Her gut tightened. He certainly didn't need to know that. And, anyway, her name was her own and it was hers to give. No one had the right to know it.

Why don't you give him a fake one, then?

She could. But that would be giving in, regardless of whether it was a fake name or not, and something inside her wouldn't let her do that.

What was it about him that had her wanting to fight him all the time? She'd never had such strong reactions to a man before. Admittedly, she hadn't come into contact with a lot of men, since it was better safety-wise to avoid them, but the few she'd had run-ins with hadn't endeared themselves to her. But this man…

He made her want to fight, to stand her ground, kick back. He also made her feel physical things she hadn't felt before in her entire life. A kind of shivery ache. A prickly restlessness. The stupid desire to poke at him just to see what he'd do. What on earth was that?

You know what it is.

But Leonie didn't want to think about it. She couldn't afford to—not when she was seconds away from catastrophe. Who knew how long this job would last? Or when she'd be turned out back on to the streets again?

She'd got herself into this situation, and if she was very lucky it would mean good things for her. So the most logical thing to do now was to be careful with the dangerous panther that lounged on the branch above her head. To keep her head down and perhaps not present herself as so much prey. Keep a low profile and not struggle. If she did that well he might even forget she existed and leave her alone.

So she said nothing, dragging her gaze away from him and looking at the ground instead.

'Ah, so that's how it's to be, hmm?'

Again, he sounded just like that panther—all low and purring and sleek.

'Come to my study when you finish up today. I'll tell Camille that you're expected.'

She nodded silently, and when she finally looked up the doorway was empty.

He'd gone.

CHAPTER FOUR

CRISTIANO FROWNED AT the clock on the mantelpiece, an unexpected impatience gathering inside him. Leonie was late and he suspected it was intentional, since Camille wouldn't have kept her working if she was expected to attend a meeting with him.

And she was definitely expected to attend.

He supposed he could have had the conversation with her in the library earlier that day, rather than make a performance of it over dinner. But trust was a difficult thing. You couldn't compel it and you couldn't buy it— it could only be given.

Which made him a liar in some respects, because he was absolutely planning a seduction. Except sex wasn't the goal. He was planning on seducing her curious mind instead.

He found himself energised by the prospect. It had been a long time since he'd had to exert himself for a woman— for anyone, for that matter—and the idea was more exciting than he'd anticipated. Lately his life of unmitigated pleasure had begun to pall, and it made a nice change to have to put his brain to good use instead of his body.

The thought of de Riero's shock as his daughter was revealed was…

The feeling of satisfaction was vicious, hot, and he had to force it back down—hard. He couldn't let emotion rule him. Not given the mistake he'd made the last time he'd tried to confront de Riero, blundering around in a blind rage, sending his son straight back into the other man's arms.

This time he needed to be casual, detached. Keep his revenge cold.

Mastering himself once more, Cristiano checked the time again, allowing himself some amusement at his own impatience, then crossed over to his desk. Since she was late, he might as well do something. It wouldn't do for her to find him cooling his heels and watching the clock for her arrival; he wasn't a man who waited for anyone, still less looked as if he was.

There were a few business matters he had to attend to, a few calls to make, and he made them, keeping an ear out for the door. And sure enough, ten minutes later, while he was in the middle of a conversation with a business acquaintance, he heard a soft knock.

'Enter,' he said, then turned his chair around so his back was to the room, continuing with his call.

It was petty, but he'd never been above a little pettiness. It would do her good to wait for him—especially since he'd spent the last ten minutes waiting for her.

He carried on with his call in a leisurely fashion, in no hurry to end it since his acquaintance was amusing, and only when the other man had to go did he end the call and turn his chair back around.

Leonie was standing near one of the ornate wooden shelves he kept stocked with his favourite reading material—business texts, philosophy, sociology and a few novels thrown in the mix—staring fixedly at the spines.

She held herself very tense, her shoulders and spine stiff, that waterfall of beautiful hair lying sleek and silky down her back.

He had the sense that she wasn't actually looking at the books at all. She was waiting for him. Good.

'Good evening, *gatita*,' he said lazily, leaning back in his chair. 'You're late.'

Slowly, she turned to him, and his gaze was instantly drawn to the dark circles beneath her eyes. Her pretty face looked pale, her big violet-blue eyes shadowed. One hand was in the pocket of her black trousers—clutching that knife, no doubt.

A feeling he wasn't expecting tightened in his chest. He ignored it, raising a brow at her. 'Well? Any particular reason you're late to your job interview?'

Her determined little chin lifted. 'Because you distracted me in the library I didn't get my work done on time, so I had to make it up at the end of the day.'

He almost laughed. She did like testing him, didn't she? 'I see. Nothing whatsoever to do with the fact that I caught you reading, hmm?'

Colour bloomed across her delicate cheekbones. 'No.'

Which was an outright lie and they both knew it.

Highly amused, he grinned. 'And you took some time to go back to your room for you knife, also, I think?'

Her forearm flexed above where her hand disappeared into her pocket, as if she was squeezing her fingers around the handle of something. But this time she didn't deny it.

'You said I could bring it.'

'It's true. I did.'

He got up from the chair and came around the side of his desk, noting the way she tensed at his approach. She was very wary of him. As wary as she'd been the night before. Understandable, of course, and it was an obvious sign of distrust. In fact, he could probably gauge her progression in trusting him through the way she acted around him physically.

It made him wonder, though, exactly what had happened to her out there on the Parisian streets. How she'd managed to survive. What had happened to Hélène? Why hadn't she gone to her father and told him she was still alive…?

So many questions.

If he wanted answers, he had some work to do.

He moved over to the fireplace against one wall, opposite the bookshelves. He'd had one of his staff light a fire even though it wasn't particularly cold, mainly because it made the room feel more welcoming. The fire crackled pleasantly, casting its orange glow over Leonie's beautiful hair.

She watched him as if he was a dangerous animal she had to be cautious about, yet her gaze kept flicking to the fire as if she wanted to get close to it. As if she was cold.

'You're afraid of me,' he said, and didn't make it a question. 'I can assure you that you have no need to be.'

Her gaze flickered. 'I'm not afraid.'

But the response sounded as if it had been made by rote—as if that was always her answer, whether it was true or not. It made sense, though. When you were small and female you were viewed as prey by certain people, which meant fear wasn't something you could afford. Fear was weakness. Especially when there was no one to protect you.

Had she ever had anyone to protect her? Or had she had to do it herself?

That tight feeling in his chest shifted again. It had been such a long time since he'd felt anything remotely resembling pity or sympathy that he wasn't sure what it was at first. But then he knew. He didn't like the idea of her being on her own. He didn't like the idea of her not being protected. How strange.

'Then come closer.' He thrust his hands in his pockets so he looked less intimidating. 'You want to be near the fire. Don't think I hadn't noticed.'

She didn't like that—he could see the tension ripple through her. Perhaps he was wrong to test her. But if he wanted her trust he had to start somewhere, and having her be less wary around him physically was certainly one way of doing it.

He remained still, not moving, keeping his hands in his pockets, silently daring her. She was brave, not to mention stubborn, and he suspected that if he kept challenging her she'd rise to it.

Sure enough, after a couple of tense moments, she gave a shrug, as if it didn't matter, and then came slowly across the room to stand on the opposite side of the fireplace. Her expression was carefully blank, and when she got closer to the flames she held out her hands to warm them.

Ostensibly she looked as if nothing bothered her and she was perfectly comfortable. But she wasn't. He could feel the tension vibrating in the air around her.

She was like a wild animal, ready to start at the slightest sound or motion.

'There,' he murmured. 'That's not so bad, is it?'

She flicked him an impatient look. 'I'm not afraid of you. I have a knife.'

'Good. Keep that knife about your person at all times.'

He turned slightly, noting how she tensed at his movement. 'So, nameless *gatita*. I suppose my first question to you is why on earth were you spray-painting my limo at two in the morning?'

Her attention was on the flames, but he suspected she was still very aware of him. 'Why shouldn't I be spray-painting your limo at two in the morning?'

'That's not the correct answer,' he reproved mildly. 'Don't you think I'm owed an explanation, considering it was my property you vandalised?'

Irritation crossed her features. 'Fine. The people I was with dared me to. So I did.'

'And if they dared you to jump off the Eiffel Tower you'd do the same?'

'Probably.' She gave him a sidelong glance. 'You can't back down—not even once. Not if you don't want to be a target.'

Ah, so now they were getting to it. 'I see. And these people are your friends?'

He thought not. Not considering how a one-hundred-euro note had been enough to pay for her name.

She shook her head. 'Just some people I was hanging around with.'

'At two in the morning? Didn't you have somewhere else to go?'

Her lashes fell, limned in gold by the firelight. 'It's… safer to be around other people sometimes.'

The tight thing coiled in his chest shifted around yet again, because even though she hadn't said it outright he knew. No, she didn't have anywhere to go, and she didn't want to admit it.

Proud *gatita*.

'I'm not sure those people were very safe,' he murmured. 'Considering how your night ended.'

She gave a shrug. 'Could have been worse.'

'Indeed. You could have spent another night on the streets.'

There was no response to that, though he didn't expect her either to confirm or deny it—not given how reluctant she was to give him any information about herself. Clearly telling her that he knew who she was wouldn't go down well, so he definitely wasn't going to reveal that in a hurry.

A small silence fell, broken only by the crackling of the fire.

'Will you sit down?' he asked after a moment. 'The chair behind you will allow you to stay close to the fire if you're cold.'

She gave him another sidelong glance, then made a show of looking around the room, as if trying to locate the chair. Then, without any hurry, she moved over to it and sat down, leaning back, ostensibly relaxed, though she'd put her hand in her pocket again, holding on to her knife.

There was another armchair opposite hers, so he sat down in that one. A low coffee table was positioned between them, which should present her with a safety barrier if she needed it.

'So what now?' she asked, staring at him, her chin set at a stubborn angle.

'Tell me a little about yourself. If not your name, then at least a few things that will give me an idea about the kind of person I've just employed.'

'Why do you want to know that?'

He smiled. 'This isn't supposed to be a debate—merely a request for information.'

'Why do you need information?'

Persistent, wasn't she? Not to mention challenging. Good. His life had been without any challenges lately, and he could use the excitement.

'Well, since you won't give me your name, I need some indication of whether you're likely to make off with all the silverware.' He paused, considering whether or not to let her know just how much leeway he was allowing her. Why not? If she was testing him, he could test her. 'I do a background check on all employees who are granted access to my house, in other words. For safety reasons, you understand?'

A little crease appeared between her red-gold brows. 'How can you be unsafe? Here?'

Of course she'd find that surprising. Especially if she was living on the streets. She no doubt thought nothing could harm him here, and to a certain extent she was right. Physically, he was safe. But four walls and body-guards—even if he employed any—didn't equal safety. You could have all the physical protection in the world and still end up broken and bleeding.

Luckily for him, his wounds had healed. And no one could see the scars but him.

'You can be unsafe anywhere,' he said dryly. 'In my experience you can never be too careful.'

'And what is your experience?'

He almost answered her. Almost. Sneaky kitten.

Cristiano smiled. 'It's supposed to be your job interview, *gatita*, not mine. I already have a job.'

'And so do I. You gave it to me, remember?'

'I do. Which means I can take it back whenever I like.'

She sniffed, glancing over to the fire once more. 'I might be more inclined to answer your questions if you answered some of mine.'

Well, this was an interesting tactic…

'That's not how a job interview works,' he said, amused by how she kept on pushing. 'Also, if you'll remember, I gave you my name last night.'

An irritated expression flitted across her face. She shifted in her seat and he didn't miss how her hand had fallen away from the pocket where her knife was kept.

So. Progress.

'I don't know why you keep asking.' Her sweet, husky voice had an edge to it. 'Not when you could just threaten me and be done with it.'

'Threats are effective, it's true. But ultimately they're not very exciting.' He watched her face. 'Not when it's much more fun to convince you to give it to me willingly.'

She flushed. 'You're very sure of yourself.'

'Of course I'm sure of myself. I'm a duke.'

'Duke of what?'

Good question. And because he was enjoying himself, and because it had been a long time since any woman had provided him with this much amusement, he answered it.

'Weren't you listening last night? I'm the Fifteenth Duke of San Lorenzo. It's a small duchy in Andalusia.'

She gave him a measuring look. 'What are you doing in Paris?'

'Business.' He smiled. 'Catching vandals spray-painting rude words on my limo.'

She gave another little sniff at that, but the colour in her cheeks deepened—which was a good thing considering how pale she'd been.

'You didn't sleep well, *gatita*,' he observed quietly.

'But I did tell Camille to let you sleep in a little this morning.'

She blinked and looked away, shifting around in her seat. 'The bed was...uncomfortable. And I'd had a long shower—too long.'

Well, he knew for a fact that the bed wasn't uncomfortable, since he had the same one in his room here. And as for the shower...that may have been the case. But he suspected she hadn't slept well because she wasn't used to having a bed at all.

'What do you care anyway?' she added irritably.

'I care because I like my employees to do a good job. And they can't if they're not well rested.'

'Or well fed,' she muttered.

He thought she probably hadn't meant him to hear that, but unfortunately for her he had excellent hearing. So she was hungry, was she? Again, understandable. If she lived on the streets, decent food must be hard to come by.

How lucky, then, that he'd organised a very good dinner.

Right on cue, there was a knock at the door.

She sat up, tension gathering around her again, instantly on the alert.

'Enter,' he said, watching her response as several staff members came in, bearing trays of the food he'd ordered.

Her eyes went wide as he directed them to put the food on the coffee table between them, including cutlery and plates, not to mention a couple of glasses and a bottle of extremely good red wine from his cellar.

'I told you there would be dinner,' he murmured as his staff arranged the food and then quietly withdrew.

Leonie had sat forward, her gaze fixed on the food on the table. It was a simple meal—a fresh garden salad and excellent steak, along with some warm, crusty bread and salted butter. All her earlier wariness had dissipated, to be replaced by a different kind of tension.

Her hands were clasped tightly in her lap.

She was hungry.

He became aware that her cheeks were slightly hollow, and her figure, now it wasn't swamped by that giant hoodie, was very slender. Probably too slender.

No, she wasn't just hungry—she was starving.

That tightness in his chest grew sharp edges, touching on that dangerous volcanic anger of his. Anger at how this lovely, spirited woman had ended up where she had. On the streets. Left to fend for herself with only a knife.

Left to starve.

Hélène had taken her and disappeared, letting Victor de Riero think she and his daughter were dead, but what had led her to do that? Had de Riero treated them badly? Was there something that had stopped Leonie from seeking him out?

A memory trickled through his consciousness...a small green-eyed boy running into de Riero's arms in fear...

Fear of you.

Red tinged the edges of Cristiano's vision and it took a massive effort to shove the rage back down where it had come from, to ignore the memory in his head. He had to do it. There would be no mistakes, not this time.

But her challenging him so continually was dangerous for them both. It roused his long-dormant emotions and that couldn't happen. Which meant she had to give him the answers he needed. Tonight. Now.

As she reached out towards the food Cristiano shot out a hand and closed his fingers around her narrow wrist.

'Oh, no, *gatita*. I've given you enough leeway. If you want to eat, you must pay me with some answers first.'

Leonie froze, her heart thudding hard in her ears, panic flooding through her. When his fingers had tightened her free hand had gone instantly to her knife, to pull it out and slash him with it.

'No,' he said, very calmly and with so much authority that for some strange reason her panic eased.

Because although his grip was firm, he wasn't pulling at her. He was only holding her. His fingers burned against her skin like a manacle of fire—except that wasn't painful, either. Or rather, it wasn't pain that she felt but a kind of prickling heat that swept up her arm and over the rest of her body.

She felt hypnotised by the sight of his fingers around her wrist. Long, strong and tanned. Competent hands. Not cruel hands.

'You'd stop me eating just to get what you want?' she asked hoarsely, not looking at him, staring instead at that warm, long-fingered hand gripping her wrist.

'No,' he repeated, in that deep, authoritarian voice. 'But I've given you food and a bed. A job that you'll be paid for. I haven't touched you except for twice—once when I grabbed you last night, and once now. I've given you my name and told you a few things about me. I have let you into my home.'

He paused, as if he wanted those words to sink in. And, as much as she didn't want them to, they did.

'I'm not asking for your date of birth or your passport number, or the number of your bank account. I'm not even asking for your surname. All I want is your first name. It's a small thing in return for all that, don't you think? After all, it was you who decided to deface my car, not me.'

Then, much to her shock, he let her go.

Her heart was beating very fast and she could still feel the imprint of his fingertips on her skin. It was as if he'd scorched her, and it made thinking very difficult.

But he was right about one thing. He wasn't asking for much. And he hadn't hurt her or been cruel. He *had* given her a bed and a job, and now there was food. And he hadn't withheld his name from her the way she had withheld hers from him.

She didn't trust him, but giving him this one small thing wouldn't hurt. After all, there were probably plenty of Leonies around. He couldn't know that she was Leonie de Riero, the forgotten daughter of Victor de Riero, the rich Spanish magnate, who'd tossed her and her mother out because he'd wanted a son. Or at least that was what her mother had told her.

'Leonie,' she said quietly, still staring at her wrist, part of her amazed she didn't have scorch marks there from his hand. 'My name is Leonie.'

There was a silence.

She glanced up and found his green gaze on hers, deep and dark as forests and full of dangerous wild things. She couldn't look away.

There was a kind of humming in the air around them, and the prickling heat that had swept over her skin was spreading out. Warming her entire body. Making her feel restless and hot and hungry. But not for food.

'Thank you,' the duke said gravely.

He was not triumphant or smug, nor even showing that lazy amusement she'd come to associate with him. It was as if her name had been an important gift and he was receiving it with all the solemnity that entailed.

'Pleased to met you, Leonie.'

Just for a moment she thought he might reach out and take her hand, shake it. And, strangely, she almost wanted him to, so she could feel his fingers on her skin again. How odd to want to touch someone after so long actively avoiding it.

But he didn't take her hand. Instead he gestured to the food.

'Eat.' His mouth curled. 'Not that I was going to stop you from eating.'

Leonie decided not to say anything to that. She was too hungry anyway.

Not wanting to draw his attention, she didn't load her plate with too much food and she tried to eat slowly. It was all unbelievably delicious, but she wanted to pace herself. It had been a while since she'd eaten rich food and she didn't want to make herself sick. But it tasted so good—especially the fresh vegetables.

The duke poured her a glass of wine and she had a sip—and her toes just about curled in the plain black leather shoes she'd been given. Everything tasted amazing. She wanted to eat and drink all of it.

He didn't eat—merely sat there toying with a glass of wine in a leisurely fashion and studying her. It was disconcerting.

'You're not hungry?' she asked, feeling self-conscious.

Had she been gorging herself? She didn't want to give away how starving she was, wary of him asking more questions that she wasn't prepared to answer.

What does it matter if he knows you're homeless?

Perhaps it didn't matter. Perhaps it was only instinct

that prevented her from revealing more, the long years of being wary and mistrustful settling into a reflex she couldn't ignore. Then again, there were reasons for her mistrust and wariness. She'd seen many young women in the same situation as herself fall victim to unscrupulous men because they'd trusted the wrong person, revealed the wrong thing.

Easier to keep to oneself, not let anyone close and stay alive.

It was a habit her wary, bitter mother had instilled in her long before she was on the streets anyway, and she'd seen no reason to change it.

Then again, although trusting this particular man might be a bridge too far, it was clear he wasn't here to hurt her. He'd had ample opportunity to do so and hadn't, so either he was saving it for a specific time or he wasn't going to do anything to her at all.

Maybe she could relax a little. Perhaps part of her reluctance to tell him anything had more to do with what he'd think of her, a dirty Parisian street kid, than whether he'd harm her. Not that she cared what he thought of her. At all.

'No, not hungry right now.' He leaned back in his chair, his wine glass held between long fingers. 'Did Camille not feed you enough?'

Despite all her justifications, she could feel her cheeks get hot. When she'd been turned out of the dilapidated apartment she'd shared with her mother, after her mother hadn't ever returned home, she'd had to fend for herself. And that hadn't allowed for such luxuries as pride. So why she was blushing now because he'd spotted her hunger, she had no idea.

'Just hungry today,' she muttered, not willing to give

him anything else just yet. Mainly because she'd been doing nothing but resist for so long she couldn't remember how to surrender.

'I think not.' His tone was casual. 'I think you're starving.'

She tensed. Had the way she'd been eating given her away? 'I'm not—'

'Your cheeks are hollow and you're far too thin.' His gaze was very sharp, though his posture was relaxed. 'You're homeless, aren't you?'

Did you really think you could keep it from him?

Damn. Why did he have to be so observant? Why couldn't be like all the other rich people in the world who never saw the people living on the streets? Who were blind to them? Why couldn't he have simply called the police when he'd grabbed her the night before and got her carted away to the cells?

Why do you even care?

She had no answer to that except to wish it wasn't true. Sadly, though, it was true. She did care. She didn't want him to know that she was homeless—that she had no one and nothing. And she especially didn't want him to know that she'd once been the daughter of a very rich man who'd left her to rot on the streets like so much unwanted trash. Her mother had been very clear on that point.

Except, all the wanting in the world wasn't going to change the fact that he'd picked up on a few things she'd hoped he wouldn't see and had drawn his own conclusions. Correct conclusions. So was there any point in denying it now? She could pretend she had a home and a family, but he'd see through that pretty quickly. He was that kind of man.

So, since pretending was out, Leonie decided on belligerence instead. She stared back at him, daring him to pass judgement on her. 'And if I am?'

His gaze roamed over her face, irritatingly making the heat in her cheeks deepen even more. 'And nothing,' he said at last. 'It was merely an observation.'

'Don't you want to know where and why and how it happened? Whether I'm a drug addict or an alcoholic? Why haven't I found somewhere to go or a shelter to stay in?'

'Not particularly.' His green eyes gleamed. 'But if you want to tell me any of those things I'm happy to listen.'

That surprised her. She'd been expecting him to push for more information since he'd been so emphatic about her name before. Yet apparently not.

A strange feeling settled in her gut. Almost as if she'd wanted him to ask so she could tell him and was disappointed that he hadn't.

To cover her surprise, she reached for another piece of bread, spreading it liberally with the delicious butter and eating it in slow, careful bites.

'I'll have Camille make sure you get enough to eat,' he said after a moment. 'I won't have you going hungry here.'

She swallowed the last bit of bread. 'Don't tell her—'

'I won't. Your secret's safe with me.'

She didn't want it to be reassuring, yet it was. Not that she cared about what Camille thought, but still… Questions would be asked and she didn't want questions. She didn't want to have to explain her situation to anyone—including this powerful, yet oddly reassuring duke.

He could protect you.

The thought was a discomforting one. She'd protected

herself well enough for nearly six years, so why would she need him?

You need someone, though.

No, she didn't.

She picked up her wine and took another sip, allowing the rich, dark flavour to settle on her tongue. It made her a little dizzy, but she didn't mind that.

He began to ask her a few more questions, though these were solely about how she'd found the work today and whether she had what she needed to do her job, so she answered them. Then they had a discussion about what other tasks she might like to tackle and how she'd prefer to be paid—cash, since she didn't have a bank account.

The conversation wasn't personal, his questions were not intrusive, and he didn't make any more of those un-expected movements. And after maybe another half an hour had passed his phone went. Since it was apparently urgent, he excused himself to answer it.

Leonie settled back in the chair and finished her wine. It was very warm in the room, and she was very full, and since they were both sensations she had almost never felt she wanted to enjoy them for a little while.

The deep, rich sound of his voice as he talked to who-ever he was talking to was lulling her. There was warmth and texture to that voice, and it was comforting in a way she couldn't describe.

Maybe it was that voice. Or maybe it was the wine and food. Maybe it was fire crackling pleasantly in the fire-place. Or maybe it was simply the fact that she'd barely slept a wink the night before, but she found her eyes be-ginning to close.

It took a lot of effort to keep them open.

Too much effort.

She closed them, all her muscles relaxing, along with her ever-present vigilance.

And then she fell asleep.

At some point she became aware that she was in someone's arms and was being carried somewhere. Normally that would have been enough to have her struggling wildly and waking up. But a familiar warm and spicy scent wound around her, and a comforting heat against her side was easing her instinctive panic.

And instead of struggling she relaxed. Letting the heat and that familiar scent soothe her. Feeling those arms tighten around her.

Where she was being carried, she didn't know, and a minute or so later she didn't care.

She was already asleep again.

CHAPTER FIVE

CRISTIANO MADE AN effort over the next week to keep an eye on Leonie in an unobtrusive way, stopping by wherever she was working to exchange a few words with her. Sometimes it was just that—a few words—and sometimes it was more of a conversation.

And slowly she began to relax around him. She no longer tensed when he appeared, and during the last two visits, she hadn't even scowled.

He counted it a victory.

Of course the real victory had been that night in his study, when she'd finally given him her name.

Reaching out to grab her wrist had been a gamble, but she'd had to learn that he meant business and that he had his limits. He wasn't a man to be toyed with. Besides, he hadn't been asking for much—just her name.

She'd seemed to understand and the gamble had paid off. She hadn't given him anything else, but he hadn't pushed. He knew when to insist and when to back off. She'd eventually give him what he wanted—he was sure of it.

He'd been even more sure when he'd finished his phone call and turned around to find that she'd fallen asleep in her chair. He hadn't wanted to wake her, since the shadows under her eyes had been pronounced, but nor had he wanted to leave her sleeping in an uncomfortable position. So, compelled by an instinct he hadn't felt in years, he'd gathered her into his arms and carried her up to her room.

Another gamble, considering how hyper-vigilant she was. But she hadn't woken. Or at least she hadn't panicked. Her lovely red-gold eyelashes had fluttered and her muscles had tensed, and then, just as quickly, she'd relaxed against him. As if she'd decided she was safe.

A mistake on her part, because he wasn't safe—not in any way—but he'd liked the way she'd felt in his arms. Liked the way she'd relaxed against him as if she didn't need to fear him. Liked it too much, truth be told.

Anna had never nestled sleepily in his arms. She'd never been comfortable with his displays of affection. But he was a deeply physical man and that was how he expressed it. She had also known his darkest secret, known the damage he was capable of, and although she'd never said it outright he knew she'd always judged him for it.

He'd tried to contain himself for her, change himself for her, but it hadn't been enough in the end. Victor de Riero had offered her what Cristiano hadn't been able to, and so she'd left him.

But it was dangerous to think of Anna, so he'd shoved his memories of her away and ignored the way Leonie had felt in his arms.

Leonie hadn't mentioned it the next day when he'd stopped by the room where she was dusting, so he hadn't mentioned it, either, merely giving her a greeting and then going on his way.

Which was what he'd done the next couple of days, too, only stopping for longer on the subsequent days after that. And the day before, not only had he not had a scowl, but he thought he might have had a smile. Or at least the beginnings of one.

It was very definitely a start.

But he needed to do more.

He wasn't normally an impatient man, since he never wanted anything enough to get impatient about it, but the thought of revenge had definitely put him in an impatient mood. He needed to gain her trust and then either get her to tell him who she was or reveal that he already knew in a way that wouldn't frighten her off.

After that, he had to ascertain her feelings about her father and find out whether she'd agree to let him widen her job description, as it were. In return for a sizeable bonus, naturally.

It was a good plan, and one he was sure would work, but it would require a certain delicacy. So far he'd done well, but more needed to be accomplished—and faster.

It was a pity trust wasn't one of those things that could be compelled.

He was reflecting on that as he arrived back home late one night the following week. He'd come from a party that had started out as tedious, only to descend into unpleasant when he'd heard Victor de Riero's name being bandied about in a business discussion.

Normally that wouldn't have caused him any concern. He'd detached himself so completely from what had happened fifteen years ago that he could even have attended the same party as the man and not felt a thing.

Yet tonight even the sound of that name had set his anger burning so fiercely that some disconnected part of him had been amazed at the intensity of his emotions when for so long he'd felt nothing. It had been disturbing, and it had made him even more certain that he must move his revenge plan on faster—because the quicker he dealt with it, the easier it would be to put out the fire of his anger once and for all.

He'd left the party early, full of that intense directionless anger, and was still in a foul temper now, as he arrived home. He'd been intending to sit in the library alone, with a very good Scotch, so his mood was not improved when he found that the library was already occupied by Leonie, kneeling on the floor in front of the bookshelves once again.

She was still in her uniform, and there were cleaning implements next to her, even though it was nearly midnight and she should be in bed, asleep. Something jolted in his chest at the sight of that familiar red-gold skein hanging down on her back.

He remembered carrying her to bed that night— how that hair had brushed against his forearm and then drifted over the backs of his hands as he'd bent over to lay her down on the mattress. It had felt very silky, and the urge to touch it, to sift his fingers through it, had gripped him once again. She'd felt light in his arms, but very soft and warm and feminine, and she'd smelled subtly of the rose-scented soap her bathroom had been stocked with.

He'd been very good at not paying attention to his physical reactions around her. Very good at not thinking about that moment of chemistry in his study that night when he'd put his fingers around her wrist, touched her soft skin. And it had been soft, her pulse frantic beneath his fingertips.

It hadn't been a problem before. He was always in complete control of himself, even when it looked to the rest of the world as if he wasn't. Yet right now, looking at her kneeling there, that control seemed suddenly very tenuous.

There'd been enough beautiful women at the party tonight for him to take his pick if it was sex he wanted. He didn't have to have her. She'd be a virgin, too—he'd bet his dukedom on it—and he wasn't into virgins. They were complicated, and the last thing he needed was more complications.

Yet that didn't put a stop to the hunger that gripped him, and his temper, already on a knife-edge, worsened.

Meirda, what was she doing here? Hadn't she finished her work? There were plenty of chairs around. Why wasn't she sitting on one of them? But, most importantly, why wasn't she safely in bed and out of his reach? And why did he always find her poring over a book?

He prowled up behind her, where she knelt, but she didn't look around, once again absorbed in whatever she was reading.

'You can take that upstairs if you want,' he said, unable to keep the growl out of his voice. 'You don't have to sit on the floor.'

She gave a little start, then sprang to her feet, turning around quickly. Her violet-blue eyes were very wide, and one hand automatically went to her pocket—as if her knife was still there and not where he'd seen it last, on her bedside table.

And then, as she took in his presence, her posture relaxed as quickly as it had tensed. 'Oh…' she breathed. 'It's you.'

He should have been pleased by how quickly she'd calmed, since it indicated more progress towards her trusting him. But tonight he wasn't pleased. Tonight it rubbed against his vile temper like salt in a wound. She was the daughter of his enemy and he was going to use her to get his revenge on that *hijo de puta*. She should be afraid of him. He was dangerous—and most especially when he was angry.

Hadn't Anna always told him that he frightened her? She'd been right to be scared. He was capable of such destruction when he let his emotions get the better of him. This little kitten should be cowering, not relaxing as if she was safe.

'Yes, it is,' he agreed, his temper burning with a sullen heat. 'What are you doing in the library at this time of night?' It came out as an accusation, which wasn't helpful, but he didn't bother to adjust his tone. He wasn't in the mood for adjusting himself for anyone tonight. 'You should go to bed.'

'I was working late.' Her forehead creased, her violet-blue gaze studying him. 'Are you all right?'

A dart of something sharp he couldn't identify shot through him. Was his temper that noticeable? Maybe it was. He hadn't exactly been hiding it after all. Still, he hadn't been asked that question in a very long time. Years, possibly. Not by his staff, not his few close friends, not his lovers. And the fact that this homeless girl should be the first one to have even a fleeting concern for his wellbeing annoyed him all the more.

He smiled without humour. 'Of course. Why would you imagine I'm anything other than all right?'

'Because you're...' She made a gesture at him.

'Because I'm what?' He took a leisurely step towards her. 'Have you been watching me, *gatita*?'

Her cheeks flooded with telltale colour. 'No, I haven't.'

A lie. She *had* been watching him. How interesting.

You should order her upstairs. Away from you. Nothing good comes from your temper—you know this already.

Oh, he knew. He knew all too well. But he was tired of having to do what he always did, which was to shove that temper away. Beat it down so no one would ever know it was there. Tired of having to pretend he didn't feel it, of having to restrain himself all the time.

Dios, she was the one who'd brought all this to the surface again. This was her fault if it was anyone's.

So what are you going to do? Punish her?

He ignored the thought, taking another step towards her. 'I think you have. I think you've been watching me. And why is that?' He let his voice drop to a low purr. 'Do you see something you like?'

Something flickered through her eyes, though he couldn't tell what it was. It wasn't fear, though, and he didn't understand. She was normally wary, and yet she wasn't wary now, which was strange. Had he done his job already? Did she trust him?

Silly *gatita*. Perhaps he should show her what she had to be afraid about.

He closed the distance between them, crowding her very purposefully back against the bookshelves, and this time obvious alarm rippled across her pretty face. He was standing close enough to feel the warmth of her body and inhale the faint, sweet scent of roses. Close enough to see the pulse beating fast beneath the pale skin at the base of her throat.

Fool. Giving in to your temper will undo all the progress you've made, and you swore you wouldn't make any more mistakes this time.

Cold realisation swept through him—of what he was doing and how badly he'd allowed his control to slip. She was supposed to trust him, supposed to feel safe with him—that was the whole point. And he wasn't supposed to make any more mistakes.

'You should leave,' he forced out, trying to handle the fury that coursed through him. 'I'm not fit company right now.'

She gave him another of those wary looks, but didn't move. 'Why not?'

'Too much wine, too many women, and not enough song.' He tried to hold on to his usual lazy, casual demeanour, baring his teeth in what he hoped was a smile, but probably wasn't. 'Leave, Leonie. I'm not in the mood to be kind.'

Yet again she made no move, only studied him as if he was a mystery she wanted to unravel and not a man she should be afraid of. A man whose passions ran too hot for anyone's comfort.

'Why?' she asked again. 'What happened?'

His fury wound tighter. He didn't want to talk about this with her and he didn't know why she was even interested. She shouldn't be wanting to know more; she should be running back upstairs to the safety of her room.

'I commend your interest in my wellbeing, *gatita*. But I think it is a mistake.' He moved closer since she wasn't getting the message. 'I'm telling you to leave for a reason.'

She was still pressed up against the bookshelves behind her but, strangely, her earlier alarm seemed to have vanished. Instead she was frowning slightly, searching his face as if looking for something, her gaze full of what looked like...concern, almost.

You've done nothing to deserve it.

No, he hadn't. Not a single damn thing.

Her scent wrapped around him and he was aware that the black T-shirt of her uniform was very fitted, outlining to perfection the soft curves of her breasts. They were round and full, just the right size for his hands. Would they be sensitive if he touched them? If he put his mouth to them? Kissed them and sucked on her nipples? Some women were very sensitive there, the slightest touch making them moan, while others needed firmer handling…

'What reason is that?' Leonie asked, and her sweet husky voice did nothing to halt the flood of sexual awareness coursing through him.

There was no alarm in the question, and her gaze was direct. Almost as if she was challenging him. Which would be either very brave, or very foolish, especially when he was in this kind of mood.

'You don't want to know,' he said roughly. 'It might frighten you.'

A spark glowed suddenly in the depths of her eyes. 'I'm not scared of you.'

It was fascinating, that spark. It burned bright and hot and he couldn't drag his gaze from it. Yes, this time it was definitely a challenge, and all he could think about was the fact that Anna had never looked at him that way. Anna had never challenged him—not once.

'You should be.' His voice had deepened, become even rougher, and his groin tightened in response to her nearness. 'I've told you before. I'm not a kind man.'

'That's a lie.' She gave him another searching look, apparently oblivious to the danger. 'You've been nothing but kind since I got here.'

Naturally she'd think that. She wasn't to know that he was being kind only because he wanted something from her. That he wasn't doing this out of the goodness of his heart, but to appease his own desire for vengeance.

Tell her, then. Tell her so she knows.

But if he told her she might run, and he couldn't afford for her to do that. Not yet.

She might run from you anyway if you keep on like this.

It was true. Which meant he needed to pull himself together—perhaps call one of those women who'd indicated interest tonight. It had been a while since he'd taken anyone to bed, so maybe it was that getting to him. Sex had always been his go-to when it came to working out his more primitive emotions. That was why he revelled in it.

'My kindness has a threshold,' he said instead. 'And you're approaching it.'

Her head tilted, her gaze still bright. Almost as if she was pushing him.

'Why? What have I done? You're not very good at answering questions, are you?'

He should have moved—should have stepped away. Should definitely not still be standing there, so close to her, now he'd decided he was going to find some alternative female company.

Yet he couldn't bring himself to move. He was caught by the bright spark in her eyes and by her sweet scent. There was colour in her cheeks still and the pulse at the base of her throat was beating even faster. Her mouth was full and red. Such temptation.

He could kiss that mouth. He could stop her questions and her ill-considered challenges simply by covering it with his own. Would she taste sweet? As sweet as she smelled?

'You haven't done anything but be where you shouldn't

be.' He lifted his hand before he could stop himself and gently brushed her bottom lip with his fingertips. 'Which is a mistake, *gatita*.'

Her mouth was as soft as he'd thought it would be, and velvety like rose petals. She stilled, her eyes going wide. But she didn't pull away.

Aren't you going to find yourself another woman?

He was. So why he wasn't—why he was standing here and touching *this* woman he had no idea. It shouldn't matter which woman he touched, and since Anna he'd made sure it didn't. He didn't need someone who was his—not again.

Not when you can't be trusted with them.

The thought should have made him move away. But it didn't. Instead, he put one hand on the bookshelf behind her head, leaning over her while he dragged the tip of his finger across the softness of her skin, tracing the line of her lower lip.

She shivered, taking another audible breath, her gaze never leaving his face. Her body was stiff with tension and yet she didn't move, the spark in her eyes leaping higher.

'Why are you touching me?' Her voice had become even huskier than normal.

'Why do you think?'

Every muscle in his body had tightened; his groin was aching. His anger had dulled. Physical desire was smoothing the sharp edges and making it less acute. Replacing it with another, safer hunger.

'This is the reason you should have left, Leonie.' He dragged his finger gently over her bottom lip once more, pressing against the full softness of it. 'Because you're a lovely woman and I'm a very, *very* bad man.'

* * *

Leonie couldn't move. Or rather, she probably could—it was more that she didn't want to. And she didn't understand why, because what the duke was doing to her should have sent her bolting from the room in search of her knife.

A week ago it would have.

But that had been before she'd spent a whole week in his house, cleaning the rooms she'd been assigned to. A whole week of a comfortable bed and good food, of being clean and dry and warm. A whole week of being safe.

A whole week of him stopping by every day to visit her—sometimes just to say hello, sometimes to chat.

She hadn't realised how much she liked his little visits until the fourth day, when he hadn't stopped by the room she was cleaning and she'd begun to feel annoyed, wondering if she'd missed him. Wondering if she'd been forgotten.

If she'd still been the Leonie of a week ago being forgotten would have been preferable. But she wasn't that Leonie. Not since she'd fallen asleep in his study that night and he'd gathered her up in his arms and put her to bed.

She'd woken the next morning disorientated and restless, panicking slightly when she'd realised what had happened. But when she'd jerked back the quilt she'd found she was still fully clothed. Only her shoes had been removed. She'd been asleep, at her most vulnerable, and all he'd done was tuck her into bed.

Perhaps that was why she felt no fear now, even though he was definitely touching her and threatening her into the bargain. But it wasn't a threat like those she'd experienced before, that promised only violence and pain. No, this was different. This promised something else, and she wasn't at all sure she wouldn't like whatever it was he was promising.

Especially if it was this prickling kind of heat sweeping over her, making her mouth feel full and sensitive. Making something inside her pulse hard and low, with that same hunger she'd felt the night he'd gripped her wrist.

Unfamiliar feelings. Good feelings.

She didn't want to move in case they vanished, as everything good in her life always seemed to do.

She tipped her head back against the bookshelf, staring up him, right into those intense green eyes. There was a flame burning there, giving out more heat than the fire that night in his study, and she wanted more of it. More of the heat of his tall, powerful body so close to hers.

Men had never been anything but threatening to her before, and sex something only offered as a transaction or taken with violence. She knew that there was more to it than that, because she'd watched couples holding hands in the streets. Couples hugging. Couples kissing.

She'd once been interrupted by a well-dressed man and woman slipping into the alley she'd been sleeping in at the time, and had watched unseen from behind a pile of boxes as the man had gently pressed the woman to the brick wall of the alley and lifted her dress. The woman had moaned, but not in protest. Her hands had clutched at the man, pulling him to her, and when she'd cried out it hadn't been in pain.

Leonie had wondered what it would be like to be that woman, but she knew she never would be. Because to be that woman she'd have to be clean and wear a nice dress. To be that woman she'd have to be cared for, and the only person who'd ever cared for her was herself.

So, since physical pleasure was not for people like her, she'd had to settle on invisibility instead. Blending into the background and never calling attention to herself, staying unnoticed and unseen, the way her mother had always taught her.

Except she wasn't unseen now. The duke had seen her, and continued to see her, and with every brush of his finger he made her more and more visible. More and more aware of how she liked that touch, how she wanted it. How cold she'd been before, and also how lonely.

And now he was here, with his hot green eyes and his hard, muscular body, and he was touching her.

He was turning her into that woman in the pretty dress in the alley and she liked it. She didn't want to run away. She wanted to be that woman. The woman who deserved pleasure and who got it.

'I don't think you're bad.' She held his gaze, every nerve-ending she had focused on the touch of his finger on her mouth. 'If you were that bad you wouldn't have told me to leave.'

'I don't think you know bad men, in that case.'

His gaze was all-consuming, a dark forest full of secrets, making her want to journey into it, discover what those secrets were.

'Of course I do.' Her mouth felt achingly sensitive. His touch was so light it was oddly maddening. 'I see them all the time on the streets. And I avoid them whenever I can.'

'So why aren't you running now?'

He shifted, leaning a fraction closer, bracing himself on the bookshelf behind her while his fingers moved on her mouth, his thumb pressing gently on her lip as if testing it.

'Or perhaps it's because you can't see past a warm bed and good food.'

That could be true. He might have lulled her into a false sense of security. She'd been wrong a couple of times before. But she didn't think she was wrong now. He'd had plenty of opportunity to touch her, to take what he wanted, and he hadn't. He had no reason to do so now.

Yes, so why now?

Good point. His obvious sexual interest was rather sudden. Perhaps he didn't want her the way she thought he did. Perhaps he was only trying to frighten her away.

After all, he'd been in a strange mood when he'd come in, with a sharp, raw energy to him, his eyes glittering like shards of green glass. Anger, she was sure, though she wasn't sure why.

Perhaps he'd come into the library hoping for some time to himself and found her there instead, intruding. Ignoring him when he told her to leave. And now he'd had to take more drastic steps to scare her off.

He doesn't want you, idiot. Why would he?

Her stomach dipped, an aching disappointment filling her. There was no reason for him to want her. She was just a homeless person he'd rescued from the streets and for some reason been kind to. And because she hadn't taken the hint and left when he'd asked her to he'd had to be more explicit. All this touching and getting close to her wasn't actually about *her*, and she'd be an idiot to think otherwise.

She tore her gaze away, not wanting him to see her disappointment or the hurt that had lodged inside her. 'Perhaps you're right. Perhaps you're really not all that kind after all.' She tried to sound as level as she could. 'If you want me to go, you'd better move.'

Yet the hard, masculine body crowding her against the bookshelves didn't move. She stared at the fine white cotton of his shirt—he was in evening clothes tonight, so it was obvious he'd been to some fancy party or other—her heartbeat thudding in her ears, a sick feeling in her gut.

Then the finger stroking her mouth dropped, as did the arm near her ear, and the duke straightened up, giving her some room.

The feeling of disappointment deepened.

She pushed herself away from the bookshelf, wanting to get away now, to get some distance from him. But before she could go past him, his fingers closed around her upper arm.

Her bare upper arm.

Leonie froze. His fingers burned against her skin the way they had that night in his study, making her breath catch and that restless heat sweep over her yet again.

She didn't look at him, staring straight ahead, her pulse racing. 'I thought you wanted me to go?'

'I thought I did, too.' His voice was dark, with threads of heat winding through it. 'You're really not scared of me, are you?'

'Does it matter?' She tried not to shiver in response to the sound of his voice, though it was difficult. 'I'm sorry I was here when you came in. I know you wanted to be alone, and I shouldn't—'

His fingers tightened around her arm abruptly and she broke off.

'Why did you think I wanted to be alone?' he demanded.

'You looked angry, and I shouldn't have been in here.'

'You're fine to be in here. Also, yes, it does matter.'

His fingers felt scorching. 'You should let me go.' She

kept her gaze on the wall opposite, trying to ignore his heat and the delicious scent of his aftershave. 'I know you were trying to scare me away—but, for the record, it won't work.'

There was a tense silence, full of the same humming tension that had surrounded them last week in his study.

'It won't, hmm…?'

Unexpectedly, his thumb stroked the underside of her arm in a caress that sent goosebumps scattering all over her skin. 'That's something you shouldn't have told me.'

'Why not?'

'Because it only makes me want try harder to scare you, of course.'

The sound of her heart hammered in her ears. She stared blindly across the room, every sense she possessed concentrated on the man standing beside her, holding her.

Was that another warning? And if it was, why was he still holding her? If he really wanted her to leave he only needed to open his hand and she'd be free.

Yet he hadn't.

She tried to process what that meant, but it was difficult when his thumb was pressing against the sensitive flesh of her under-arm, caressing lightly.

You could pull away. You don't have to stand here.

That was true. She didn't need to stand there being reminded of how empty and cold her life was, of all the good things she was missing out on. She didn't need to be reminded of how unwanted and unneeded she was.

Anyway, she had a warm bed, and food, and a job. Wanting more than that was just being greedy. She should be happy with what she had.

'All this talk of scaring me and being bad—yet you're not doing anything but hold on to me.' She kept her gaze resolutely ahead. 'I know you don't really want me. So why don't you just be done with it and let me go?'

There was a moment of silence and then she was being tugged around to face him, his glittering green gaze clashing with hers.

'What on earth makes you think I don't want you?' he demanded.

'Why would you?' She lifted her chin, prepared for the truth, ignoring the hurt lodged deep inside her. 'I'm just some poor homeless woman you picked up from the streets. No one else has ever wanted me so why should you?'

The hot flame in his eyes leapt, an emotion she couldn't name flickering over his handsome face. *'Gatita...'*

He looked as if he might say something more, but he didn't. Instead he jerked her suddenly towards him.

Not expecting it, she flung up her hands, her palms connecting with the heat and hardness of his broad chest. His fingers had curled around both her upper arms now, keeping her prisoner, and he'd bent his head, so his green eyes were all she could see.

'You are very foolish indeed if you think that,' he said, in a soft, dangerous voice.

Then, before she could say anything more, his mouth covered hers.

She froze in shock. She'd never been kissed before— had never wanted to be. Although sometimes, when the nights were very dark and she was especially cold, she'd remember that man and woman in the alleyway. Remember how the woman had cried out and how the man had kissed her, silencing her. And she'd wonder what it would feel like to have someone's mouth touching hers. Kissing her...

Now she knew. And it became very clear why that woman had clutched at the man kissing her.

The duke's lips were warm, so much softer than she'd expected a man's lips to be, and the subtle pressure and implicit demand were making a river of unfamiliar heat course the length of her spine.

She trembled, curling her fingers into the warm cotton of his shirt, her own mouth opening beneath his almost automatically. And he took advantage, his tongue pushing inside, tasting her, coaxing her, beginning to explore her.

A low, helpless moan escaped her. The delicious flavour of him was filling her senses and making her want more. She clutched at his shirt tighter, pressing herself closer. The heat of his kiss was melting all the frozen places inside her. All the lonely places. Lighting up all the dark corners of her soul.

Her awareness narrowed on the heat of his mouth, the slow exploration of his tongue, the dark, rich flavour that was all him and the iron-hard body she was pressed against.

It was overwhelming.

It was not enough.

It was everything she'd missed out on, all the good things she'd never had, and now she'd had a taste she wanted more.

She wanted them all.

'Cristiano…' she murmured against his mouth. And the name he'd given her, that she'd only used once before now, came out of her as easily as breathing. 'Please…'

CHAPTER SIX

HE SHOULDN'T HAVE kissed her. Yet now her mouth was open beneath his, the sweet taste of her was on his tongue and the slender heat of her body was pressed against him, he couldn't stop.

She was right in thinking he'd been trying to scare her. And he'd expected it to be easy—that a blatantly sexual touch would have her jerking away from him and leaving the room.

But she hadn't run as he'd anticipated. Because it seemed she never did the thing he anticipated.

Instead she'd only stayed where she was and let him touch her. Let his fingers trace her soft mouth, looking up at him, her eyes darkening with what could only be arousal.

He should have let her go. He hadn't needed to keep holding on to her and he wasn't sure why he had. He certainly shouldn't have compounded his mistake by covering her mouth with his—not when he'd already decided that he wasn't going to have her.

But something in his heart had stopped him. Because the way she'd looked so defiantly up at him, telling him that no one had ever wanted her before and why should he… Well, he hadn't been able to stand it.

A kiss to prove her wrong—that was all it was supposed to be. A kiss to ease the hurt she hadn't been able to hide. And maybe, too, a kiss to frighten her away once and for all.

No, you kissed her because you wanted to, because you wanted her.

Whatever the reason, it didn't matter. What did matter was the furnace that had roared to life inside him the minute her mouth was under his. The very second he'd felt her soften and melt against him, a throaty, husky moan escaped her.

And he wasn't sure why, or what it was about her that had got him burning hot and instantly hard. Yet as she arched against him, her fingers tugging on his shirt, the desire that just about strangled him was as if he hadn't had a woman in months. Years, even.

He could taste her desperation, could feel it in the way she pressed against him, in the sound of his name whispered in her husky voice, so erotic it felt as if she'd reached inside his trousers and wrapped her fingers directly around his shaft.

Anna had never done any of those things during sex. She'd never clutched at him, never moaned his name or pressed herself against him. She'd found his brand of earthy, physical sexuality uncomfortable, telling him he was too demanding. He'd tried to be less so, restraining himself to make her comfortable, turning sex from something passionate into something softer, more palatable, and thus more acceptable. Though it still hadn't been enough for her.

Since she'd left, and since his son had been claimed by another, he'd lost his taste for passion. Something easy, fun and pleasurable—that was all he wanted from sex, nothing more. His lovers could touch his body but they touched nothing else, and that was the way he made sure it always was.

But there was something about the way Leonie clutched at his shirt, her mouth open and hungry beneath his, whispering his name against his lips, that reached inside him, unleashing something he'd kept caged for a long time.

Raw, animal passion.

Perhaps it was because she wasn't a random woman he'd met at a party, or some pretty socialite he'd picked up at a bar. A woman who didn't want more from him than one night and a couple of orgasms, and that was all.

Perhaps it was the wrongness of it. Because there were so many reasons why it was a bad idea. She'd been living on the streets. She was homeless. She was a virgin. She was the daughter of his enemy and he was going to use her to get his revenge. He should not be hard for her, let alone kissing her hungrily late at night in his study.

And yet when she whispered, 'Cristiano... Please...' and arched against him, the soft curves of her breasts pressing against his chest, the sound of his name spoken in her husky voice echoing in his ears, all he could think about was giving her exactly what she was begging for.

After all, who was he to deny her? He'd never been a man to refuse anyone when it came to sex, still less one bright and beautiful woman whom he wanted very much.

Besides, perhaps taking her would cement what trust there was between them rather than break it. And when desire was this strong it was always better not to fight it. Always better to take command and sate it so it was easier to control later on.

That all sounds like some excellent justification.

But Cristiano was done listening to his better self.

He dropped his hands from her upper arms to her hips, letting them rest there a second to get her used to his touch. Then he slid them higher, until his palms were gently cupping her breasts.

She gave another of those delicious little moans, shuddering and then arching into his hands like a cat wanting to be stroked. He kept his mouth on hers, making the kiss teasing as he traced her soft curves with his fingertips before brushing his thumbs over the hard outlines of her nipples.

She gasped and he wanted to devour her whole, but he forced himself to lift his mouth from hers instead, to stare down into her face to check if she was still with him. Her cheeks were deeply flushed, her lips full and red from the kiss.

'Why did you stop?' she asked breathlessly. 'Please don't.'

Oh, yes, she was with him.

Satisfaction pulsed through him and he took her mouth again, nipping at her bottom lip at the same time as he pinched her nipples lightly, making her jerk and shudder against him.

His own heartbeat roared in his ears; his groin was aching. He wanted her naked, wanted her skin bare to his touch, wanted her hands on him, clutching at him. He wanted her desperate for him.

He'd given her food and drink. Given her a job. Given her a bed. And now he wanted to give her pleasure, too. He didn't pause to examine why this was important to him—he just wanted to.

Dangerous. You know how you get when you give in to your passions.

Ah, but this was only sex. It wouldn't touch his emotions in any way. He'd make sure of it.

'*Gatita*,' he murmured roughly against her hungry mouth. 'In ten seconds I'm going to have you naked on the floor, so if that's not what you want you'd better tell me right now.'

'I want it.' There was no hesitation in her voice, no coy dancing around the subject. 'Cristiano, please—I want it.'

Desire soaked through every husky word, and when he lifted his head and looked down into her eyes a part of him was shocked by the nakedness of her desire. Because she made no effort to hide it. Everything she felt was laid bare for him to see, exposing a vulnerability he was sure she hadn't meant to expose.

He could use that against her if he chose—get her to do anything he wanted if he handled it right. Even convince her to be his wife, for example. And if he'd been a more unscrupulous man...

What are you talking about? You are an unscrupulous man.

Oh, he was. But there was something innocent about Leonie, an honesty that he found almost painful. And he could not bring himself to take advantage of it.

Though she should know better than to let herself be so vulnerable—especially with a man like him. He was dangerous and hadn't he told her that? She needed to be more wary, more on her guard.

He bent his head further, moving his mouth to her jaw, kissing down the side of her neck and nipping her again in sensual punishment. But, again, she didn't push him away, only pulled harder on his shirt instead, as if she wanted more.

It was like petrol being poured over an already blazing fire, making his own passion leap high and hot.

Without another word, he lifted her into his arms and carried her over to the soft silk rug in front of the empty fireplace. Then he laid her down on it and took the hem of her T-shirt in his hands, dragging it up and over her head.

She didn't stop him, and a wave of gorgeous pink swept down her throat and over her chest as he uncovered her. The colour turned her eyes a vivid blue and made the plain black bra she wore stand out. But not for long. He undid the catch and stripped that from her, too, leaving her upper body bare.

Instantly her hands went to cover herself, but he caught her wrists, preventing her. 'No,' he said roughly, unable to keep his voice level. 'I want to look at you.'

She swallowed, but there was no resistance in her as he pushed her down onto her back, taking her arms above her head and pinning them to the rug, gripping her crossed wrists in one hand.

Lying there stretched out beneath him, all silky pale skin, her breasts exposed, hard nipples flushed a deep pink, she was the most delectable thing he'd ever seen.

He stared down into her eyes, watching the passion that burned there burn even higher as he stroked his free hand up and down her sides.

'Cristiano…' she said breathlessly, shivering.

'What it is, *gatita*? Do you need more?' He moved his hand to cup one of those perfect breasts, felt her skin hot against his palm. 'This, perhaps?'

'Oh…' she sighed. 'That's so—'

She broke off on a gasp as he rubbed his thumb over one hard nipple before pinching it, watching the pleasure chase itself over her lovely face. Her body arched beneath his hand, her lashes half closing.

'Oh…that's so good. More…'

His little kitten was demanding.

Yours? Already?

Maybe. And why not? No one else had claimed her, so why couldn't he? She was so very responsive, so very rewarding. Making her gasp like that might even become addictive.

He pinched her again, rolling her nipple between his thumb and forefinger, making her writhe. 'You'd best be more respectful,' he murmured, teasing the tip of her breast relentlessly. 'Please and thank you are always welcome.'

'Please…' She moaned softly, arching yet again beneath him. 'Please, more…'

'So obedient.' He eased his hand lower, over the soft skin of her stomach to the fastening of her plain black trousers. 'I like that, though. I like how you beg for me.'

Flicking open the button of her trousers, he grabbed the zip and drew it down. Then he pushed his hand beneath the fabric and over the front of her underwear. She shuddered as his fingers traced her through the damp cotton, pleasure and a certain wonder making her eyes glow. She was looking at him as though he'd shown her something amazing, the most precious thing in all the universe.

'Oh…' Her eyes went very wide as he pressed a finger gently against the most sensitive part of her and then circled around it, making her hips shudder and lift. 'What are you doing?' She didn't sound alarmed, only a little shocked.

'Giving you pleasure.' His voice came out rougher

than he'd intended. 'Does it feel good, Leonie? Does it feel good when I touch you?'

'Yes, oh, yes...' The breath sighed out of her and her gaze fixed to his, more wonder and amazement in her eyes. 'I never thought...it would...feel like this.'

She was so unguarded, so sincere. This woman had been denied a lot of things—warmth and comfort and safety. She'd been denied physical pleasure, too, and that was a crime. Because it was becoming apparent to him that she was a creature of passion, greedy for all the pleasure he could give her. And he had a lot of that to give.

Pleasure wasn't new to him, but for some reason introducing her to it was completely addictive. From the way she shivered under his hand to the flush in her silky skin. From the sounds she made to the wonder of discovery as she looked at him.

It was a discovery for him as well, he realised. It had been a long time since he'd been engaged in bed. He always gave his partners pleasure, but only in so far as it affected his own reputation. It was never about the woman in particular.

But now it was about this woman. He wanted to give her something she'd never had before—wanted to show her something new. He wanted her to look at him exactly the way she was looking at him now, as if she'd never seen anything or anyone so amazing in all her life.

The way no one, not even Anna, had ever looked at him.

You can't give that up.

A dark, ferocious thing stretched out lazily inside him, flexing its claws.

Well, maybe he didn't have to give it up. Why should he? She wanted him—that was obvious—and passion like hers didn't stay sated. This needn't be a one-off thing. He was planning on marrying her anyway, so why not make it a true marriage for a time?

Are you sure that's a good idea? Look what happened last time with Anna.

Yes, but that had only been because those dangerous emotions of his had been involved, and they weren't here. He didn't love Leonie and she didn't love him. He was simply taking advantage of their intense physical chemistry, nothing more.

She might not feel that way when you tell her you've known who she is all along.

Cristiano ignored that thought, slipping his hand beneath the fabric of her underwear, then sliding his fingers over her slick, wet flesh. She gave a little cry, pushing herself into his touch, her eyes darkening as her pupils dilated.

Satisfaction deepened inside him. He could have watched the pleasure rippling over her face for ever. 'You like that, *mi corazón*? Do you like it when I stroke you here?'

He found the small, sensitive bud between her thighs and brushed the tip of his finger over and around it. She gasped, shivering.

'And here?'

He shifted his hand, put his thumb where his finger had been, then slid that finger down through the slick folds of her sex to the entrance of her body, easing gently inside.

'Do you like it when I touch you here?'

Her cheeks were deeply flushed and she moved restlessly, unable to keep still. 'Yes...' Her voice had become even more hoarse. 'Oh, yes... Cristiano... I need...'

He could become addicted to hearing his name spoken like that...husky and soft and desperate. Just as he could become addicted to the silky, slippery feel of her flesh and the hot grip of her body around his finger. To the way she shook and gasped and arched. To the obvious pleasure she was feeling and didn't hide.

His groin was aching, his own desire winding tight, and he wanted to be inside her with a desperation he hadn't thought possible.

But he wanted to watch her come even more. So he eased his fingers in and out of her, adding more pressure and friction with his thumb until her eyes went wide and her mouth opened and her body convulsed.

She cried out in shocked pleasure as her climax hit, and he leaned down and kissed her, tasting that pleasure for himself.

Cristiano's mouth on hers was so hot and so delicious she could hardly bear it. Waves of the most intense pleasure were shaking her, and all she could do was lie there and let them wash over her.

She'd told him the truth when she'd said she'd had no idea it would feel like this. She really hadn't. Had the woman against that wall felt the same pleasure? Was it this that had made her cry out? Because, yes, *now* she understood. Now she got it completely.

When Cristiano had touched her she'd felt as if something was blooming inside her. A flower she'd thought had died, which had turned out to be only dormant, waiting for the sun, and now the sun was shining and she was opening up to it, revelling in it.

She hadn't been afraid. His kiss had been hot but his hands gentle, and when a fit of modesty had overcome her when he'd taken her bra off he'd been very clear that he wanted to look at her. That he liked looking at her.

And so she'd let him. And the longer he'd looked, the more she'd wanted him to. Because she'd seen the effect she'd had on him, the heat burning in his eyes, and it had made her feel…beautiful. She'd never felt that before, nor ever been conscious of her own feminine power. Her ability to make him burn as much as he made her.

Then he'd touched her, and the world around her had turned to fire.

Perhaps she should be ashamed that she'd been so open with her responses. Perhaps she should have been more guarded. But the pleasure had been too intense, and she simply hadn't been able to hide her feelings.

He'd touched her as if she wasn't some dirty forgotten kid that he'd found on the streets of Paris. He'd touched her as if she was precious…as if she was worth something. He'd touched her as if he cared about her, and she realised that she wanted him to.

It didn't make any sense—not when she hadn't known him long—yet every touch had only made her more certain. He'd given her many things she'd been missing in her life and now he was giving her another—something she'd never thought she'd want.

And, despite the fact that he'd seemed so angry when he'd come into the library earlier, he wasn't taking that anger out on her. He wasn't taking from her at all.

He was giving to her. Giving heat and a shivery desperation. A delicious need. Pleasure to chase away the cold and the dark, the fear and the loneliness. So much pleasure…

She wanted more of it.

She tried to pull her hands away from his restraining

hold, but his grip only firmed as his glittering green eyes scanned her from head to foot.

'Are you okay?'

His voice was a soft, roughened caress, whispering over her skin like velvet.

'Did you like that?'

'Yes. Very much.' She didn't sound much better herself. 'But I want you. I want to touch you.'

There was no hiding it so she didn't bother.

He swept his free hand down the length of her body in a long stroke that soothed her at the same time as it excited her.

'There will be time for that. But first, you're wearing far too many clothes.'

With practiced, careful hands he stripped the rest of the clothing from her body, finally baring her.

She'd thought she might feel terribly vulnerable and exposed, being naked in front of a man. Being naked in front of anyone, really. But she didn't feel either of those things. Only strangely powerful as he pulled the fabric away from her and she saw the look on his face became hungrier, sharper, as if the sight of her was something he'd been waiting lifetimes for.

And when she was finally naked, lying back on the rug, he knelt over her, his gaze roaming all over her body, and she felt for the first time in her life as if maybe there was something worthwhile about her after all.

What it was, she didn't know. But it was certainly something that had this powerful duke looking at her as if she was the Holy Grail itself.

He ran his fingertips lightly all over her, inciting her, watching her face as he did so, gauging her every response as if there was nothing more important in the world than discovering which touches made her shiver and which made her moan. Which ones made her pant his name.

She'd long since lost any shyness by the time he pushed apart her legs, brushing his mouth over her trembling stomach before moving further down. And then all she could do was thread her fingers in his hair as he put that clever mouth of his between her thighs.

Pleasure exploded through her as he began to explore, his fingers delicately parting her wet flesh while his tongue licked and caressed, driving her higher and higher. Making her cry out as the most delicious ecstasy threaded through her.

She'd never thought this feeling would be hers. Never thought that sex could be something so intense, so incredible, that it would feel so good. She'd never thought it would make her feel treasured and desired rather than dirty and worthless, but with every flick of his tongue and stroke of his hand that was what he made her feel.

She pulled on his hair, crying his name as he pushed his tongue inside her and she shattered for a second time, her climax so all-consuming that all she could do was lie there with her eyes closed as it washed over her, feeling him stroke her gently as he moved away.

Then there came the rustle of clothing and the sound of a zip being drawn down, the crinkle of foil. And then the brush of hot skin on hers, setting every nerve-ending to aching life once again.

She opened her eyes.

The duke was kneeling between her spread thighs, tall, powerful and extremely naked. And somehow he seemed even more intimidating without his clothes on, because all that lazy amusement, the studied air of ennui, had vanished completely as if it had never been.

It was a smokescreen, she realised. A distraction. A disguise hiding the true nature of the man beneath it.

She'd imagined him as a panther, lazily sunning himself on a branch, and he was that. But a panther was a predator—and that was what she was looking at now, not the lazy cat.

He was all velvet tanned skin drawn over sharply defined muscle, broad and powerful and strong. A work of art. A Greek statue come to life. As hard as the bronze from which he'd been fashioned yet not cold, but hot. Heated metal and oiled silk.

And his beautiful face was drawn tight with hunger and intent. His eyes had narrowed; hot emerald was glittering from between silky black lashes. The panther ready to pounce. The predator ready to feast.

A delicious shiver chased over her body and she allowed herself to look down to where he was hot and hard and ready for her. She'd never thought that could be beautiful as well, but it was. She pushed herself up on one hand and reached to touch him, and he made no move to stop her, letting her fingers brush along the velvet-smooth skin of his shaft.

She looked up at his face as she did it, wanting to see what effect her touch had on him, and was thrilled to see a muscle jump in the side of his impressive jaw.

'No playing, *gatita*,' he murmured, his rich voice dark and thick with heat. 'Like I said, my patience is limited.'

'I want to touch you, though.' She closed her fingers around him, marvelling at how hard he was and yet how soft and smooth his skin felt. 'You're so hard…' She squeezed experimentally.

He hissed, and then suddenly everything was moving very quickly. He pulled her hand away and pushed her down on her back, his long, muscular body settling over hers. She protested, but he shook his head, the smile he gave her sharp and edged.

'You can touch me later. Seems I have limited patience where you are concerned.'

She liked that. Liked the way her touch could incite him the way his could incite her.

She wanted to help him with the protection, too, but he gave a sharp shake of his head, dealing with it himself. And then his hands were sliding beneath her bottom, gripping her tight and lifting her, and he was positioning himself so he was pressing gently at her entrance.

'Are you ready for me?'

His jaw was set and hard, every muscle in his body drawn tight and ready. All that strength and power was held back, and not without effort. But it was definitely held back. For her.

'Answer me. I'm not made of stone.'

What a lie. He *was* made of stone. Not bronze after all, but hard, living rock that she couldn't stop touching. Enduring and powerful. She could shelter beneath him right here and nothing would touch her.

The feeling was so intense she put her hands on his chest and spread out her fingers, stroking up over all that hard muscle to his strong shoulders. Holding on.

'I'm ready,' she whispered.

And he didn't hesitate, his fingers tightening as he pushed into her. She gasped as she felt her flesh part for him, in an intense yet delicious stretch, and tensed, ready for pain, because this was supposed to hurt. Yet apart from a slight pinch there was nothing. Only more of that sensual stretch that had her panting and twisting in his arms as she tried to adjust to the sensation.

'Look at me,' he ordered. 'Look at me, Leonie.'

So she did, staring straight up into his eyes, and suddenly everything clicked into place. She was made for him. Her body was made especially for him—for his hands and his mouth, for the hard, male part of him, and he was where he was supposed to be. He might be holding her, but she was also holding him.

'Cristiano...' She lingered over the sound of it, loving how it felt to say it. Loving, too, the way his eyes flared as she said it. So she said it again, digging her nails into his skin, lifting her hips, because she was ready for him to move. Ready for him to take her on another journey.

'Demanding, *gatita*,' he growled. 'You are perfect.'

Then he covered her mouth in a kiss so hot and blinding she trembled and he began to move, the long, lazy glide of him inside her making more of that intense, delicious pleasure sweep over her.

She tried to press herself harder against him, because it wasn't quite enough and she didn't know how to get more, and then he reached down and hooked one hand behind her knee, drawing her leg up and around his hip, allowing him to sink deeper, and she moaned in delight against his mouth.

He felt so good. The glide of his hips, the silk of his skin, the flex and release of all those powerful muscles as he thrust in and out. The warm spice of his scent was cut through with the musk of his arousal. It was delicious.

She sank her teeth into his lower lip, hardly aware of what she was doing, only knowing she wanted even more of him and this insanely pleasurable movement.

He growled in response—a deep rumble in his chest that sent chills through her.

Yes, she wanted the panther. The raw untamed part of him, not the lazy, civilised man he was on the outside. Not the smokescreen. Did anyone else know he was this way? Was he like this when he made love to other women?

She didn't like that thought—not at all. She wanted him to be like this with her and only her.

She bit him again, scratching him with her nails, thrilled when he grabbed her hands and held them down on either side of her head.

He lifted his mouth from hers and looked into her eyes as he thrust hard and deep. 'You like showing me your claws, don't you?' He sounded breathless. 'What's that all about, hmm…?'

'You're not the only one who's bad.' She put a growl of her own into her voice as she pulled her hands away, running her nails down his back in a long scratch, lifting her hips to meet his thrust. 'You're not the one who's dangerous.'

'Is that so?' He thrust harder, pushing deeper, making her gasp and arch her back, her nails digging in. 'Show me how bad you are, then, *leona*. Show me your teeth.'

Pleasure twisted inside her and she turned her head, bit his shoulder, tasting the salt and musk of his skin, loving how he gave another growl deep in his throat and moved faster.

She clung to him, licking him, biting him, scratching him as pleasure drew so tight that she didn't think she could bear it. She called his name desperately and he answered, shifting one hand down between them and stroking her where she needed it most. And then she had to turn her face against his neck as everything came apart inside her. Tears flooded her eyes and she was sobbing his name as ecstasy annihilated her.

She had a dim sense of him moving faster, harder, and then she heard his own roar of release, felt his arms coming around her and holding her, his big, hot body over her and around her, inside her.

Protecting her.

CHAPTER SEVEN

CRISTIANO PULLED A shirt on, slowly doing up the buttons, then methodically starting on the cuffs. He stood at the window of his bedroom while he did so, his attention on the garden below, though he wasn't looking at the view.

He was too busy thinking about what he was going to say to the woman still asleep in the bed behind him. His little *gatita*. Though she wasn't really a kitten. Not after last night. Last night he'd discovered she was a lioness, and he had the scratches down his back to prove it.

It would have made him smile if he'd been in a smiling mood, but he wasn't.

There were a number of things he wanted to do, and he couldn't do any of them until he'd told her that he'd known who she was from the moment he'd taken her home. And that he intended to marry her to take his revenge on her father.

She probably wasn't going to take either of those things well.

Are you sure it's wise to tell her now?

He frowned at the garden for a moment, then turned around.

Leonie was curled up in the centre of his bed, her hair a scatter of brilliant red-gold across his white pillows.

She was fast sleep, with the sheet falling down off her shoulders a little, revealing pale, milky skin.

Last night she'd felt like pure joy in his hands, passionate and generous and honest. Pleasure had been a discovery and she a fascinated explorer. She'd denied him nothing, taken everything he'd given, and now all he could think about was doing it again. And again and again.

He hadn't had sex like that in years—if ever.

Leonie hadn't found his passion frightening or uncomfortable, the way Anna had. No, she'd demanded it. And then, when he'd given it to her, she'd demanded more.

His groin hardened, and the decision he'd made in the early hours of the morning, when he'd had to get up and have a cold shower so he could sleep, was now a certainty.

He'd take her back to San Lorenzo, his ancestral estate. There he would have her all to himself. He could certainly tell her about his plans here, but perhaps it would be better if she was at home in Spain. Where he could keep an eye on her.

The chances of her running away or not wanting anything to do with him once she found out about his plans were slim—or so he anticipated—but it was better to be safe than sorry.

Plus, marrying her in the ancient Velazquez family chapel would no doubt rub further salt in the wound for Victor de Riero. A further declaration of Cristiano's possession.

And if she refuses to marry you?

He would just ensure that she wouldn't. Everyone had a price, and no doubt so did she.

Finishing with his cuffs, he moved over to the bed and bent, stroking his fingers along one bare shoulder, smiling as she shivered. Her red-gold lashes fluttered and then she let out a small sigh, rolling over onto her back. The sheet fell all the way to her waist, exposing those small, perfect breasts and their little pink nipples.

He was very tempted to taste one of them, to make her gasp the way he had the night before. But that wouldn't get them any closer to San Lorenzo, and now he'd decided to go he saw no reason to linger in Paris.

'Wake up, sleepy *gatita*,' he murmured, unable to stop himself from brushing his fingers over one pert nipple, watching as it hardened, feeling his own hunger tighten along with it.

She sighed and lifted her arms, giving such a sensual stretch he almost changed his plans right there and then in favour of staying a few more hours in bed with her.

Her eyes opened, deep violet this morning, and she smiled. It took his breath away.

'Good morning.' Her gaze dropped down his body before coming to his face again. 'You're dressed. That's unfortunate.'

He smiled, the beast inside him stretching again, purring in pleasure at her blatant stare. 'Hold that thought. I have plans for us today.'

'What plans?' Her eyes widened and she sat up suddenly. 'What's the time? Am I late for work? Where are my—?'

'There will be no work for you today. Or perhaps any other day.'

He saw shock, hurt and anger ripple across her lovely face. 'Why not? I thought I—'

'Relax, *mi corazón*. I have another position in mind for you.' He sat on the side of the bed and reached for her small hand, holding it in his. 'I'm planning to return to my estate in Spain.'

'Oh.' Her expression relaxed. And then she frowned. 'Why?'

Naturally she would have questions. She was nothing if not curious.

'I have some things that need attention and I haven't been back for a while.'

Years, in reality. Fifteen of them, to be exact. But she didn't need to know that.

He turned her hand over in his, stroking her palm with his thumb. 'It would please me very much to take you with me.'

She glanced down at her hand, enclosed in his. 'But what about my job here? Camille wouldn't like it if I suddenly left with no word.' Another troubled expression crossed her face. 'She wouldn't like it if she knew what I...what we...'

'Leave Camille to me.' He stroked her palm reassuringly, noting how she shivered yet again. 'And, like I told you, I have another position in mind for you.'

She looked up at him, her gaze very direct. 'What position? Your lover?'

There was a challenging note in her voice and he couldn't help but like how unafraid she was to confront him. She was strong, that was for certain, and although she might have been an innocent when it came to sex, she wasn't an innocent in anything else. She'd lived for years on the streets. She would have seen all kinds of cruel things, seen the basest of human nature. She knew how the world worked and knew that it was not kind.

If you tell her the truth she'll understand. She, more than anyone, will know what it's like to lose everything.

It was true. And if she didn't—well, there was always the money option. Either way, it wouldn't be an issue.

'Is there a problem with that?' he asked casually. 'You seemed to enjoy it well enough last night.'

She glanced down once again at her hand resting in his, at his thumb stroking gently her palm. 'So will that now be my job?'

The question sounded neutral, but he knew it wasn't.

'To be your whore?' The word was like a stone thrown against glass, jagged and sharp. 'Will you pay me more to be in your bed, Cristiano?'

The question sounded raw in the silence of the room. It wasn't a simple challenge now, because there was something else in her tone. She sounded...vulnerable, and he had the sense that he'd hurt her somehow.

You have hurt her.

Anger twisted sharply inside him and he dropped her hand and pushed himself off the bed, striding restlessly over to the window, trying to get his thoughts in order and his ridiculous emotions safely under control again.

The issue, of course, was that she was right. That was exactly what he'd been planning to do. Pay her to be his wife. And since he was also thinking their marriage would include sex, essentially he was paying her to sleep with him.

'Would that be so very bad?' he asked harshly.

There was a brief silence, and then she said in a small voice, 'So that's all last night was? Just a...a transaction?'

Ah, so that was what this was about. She thought the sex had meant something.

It did.

No—and he couldn't afford it to. His emotions had to remain detached, and already they were more engaged than he wanted them to be. His anger was far too close to the surface and she had an ability to rouse it too easily. He had to make sure he stayed uninvolved—that his feelings for her didn't go beyond physical lust.

'I thought last night was all about mutual pleasure,' he said, keeping his tone neutral. 'Though if there was anything transactional about it I apologise.'

'Oh.' Her voice sounded even smaller. 'I see.'

Cristiano's jaw tightened. He hadn't thought about her feelings and he should have. Because of course the sex for her wouldn't simply have been physical. It had been her first time, and she didn't have the experience to tell the difference between great sex and an emotional connection.

Are you sure you do?

He shoved that thought away—hard. Oh, he knew the difference. He wasn't a boy any more. But he couldn't have her thinking that the sex between them had meant more than it had. He also couldn't have her getting under his skin the way she was currently doing.

Which left him with only one option.

He would have to give her the truth.

It would hurt her, but maybe that would be a good thing. Then she would know exactly what kind of man he was. Which was definitely not the kind of man she could have sex that meant something with.

She might not want to have anything to do with you after that.

His chest tightened with a regret and disappointment he didn't want to feel, so he ignored it, placing his hands on the sill and staring sightlessly at the rooftops of Paris.

'I was married years ago,' he said into the silence. 'Both of us were very young—too young, as it turned out. She found me…difficult. And I *was* difficult. But I didn't know that she was so unhappy.' He paused, the words catching unexpectedly in his throat. 'At least not until she left me for someone else.'

Leonie was silent behind him.

'That someone else was an old enemy of my family's,' he went on. 'Someone who befriended me after my parents died and became a mentor to me. I told him about my marriage difficulties in the hope that he'd give me some advice, and he did. All the while using what I said to seduce my wife away from me.'

His grip on the sill tightened, his nails digging into the paintwork.

'And that's not all. I didn't realise that Anna was pregnant when she left me for him. In fact, I only found out when he came to tell me that not only was the baby mine, but he'd organised it so that legally he was the baby's father. I could never claim him.'

There was a soft, shocked sound from behind him, but he ignored it.

'This enemy was a powerful man,' he said roughly, 'and even though I tried to uncover what he'd done I was unable to. I was young and had no influence, no power and no money.'

He paused yet again, trying to wrestle the burning rage that ate away at him under his control again.

'I felt I had no choice. If I wanted my son I would have to take him by force. And so I planned to do that. I crashed a party they were giving and tried to confront the man who'd taken my child. But I was…angry. So very angry. And I ended up frightening my son. He ran straight into my enemy's arms—'

His voice cracked and he had to fight to keep it level.

'I knew then I had to let him go,' he went on, more levelly this time. 'That I had to let everything go. And so I did.'

Even though it had cut him in half. Even though it had caused his heart to shrivel up and die in his chest.

'I cut my marriage and my son out of my life, out of my memory. I pretended that it never happened, that he never existed. And then...then I found a woman in the streets. A woman who was defacing my car. I found out her name. Leonie de Riero. The long-lost, much-loved daughter of Victor de Riero.'

Cristiano let go of the windowsill and turned around to face the woman in the bed.

'Victor de Riero is the man who first stole my wife and then stole my child from me. And he owes me a debt that I will collect.' He stared at her, let her see the depth of his fury. 'With you.'

Leonie clutched the sheet tight in her hands, unable to process what Cristiano had just told her.

He stood with the window at his back, his hands at his sides, his fingers curled into fists. His beautiful face was set in hard lines, the look in his emerald eyes so sharp it could cut. The smokescreen had dropped away entirely. He looked fierce, dangerous, and the fury rolling off him took her breath away.

What little breath she had, given that apparently all this time he'd known who she was. Known *exactly* who she was.

That's why he picked you up off the streets. That's why he gave you a job. You were never anything to him but a means to an end.

Pain settled inside her, though she ignored it. As she

ignored the cold waves of shock and the sharp tug of pity because there was so much to take in.

He'd been married. He'd had a child. A child that had been taken from him. God, she could still hear his voice cracking as he'd told her what had happened, and that pity tugged harder at her heart.

But she didn't want to feel pity for him.

'You knew,' she said thickly, focusing on that since it was easier than thinking about the rest. 'All this time, you knew.'

His expression was like granite. 'Yes. I went to get my driver and found him playing a dice game with one of your friends. I gave the kids a hundred euros to tell me what your name was.' His mouth quirked in a humourless smile. 'Everyone has their price.'

She felt cold. But it was a cold that came from the inside, something that no amount of blankets or quilts could help. 'But…how could you know who I was from my first name?'

His gaze went to her hair, spilling down her back. 'You were familiar to me and I couldn't put my finger on why. But the colour of your hair gave it away. Anna and I used to go to many events hosted by your father and you attended some of them.'

Her stomach dropped away. Her memories of that time were so dim they were only blurry impressions. A pretty dress. A crowd of adults. Nothing more.

But Cristiano had been there. She must have seen him and clearly he'd remembered her.

She stared at him, her heart pounding. Before, she'd noted that he was older, certainly much older than she was, but she hadn't thought about it again. She hadn't thought about it last night, either—had been too desperate for him.

There had been a vague familiarity to his name when she'd first heard it, but she hadn't remembered anything. She'd been too young.

'Why...?' She stopped, not sure which question to ask first since there were so many.

'Why did I bring you here? Why did I not tell you I knew?' He asked them for her. 'Because you were familiar and I wanted to know why. And when I discovered who you were I didn't tell you because I wanted you to tell me. I wanted you to trust me.'

A sudden foreboding wound through her. 'What do you want from me?'

He smiled again, his predator's smile, and it chilled her. 'What do I want from you? I want you to help me get my revenge, of course.'

Ice spread through her.

Did you think he wanted you for real?

She fought to think, fought her pity for him and for what had happened to him.

'How? I don't understand.'

'I'm going to marry you, Leonie. And I'm going to invite your father to our wedding, to watch as a Velazquez takes a precious de Riero daughter the way he took my son.'

The ferocity on Cristiano's face, gleaming in his eyes, made the ice inside her deepen, yet at the same time it gave her a peculiar and unwanted little thrill.

'You will be mine, Leonie. And there will be nothing he can do to stop it.'

You want to be someone's.

The thought tangled with all the other emotions knotting in her chest, too many to sort out and deal with. So she tried to concentrate only on the thing that made any kind of sense to her.

'It won't work,' she said. 'My father doesn't care. He left me to rot in the streets.'

Something flickered across Cristiano's intense features. 'No, he didn't. He thought you were dead. Didn't you know?'

Her stomach dropped away. Dead? He thought she was dead?

'What?' she whispered, hoarse with shock. 'No, my mother told me he got rid of us. That he'd wanted a son, and she couldn't have any more children. And he…he…' She trailed off, because it couldn't be true. It couldn't.

Maybe it is and your mother lied to you.

This time the expression on Cristiano's face was unmistakable: pity.

'He didn't get rid of you,' he said quietly. 'I know. I was there. Your mother left him, and took you with her, and you both disappeared. A week or so later he got word that you'd both died in a fire in Barcelona.'

'No,' she repeated pointlessly. 'No. We came to Paris. Mamá had to get a job. I wanted to go home, but she told me we couldn't because Papá didn't want us. She couldn't give him the son he'd always wanted so he kicked us out.' Leonie took a shaken breath. 'Why would she say that if it wasn't true?'

Cristiano only shook his head. 'I don't know. Perhaps she didn't want you to find out that he'd been having an affair with my wife.'

Does it matter why? She lied to you.

The shock settled inside her, coating all those tangled emotions inside her, freezing them.

'All this time I thought he didn't look for me because he didn't care,' she said thickly. 'But it wasn't that. He thought…he thought I was dead.'

Cristiano's anger had cooled, and a remote expression settled over his face. 'I wouldn't ascribe any tender emotion to him if I were you. He didn't demand proof of your deaths. He merely took some stranger's word for it.'

A lump rose in Leonie's throat. There was a prickling behind her eyes and she felt like crying. Okay, so not only had her father thought she'd died, and hadn't much cared, but her mother had lied to her. Had lied to her for years.

Does knowing all that really change anything?

No, it didn't. She was still homeless. Still in this man's power. This man who'd known who she was all this time and hadn't told her. Who was planning to use her in some kind of twisted revenge plot.

It made her ache, made her furious, that all the heat and passion and wonder of the night before had been a lie. The joy she'd felt as he'd touched her as if she mattered was tainted.

He'd lied to her the way her mother had lied to her.

Bitterness and hurt threatened to overwhelm her, but she grabbed on to that thread of fury. Because fury was easier than pain every single time.

'So that's why you slept with me?' She fought to keep the pain from her voice. 'To make sure I'd do what I was told?'

Something flickered through his green eyes, though she didn't know what it was.

'No, sleeping with you was never the plan. I was going to make sure you trusted me and then I was going to put it to you as a business proposition. If you'd agree to marry me I would pay you a certain amount, and then in a few years we would divorce.'

'I see.' Carefully she drew the sheet around her, though it didn't help the numbness creeping through her. 'The sex was part of building trust, then?'

A muscle flicked in his jaw. 'That wasn't the intention.'

But it was clear that he wasn't unhappy that it had happened between them.

Of course he wasn't. It was another thing for him to use. And you thought you could trust him...

The cold in the pit of her stomach turned sharp, digging in, a jagged pain. She was a fool. The last person she'd trusted had been her mother and look how that had turned out. She'd thought after that she'd be more careful about who she gave her trust to, but apparently she'd learned nothing.

Though, really, what did it matter? The sex had been amazing, but so what? It was only sex and he wasn't different. He was a liar, like everyone else. And one thing was certain: he would never touch her again.

'Then what was your intention?' She was pleased with how level her voice was.

He stared at her for a long moment, his gaze unreadable. 'You're beautiful, Leonie. And I thought—'

'You thought, *Why not? A girl from the streets could be fun? Something a bit different.*'

Bitterness was creeping in now, which wasn't supposed to happen, so she forced it out.

'It doesn't matter,' she went on dismissively. 'It was a nice way to pass the evening.'

Shifting, she slid out of the bed, keeping the sheet

wrapped around her as she took a couple of steps towards him, then stopped.

'You didn't need to bother, though. If you'd asked me the night you picked me up if I wanted to help you get revenge on my father I would have said yes. Especially if you're going to pay me.'

Cristiano didn't move, but the line of his shoulders was tense, his jaw tight. His gaze was absolutely impenetrable.

'You have no loyalty to him, then?'

'Why should I? I barely remember him. Money is what I need now.'

There was silence as he stared at her and she couldn't tell what he was thinking.

'For what it's worth,' he said quietly, 'I slept with you last night because you're beautiful and I wanted you, Leonie. Because I couldn't stop myself.'

She hated him a little in that moment, and part of her wanted to throw it back in his face. But that would give away the fact that their night had mattered to her, and she didn't want him to know that. She didn't want him to know *anything*.

Last night she'd trusted him, but she certainly wasn't going to make that mistake again. His money, on the other hand, was a different story. She could buy herself a new life with money like that. Buy that little cottage in the country, where she'd live with the only person she trusted in the entire world: herself.

So all she did was lift a shoulder as if she didn't care and it didn't matter. 'Fine—but I want the money, Cristiano.'

His features hardened. 'Name your price.'

She thought of the most outrageous sum she could and said it out loud.

'It's yours,' he replied without hesitation.

'There's a condition,' she added.

His granite expression didn't change. 'Which is?'

'You can never touch me again.'

The muscle in the side of his jaw flicked, and there was a steady green glitter in his eyes. 'And if I don't like that condition?'

'Then I'll refuse to help you.'

He said nothing, and didn't move, but she could sense the fury rolling off him in waves. He didn't like her condition. Didn't like it one bit.

'I could make you change your mind.'

The words were more a growl than anything else, and the fighter in her wanted to respond to that challenge, relished it, even.

'Could you?' She gave him a very direct look. 'Why would you bother? I'm just a girl from the streets. You could get better with a snap of your fingers.'

'It's true, I could.' His gaze clashed with hers. 'But I don't want better. I want you.'

That shouldn't have touched her own anger, shouldn't have made it waver for even a second. But it did. Not that she was going to do anything about it. He was a liar, and even though that nagging pity for him still wound through her anger she ignored it.

'That's too bad.' And then, because she couldn't help herself, 'Feel free to try and change my mind if you can. But you won't be able to.'

The flame in his eyes blazed and he pushed himself away from the window, straightening to his full height.

A wild thrill shot straight down her spine. Oh, yes, challenge accepted.

'You shouldn't say things like that to men like me,' he murmured. 'But, fine, you'll have your money. You'll have to come to San Lorenzo with me if you want it, though. We'll be married in my family chapel.'

Leonie didn't think twice. She wanted the money—what did she care if she had to return to Spain to get it?

Are you sure it's a good idea to be near him?

Why wouldn't it be? She didn't care about him—not now. She didn't care about her father, either. Now all she cared about was the money, and she had no problem with using Cristiano the way he'd used her.

'Fine,' she said, shrugging. 'I don't care.'

'Good.' He moved, striding past her to the door of his bedroom without even a glance. 'Prepare to leave in an hour.'

And then he went out.

CHAPTER EIGHT

CRISTIANO FILLED THE flight to Spain with business. It was the only way to distract himself from the fact that Leonie was right there, sitting casually in one of his jet's luxurious leather seats, leafing through a magazine as if the night before and the morning after had all been just a passing encounter for her.

It was a performance worthy of himself.

It also drove him mad enough that he stayed on the phone even as the car they'd transferred to from the small airport where they'd landed wound its way through the sharp crags of the mountains on the road to San Lorenzo.

He could think of no other way to handle having her in his vicinity and not touching her.

Since she had no other clothes, she wore the black T-shirt and black trousers of his staff uniform, the small bag at her side containing only her old clothes and her useless phone—items she'd insisted on bringing with her for no reason that he could see.

He hadn't argued. She could bring them if she wanted to. He was planning on providing her with a proper wardrobe anyway, once they'd got to his estate, since if she was going to be his duchess he would need her to look the part.

But even that plain black uniform didn't stop memories of the night before rolling through him. Of her silken skin beneath his fingers, of the cries she'd made, of how tightly she'd gripped him as he'd slid inside her, of the look in her eyes as she'd stared up at him.

He'd told himself that the sex didn't matter, that it was physical, nothing more, and yet he couldn't get it out of his head. Couldn't get the memory of her white face as he'd told her the truth that he'd known who she was all this time out of his head, either.

He'd been right. Not only had he shocked her, he'd hurt her, too. She hadn't even known that her father thought she was dead. And what had been worse was the feeling that had swept through him as those big violet eyes had stared back at him in shock and betrayal. The need to go to the bed and sweep her into his arms had been strong. To hold her. Soothe her. Comfort her.

But he hadn't allowed himself to give in to those feelings. Instead he'd watched as his little *gatita* had drawn on some hidden core of strength, her pain and shock vanishing beneath her usual stubborn belligerence and an emotion he was all too familiar with.

Anger.

He'd hoped telling her the truth would make her aware of what kind of man he was and put some distance between them, and it had. He just hadn't expected to feel quite so disappointed about that—or disappointed in her demands. The money wasn't important—it wasn't an outrageous sum—it was the fact that she didn't want him to touch her again that he cared about. Which was especially enraging since he wasn't supposed to care.

Your emotions are involved with her whether you like it or not.

Yes, which meant he had to *un*-involve them.

Difficult when touching her was all he wanted to do.

The car wound through yet another green valley, with vineyards spread out on either side, almost to the foothills of the sharp, jagged mountains rising above them. But Cristiano wasn't watching the homeland he hadn't been to in years unroll before him. He was too busy watching the woman sitting beside him.

She had her head turned away, and was staring at the view outside. The sun was falling over the fine grain of her skin and turning her hair to fire.

Beautiful *gatita*.

He couldn't stop the sound of her voice replaying in his head, even huskier than it normally was, telling him how her mother had told her that her father hadn't wanted her, that he'd wanted a son instead.

Cristiano didn't know what to think about that, because it was certainly something that Victor de Riero had wanted. And maybe it had been true that Hélène couldn't have any more children. Maybe that had been part of the reason for de Riero targeting Anna. He'd wanted a new, more fertile wife for an heir.

'I thought he didn't look for me because he didn't care...'

A deep sympathy he didn't want to feel sat in his chest like a boulder, weighing him down. All those years she'd been on the streets, thinking herself unwanted. Where had Hélène been? Gone, it was clear, leaving Leonie to fend for herself. Alone.

He knew that feeling. He knew what it was to be alone. He'd had it all his childhood, as the only child of a man who'd cared more about his duties as duke than being a father, and a woman who'd preferred socialite parties to being a mother.

No wonder you scared Anna away. You were an endless well of need.

Cristiano dragged his gaze from Leonie and tried to concentrate on his phone call instead of the snide voice in his head.

Another reason not to care—as if he needed one. His emotions were destructive, and he had to make sure he stayed detached from them, which meant caring about Leonie wasn't something he should do.

He shouldn't give in to this sexual hunger, either, no matter how badly he wanted to. Letting one little kitten get the better of him just wasn't going to happen.

He leaned back in his seat, shifting slightly, uncomfortable with being so long in the car. Then he noticed that Leonie had tensed. Her gaze was flicking from the window to him, her hand lifting an inch from her thigh before coming down again. Colour crept into her cheeks as she turned towards the window again.

Interesting. So she was physically aware of him, perhaps as painfully as he was aware of her, which made sense. Because she'd loved everything he'd done to her and had answered his passion with her own fierce, untutored desire. A hunger like that, once released, didn't die. It burned for ever. She wouldn't be able to ignore it the way she had on the streets.

Cristiano didn't smile, but he allowed himself a certain satisfaction, filing away her response for future reference. Then he focused completely on his phone call as the car wound its way through another vineyard and then the tiny ancient village that had once been part of his estate. They moved on up into the mountains, and from there down a rocky, twisting driveway that led at last to the *castillo* he'd been born in.

The *castillo* he'd grown up in.

The big, empty *castillo* that had echoed with nothing but silence after his parents had been killed.

And that was your fault, too.

Cristiano tensed as the car cleared the trees and Leonie sat forward as the *castillo* came into view.

'You live here?' she asked, in tones of absolute astonishment. 'In a castle?'

It was literally a castle, built into the hillside. A medieval fortress that his warlord ancestors had held for centuries. Had it really been fifteen years since he'd been back?

After Anna had gone, and he'd lost his son, it had felt too big and too empty. It had reminded him of being seventeen once again, of losing his parents and walking the halls, feeling as if the silence and the guilt was pressing in on him. Crushing him.

After Anna, he hadn't been able to get out of the place fast enough, filling up his life with music and talk and laughter. With the sound of life.

A cold sensation sat in his gut as the car drew up on the gravel area outside the massive front doors. Why had he thought coming back was a good idea? He didn't want to go inside. The whole place had felt like a tomb the last time he'd been here and nothing would have changed.

Something's changed. You have Leonie.

She was already getting out of the car, walking towards the doors, looking up in open amazement at the *castillo* towering above her.

Ah, but he didn't have her, did he? She wasn't his. She'd made that very clear.

Still, if he was going to make her his duchess he

wanted it to happen on Velazquez ground, and he'd already sent messages to his PR company to let them know he'd be bringing his 'fiancée' back to his estate, and that more information would follow. They were naturally thrilled that the duke of San Lorenzo, infamous for his pursuit of pleasure, would be marrying again. The press would be ecstatic.

Gathering himself, Cristiano got out of the car and strolled after Leonie, letting none of his unease show. He'd called his staff here before he'd left Paris, telling them to prepare for his arrival, so everything should be in place.

Sure enough, they were greeted in the huge, vaulted stone entrance hall by one of his family's old retainers. The woman spoke a very old Spanish dialect that no one spoke outside the valley, and the memories it evoked made the cold inside him deepen.

He answered her in the same language, issuing orders while Leonie wandered around, looking up at the bare stone walls and the huge stone staircase that led to the upper levels. Portraits of his ancestors had been hung there. He'd always hated them—dark, gloomy paintings of stone-faced men and women who looked as if they'd never tasted joy in their entire lives and perhaps hadn't.

Leonie had started climbing the stairs to look at them and he walked slowly after her, the familiar cold oppressiveness of the ancient stones wrapping around him, squeezing him tight.

'Are these people your family?' she asked, staring at the portraits.

'Yes. Miserable bunch, aren't they?'

'They don't look that happy, no.' She frowned. 'But… they're so old. How long has your family been here?'

He climbed up a little way, then stopped one step below her, looking at her since that was better than looking at those ghastly portraits. She was all pale skin, bright hair and deep blue-violet eyes. Life and colour. Unlike these dim, dark portraits of people long dead.

'Centuries.' He thrust his hands in his pockets, his fingers itching to touch her. 'Since medieval times, if not before.'

'Wow...' she breathed, following the line of portraits on the walls. 'And what about this one?'

She pointed at the last picture, the most recent—though it didn't look like it, given it had been painted in the same dark, gloomy style. Her earlier anger at him seemed to have faded away, and interest was alight in her face.

Cristiano didn't look at the picture. He knew exactly which one it was. 'That one? Those are my parents. They were killed in a car accident when I was seventeen.'

She flicked him a glance, a crease between her brows. 'Oh. I'm sorry.'

It sounded almost as if she really meant it—not that he needed her sympathy. It had happened so long ago he barely remembered it.

That's why you can never escape the cold of this place. That's why you carry it around with you wherever you go. Because you can't remember how you tried to warm it up...

Cristiano shoved the thoughts away. 'It was a long time ago.'

'Your mother was pretty.' She leaned closer, studying the picture. 'Your father was handsome, too. But he looks a little...stern.'

'If by "stern" you mean aloof and cold, then, yes. He

was. And my mother was far more interested in parties than anything else.' He was conscious that he hadn't quite managed to hide the bitter note in his voice.

Leonie straightened and turned, studying his face. 'They weren't good parents?'

He didn't want to talk about this. 'What happened to Hélène, Leonie?' he asked instead. 'What happened to your mother?'

Her lashes fluttered; her gaze slid away. 'She left. I was sixteen. I came home from school one day and she was just…gone. She left me a note, saying she was leaving and not to look for her. But that was it.'

His fingers had curled into fists in his pockets, and that same tight sensation that Leonie always seemed to prompt was coiling in his chest. 'She just left? Without saying why?'

'Yes.' Leonie was looking down at the stairs now. 'I'll never know why.'

So. She'd effectively been abandoned by the one person in the world who should have looked after her. At sixteen.

'What did you do?' he asked quietly.

She lifted a shoulder. 'Eventually I was evicted from our apartment. No one seemed to notice I was gone.'

He felt as if a fist was closing around his ribs and squeezing, and he wanted to reach out, touch that petal-soft cheek. Tell her that he would have noticed. That he would have looked for her.

But then she glanced up at him again, a fierce expression in her eyes. 'Don't you dare pity me. I survived on my own quite well, thank you very much.'

'Survived, maybe,' he said. 'But life isn't just survival, Leonie.'

'It's better than being dead.'

Proud, stubborn girl.

'You should have had more than that.' This time it was his turn to study her. 'You deserved more than that.'

Colour flooded her pale cheeks, shock flickering in her eyes. 'Yes, well, I didn't get it. And you didn't answer my question.'

'No,' he said. 'Mine were not good parents.'

She blinked, as if she hadn't expected him to capitulate so quickly. 'Oh. Do you have brothers or sisters?'

'No.'

'So it was just you? All alone in this big castle by yourself?' There was a certain knowledge in her eyes, an understanding that he'd never thought he'd find in anyone else.

She knew loneliness—of course she did.

'Yes.' He lifted a shoulder. 'I was alone in this big castle by myself. This mausoleum was my inheritance.'

'Is that what it felt like? A mausoleum?'

'Don't you feel it?' He moved his gaze around the soaring ceilings and bare stone walls. 'All that cold stone and nothing but dead faces everywhere. I never come here if I can help it. In fact, I haven't been here in fifteen years.'

There was silence, but he could feel her looking at him, studying him like an archaeologist studying a dig site, excavating him.

'What happened here, Cristiano?'

That was his *gatita*. Always so curious and always so blunt.

'Do I really have to go into my long and tedious history?' he drawled. 'Don't you want to see where you're going to be sleeping?'

'No. And isn't your tedious history something I should know? Especially if I'm going to be marrying you.'

He looked at her. She was so small; she was on the stair above him but she was still only barely level with him. He didn't want to talk about this any more. He wanted his hands on her instead. He wanted her warmth melting away the relentless cold of this damn tomb.

'What is there to say?'

He kept his gaze on her, hiding nothing. Because she was right. She should know his history. So she knew what to be wary of.

'It was my seventeenth birthday, but my parents had some government party they had to attend. I was lonely. I was angry. And it was the second birthday in a row that they'd missed. So I took a match to my father's library and set it on fire.'

Leonie's gaze widened. 'What?'

'You think that's the worst part? It's not.' He smiled, but it was bitter. 'One of my father's staff called him to let him know the *castillo* was on fire. So he and my mother rushed back from the party. But he drove too fast and there was an accident. They were both killed.'

She hadn't understood until that moment why he so obviously hated this place, with its ancient stones and the deep silence of history. She'd thought it was wonderful— a fortress that no one could get into. A place of security and safety. She'd never been anywhere so fascinating and she wanted to explore it from top to bottom.

But it was clear that Cristiano did not feel the same. It was obvious in every line of him.

This man had used her, hurt her, and no matter that he'd said their night together had been because he'd wanted her, she couldn't forget her anger at him and what he'd done.

Yet that didn't stop the pulse of shock that went through her, or the wave of sympathy that followed hard on its heels.

There was self-loathing in his voice, a bitterness he couldn't hide, and she knew what that meant: he blamed himself for his parents' death.

No wonder he hated this place. No wonder he thought it was a tomb. For him, it was.

'You blame yourself,' she said. 'Don't you?'

He gave another of those bitter laughs. 'Of course I blame myself. Who else is there? No one else started a fire because he couldn't handle his anger.'

Her heart tightened. Although their stations in life were so far removed from each other that the gulf between them might have been the distance from the earth to the sun, they were in fact far closer than she'd realised.

He'd lost people the same as she had.

'For years after Mamá left I blamed myself,' she said. 'I thought that maybe it was something I'd done that had made her leave. Perhaps I'd asked too many questions, disobeyed her too many times. Nagged her for something once too often.' Her throat closed unexpectedly, but she forced herself to go on. 'Or...been a girl instead of a boy.'

The bitter twist to his mouth vanished. 'Leonie—' he began.

But she shook her head. 'No, I haven't finished. What I'm trying to say is that in the end I didn't know why she'd left. I'll never know, probably. And I could have chosen to let myself get all eaten up about what I did or didn't do, or I could accept that it was her choice to leave.' Leonie stared at him. 'She didn't have to leave.

I didn't make her. She choose that. Just like your father chose to return here.'

Cristiano's expression hardened. 'Of course he had to return. His son had just set fire to the—'

'No, he didn't,' she interrupted. 'He could have got a staff member to handle it. He could have decided he wasn't fit to drive and had your mother drive instead. He could have called you. But he didn't do any of those things. He chose to drive himself.'

Cristiano said nothing. He was standing on the step below her but still he was taller than she was, all broad shoulders and hard muscle encased in the dark grey wool of his suit. He wasn't wearing a tie, and the neck of his black shirt was open, exposing the smooth olive skin of his throat and the steady pulse that beat there.

She didn't know why she wanted to help him so badly—not after he'd hurt her the way he had. But she couldn't help it. She knew loneliness and grief, and she knew anger, too, and so much of what had happened to him had also happened to her.

'You are very wise, *gatita*,' he said at last, roughly. 'Where did you learn such wisdom?'

'There's not much to do on the streets but think.'

'In between all the surviving you had to do?' A thread of faint, wry amusement wound through his beautiful voice.

You deserved more than that...

A shiver chased over her skin. He'd said it as if he meant it, as if he truly believed that she had. But why would she trust what he said about anything?

'Yes,' she said blankly, her gaze caught and drawn relentlessly to the pulse at the base of his throat once again. 'In between all that.'

She'd put her mouth over that pulse the night before. She'd tasted his skin and the beat of his heart, had run her hands over all that hard muscle and raw male power.

A throb of hunger went through her.

She'd spent most of the day trying to ignore his physical presence. She'd thought it would be easy enough to do since he'd ignored her, spending all his time on the phone. She'd been fascinated by all the new sights and sounds as they'd left Paris and flown to Spain, so that had made it easier.

But despite that—despite how she should have been concentrating on her return to her long-forgotten homeland—all she'd been conscious of was him. Of his deep, authoritative voice on the plane as he'd talked on his phone. Of his hard-muscled thigh next to hers in the car. Of the spice of his aftershave and the heat in his long, powerful body.

And she'd realised that she might ignore him all she liked, but that didn't change her hunger for him, or her innate female awareness of him as a man. It couldn't be switched off. It pulsed inside her like a giant heartbeat, making her horribly conscious that her declaration of how she wasn't going to let him touch her again had maybe been a little shortsighted.

That was another thing she hadn't understood before, yet did now. Sexual hunger hadn't ever affected her, so she'd imagined that refusing him would be easy. But it wasn't, and she felt it acutely now as he stood there staring at her, his jungle-green eyes holding her captive. As if he knew exactly what she was thinking.

Her heartbeat accelerated, the ache of desire pulsed between her thighs, and she knew her awareness of him was expanding, deepening.

He wasn't just a powerful and physically attractive man. He was also a man who seemed not to care about very much at all on the surface, yet who burned on the inside with a terrible all-consuming rage. And a rage like that only came from deep caring, from a man with a wounded heart who'd suffered a terrible loss.

At least after the deaths of his parents he'd been able to grieve. But how could he grieve a child who wasn't dead? Who was still alive and who had no idea that Cristiano was his father?

He hasn't grieved. Why do you think he's so angry?

'You'd better stop looking at me that way, *gatita*,' he murmured. 'You'll be giving me ideas.'

She ignored that, feeling her own heart suddenly painful in her chest. 'I'm sorry about your parents,' she said. But she wanted him to know that although his son might not be aware of Cristiano, she was. And that she acknowledged what the loss had meant for him. 'And I'm so sorry about your son.'

A raw emerald light flared in the duke's eyes. That wry amusement dropped away, his whole posture tightening. 'Do not speak of it.' His voice vibrated with some intense, suppressed emotion.

She didn't want to cause him pain, yet all of a sudden she wanted him to know that she understood. That she felt for him. And that to a certain extent she shared his loss—because she, too, had lost people she'd once felt something for: her mother and her father.

So she lifted a hand, thinking to reach out and touch him, having nothing else to give him but that.

'No, Leonie,' he ordered.

The word was heavy and final, freezing her in place. 'I have respected your wishes by not touching you, but don't think for one moment that it doesn't go both ways. Not when all I can think about is having you on these stairs right now, right here.'

Her heart thudded even louder. He had respected her wishes. He hadn't made one move towards her. And she... Well, she'd never thought that even though he'd broken her fledgling trust she'd still want him—and quite desperately.

So have him. It doesn't have to mean anything.

It didn't. And now there were no secrets between them, no trust to break, it could be just sex, nothing more. After all, she'd been denied so many good things—why should she deny herself this?

He'd told her she deserved better and he was certainly better than anything she'd ever had. So why couldn't she have him?

She lifted her hand and, holding his gaze, very deliberately placed her fingertips against the line of his hard jaw, feeling the prickle of hair and the warm silk of his skin.

'Then take me,' she said softly.

He was completely still for long moments, unmoving beneath her hand. But his eyes burned with raw green fire.

'Once you change your mind there will be no coming back from it, do you understand me?' His voice was so deep, so rough. The growl of a beast. 'This is the place of my ancestors, and if I have you here that makes you mine.'

He was always trying to warn her, to frighten her. Letting her see the fire burning in the heart of the man he was beneath the veneer of a bored playboy. But Leonie had never been easily frightened. And the man behind that veneer, with his anger, his passion and his pain, was far more fascinating to her than the playboy ever had been.

She wanted that man. And she wasn't frightened of him. After all, she'd always wanted to be someone's. She might as well be his.

'Then I'll be yours,' she said simply.

Cristiano didn't hesitate. Reaching out, he curled his fingers around the back of her neck and pulled her in close, his mouth taking hers in a kiss that scoured all thought from her head. He kissed her hungrily, feverishly, his tongue pushing deep into her mouth and taking charge of her utterly.

But his wasn't the only hunger.

Desire leapt inside her and she put her hands on his chest, sliding them up and around his neck, threading her fingers in the thick black silk of his hair and holding on tight. She kissed him back the way she had the night before, as hard and demanding as he was, showing him her teeth and her claws by biting him.

He growled deep in his throat. His hands were on her hips, pushing her down onto the cold stone of the stairs so she was sitting on one step while he knelt on the one below her.

He didn't speak, making short work of the fastenings of her trousers and then stripping them off her, taking her underwear with them. The stone was icy under her bare skin, but she didn't care. She was burning up. Everywhere he touched felt as if it was being licked by flame.

His mouth ravaged hers, nipping and biting at her bottom lip before moving down her neck to taste the hollow of her throat. She sighed, her head falling back as he cradled the back of it in his palm. His hand slid between her bare thighs, stroking and teasing, finding her slick and hot for him.

Leonie moaned, desperate for more pressure, more friction. Desperate for more of him.

And it seemed he felt the same, because there were no niceties today, no slow, gentle seduction. He ripped open the front of his trousers, his hands falling away from her as he grabbed for his wallet and dealt with the issue of protection. Then his hot palms were sliding beneath her buttocks, lifting her, positioning her, before he pushed into her in a hard, deep thrust.

The edge of the stair above her was digging into her back. She didn't care, though, was barely conscious of it as she gasped aloud, staring up into his face. Again, he was nothing but a predator, his eyes glittering with desire, his sensual mouth drawn into a snarl as he drew his hips back and thrust again.

All she could see was that hot stare and the possessive fire in it, and it twisted the pleasure tighter, harder. She wanted to be possessed. She wanted to be taken. And she wanted to take in return. Because, as much as he wanted her to be his, she wanted something to call her own.

He could be that for you.

Her heart slammed against her ribs and she curled her legs around his lean waist, holding him tightly to her, forgetting how he'd hurt her, how he'd lied to her in that moment.

'You could be mine, too,' she whispered hoarsely as he thrust into her again, making her gasp in pleasure. 'You could be, Cristiano.'

He didn't reply, but the fire in his eyes climbed higher. His fingers curled into her hair, protecting her head from the hard stone of the stairs, but he gave her no mercy from the brutal thrust of his hips. As if he could impress himself into her. As if he was trying to make her part of the stones of the castle itself.

And beneath the passion she could feel his need, could sense it in some deep part of her heart. The need for touch and warmth and connection. So she gave it to him, wrapping herself around him, and he took it, holding tight to her as he gave her the most intense pleasure in return.

It didn't take long.

He grabbed one her hands and guided her own fingers between her thighs, holding it down over that tight, aching bundle of nerves. And then he thrust again, deeper, harder, as he held her fingers there until the desperation inside her exploded into ecstasy and the entrance hall rang with the sounds of her cries.

She was hardly aware of his own growl as he followed her, murmuring her name roughly against her neck.

For long moments afterwards she didn't want to move, quite happy to sit on the cold stone of the stairs, with Cristiano's heat warming her through. But then he was shifting, withdrawing from her, dealing with the aftermath. Only after that was done did he reach for her, gathering her up into his arms and holding her close against his chest as he climbed the rest of the way up the stairs.

He carried her down a long and echoing stone corridor and into a room with a massive four-poster bed pushed against one wall. There he stripped her naked, put her down on it, and proceeded to make her forget her own name.

CHAPTER NINE

CRISTIANO FINISHED UP the phone call he was on with his PR people then leaned back in the old hand-carved wooden chair that sat behind his father's massive antique desk, reflecting once again on how hideously uncomfortable it was.

His father had liked the chair—his father had liked all the heavy old wooden furniture in the ducal study—but Cristiano had already decided that the chair had to go. Especially if he was going to make his home here—and he was certainly considering it.

The *castillo* was different with Leonie in it. She'd spent the past week investigating every corner of the ancient stones, exclaiming over things like the deep window seat in the library that could be enclosed when the heavy velvet curtains were drawn. Like the big bathroom that had been modernised to a point, but still retained a giant round bath of beaten copper. The cavernous dining room, where he'd had many a silent dinner with his parents, now filled up with Leonie's questions about the history of the estate and the *castillo* itself. Like the tapestries on the walls and the huge kitchen fireplace that was large enough to roast a whole cow in and probably had. The courtyard with the overgrown rose garden, the orchard full of orange trees, and the meadow beyond where he'd used to play as a child, pretending he had brothers and sisters to play with him.

But those memories seemed distant now—especially now he'd created new ones. Memories that were all about her laughter, her husky voice, her bright smile. Her cries of pleasure. Her bright hair tangled in his fingers and her warmth as he took her in yet another of those old, cold rooms.

He'd even taken her in that window seat in the library, and the memories of books flaming and shelves burning as bright as his anger were buried under flames and heat of a different kind.

It was better—much better. And the castle didn't feel so cold any more, or so silent. In fact, it felt as if summer had come to stay in the halls, making the place seem warmer and so much brighter than he remembered.

He was even considering staying on here with her after the wedding—and why not? She would be his wife, after all, and now they were spending every night, not to mention quite a few days, exploring the chemistry between them, it seemed only logical to indulge in a honeymoon, as it were. Maybe even beyond that.

He'd thought about the possibility of having an heir with her and tainting that precious de Riero bloodline even before they'd left Paris, and the idea certainly still held its appeal. He could create a home here with her. Create a family the way Victor de Riero had created a family.

You really want to have another child?

Something jolted inside him, a kind of electric shock, and he had to push himself out of his chair and take a couple of steps as restlessness coiled tight through his muscles.

Another child...

Intellectually, the idea was a sound one, and it would certainly make his revenge all the sweeter—so why did the thought make him feel as if ice was gathering in the pit of his stomach?

'I'm so sorry about your son...'

The memory of Leonie's voice on the stairs drifted back to him, the sound husky with emotion, her eyes full of a terrible sympathy, bringing with it another hard, electric jolt.

It had felt as if she was cutting him open that day, and he'd told her not to speak of it before he'd been able to stop himself. Before he'd been able to pretend that the thought of his child no longer had the power to hurt him.

So much for detachment.

His hands dropped into fists at his sides and he took a slow breath.

Yes, he could recognise that the thought of having another child was difficult for him, but he also had to recognise that this situation was different. Any child he had with Leonie would be born in pursuit of his revenge, nothing more. It would not be for him. Which meant it was perfectly possible for him to remain detached.

He would simply choose not to involve himself with any such child, and that would be better for the child, too. Certainly he wouldn't love it—not when love led to nothing but pain and destruction. The cost of love had been too high the first time; he wouldn't pay it again.

At that moment the heavy wooden door of the study burst open and he turned to find Leonie sweeping in, a blur of shimmering white silk and silvery lace, her hair in a loose, bright cascade down her back. She came to a stop in front of him, her cornflower-blue eyes alight with excitement, and put her hands on her hips.

'Well?' she asked. 'What do you think of this?'

He stared, all thoughts of children vanishing, his chest gone tight.

She was wearing a wedding gown. It was strapless, the gleaming white silk bodice embroidered with silver and cupping her breasts deliciously. Then it narrowed down to her small waist before sweeping outwards in a white froth of silky skirts and silver lace.

She looked beautiful—a princess from a fairy-tale or a queen about to be crowned.

'You forgot, didn't you?' she said as he stared at her in stunned silence. 'The designer's here with a few of the dresses we picked last week.'

He *had* forgotten. He and Leonie had sat down the previous week to choose a gown for her—not that he'd been overly interested in the details of the wedding, since it was the revenge that mattered. But Leonie had been excited, and had enjoyed choosing a gown for herself, and he'd surprised himself by enjoying helping her, too.

'So I see.' He tried to calm his racing heartbeat, unable to take his eyes off her. 'I'm not supposed to see the final gown before the wedding, am I?'

'Well, it's your revenge. I thought you might want to make sure the dress is…' she did a small twirl, the gown flaring out around her '…revengey enough.'

Her excitement and pleasure were a joy, and yet they only added to that tight sensation in his chest—the one he hadn't asked for and didn't want, and yet had been there since the night he'd picked her up off the street.

He fought it, tried to ignore it. 'You like it, don't you?'

She smiled, her expression radiant, her hands smoothing lovingly over the silk. 'I love it. I've never had anything so pretty or that's felt so lovely.'

She'd been like this over the past couple of weeks as he'd bought clothes and other personal items to add to her meagre stock of belongings, greeting each new thing with a thrilled delight that was immensely gratifying. And it didn't matter whether it was expensive or not—the fact that she had something of her own seemed to be the most important thing.

It made sense. She'd literally had nothing when he'd found her that night on the streets of Paris except for a very old cellphone and some dirty clothes. Now she had a wardrobe full of items she'd chosen with great care herself and a new phone, not to mention shoes and underwear and perfume and lots of other pretty girly things.

But he hadn't felt like this when he'd given her those things and she'd smiled at him. Not like he did now, with her so radiantly lovely in a wedding gown, full of excitement and joy. He hadn't felt as if he couldn't breathe… as if the world was tilting on its axis and he was going to slide right off.

All he could think about was the day they'd arrived here and how he'd told her that once he took her here, in the place of his ancestors, she'd be his. And how she'd surrendered to him as if she'd never wanted to be anyone else's, all the while whispering to him that he was hers, too.

You want to be hers.

No, he didn't. He couldn't be anyone's—just as he couldn't have anything that was his. Not any more. Not when he couldn't trust himself and his destructive emotions. And this tight feeling in his chest, the way he couldn't breathe...

You're falling for her.

Absolutely not. He had to stay detached and uninvolved. Keep it all about revenge. Because that, in the end, was the whole point of this charade: a cold and emotionless revenge against the man who'd taken his wife and son from him.

Which meant he had to keep his emotions out of it.

Yet still he couldn't stop himself from touching her, reaching out to brush his fingers over the lace of her bodice, watching as her eyes darkened with the passion that always burned so near the surface. She was always ready for him. She never denied him.

'You are beautiful, *gatita*,' he murmured. 'You are perfect in every way.'

She flushed adorably, giving him a little smile. 'Thank you.' Then that smile faded, a look of concern crossing her face. 'Are you all right?'

How she'd picked up on his unease he had no idea, because he was sure he'd hidden it. Then again, she was incredibly perceptive. Too perceptive in many ways.

'What? I can't give my fiancée a compliment without my health being questioned?' he asked, keeping his voice casual. 'Whatever is the world coming to?'

She didn't smile. 'Cristiano...'

The tight thing in his chest tightened even further, like a fist. 'You know this will be a proper marriage, don't you?' They hadn't had this conversation and they needed to. It might as well be now. 'You'll be my wife in every way?'

'Yes,' she replied without hesitation. 'You made that clear.'

'I will want children, too.'

This time her gaze flickered. 'Oh.'

'It makes my revenge even more perfect, *gatita*. Don't you see? He took my son and I will have another with his daughter.'

An expression he couldn't catch rippled over her face, then abruptly her lashes lowered, veiling her gaze. 'I do see, yes.' Her tone was utterly neutral.

He stared down at the smooth, silky curve of her cheek and the brilliant colour of her lashes resting against her pale skin. She seemed a little less bright now, her excitement dimming, disappearing.

'You don't like the idea of children?' he asked.

'No. I just…just hadn't thought of them before.'

He couldn't blame her. She was young, and probably hadn't considered a future with a family. But still, he didn't think it was surprise she was trying to hide from him—and she was definitely hiding something.

Reaching out, he took her chin between his thumb and forefinger and tilted her face up so he could look into her eyes. 'This bothers you. Why?'

She made no attempt to pull away, her violet gaze meeting his. 'You'd really want another child? After what happened with your son?'

Ah, she never shied away from the difficult questions, did she?

'It will be different this time.' He stroked her chin gently with his thumb, unable to resist the feel of her satiny skin. 'Because the child won't be for me. The child will be for the pleasure of seeing Victor de Riero's face when I tell him he will have a Velazquez grandchild.'

That way he could retain his distance. He'd never have to feel what he'd felt for his son for another child again. Never have to experience the pain of another loss. Anger was the only emotion he could allow himself to have.

Some expression he couldn't name shifted in her eyes. 'That's a terrible reason to have a child, Cristiano.'

The flat note of accusation in her voice burrowed like a knife between his ribs, making him realise how cold and callous he'd sounded.

He let go of her chin, felt the warmth of her skin lingering against his fingertips. 'Too bad. That's the only reason I'll ever have another.'

Cold and callous it would have to be. He couldn't afford anything else.

'Revenge…' The word echoed strangely off the stone walls of the room, her gaze never leaving his. 'Don't you want more than that?'

Something inside him dropped away, while something else seemed to claw its way up. Longing. The same kind of longing that had gripped him the day he'd taken her on the staircase of this *castillo*. The need for her touch, for the feel of her skin and the taste of her mouth. The heat of her body burning out the cold.

The need for *her*.

He couldn't allow that. Need had caused him more pain than anything else ever had, so he'd cut it out of his life. Successfully. He had no desire to let it back in again.

'No.' He kept his voice cold. 'I don't.'

But she only looked at him in that direct, sharp way. Seeing beneath the armour of the playboy duke that he wore, seeing the man beneath it. The desperate, lonely man…

'Yes, you do,' she said quietly. 'Would it really be so bad? To let yourself have more?'

Ah, his *gatita*. She couldn't leave well enough alone, could she? She should really learn when to stop pushing.

'I had more once,' he said. 'And I lost it. I do not want it again.'

Those big violet eyes searched his. 'Because of your son? Because of Anna?'

He should have laughed. Should have lifted a shoulder and made a joke. Should have closed the distance between them and put his hands on her, distracted her the way he knew so well how to do.

But he didn't do any of those things. He turned away from her instead and moved around his desk. 'I told you before—do not speak of them. They have nothing to do with our wedding.'

He sat down in his father's uncomfortable chair, ignoring the way his heart was beating, ignoring the pain that had settled in his heart for absolutely no reason that he could see.

'Now, if there's nothing else, I have some work to do.'

Except Leonie didn't move. She just stood there in the lovely gown, looking at him. Sympathy in her eyes. 'It wasn't your fault, Cristiano. What happened with my father and Anna…with your son.'

The knife between his ribs sank deeper, pain rippling outwards, and he found he was gripping the arms of the chair so hard his knuckles were white. 'I told you. Do not—'

'You were young and you didn't know.' Leonie was suddenly standing right in front of his desk, that terrible piercing gaze of hers on him. 'You were used. You were betrayed by someone you thought you could trust.' There was blue flame burning in her eyes, conviction in her voice. 'And you had every right—*every right*—to be angry.'

'No,' he heard himself say hoarsely, and then he was on his feet, his hands in fists, fury flooding through him. 'Maybe I did have every right, but I should have controlled it. Controlled myself. I barged into that party, shouting like a monster, and I scared my son, Leonie. I *terrified* him. And he ran straight to Victor as if I was the devil himself.'

His jaw ached, his every muscle stiff with tension, and he wanted to stop talking but the words kept on coming.

'I would have taken him, too. I would have ripped him from Victor's arms if Anna hadn't stopped me. If she hadn't thrown herself in front of Victor and told me that this was why she'd left me. Because I terrified her.'

Leonie was coming, moving around the side of the desk towards him, and he shoved the chair back, wanting to put some distance between them. But she was there before he could move, reaching out to cup his face between her small hands.

'You're *not* to blame,' she insisted, her voice vibrating with fierce emotion. 'That man—my *father*—' she spat the word as if it were poison '—took your son from you. He seduced your wife from you. He had no right. And it was *not* your fault. Just like the deaths of your parents weren't your fault.'

The fire in her eyes was all-consuming, mesmerising.

'Just like it wasn't my fault my mother left and my father just accepted I was dead and never once looked for confirmation.'

Her grip held him still, her conviction almost a physical force.

'You were angry because you cared about him, Cristiano. And, yes, caring hurts—but wouldn't you rather have had the pain than feel nothing for him? Than for all of that to have meant nothing at all?'

He couldn't move. He was held in place by her hands on him. By the passion and fierce anger that burned in her lovely face. Passion that burned for *him*.

His world tilted again and he was falling right off the face of it. And there was no one to hold on to but her.

Cristiano reached for her, hauled her close. And crushed her mouth beneath his.

Leonie was shaking as Cristiano kissed her, sliding her hands down the wall of his rock-hard chest, curling her fingers into his shirt, holding on to him.

She hadn't meant to confront him. Hadn't meant to hurt him. But she knew she *had* hurt him. She'd seen the flare of agony in his green eyes as she'd mentioned his son, had heard the harsh rasp of it in his beautiful voice as he'd told her that he'd lost what he'd had. And so, no, he didn't want more.

But he'd lied. Of course he wanted more. She felt his longing every time he touched her, every time he pushed inside her. It was there in the demanding way he kissed her, in the brutal rhythm of his hips as he claimed her, stamping his possession on her. In the way he said her name when he came, and in the way he held her so tightly afterwards, as if he didn't want her to get away.

That was fine with her; she loved the way he wanted her. But she hadn't understood why he kept denying that was what he wanted until now. Until he'd tried to end the conversation.

It had all become clear to her then.

Of course he didn't want more. Because he blamed

himself for the loss of his wife and child and he thought he didn't deserve more.

She'd told him that day on the stairs that he wasn't responsible for his parents' death, but it was clear that he hadn't taken that on board. That the guilt he was carrying around extended to the loss of his son.

And she didn't know why, but his pain had felt like a knife in her own heart.

She hadn't been able to stop the fierce anger that had risen inside her on his behalf, the fierce need to make him understand that he didn't have to take responsibility for what had happened because it wasn't his fault. None of it was.

He might act as if he was frightening, as if he was bad, but he wasn't. There was nothing about him that was cruel or mean or petty. That was violent or bullying. He was simply a man whose emotions ran fathoms deep and so very strong. A man who'd lost so very much.

She couldn't bear to see him hurt.

He gripped her tight, lifting her, then turning to put her on the desk, ravaging her mouth as he did so. She spread her legs, dropping her hands to his lean hips to pull him closer, the fall of her skirts getting in the way.

'Leonie,' he said hoarsely against her mouth. 'Not like this, *gatita*. Not again.'

'But I—'

He laid a finger across her mouth and she was stunned to feel it tremble lightly against her lips. His eyes had darkened, the green almost black.

'I want to savour you, *mi corazón*. I don't want to be a beast today.'

'I like the beast,' she murmured.

But that was all he gave her a chance to say, because

then his mouth was on hers again, his hands moving down the bodice of the beautiful wedding gown, his fingers shaping her through the fabric, cupping her breasts gently in his palms.

She shivered, because there was something reverent in his touch that hadn't been there before. As if she was a work of art that he had to be careful in handling.

You're not a work of art. You're dirt from the streets—don't forget.

No, she didn't believe it. And she didn't feel it, either—not as his kiss turned gentle, teasing.

The passion between them that normally flared hot and intense had become more focused, more deliberate, settling on delicacy and tenderness rather than mastery.

He tasted her mouth, exploring it lightly before brushing his lips over her jaw and down the side of her neck in a trail of kisses and gentle nips that had her shuddering in his hands. He didn't speak but he didn't need to; the reverent way he touched her made it clear. He'd said he wanted to savour her and that was exactly what he was doing.

He unzipped the gown and slid it down her body, lifting her up so he could get it off her, then laying it carefully over the desk. He turned back to her and pushed her down over the polished wood, so she was lying across the desk next to her gown.

Slowly, carefully, he stripped her underwear from her, his fingers running lightly over every curve, and with each touch she felt something inside her shift and change. She had become something else…something more. Not the dirty, unwanted girl from the streets but someone treasured. Someone precious.

His hands swept down her body, stroking, caressing,

as if she was beautiful, wanted, worth taking time over. And, perhaps for the first time in her life, Leonie actually felt that. Tears prickled behind her lids, her throat was tight, but she didn't fight the sensations or the emotions that came along with them, letting them wash through her as he touched her, as if his hands were sweeping them away for good.

He kissed his way down her body, teasing her nipples with his tongue, then drawing them inside the heat of his mouth, making her arch and gasp. His hands stroked her sides and then moved further down, along her thighs. With each caress the dirt of the streets fell away, and with it the cold loneliness and the isolation.

She would have let him touch her for ever if she could, but soon her entire body was trembling and she wanted more from him than gentle touches. She sat up, pushed her hands beneath his shirt, stroking the hard, chiselled muscles of his stomach, glorying in the heat of his skin. Glorying too in the rough curse he gave as she dropped one hand to the fastenings of his trousers and undid them, slipping her hand inside, curling her fingers around his shaft.

'Ah, *gatita*...' he murmured roughly, letting her stroke him. 'You should let me finish proving my point.'

'Which is...?' She looked up into his green eyes, losing herself in the heat that burned there. 'That you're not a beast? I know that already.'

'No. My point is that you're worth savouring.'

'Well, so are you.' She ran her fingers lightly along the length of him, loving how he shuddered under her touch. 'You're not the only one worth taking time over.'

His gaze darkened. *'Mi corazón...'*

He didn't believe her, did he?

'Here,' she said thickly. 'Let me show you.'

And she pushed at him so he shifted back, then slid off his desk to stand before him, going up on her tiptoes to kiss the strong column of his neck and then further down, tasting the powerful beat of the pulse at his throat. Then she undid the buttons of his shirt, running her fingers down his sculpted torso, tracing all those hard-cut muscles before dropping to her knees in front of him.

Her hands moved to part the fabric of his trousers, to grasp him and take out the long, hard length of him. And then she closed her mouth around him.

His hands slid into her hair and he gave a rough groan, flexing his hips. He tasted so good, a little salty and musky, and she loved the way she could make his breath catch and his body shake. But she also loved giving him pleasure—because if she deserved to feel wanted and treasured, then he did, too.

So she showed him, worshipping him with her mouth until he finally pulled her head away, picking her up in his arms and taking her over to the butter-soft leather couch under the window. He laid her down on it, dealt with protection, then spread her thighs, positioning himself. And when he pushed inside her it felt like a homecoming, a welcome rather than something desperate and hungry.

He didn't move at first, and she lost herself in the green of his eyes and the feel of him inside her, filling her. There was a rightness to this. A sense of wholeness. As if she'd been waiting for this moment, for him, her entire life.

You're in love with him.

Something shifted in her chest, a heavy weight, and it made her go hot and cold both at the same time. Made her dizzy and hungry, bursting with happiness and aching with despair all at once.

Was what she felt love? How would she know? No one had ever given her love. She'd never even contemplated it before.

Yet the hot, powerful thing inside her, pushing at her, was insistent, and she had no other name for it. And it was all centred on him. On his beautiful face and the heat in his eyes. On his smile and the dark, sexy sound of his laughter. On the way he touched her, the way he made her feel. As if she wasn't broken or dirty, but beautiful and full of light. A treasure, precious and wanted.

He began to move inside her and she couldn't look away. The feeling suffusing her entire body was making her ache. She'd never known till that moment that pain could have a sweet edge.

Words stuck in her throat. Part of her wanted to tell him. Yet something held her back.

'I had more. And I lost it.'

And she was simply a replacement for what he'd lost, wasn't she? A handy vehicle for his revenge. He pitied her and wanted her, that was clear, but that was all she was to him.

Why don't you just ask him?

But she didn't want to ask him. She would lose this moment, and the moment was all she'd ever had. The moment was all there was.

So she ignored the heavy feeling in her heart, in her soul, and pulled his mouth down on hers. Losing herself to his heat and his kiss and the pleasure he could give her and letting the future take care of itself.

CHAPTER TEN

CRISTIANO WAITED IN a small side room in the ancient chapel that had once been part of the Velazquez estate. Many of his ancestors had been christened and married in this same place, before making their final journey from there to the small cemetery at the back.

He'd waited for a bride here before, his heart beating fast with happiness and excitement as he'd watched through the window for her arrival.

Today, although he was waiting for another bride, it wasn't her he was watching for, and he felt neither excitement nor happiness. He felt cold, and a bone-deep anger was the only thing warming him as he watched for de Riero.

Initially there had been some doubt as to whether the man would accept the invitation, but curiosity and perhaps a chance to gloat had clearly won out, because he'd passed on his acceptance to one of Cristiano's staff.

Guests were already streaming in, and journalists were gathering as per his instructions to his PR people. He wanted as many news media people there as possible to record the moment when he would lift Leonie's veil and reveal her for the first time. To record Victor's face when he realised that it was his daughter standing at the altar.

The daughter who was supposed to be dead.

The daughter who was now his hated enemy's bride.

The daughter who doesn't deserve this pettiness.

Cristiano gritted his teeth, shifting restlessly as he watched the guests enter the chapel.

It wasn't pettiness. It was necessary. How else was he to deal with losing everything that had ever meant something to him?

Doesn't she also mean something to you?

The memory of Leonie's touch wound through him. Not her mouth on him, but her hands cupping his face. That fierce, passionate gaze staring up into his, telling him that none of it was his fault. As if it was vitally important to her that he understand that. As if *he* was important to her.

His hands closed into fists as he gazed sightlessly through the window.

No, he couldn't think about this—about her. It was vital his emotions stay out of it. The important thing was that he was very close to finally getting the satisfaction he craved from de Riero—payback for the agony he had caused him—and nothing was going to stop him from getting it.

And after that?

Cristiano ignored the thought, focusing instead on the long black car that now drew up in the gravel parking area outside the chapel and the tall man that got out of it.

De Riero.

Cristiano began to smile.

And then de Riero turned as another person got out of the car. A tall, gangly teenager with a shock of black hair. De Riero said something and the boy straightened up, looking sullen. Then he reached to adjust the boy's tie, and he must have said something else because the boy lost his sullen look, grinning reluctantly.

An arrow of pure agony pierced Cristian's heart.

His son.

He couldn't move, couldn't tear his gaze away. He purposely hadn't looked at any pictures of the boy, or read any news stories about him. He'd simply pretended that the child had never existed.

But he did exist. And now he was here. And he was tall, handsome. He'd grow into those shoulders one day, just as he'd grow into his confidence, and then the world would be his oyster. He'd be a credit to his parents…

But Cristiano would not be one of those parents.

Pain spread outwards inside him, a grief he wasn't prepared for. Why had de Riero brought the boy? To gloat? To rub salt in the wound? As a shield? Why?

And then another person got out of the car—a woman with dark hair in a dark blue dress. Anna.

She came to stand by her son, smiling up at him, saying something to both him and de Riero that made them laugh. De Riero put a hand at the small of her back and leaned in to kiss her cheek while Anna's hand rested on her son's shoulder.

Something else hit Cristiano with all the force of a quarrel shot from a crossbow.

They were happy.

His son was happy.

You will destroy that. Publicly.

Realisation washed over him like a bucket of ice water and he found himself turning from the window and striding into the middle of the room, his hands in fists.

Anger was a torch blazing inside him. Of course de Riero had brought the boy. Yes, he *was* here as a shield—

to protect de Riero against anything Cristiano might do. The coward. Well, he was mistaken. This wedding would go ahead, and Cristiano would parade his daughter in front of him, and...

In front of your son.

Cristiano took a breath, then another, adrenaline pumping through him, anger and bitterness gathering in his throat, choking him.

He couldn't stop thinking about it—about what would happen when Leonie was revealed. What de Riero would do and, more importantly, what his son would do. Did he know he had a stepsister? If he did, how would he react to the knowledge that she wasn't dead, but alive? And if he didn't what would he think about the fact that his so-called father hadn't told him?

That happiness you saw outside... You will destroy it. In front of the world.

The breath caught in his throat, an arrow reaching his heart.

He couldn't do it.

He couldn't destroy his son's happiness.

He'd already done it once before, when the boy had been small, frightening him and sending straight into de Riero's arms. He couldn't do it again.

And all the revenge in the world wouldn't give him back what he'd lost. That was gone. For ever.

Love. That was the problem. That had *always* been the problem.

He'd loved his parents and, no matter what Leonie said, that love had destroyed them. He'd loved Anna once, and had nearly destroyed her. And this love he had for his son—well, now he was on the brink of nearly destroying him, too.

This revenge wasn't cold. It burned like the sun and that was unacceptable.

Love. He was done with it.

And Leonie? What about her?

Yes, she was another casualty of his caring. He'd drawn her into his orbit and kept her there—a tool he could use, a weapon he could wield against Victor de Riero.

Lovely, generous, passionate Leonie, who didn't deserve the use he'd put her to.

Who deserved so much more than being tied to man who only saw her only as something he could use.

He was selfish and he'd hurt her. And he would keep on hurting her. Because that was all he knew how to do.

Hurting people was all he ever did.

Certainty settled down inside him, along with a bone-deep pain and regret. He should never have picked her up off the street and taken her home. Or at least he should have found her a place to live and a job far away from him, where she would have been able to create the kind of life she wanted, not be dragged into his own self-centred plans.

Anna was right to be afraid of you.

His hand was shaking as he grabbed his phone from his pocket and called one of his assistants to get Leonie's location. Luckily she was still a few minutes away, so he ordered the assistant to get the driver to bring the car around to the back of the chapel instead of the front. He'd get another member of staff to intercept her and bring her here, where he could talk to her, tell her what he intended to do.

He paced around for ten minutes, conscious that the moment when they were supposed to exchange vows was getting closer and closer, and that the sooner he made an announcement the better. But he needed to tell her first. She deserved that from him at least.

Finally the door opened and Leonie was ushered in.

His heart shuddered to a complete halt inside his chest.

She was in that gorgeous wedding dress, a princess out of a fairy-tale. The veil that covered her face was white lace, densely embroidered with silver thread, and all that could be seen was the faint gleam of her red-gold hair. In one hand was a spray of simple wildflowers, gathered from the meadow near the castle, while the other held her skirts out of the way so she could walk.

His beautiful *gatita*.

She will never be yours.

He hadn't thought that particular truth would hurt, but it did, like a sword running through him. He ignored the pain. He wouldn't be the cause of any more hurt for her. She'd had enough of that in her life already.

'What's happening?' Leonie pushed back her veil, revealing her lovely face, her cornflower-blue eyes wide and filling with concern as they saw his face. 'What's going on, Cristiano? Are you okay? You look like you've seen a ghost.'

The deep violet-blue of her eyes was the colour that he only ever saw on the most perfect days here in the valley. The warmth of her body was like the hot, dry summers that were his only escape from the silence and the cold. Her rich, heady scent was like the rose garden hidden in the courtyard, where he'd used to play as a child.

She was everything good. Everything he'd been searching for and never known he'd wanted.

Everything he could never have—not when he'd only end up destroying it.

He stood very still, shutting out the anger and the pain, the deep ache of regret that settled inside him. Shutting out every one of those terrible, raw, destructive emotions.

'I'm sorry, *gatita*,' he said. 'But I'm going to have to cancel the wedding.'

Leonie stared at the man she'd thought she'd be marrying today, shock rippling through her. She'd been nervous that morning as a couple of Cristiano's staff had helped her prepare for the ceremony, doing her hair and make-up, preparing her bouquet and finally helping her into the gown.

But she wasn't nervous about finally seeing her father after all these years. In fact, she'd barely thought about him, and even when she had it had only been with a savage kind of anger. Not for herself and what he'd done to her, but for what he'd done to Cristiano.

No, it was marrying Cristiano that she was nervous about. And she was nervous because she was hopelessly in love with him and had no idea what that was going to mean. Especially when she was certain he didn't feel the same about her.

She'd had a battle with herself about whether or not to tell him about her feelings and had decided in the end not to. What would telling him achieve? Who knew how he'd take it? Perhaps things would change, and she didn't want that.

Anyway, she knew that he did feel something for her, because he showed her every night in the big four-poster bed in his bedroom. It was enough. She didn't need him to love her. She'd survived for years without love, after all, and she'd no doubt survive the rest of her life without it, too.

Of course there had been a few nagging doubts here and there. Such as how he'd mentioned having children, but said they wouldn't be for him. They'd only be in service to his grand revenge plan. That had seemed especially bleak to her, but then she couldn't force him to care if he didn't want to. She would just love any children they had twice as much, to make up for his lack.

What was important was that now she had her little cottage in the countryside—although the cottage had turned out to be a castle and she had a genuine duke at her side. She had more than enough.

More than the homeless and bedraggled Leonie of the streets had ever dreamed of.

Except now, as she stood there in her wedding gown, staring at the man she'd been going to marry, whose green eyes were bleak, she suddenly realised that perhaps all of those things hadn't been enough after all.

'What do you mean, cancel the wedding?' Her voice sounded far too small and far too fragile in the little stone room. 'I thought you were going to—?'

'I thought so, too,' he interrupted coolly. 'And then I changed my mind.'

She swallowed, trying to get her thoughts together, trying not to feel as if the ground had suddenly dropped away beneath her feet. 'Cristiano—' she began.

'De Riero has arrived,' he went on, before she could finish. 'And he has brought my son and my ex-wife with him.'

Leonie stared at him. 'You…weren't expecting them?'

'I didn't even think about them.' He was standing so still, as if he'd been turned to stone. 'Until I saw them get out of the car. And then there he was—my son. And Anna. De Riero's *family*.'

He said the word as if it hurt him, and maybe it did, because it was definitely pain turning his green eyes into shards of cut glass.

'They are happy, Leonie. My son is happy. And going through with this will hurt him. Publicly. I have no issue with doing that to de Riero, but I cannot do that to my child.' He paused a moment, staring at her. 'And I cannot do that to you, either.'

She blinked. 'What? You're not hurting me. And as for my father—'

'It won't bring my son back,' Cristiano cut her off, and the thread of pain running through his voice was like a vein of rust in a strong steel column. 'It won't make up for all the years I've missed with him. And I've already hurt him once before, years ago. Revenge won't make me his father, but...' A muscle ticked in his strong jaw, his eyes glittering. 'Protecting him is what a father would do.'

Something twisted in her gut—sympathy, pain.

How could she argue with him? How could she put herself and what she wanted before his need to do what was right for his son?

Because that was the problem. She wanted to marry him. She wanted to be his.

'I see,' she said a little thickly. 'So what will happen? After you cancel the wedding?'

He lifted a shoulder, as if the future didn't matter. 'Everyone will go home and life will resume as normal, I expect.'

'I mean what about us, Cristiano? What will happen with us?'

But she knew as soon as the words left her mouth what the answer was. Because he'd turned away, moving over to the window, watching as the last of the guests entered the chapel.

'I think it's best if you return to Paris, Leonie,' he said quietly, confirming it. 'It's no life for you here.'

Why so surprised? He was only ever using you and you knew that.

No, she shouldn't be surprised. And it shouldn't feel as if he was cutting her heart into tiny pieces. She'd known right from the beginning what he wanted from her, and now he wasn't going to go through with his revenge plan he had no more use for her.

He'd told her she was his. But he'd lied.

Her throat closed up painfully, tears prickling in her eyes. 'No life for me? A castle in Spain isn't as good as being homeless on the streets of Paris? Is that what you're trying to say?'

He glanced at her, his gaze sharp and green and cold. 'You really think I'd turn you back out onto the streets? No, that will not happen. I'll organise a house for you, and a job, set up a weekly allowance for you to live on. You won't be destitute. You can have a new life.'

She found she was clutching her bouquet tightly. Too tightly. 'I don't want that,' she said, a sudden burst of intense fury going through her. 'I don't want *any* of those things. I'd rather sleep on the streets of Paris for ever than take whatever pathetic scraps you choose to give me!'

He looked tired all of a sudden, like a soldier who'd been fighting for days and was on his last legs. 'Then what do you want?'

She knew. She'd known for the past few weeks and hadn't said anything. Had been too afraid to ask for what she wanted in case things might change. Too afraid to reach for more in case she lost what she had.

But now he was taking that away from her she had nothing left to lose.

Leonie took a step forward, propelled by fury and a sudden, desperate longing. 'You,' she said fiercely. 'I want you.'

His face blanked. 'Me?'

And perhaps she should have stopped, should have reconsidered. Perhaps she should have stayed quiet, taken what he'd chosen to give her and created a new life for herself out of it. Because that was more than enough. More than she'd ever dreamed of.

But that had been before Cristiano had touched her, had held her, had made her feel as if she was worth something. Before he'd told her she deserved more than a dirty alleyway and a future with no hope.

Before he'd told her that she was perfect in every way there was.

'Yes, you.' She lifted her chin, held his gaze, gathering every ounce of courage she possessed. 'I love you, Cristiano. I've loved for you for weeks. And the kind of life I want is a life with you in it.'

For a second the flame in his eyes burned bright and hot, and she thought that perhaps he felt the same way she did after all. But then, just as quickly, the flame died, leaving his gaze nothing but cold green glass.

'That settles it, then,' he said, with no discernible emotion. 'You have to leave.'

She went hot, then cold, an endless well of disappointment and pain opening up inside her.

You always knew he didn't want you. Come on—why would he?

She ignored the thought, staring at him. 'Why?' she demanded.

His eyes got even colder. 'Because I don't love you and I never will. And I have nothing else but money to give you.'

The lump in her throat felt like a boulder, the ache in her heart never-ending. She should have known. When he'd told her that any children they had wouldn't be for him, it had been a warning sign. If he had no room in his heart for children, why would he have room for her?

'So everything you said about me deserving better?' she said huskily. 'That was a lie?'

An expression she couldn't interpret flickered over his face.

'You do deserve better. You deserve better than me, Leonie.'

'But I don't want better.' Her voice was cracking and she couldn't stop it. 'And what makes you think you're not better anyway?'

'What do you think?' His face was set and hard. 'I hurt the people I care about. I destroyed my parents, I nearly destroyed Anna, and I almost destroyed my son.' There was nothing but determination in his gaze. 'I won't destroy you.'

Her heart shredded itself inside her chest, raw pain filling her along with a fury that burned hot. She took a couple of steps towards him, one hand crushing the stems of her bouquet, the other curled in a fist.

'Oh, don't make this about protecting me,' she said, her voice vibrating with anger. 'Or your son. Or Anna. Or even your parents.' She took another step, holding his gaze. 'This is about you, Cristiano. You're not protecting us. You're protecting yourself.'

Something flickered in the depths of his eyes. A sudden spark of his own answering anger. 'And shouldn't I protect myself?' he demanded suddenly, tension in every line of him. 'Shouldn't I decide that love is no longer something I want anything to do with? Losing my son just about destroyed me. I won't put myself through that hell ever again.'

Her throat closed up, her heart aching. She had no answer to that, no logical or reasonable argument to make. Because she could understand it. He had been hurt, and hurt deeply, and that kind of wound didn't heal. Certainly she couldn't heal it.

You will never be enough for him.

Her anger had vanished now, as quickly as it had come, leaving her with nothing but a heavy ache in her chest and tears in her eyes. But still she tried, reaching out to him, trying to reach him in some way.

He caught her by the wrist, holding it gently. 'No, *gatita.*'

His touch and that name. It hurt. It hurt so much.

Her heart filled slowly with agony as tears slid down her cheeks, but she refused to wipe them away. Instead she tugged her hand from his grip and stepped away.

She wouldn't beg. She had her pride. He might not want her, but that didn't change what she felt for him, and she wouldn't pretend, either.

Leonie drew herself up, because to the core of her aching heart she was a fighter and she never gave up. 'I love you, Cristiano Velazquez, Duke of San Lorenzo. I know I can't change the past for you. I can't ever replace what you lost. And I can't heal those wounds in your soul. And I know you don't love me back. But…' She lifted her chin, looked him in the eye. 'None of that matters. You made me see that I was worth something. You made me want something more and you made me think that I deserved to have it. I think we both do.'

A raw expression crossed his face and she couldn't help it. She reached up and touched one cheek lightly, and this time he didn't stop her.

'I just wish… I just wish you believed that, too.'

But it was clear that he didn't.

She dropped her hand and stepped away.

Her poor heart had burned to ash in her chest and there were tears on her cheeks, but her spine was straight as she turned away.

And when she walked out she didn't falter.

CHAPTER ELEVEN

CRISTIANO DIDN'T ARRIVE back at the castle till late that night. Stopping a wedding certainly took less time than planning one, but still it had taken hours of explaining and arranging things until everyone's curiosity had been satisfied.

It would be a scandal, but he didn't care.

He'd told everyone that his bride had taken ill unexpectedly and that the wedding would have to be postponed.

He would naturally cancel everything once the fuss had died down.

The first thing he'd done on arriving back was to see where Leonie was. He'd given orders that she was to be granted anything she wanted, and he'd expected that she'd probably have holed herself up in one of the *castillo*'s other guest rooms.

But what he hadn't expected was to find that she had gone and no one knew where she was. She'd come back from the chapel, disappeared into the bedroom to change and then had apparently vanished into thin air.

When he found out he stormed upstairs to the bedroom, to see if she'd taken anything with her, and was disturbed to find that she hadn't. Not even the new handbag and purse he'd bought her, with all the new bank cards he'd had set up for her.

In fact, she hadn't taken anything at all.

She'd simply…gone.

He got his staff to check every inch of the castle, and then the grounds, and then, when it was clear she wasn't anywhere on the estate, he called his staff to start searching the entire damn country.

He wanted her found and he wouldn't rest until she was.

Why? She's gone and that's how you wanted it. You threw her heart back in her face. Did you really expect her to stick around?

Something tore in his chest, a jagged pain filling him.

He could still feel the imprint of her skin on his fingertips as he'd taken her wrist in his, still see the pain in her eyes and the tears on her cheeks. See her courage as she'd lifted her chin and told him that it didn't matter if he didn't love her. That she loved him anyway.

Dios, she was brave. It wasn't her fault he didn't deserve that love and never would. That he never wanted anything to do with love and the pain it brought, the destruction it wreaked, not ever again.

It's not her fault you're a coward and ended up hurting her anyway.

The tearing pain deepened, widened, winding around his soul.

He shoved himself out of his uncomfortable chair and paced the length of his study, his fingers curled tight around his phone, ready to answer it the second someone called, telling him they'd found her.

He didn't want to think about what she'd said. He only wanted to think about whether or not she was safe.

And she would be, surely? She could look after herself. After all, she had for years before he'd taken her from the streets, so why wouldn't she be safe now?

Yet he couldn't relax. Couldn't sit still. Couldn't escape the pain inside him or the cold feeling sitting in his gut.

It's too late. Too late not to love her.

He stopped in the middle of his study, staring out at the darkness beyond the window as the cold reached into his heart.

Because he knew this feeling. It was familiar. He'd felt it once for Anna and for his son. Fear and pain, and longing. An all-consuming rage. An endless well of need that no one could ever fill.

She can. She did.

Cristiano froze, unable to breathe.

Leonie, her face alight with passion as she took his face between her small hands…

Leonie, touching him gently, as if he was precious to her…

Leonie, filling his *castillo* with sunshine and warmth, with her smile and her laughter.

Leonie, whose love wasn't destructive or bitter, despite the long years she'd spent on the streets. Whose love was open and generous and honest, with nothing held back or hidden.

Leonie, who loved him.

She's what you need. What you've always needed.

Everything hurt. It was as if every nerve he had had been unsheathed, sensitive even to the movement of air on his skin.

Love was destructive, but hers wasn't. Why was that? *You know.*

Cristiano closed his eyes, facing a truth he'd never wanted to see.

It wasn't love that was destructive, because there had been nothing destructive about the way Leonie had looked at him. Nothing cruel in the way she'd touched him gently as he'd thrown her love back in her face. Nothing angry.

Because it was anger that destroyed. Anger that frightened. Anger that made him bitter and twisted and empty inside.

Anger that made him a coward.

Anger that had hurt her.

He took a shuddering breath.

His proud, beautiful *gatita*. He'd hurt her and she'd simply touched his cheek. Told him that she wished he could see what she saw when she looked at him.

His brave Leonie. Walking away from him with a straight back, unbowed. A fighter in every sense of the word. But alone. Always alone.

Not again.

It was the only thought that made sense. He'd made mistakes in his life—so many mistakes—but the one mistake he'd made, that he kept making over and over again, had been to let his anger win. And he couldn't let it.

Once…just this once…he would let love win.

And he loved her.

Perhaps he had loved her the moment he'd picked her up from the street, seen her staring at him with wide blue eyes, her hair a tangled skein down her back.

He'd tried to deny the emotion, tried to ignore it. Tried to squash it down and contain it because his love had always been such a destructive thing. But he couldn't stop it from pouring through him now, intense and deep. A vast, powerful force.

He remembered this feeling—this helpless, vulnerable feeling. And how he'd fought it, tried to manage it, to grab control where he could. The anguish of wanting something from his parents that they were never going to give, and their instinctive withdrawal from him and his neediness. The pain of it as he'd tried to hold on to Anna. As his son had slipped through his fingers.

The vulnerability that he'd turned into anger, because that was easier and he'd thought it more powerful.

But it wasn't. This feeling was the most powerful. It was everything and he let it pulse through him, overwhelm him, making everything suddenly very, *very* clear.

He had to find her. She thought that they both deserved more. He wasn't sure that was true for him. But she definitely did. And though he had nothing to give her but his own broken, imperfect heart, it was all he had.

He just had to trust it was enough.

Cristiano turned and strode out of the study, his heart on fire, his phone still clutched in his hand.

Leonie waited outside in the garden of the tiny hotel in San Lorenzo, hiding in the darkness. She'd gotten good at it in Paris, and it seemed she still had the gift since no one had spotted her.

It was a long wait. But she had nowhere to go, and nowhere to be, so she stood there until at last the door to the wide terrace opened and a man came out to stand there, gazing out over the garden.

De Riero.

She really didn't know why she was here, or what she intended to do by coming—maybe just see him. Her memories of him were very dim, and they were still dim now. She didn't recognise his face. He was a stranger.

After she'd left the castle, walking to the village in the dark, she'd thought she'd probably have to hitchhike or stow away in a truck or something in order to leave San Lorenzo. The thought hadn't worried her. She just wanted to get as far away from Cristiano and his cold green eyes as she could.

But then, outside the small village hotel, she'd spotted a tall boy with vaguely familiar features and vivid green eyes and she'd known who it was. And who the tall man beside him must be, too.

And she hadn't been able to go any further.

She hadn't wanted to go into the hotel, so she'd slunk into the gardens and skulked in the shadows, watching the hotel terrace.

Waiting for what, she didn't know, but she hadn't been able to leave all the same.

De Riero reached into his jacket and took out a cigarette, lit it, leaning on the stone parapet of the terrace.

She could step out of the shadows now, reveal herself. Show him that she was still alive—though at the moment 'alive' was relative. Especially when she felt so hollow and empty inside.

What do you want from him?

She didn't know that, either. An apology? An acknowledgement? To be welcomed into his family with open arms?

Her father leaned his elbows on the parapet, his cigarette glowing.

Would he be disappointed if he found out she wasn't dead after all? Would he be angry with her for disrupting his family? Or would he be grateful? Happy?

Does it matter?

Her throat closed and her chest ached. And she knew the truth. It wouldn't change a thing. Because her heart was broken and it had nothing to do with her father. Nothing to do with his acknowledgement of her or otherwise. She felt nothing for him. Nothing at all.

Because her heart wasn't with him. It was with another man. A man who didn't want it and yet held it in his strong, capable hands anyway.

Whether her father wanted her or not, it wouldn't change that feeling. Wouldn't alter it. Which meant it wasn't this man's acceptance that would make her whole.

Only Cristiano could.

The boy came out onto the terrace, tall and already broad, joining the man. Cristiano's son.

The sounds of their voices carried over the garden, and then their laughter. There was happiness in their voices, an easy affection, and Leonie knew she wasn't going to reveal herself. That she would stay out of it.

That wasn't her family. Not any more.

It felt right to melt away into the shadows and leave them behind.

Her future wasn't with them.

A certain calmness settled inside her, along with determination.

She would find her own family and her own future. She would carve it with her bare hands if she had to, but find it she would. Her future wasn't as a de Riero and it wasn't as a Velazquez, but she would find something else.

She wasn't lost. She'd found herself.

Slowly she walked down the tiny street of San Lorenzo, alone in the dark. And then a car came to a screeching halt beside her and a man leapt out of it.

'Leonie!' a dark, familiar voice said desperately. 'Stop!'

She stilled, staring as Cristiano came towards her, his hair standing up on end, his wedding suit rumpled, the look on his face as raw and naked as she'd ever seen it.

He stopped right in front of her, staring at her, breathing hard. 'Don't leave,' he said hoarsely before she could speak. 'Please don't leave me.'

Shocked tears pricked her eyes, her heart aching and burning. What was he doing here? He'd been very clear on what he'd wanted and it wasn't her, no matter what he was saying now.

Resisting the urge to fling herself into his arms, she drew herself up instead, lifting her chin. 'What are you doing here, Cristiano?' Her voice was hoarse, but she was pleased with how calm she sounded.

'What you said in the chapel…' The look in his eyes burned. 'About deserving more.'

'What?'

'You told me that we both deserved more and that you wished I could believe it, too.' He stared at her. 'I want to know why.'

She blinked her tears back furiously. 'Does it matter?'

He moved then, taking her face between his big, warm palms, his whole body shaking with the force of some deep, powerful emotion. 'Yes,' he said fiercely. 'It matters. It matters more than anything in this entire world.'

His touch was so good. The warmth of it soothed all the broken edges of her soul, making her want to lean into his hands. Give him everything she had.

But he didn't love her, did he? And he never would. And that wasn't enough for her any more. It just wasn't.

'Why?' She forced away the tears. 'Why does it matter to you?'

The street lights glossed his black hair, made his eyes glitter strangely. 'Because you matter, *gatita*. You matter to me.'

Her breath caught—everything caught. 'What?' The question came out in a hoarse whisper.

'I came back and you were gone, and no one knew where you were.'

There was something bright and fierce in his expression.

'I couldn't rest and I couldn't sit still. I was afraid for you. And I knew it was too late. I've been trying not to love you, my little *gatita*. I've been trying not to care, trying to protect myself. But you're so easy to love, and I fell for you without even realising that I'd fallen.'

His thumbs moved gently over her cheekbones, wiping away tears she hadn't known were there.

'I resisted so hard. Love is so destructive, and I've hurt so many people. But it was you who showed me another way. You made me see that it wasn't love that destroyed things, it was anger. My anger.'

He loved her? He really loved her?

Everything took on a strange, slightly unreal quality, and she had to put her hands up and close her fingers around his strong wrists to make sure he was real.

'How?' she asked hoarsely. 'I didn't do—'

'You've spent years on the streets. Years fighting for your survival. Years with nothing and no one. And, yes, you're angry—but you haven't let it define you. You haven't let it make you bitter. No, it's your love that defines you. Your joy and your passion. And that's what

I want, *mi corazón*. I want you to teach me how to love like that…teach me how to love *you* like that.'

She was trembling, and she didn't want to look away from him in case this wasn't real. In case he disappeared, as all the good things in her life seemed to do.

'You don't need me to teach you,' she whispered in a scratchy voice. 'You already know how to love, Cristiano. You just have to let go of your anger.'

He said nothing for a long moment, staring down into her face, holding her as if he was afraid of exactly the same thing she was: that this thing they were both within touching distance of would vanish and never come back.

'Is that what you see?' he asked roughly. 'When you look at me? How do I deserve anything if anger is all there is?'

His face blurred as more tears filled her vision and she had to blink them away fiercely. 'That's not all there is. You're a good man, a kind man. A man who feels things deeply and intensely. A protective man desperate for something to protect.'

She slid her hands up his wrists, covering the backs of his where they cupped her face.

'A man who wants someone to be his—and you deserve that, Cristiano. More, I think you need it.'

'I don't know that I did to deserve it. But I'm willing to spend my life trying.' His eyes burned with an intense green fire. 'Will you be mine, Leonie?'

'You don't have to try,' she said thickly. 'And I'm already yours. I've never been anyone else's.'

'Then please come back to me, *gatita*.' He searched her face as if he couldn't quite believe her. 'Please come home.'

But she didn't need him to plead. She'd already decided.

She went up on her toes and pressed her mouth to his, and when his arms came around her and held her tight she became whole.

With him she would never be homeless.

Because he was her home.

EPILOGUE

CRISTIANO PAID THE bill and pushed back his chair, standing up. The restaurant was very crowded and no one was looking at them, too involved with their own conversations to pay attention to the tall man with green eyes and the other, much younger man opposite him, who also stood, and who also had the same green eyes.

The lunch had gone surprisingly well, but it was too soon for an embrace so Cristiano only held out his hand, looking his son in the eye. 'It was good to meet you, Alexander.'

His son frowned, looked down at his extended hand, and then, after a moment, reached out and took it, shaking it firmly. 'I can't call you Papá—you know that, right?'

'Of course not,' Cristiano said easily. 'You already have one of those.'

De Riero—which wasn't what Cristiano had either wanted or chosen, but he couldn't change what had happened twenty years ago. All he could do was let go of his anger and accept it.

It hadn't been easy, but he'd done it. With a little help from Leonie, naturally enough.

In fact, that he'd made contact with his son at all had been all down to her. After a few years—after their lives had settled down and his son had become an adult in his own right—she'd encouraged Cristiano and supported him to reach out.

De Riero hadn't liked it, but something must have mellowed him over the years, because when Alexander had asked him about his parentage he apparently hadn't denied that Cristiano was his father.

He'd even tried to make contact with Leonie, when word had got out about the identity of Cristiano's wife. She hadn't wanted to take that step yet, but Cristiano knew she would one day. When she was ready.

As for Alexander... Cristiano didn't know what de Riero had told the boy about him, but clearly nothing too bad, since he had eventually agreed to meet him.

It had been tense initially, but Alexander had eventually relaxed. As had Cristiano.

'I'd like to meet with you again,' Cristiano said after they'd shaken hands. 'Lunch? Once a month, say?'

The young man nodded, looking serious. 'I think I'd like that.' He paused, giving Cristiano another measuring look. 'You're not what I expected,' he said at last.

Cristiano raised a brow. 'What did you expect?'

'I don't know. You're just...' Alexander lifted a shoulder. 'Easier to talk to than I thought you'd be.'

Something in Cristiano's heart—a wound that hadn't ever fully healed—felt suddenly a little less painful.

He smiled. 'I'll take that.'

Ten minutes later, after Alexander had left, he stepped out of the restaurant and onto the footpath—and was nearly bowled over by two small figures.

'Papá!' the little boy yelled, flinging himself at his father, closely followed by his red-haired sister.

The pain in Cristiano's heart suddenly dissolved as if

it had never been. He opened his arms, scooping both children up. They squealed, his daughter gripping onto his hair while his son grabbed his shirt.

It was soon apparent that both of them had been eating ice cream and had got it all over their hands.

'They're too big for that,' Leonie said, coming up behind them, her face alight with amusement. 'And look what Carlos has done to your shirt.'

Cristiano only laughed. 'That's what washing machines are for.'

She rolled her eyes. She'd lost nothing of her fire and spark over the past five years, coming into her own as his duchess. Not only had she proved adept at helping him manage the San Lorenzo estate, as well as becoming the driving force behind various charities aimed at helping children on the streets, she'd also proved herself to be a talented artist. Luckily she used oils and canvas these days, rather than spray cans and cars.

She was looking at him now in that way he loved. Sharp and direct. Seeing through him and into his heart. 'How did it go?' she asked.

He grinned. 'It went well. Very well indeed.'

Her eyes glinted and he realised they were full of tears. 'I'm so glad.'

His beautiful, beautiful *gatita*. She had worried for him.

Cristiano put down the twins and ignored their complaints, gathering his wife in his arms. 'He wants to meet again. Lunch, once a month.'

'Oh, Cristiano.' Leonie put her arms around his neck and buried her face in his shirt.

He put his hands in her hair, stroking gently, his heart full as he soothed his wife while two of his children tugged at his jacket, oblivious, and the third...

The third he'd find out more about soon.

It was enough. It was more than he'd ever thought he'd have.

After winter there was summer.

And after rain there was sunshine.

After anger and grief and loss there was love.

Always and for ever love.

Cristiano kissed his wife. 'Come, Leonie Velazquez. Let's go home.'

* * * * *

COMING SOON!

We really hope you enjoyed reading this book.
If you're looking for more romance, be sure to
head to the shops when new books are
available on

Thursday 14th
May

To see which titles are coming soon, please visit

millsandboon.co.uk/nextmonth

MILLS & BOON

Coming next month

BEAUTY AND HER ONE-NIGHT BABY
Dani Collins

Scarlett dropped her phone with a clatter.

She had been trying to call Kiara. Now she was taking in the livid claw marks across Javiero's face, each pocked on either side with the pinpricks of recently removed stitches. His dark brown hair was longer than she'd ever seen it, perhaps gelled back from the widow's peak at some point this morning, but it was mussed and held a jagged part. He wore a black eye patch like a pirate, its narrow band cutting a thin stripe across his temple and into his hair.

Maybe that's why his features looked as though they had been set askew? His mouth was…not right. His upper lip was uneven and the claw marks drew lines through his unkempt stubble all the way down into his neck.

That was dangerously close to his jugular! Dear God, he had nearly been killed.

She grasped at the edge of the sink, trying to stay on her feet while she grew so light-headed at the thought of him dying that she feared she would faint.

The ravages of his attack weren't what made him look so forbidding and grim, though, she computed through her haze of panic and anguish. No. The contemptuous glare in his one eye was for her. For *this*.

He flicked another outraged glance at her middle.

"I thought we were meeting in the boardroom." His voice sounded gravelly. Damaged as well? Or was that simply his true feelings toward her now? Deadly and completely devoid of any of the sensual admiration she'd sometimes heard in his tone.

Not that he'd ever been particularly warm toward her. He'd been aloof, indifferent, irritated, impatient, explosively passionate. Generous in the giving of pleasure. Of compliments. Then cold as she left. Disapproving. Malevolent.

Damningly silent.

And now he was…what? Ignoring that she was as big as a barn?

Her arteries were on fire with straight adrenaline, her heart pounding and her brain spinning with the way she was having to switch gears so fast. Her eyes were hot and her throat tight. Everything in her wanted to scream *Help me*, but she'd been in enough tight spots to know this was all on her. Everything was always on her. She fought to keep her head and get through the next few minutes before she moved on to the next challenge.

Which was just a tiny trial called *childbirth*, but she would worry about that when she got to the hospital.

As the tingle of a fresh contraction began to pang in her lower back, she tightened her grip on the edge of the sink and gritted her teeth, trying to ignore the coming pain and hang on to what dregs of dignity she had left.

"I'm in labor," she said tightly. "It's yours."

Continue reading
BEAUTY AND HER ONE-NIGHT BABY
Dani Collins

Available next month
www.millsandboon.co.uk

LET'S TALK
Romance

For exclusive extracts, competitions
and special offers, find us online:

 facebook.com/millsandboon

 @MillsandBoon

 @MillsandBoonUK

Get in touch on 01413 063232

MILLS & BOON

THE HEART OF ROMANCE

A ROMANCE FOR EVERY KIND OF READER

MODERN

Prepare to be swept off your feet by sophisticated, sexy and seductive heroes, in some of the world's most glamourous and romantic locations, where power and passion collide.
8 stories per month.

HISTORICAL

Escape with historical heroes from time gone by. Whether your passion is for wicked Regency Rakes, muscled Vikings or rugged Highlanders, awaken the romance of the past.
6 stories per month.

MEDICAL

Set your pulse racing with dedicated, delectable doctors in the high-pressure world of medicine, where emotions run high and passion, comfort and love are the best medicine.
6 stories per month.

True Love

Celebrate true love with tender stories of heartfelt romance, from the rush of falling in love to the joy a new baby can bring, and a focus on the emotional heart of a relationship.
8 stories per month.

Desire

Indulge in secrets and scandal, intense drama and plenty of sizzling hot action with powerful and passionate heroes who have it all: wealth, status, good looks…everything but the right woman.
6 stories per month.

HEROES

Experience all the excitement of a gripping thriller, with an intense romance at its heart. Resourceful, true-to-life women and strong, fearless men face danger and desire - a killer combination!
8 stories per month.

DARE

Sensual love stories featuring smart, sassy heroines you'd want as a best friend, and compelling intense heroes who are worthy of them.
4 stories per month.

To see which titles are coming soon, please visit

millsandboon.co.uk/nextmonth

JOIN US ON SOCIAL MEDIA!

Stay up to date with our latest releases, author
news and gossip, special offers and discounts, and
all the behind-the-scenes action
from Mills & Boon...

 millsandboon

 millsandboonuk

 millsandboon

It might just be true love...